FREE PUBLIC LIBRARY
WATERTOWN MASS

PRAISE FOR ...

NATU
HIS

D0779411

Shortlisted for the British Science Fiction Award, second-place winner of the John W. Campbell Memorial Award

"[Robson's] strongest novel yet, reminiscent of Moorcock, Banks, M. John Harrison and Macleod, and should assure her position as being one of the most exciting genre writers at this present time . . . Her characters are closely portrayed and wonderfully believable yet she never takes an easy route. She is able to defy the expectations of the reader and to carefully dissect the standard assumptions of the reader. Lyrical and full of a sense of wonder, this is the highlight of the year."
—*SFRevu*

"With a clean, powerful narrative drive and a cosmological sensibility, [Robson's] clarity of vision now demonstrates itself as her major asset, making her one of the very best of the new British SF writers."
—*Guardian*

"[Robson] has really hit her stride here. It's space opera for adults, with all the imponderables, shades of grey and equivocal responses that implies."
—*Alien Online*

"What distinguishes *Natural History,* then, as with the other best examples of New Space Opera, is not that it reinvents the essentials of the form, but that it infuses those tropes with a political resonance and moral complexity, introduces major characters who can at once be deeply flawed and touching, and draws on genuinely provocative physics theory in place of the old hyperspace and FTL jargon . . . the novel lives in its brilliant details and its often beautifully crafted language."
—*Locus*

FREE PUBLIC LIBRARY
WATERTOWN MASS.
MAIN LIBRARY

Praise for the author's previous novels

MAPPA MUNDI
Shortlisted for the 2001 Arthur C. Clarke Award

"British literary sci-fi has a new star . . . ambitious,
assured and visionary."
—*SFX magazine* (five stars out of five)

"Once in a great while you stumble upon a book that gets
a firm grip on your imagination and just will not let go.
Even when you are out—driving, eating in a restaurant,
carrying on a conversation—you're thinking about that book,
anxious to get back to find out what happens next.
Enter into that restrictive list, *Mappa Mundi*."
—*SFSite*

"A thought-provoking and intriguing work
that confirms Robson's place as a major player
in the current pool of British SF talent."
—*SFRevu*

SILVER SCREEN
Shortlisted for the 1999 Arthur C. Clarke Award

"Idiosyncratic and unpredictable . . . a well-told, compelling story
tackling big ideas. Justina Robson's writing is an intriguing
example of how and why science fiction is no longer merely
generic but relevant to our scientific present. She manages
to integrate the alarmingly futuristic with a firm grasp of the
history of ideas—a novelist of real vision."
—Zadie Smith, author of *White Teeth*

"The perfect blend of excitement and thought-provoking concepts
lifts this novel far above the ordinary. Ideas and future trends
are pitched with determined realism, doing what Science Fiction
is supposed to do, and leave you thinking with considerable
anxiety about the way we're heading."
—Peter F. Hamilton, author of *Pandora's Star*

NATURAL HISTORY

JUSTINA ROBSON

SPECTRA™

Bantam Books
New York   Toronto   London   Sydney   Auckland

NATURAL HISTORY
Published by arrangement with Pan Macmillan Ltd.
A Bantam Spectra Book / January 2005

Published by
Bantam Dell
A Division of Random House, Inc.
New York, New York

"American Pie"
Words & Music by Don McLean
Copyright © 1971 Mayday Music, USA. Universal / MCA Music Limited
Elsinore House, 77 Fulham Palace Road, London W6 8JA
Used by permission of Music Sales Ltd. All rights reserved.
International copyright secured.

All rights reserved
Copyright © 2003 by Justina Robson
Cover art by Steve Stone

Bantam Books, the rooster colophon, Spectra, and the portrayal of a
boxed "s" are trademarks of Random House, Inc.

Library of Congress Cataloging-in-Publication Data

Robson, Justina.
Natural history / Justina Robson.
p. cm.
A novel.
ISBN 0-553-58741-2
1. Artificial intelligence—Fiction.   2. Interplanetary travel—Fiction.
3. Life on other planets—Fiction.   4. Women archaeologists—Fiction.
5. Women historians—Fiction.   6. Space ships—Fiction.   I. Title.
PS3618.O3366N38 2005
813'.6—dc22   2004051995

Printed in the United States of America
Published simultaneously in Canada

www.bantamdell.com

BVG 10 9 8 7 6 5 4 3 2 1

~M~ 2/05 9/3

For fun, and for my friends—you know who you are

1. ISOL AND THE ENGINE

Day's end: 5433.
Base beacon delay: 3 years, 351 days.
Speed: approaches 0.265 lights.
Fixed Stars Estimate Navigational Error: 0.0134.
Direction: Barnard's Star, holding.
Immediate Region: infestation of scattered micrometeors within density spectrum 0.001 to 0.032/m³. Bhupal halo configuration suggests ancient significant explosion. Expansion suggests incident congruent with Earth geotime 246BC: Archimedes works on his principles, Buddhism spreading over India, Punic Wars in full swing.
Crystals of water present; saturation density per cubic metre 4×10^{-6}; also frozen nitrogen, hydrogen and oxygen; also carbon in the form of complex organic molecules within outer shells of iron and non-Earthlike fullerenes. Iron ores and silicates predominate. Free gases remain as negligible traces within immediate region.
Damage sustained: catastrophic puncturing of primary skin, significant punctures of secondary skin. Heavy-particle absorption decreased to 45%. Radiation count falling by 6 rads/minute. Essential gas loss at 32%.
Condition: critical.

A long, long time ago, I can still remember how that music used to make me smile . . .

Voyager Lonestar Isol was holed like a Swiss cheese, peppered with tiny wounds like a bird caught in a blast of shot. Much more of this and her Mites would fail, her immune system become stagnant from too high a demand, her fuel absorption become disproportionate to the fuel available ahead of her.

And I knew that if I had my chance . . .

Isol continued to hurtle through the scouring degradation of the meteor field, still in shock at its sudden appearance in her path. The constant bombardment, which had felt like a rough sanding at first, was now razing her. She hurt, she bled, but her colossal inertia drove her into the grit with the force of a missile, so that pieces only micrometres in diameter pierced straight through her at whatever vector she struck them.

Even when she'd seen it, it had been far too late to turn. She'd had a warning of exactly 1.6108 seconds and, if she cared to love her numbers, by then it was a whole Golden Ratio too late—an entire Fibonacci crisis of suicidal beauty, fuck it. And in another few seconds it would be over, one way or another.

Did you write the book of love?

She'd had only two femtoseconds to realize that no diversion she could make was going to steer her clear of the ring of crap that had suddenly manifested itself. It hadn't appeared in her awareness until the last moment, due to a lack of light in this star-forsaken region. That, combined with a lack of expectation in her mind and her overconfidence in her own ultra-high-resolution optics and the data from the fixed solar scanners back home. No telescope had reported any big dusts, so she'd assumed there weren't any. Isol could process memories at fifty times the speed of an Unevolved human and have it feel like real time; but she couldn't think of what to do when she saw the problem, and by then it had been too late. Two femtoseconds wasn't even enough for the brain to make the first connection towards starting a gasp—if you had lungs.

A long, long time ago, when she was little, she'd danced in a field of poppies listening to "American Pie," not understanding a single word, around her the world as wide as a blue sky could stretch. The track had lasted half a second in those days, played as fast as she could comprehend it at the time—thinking she was some kind of genius as she dashed through one era of music after another. "American Pie" and its mystery had lasted time enough for one sharp intake of breath.

These days she could play her music at far greater speeds without losing any nuance; Earth's entire repertoire took only two years to listen to end to end—more than enough time to find favourites and make lists and endless recombinations of accompaniment to the cacophony of the universal radio.

Now she played it slower than that, one line for every second. It seemed important as never before to understand it, reviewing and discarding all the billions of databased papers already written on its lyrics in order to find her own unique take on its perfect capture of the ineffable. She wanted to hear it so loud that the sound of her own death wouldn't eclipse it.

Do you have faith in God above?

She saw the curve of her future suddenly start to veer into the cubic . . . the quartic . . . heading into its visible limit. It was too late, and it had been too late since the first day of her life when, as an extrasolar explorer, she'd been set on a track for speed and silence and the infinite depths of an ocean beyond all vastness. Even a Forged life is so short and this place is so very big. How could you stand to be late?

Do you believe in rock and roll?

A rock—much bigger than the rest—smashed through her right sailfin, punching a hole in it more than half a metre across. Numbness began to creep into her side. From the edges of the wound hydrocarbons and silicates bled out into a whitening tail behind her.

Suddenly, as if the lump had left a secret decoder in its violent passage, Isol understood the song, even the line about the levee, although she didn't know what a levee was. (Her insentient memory supplied some kind of ditch full of water runoff from green fields and a river, sodden with rain to bursting point.) It told her the song was about the death of Buddy Holly and the crash of his plane. But she knew it was for *her,* because she was the plane and the passenger and the song and the words, and the father, son and holy ghost were out beyond the light horizon.

Can music save your mortal soul?

At last she was in the clear, beyond the cloud of infinitesimal stones. But her body was failing. The damaged sailfin wouldn't eat anymore, wouldn't feel the soft breath of the solar winds or the hard blast of her reactor output. The drop in radiation made her feel a cold foreboding that was more than a physical chill. She didn't need to create the graph to know the game was done.

Slowing, she maintained course along the thread of light towards Barnard's Star. Everything about her ached with regret and fury at her hot-headedness. Now she would drift until she died, for there were no stars close enough to supply sufficient energy to solve her shortfall. Barnard's Star was to have been the first of many stops. She hadn't even got to first base.

*I was a lonely teenage broncin' buck with a pink
       carnation and a pickup truck . . .*

If only she'd *seen* it sooner. Then she might have had the time to make plans rather than simply seeing the stark promise of a detour and its deceleration. She might have had time to think, to slow down, to turn. But although her brain was made for the task, her eyes simply weren't up to the job. Not that those who had made her could have known that—they'd never tested any prototypes in the field, for there could be no prototypes, only people; when you made someone you tried to give them the best possible shot, surely, didn't you? Being among the first, she should have expected a few flaws, perhaps. But her head was made for speed and the silent heaven. She was perfect for this. Almost.

The day the music died . . .

Furious, she looked back at the debris field. All but invisible until you were right on it—positioned, as it was, far from stars and their planetary systems, far from the light of nebulae-scatter with nothing to cast its shadow upon, nothing at this range to reveal its proximity against the backdrop of glitter and dust, where worlds larger than the sun made a pinprick on her lenses no larger than an atom's width. But with a second glance she saw that this was no comet-and-rock incident. The signatures of the elements, the shapes of the pieces . . . this huge mess wasn't a cosmic accident of two bits of dumb mass colliding. It was an explosion with a centre and among its remains were fragments of complex organic material.

That strange flavour of burning that now seemed so flat on her tongues: this was carbonization. The little pieces had been *alive,* and the huge lump that had taken away her only chance of survival with a single blow was a block of highly refined metals of non-natural type that had liquefied and congealed within moments—a bit of technology that was now a lump of heat-processed slag.

For a second her astonishment outweighed her terror.

This whole savage cloud had once been *somebody.*

Bye-bye, Miss American Pie . . .

This *person* had been undergoing their violent expansion for over a thousand years. Such a short time in cosmic terms, less than a moment. Not even a gasp.

Isol turned away from her horrible intimacy with it—with them. Horror and disgust mingled with elation and made her feel sick. And here she was, dead as well, fulfilling her mission goal and her life's dream in one move.

First contact.

She laughed at the irony, deep in her core chamber where the superhot reactions of nuclear fission juddered and the unequal slams of free electrons let the elements do her sobbing for her. Eventually the reaction would eat her up if she let it run hard. Switch it off, and she could freeze solid instead.

So Isol makes the fundamental inherited goal of all explorers— contact—and in doing so is murdered accidentally by the long- dead native before introductions can be made: she often thought of herself in the third person. It was a way of looking at her in- significance. Now that seemed ludicrous, verging on the insane, as though she'd been writing her own story in a book: engineer- ing it towards the triumph and victory of a happy ending with such determination that she hadn't noticed when the plot went wrong. What a way to live.

She kept on laughing, drifting away from the field on her sin- gle, one-shot trajectory, wondering if she should tell Earth about this or keep it to herself as the final word on a life that could never have had any other purpose, although it might have had another outcome.

Mental note to Creators (you boz-eyed shitbags): beware of roadkill.

The pain from the sailfin began to ache and bite as she with- drew support from it. Cold stiffened it and froze its thin, tat- tered panes. She cut the circulation at her shoulder and kept her song on replay, humming along, eyes closed as she watched her deceleration to 0.25 lights. She felt very tired suddenly. The re- bellion in her against the Earthbound ancestors, which had pre- viously been a burning vision strong enough to fuel her through anything, exhausted itself—so much so that she longed for a sight of the planet now, blue and green and white, afloat on its prosaic round.

Her daily-link notes came in, relayed by beacons she had left behind her, their hominid-centric news mere years out of date. She deleted them.

I met a girl who sang the blues . . .

And then you get slammed by some other luckless schmuck's corpse and you realize—what?

That a piece of you is a little girl: picture her, a pink ballet dress replete with tutu and a very silly feather boa so long that it drags behind her and catches on the flowers in the field, long brown hair, a faintly, no, a *very* spoiled expression leading to a severe pout that looks utterly ridiculous. Where are the ruby slippers; three clicks to home? Why didn't I get those instead of this stupid dress?

That you're not invincible.

Dear God, the banality of all of this! A billion biographies have said as much on a lot less. Is there nothing about you that stands out and above all of that glibly mortal hyperbole, that came this far and saw so little?

The last train for the coast . . .

She switched the music off. Ahead of her lay her extinction, at a point not too far beyond the theoretical navigational marker she'd been going to hit—a virtual crossroads where the imaginary connecting lines between four "fixed" distant galaxies intersected. Her first milestone.

But looking at it again . . .

Something floated in the empty space there.

At first she thought it was simply a fault in her optics, or a reflection of one of the shattered motes behind her. But even after considerable reboots and calculations it remained out there, exactly placed on the axial crossroads, as close as she could measure.

Isol braked without hesitation this time. Anything seemed better than flinging herself headlong into nothing, even if it was only another long-dead rock.

The sailfin snapped off her abruptly. It tumbled away to one side and began to outpace her gently. In another few million years it might come within the grip of a star and burn up.

Venting and catastrophic skin repair were still consuming most of her available power. Even though it was already certain, her spirits sank as she felt the losses and the internal shrinkage they caused, the last-ditch warning systems they tripped.

For 1×10^{12} oscillations of the radiation in the caesium spectrum within her atomic clock Isol marked time as she was forced to close down part of her reactor, cooling, ebbing. She was aware of a sluggishness in herself, exhaustion, soreness from the wounds, and nausea from the build-up of repair by-products in her system. As she waited to get close enough to this new rock, she listened to the changing patterns of the light of distant stars. Their falling tones told her of her decline. She slept a lot, and sometimes couldn't tell if she were sleeping or awake except that, if anything happened meanwhile, she must have been asleep.

In her sleep she returned to a place not unlike the Dreamtime where she'd grown up, before she had a body. In her youth she'd done the common things for a Forge-born *in virtuo*: assumed many shapes, experienced the world through a range of senses, and visited places that her adult life would never subsequently have allowed her to see. One in particular, the sea-depths of Earth's ocean, she'd loved above all, no doubt because it resembled the space she was designed to inhabit.

As an octopus, her head ballooning, her limbs soft but strong, she explored the coast of Australia. As a shark she patrolled the Barrier Reef and saw the silhouettes of divers there above her, shadows from another world. As a plesiosaur in an ocean from another time she floated in the semi-darkness of tropical waters filled with algae, watching for squid, nothing in her head that would pass for thought, only the leviathan impulses of hunger and the awareness of water cold and water warm against her skin. But it was as a soft-bodied jelly that she went beyond the reach of the light and drifted down into the deepest trenches where sulphur fumaroles vented their spleen and created small, hot pockets of rising water rich with bacteria that existed nowhere else on Earth. There she knew herself home.

Here life was small and scarce. Tube worms, colourless, mouthless, lipless, eyeless, opened their digestive chambers and allowed specialized bacteria to feed on the rich minerals, absorbing their output in return. A few metres from the fumaroles' empire the rock of the sea floor stretched out, a backyard of silty death.

There were no worms here to plough fields rich with the sediments from above. Here Isol sat, silent and still, and examined a bone here and there, a piece of a thing, a tooth or the minute cogs of a long-lost watch. In this wilderness the blind forms of tiny scavengers, the relatives of prawn and crayfish, picked slowly and transferred morsels with robotic care into their untasting jaws. At these depths and pressures no bony fishes could endure. Nothing with a backbone, nothing that kept its strength on the inside.

In her dying dreams Isol found herself down there again. From miles above her the distant conversation of whales and the occasional trace of a heavy engine boomed faintly, their echoes butting against the blunt silence of her mind; the futile stammers of winter ghosts. The vibrations shivered her entire body with their undecipherable information. She identified things by touch. She burnt herself by trying to feel how hot the tip of a fumarole tower was; and again when she strayed too close to a crack in the floor where oozing tubules of fresh lava were emerging, snub-nosed and crinkly, into the icy blackness—snorting sausage-shaped chargers straight from the bowels of hell. Hell's shit. She was surprised to survive the encounter.

The bitter cold revived her. She brushed against something settled long ago into the ocean bed. It was bulkier than the usual detritus here; this was obvious from its resistance to her insensible blunder, and from the size of its surface. It tasted of metal, was coated with rust and dead barnacles, buckled out of its original shape by the weight of the water. She extended polyps and the trailing lines that were her hands, feeling its structure, identifying—after a moment of bewilderment—the crooked but unmistakable components of an internal combustion . . .

. . . *engine?*

She woke up saying this word. Her core temperature had dropped fifteen degrees in the last hour. The reactor was barely ticking over. Her drift had taken her within two hundred thousand kilometres of the crossroads. All the radiation her fansails were capturing was needed just to keep her alive. Most of her Mites were already dead.

Isol opened the containment around her reactor core, ignoring the pain and the bleat of warnings, and used it to warm herself. Organic and cellular damage was now the least of her worries when compared with keeping her mind alive a few minutes more. She tried to see what the lump of matter ahead of her was but, although it was clearer, it appeared greyish and featureless. Intense magnification showed no detail; it emitted nothing, and only reflected light in a desultory fashion. The revelation of its drabness depressed her, and she looked away to the coldly merry twinkle of stars she'd never know.

She thought she would compose a letter, just so they would know what had happened to her, but then she couldn't think who to address it to, and resorting to *Dear Sirs* seemed ridiculous. She calculated that her drift would see her eventually miss her intended destination by a narrow margin: Barnard's Star would have shifted out of her vector by the time she got there. Perhaps, she thought, like whoever had finished her off, she would get to become the piece of junk that sank another ship, someone travelling at several kilolights maybe, not seeing her as they stormed up the fast lanes . . . But then, at those speeds, who knew what would happen? Of such things she could only dream.

Isol hadn't wanted to be born, but now she definitely didn't want *this*. No poetic niceties about being as one with the stellar masses were consolation. Fuck them all for giving her such terrible eyes, and fuck the Monkeys for giving her a head full of their own silly risk-admiring strategies and what else they'd considered (in their wisdom as social and gravity-bound apes) that you needed for a life lived utterly alone in space. If she hadn't been stuck in their evolutionary tree she would have avoided this. A machine would have calculated the odds and taken the tour dispassionately, not counted the extra years of the journey as important. Wouldn't it?

Oh come on, she said to herself. *A billion animals a day die like this. In the past millions of people have vanished uncounted, all their great plans undone and no one to know or forget. What's so special about you?*

But there was a huge difference between dying someday and dying today, and her anger failed her. Isol couldn't weep, but she imagined the girl in the field, her face buried in her hands, the poppy petals against her face, so fragile and tender, red as human blood or industrial diesel. Isol wanted to live so badly that it didn't seem possible she could die.

The grey object left its bearings and moved towards her.

Startled, Isol watched its approach. She slowed again, bleeding energy, and it matched its approach speed with hers. She used the last of her reversing thrust to halt and the artefact came to rest when there were only a few metres between them. It was not as large as she had first thought; really almost a match for her own size, a small thing. She could see it very clearly now: it was quartz—silicon dioxide—but so fractured and pitted on the surface that it was utterly dulled. It had no visible means of propulsion.

She considered that this might be the same thing that had seen off that other bozo out here, but that didn't much interest her because one death now seemed as undesirable as another, and as unimportant. Freeze or be blown to smithereens—who cared?

The inert chunk, having moved this far, now sat idle. It looked a little bit like it might once have had a shape resembling some manufactured object, but had since become so battered by its long existence that it had given up on outward appearances altogether.

Isol broadcast a few mathematical constants to it on all channels in a vague gesture towards her extensive and never-used First Contact protocol, but the waves she transmitted variously penetrated and rebounded without result. The more she looked and kept on looking, the more the object seemed as though it might have been the product of technological advancement, although there was no real reason to think so except for its purposeful move. Here and there she kept noticing things about it: a hidden colour, a shape suggestive of a turbine blade or the edge of a fansail, the minute atom-shadows that might be created by field-generator patterners, their fundamental structures reflecting like the deeply buried facets of a flawed diamond.

The quartz block sat calm and unruffled by her lack of intelligence. Isol reached out with a blind desire for any kind of experience as her senses failed, seeing her spindly black arm stretching with the feeble movement of invalidity, poisoned in its blood. Her fingers opened and she touched the object's surface—expecting the savage cold of three degrees Kelvin, but finding that it had no noticeable temperature at all: that is, it was as warm as she. At that same instant she registered the radiation of its heat.

She snatched her hand back. A moment ago it had radiated nothing. Or had this been there before, but she'd been too numbed to notice? After a moment she tried again.

It felt rough, its edges undefined and brittle. But there was a shape to it that was not an accidental one.

Her exploration took many hours. From second to second the block changed not at all. In spite of this she noticed regular new features of it every few minutes. She starved as her metabolism ground down to the last of its resources in its fatal foraging for sustenance. It began to digest her, starting with her extremities. The open reactor fizzed and made her feel sick with the onset of its decline. She went through a time where she wasn't sure what was real and what was the fantasy of her own internal breakdown. Circuitry that she'd thought must be part of her heart, where her emotions were processed, began to melt. Meanwhile the object took on a shape in her hands, even though it was a clay that she hadn't the skill or the imagination to mould into the thing it became.

Eventually she woke and stared, bleary and nauseous, at her creation.

No human being had ever seen an object like this before, but that didn't prevent her from knowing exactly what it was. Never mind that she didn't grasp what half its internal structures were, nor the logic that underlay their design. Never mind that making it required a complete understanding of M-Theory, which she didn't possess—nor did any other humans or their descendants. She understood that this engine was capable of transmitting her from one point in space-time to any other, without travelling through any of the points in between.

A jump engine? Fuck the impossible mass equations of FTL. This was instant karma. It was a replicator, a giant immune injection, a factory for perfecting genetic and material design. Shove this in the backseat and in no time at all she could return to Earth, or continue her travels—made whole, made strong, made better than ever.

The only thing that bothered her was how she knew what it was, since none of these concepts had ever occurred to her before. Oh, and the fact that it was still made entirely of immobile, uninteresting silicon dioxide, a material singularly unsuited to any such functions.

Meanwhile her life ebbed away from her, and her will to question ran down with the slowing stutter of a coin spinning to fatal instability on its edge.

The engine-thing did nothing. It waited with her. She could take it up or leave it there. Perhaps it would fold back on itself and become an untouched block again, waiting for the next interstellar rover to appear. Perhaps her friend back there, stretched across ten billion kilometres, had mistakenly wished for something bad. Perhaps this was her final dream, like Pincher Martin, and she was already in the last throes of being dead.

Well, what the hell . . .

She closed down her old reactor and distended her abdomen to expel it, pointing it vaguely in the direction of a nameless green star. *Here's to your well-laid plans.* It hurt abysmally. Her flesh tore. In her mind's eye she saw panting, heaving animals, attempting to give birth. Sweat poured from them, but Isol chilled quickly with the exposure of her internal spaces to the surrounding temperature and she became stupid and clumsy with cold.

Taking in the new engine hurt less, and wasn't as tricky as she'd thought. It obediently slid up into her cavity and settled in the old space, a perfect fit. With senses dulled by the poison in her blood she felt it nestle there and burrow threads into her flesh and metal, brushing only a few pressure sensors, the odd temperature-sensitive cell. A curious new child. She didn't feel afraid. There was a rightness to this that was almost fulfilling in its simplicity: accept or die.

Isol blinked—a flash in and out of consciousness—and glimpsed her universe as the surface tension on the welling brim of a peculiar toroid undergoing constant expansion. Its inner volumes occupied seven dimensions simultaneously and each in turn exerted its effects on her ordinary four, wrapping them around itself like Christmas paper. Constrained by the fragile realspace-realtime surfaces, imaginary time ranged over immeasurable expanses of other dimensional regions. The whole Seven-D was outside realtime and realspace, but extended for the lifetime of its gigantic sister-surfaces. It touched her, through the medium of the engine, and she felt herself the still point at the heart of all things, the vanishing moment of the final breath, the source of the first inhalation. It was vaster than her ocean, smaller than the pinpoint of a single photon strike, and crossing it would take no moment at all.

Dizzied by the vision, sick with the rebellion of her mind at its demands, she longed for the safety of home.

Beneath her lay a brilliant orange sun, radiant with savage heat, and a planet both blue and grey, with white water-clouds and two moons. The place had a name she could not articulate, which meant Origin and Identity in an inextricable tangle.

Isol looked around for the Earth. It was so far away she could not find the measure for its distance.

The engine told her that the measure was Nothing.

Isol felt the breath of madness move in her. She hung still, over an unnamed ocean, and looked down at its soft gleaming reflection of the old star's light. Her fear was too big to be felt or understood. She knew her fear was there, but it had now undergone a critical fission and her circuits were blasted, and although nobody was there but herself, and nobody occupied the spaces between her and the Earth, she was not alone.

Beneath her the alien world turned slowly, beckoning her with the cloud-curled finger of a hurricane. She saw coastlines beaten by a salty sea, and where the spray smashed itself high on the rocks she saw ancient and unnatural structures clutching themselves to the stone with limpet tenacity. Nothing moved there.

She shut off her eyes. Her ears received nothing but the insensible blurt and chatter of natural radio.

Isol, said the engine, voiceless. *We were once like you.*

Corvax who was once a Roc, Handslicer class, and who was now just Corvax with a body gone weak from misuse and the addition of layer on layer of MekTek experiments, was aware of the approach of the guests before his laboratory sensors informed him of their arrival. He felt a shiver along the roots of his feathers, where tendrils of the latest batch of semi-sentient Tek were triggered by the movement of shadows on the surface of his asteroid home. What alchemy he'd used to manufacture such sensitivity belonged to him alone, as far as he knew. He'd liked to have gone to see the respectable Earthbound technicians about his own programming and his developing skills, telling them that he dreamed his machines into shape, but they'd have had a hard time believing that. Then again, they didn't possess the imagination or the versions of Uluru that he was running. No Forged wanted to share their secrets with the Unevolved anymore, and MekTek was principally an Unevolved product—the brute cybernetics of machine and AI spliced to their feeble bodies and brains to enhance capacities too ecoprecious to have been butchered together like a Forged mind. And too small to cope with a Forged consciousness.

Not that he was bitter about his lot, except for moments like this when he tried to hurry and found himself creaking along through the command gestures that summoned his holographic tool kits into life around him. He scanned the local geo-chaos and saw the silky amoeboid shape of the Ironhorse weaving nervously between the spinning clumps of rock on its final approach. It hadn't picked up any tails. Probably he should be grateful for that, although there was an itching just under his skin that was nothing to do with MekTek and everything to do with this latest line of mumbo-jumbo the Ironhorse had been explaining to him for the last hour.

Extraterrestrial life, the Timespan-class had insisted, was proven. An extra-solar Earthlike world had been its home. There were oceans, yes, and there was land, and structures made by—appendages—and there was fantastic technology beyond the dreams of blah-blah-blah . . . Corvax had stopped paying attention somewhere around then and gone to check out the library *Who's Who* on this madman. But the guide informed him that Ironhorse Timespan Tatresi had been made incarnate ten years ago, after an Uluru-upbringing of impeccable standards within Corvax's own beloved mother-father, the Forge Pangenesis Tupac. Tatresi plied the lanes from Mercury to Pluto as a fairly impressive kind of bulk carrier who also ferried passengers and specialized in fragile cargo with strict environmental requirements. He was a member of the Independence Party and leader of the Solar Transport Workers Union.

This was news that made Corvax twitchy, and he was already permanently twitchy from fending off the attentions of the Gaiasol Police and the local pirates, both keen to investigate his capabilities further. So far a nice dance of bribery, wheeler-dealing and sheer bad temper had seen him survive ten years out here in the Belt, doing good works on Uluru-programming and charitable acts of transformational surgery, but visits from virtual celebrities holding out giant lollipops with the words Wealth, Fame, Power on them were an entirely new thing to him. He didn't like the smell of it.

Nonetheless, he exchanged approach protocols with Tatresi and let him try his skill at navigating the final descent by himself. Corvax had AIs that were capable of handling almost any complication caused by the spiralling gigatonnes of stone that sheltered the laboratory from unwanted attention. They could ease the passage of a terrified passenger lifter, or ensure that nosy busybodies were made into asteroid sandwiches, but he enjoyed the spectacle of seeing something as big and vain as the Timespan negotiating this potentially fatal dance. Give him his due, Corvax grudgingly admitted, Tatresi had balls—if he had nothing else. He'd let him have five minutes for that.

With the dexterity of a much smaller vessel, the leviathan

twitched himself aside from the path of a hurtling chunk, brushed a dump of debris away from his forward sensors and matched his direction and rotation to a fixed point above the docking bay. He was saying something about the Voyager, Isol, and her fabulous journey, which to Corvax sounded not unlike a drug-fuelled fantasy—in fact, he thought he remembered experiencing one of those about seven years or so ago when doing Uluru on a mix of uppers and blissers had seemed the ultimate in erotic heaven . . .

"Do you believe her?" Corvax interrupted, trying to get the rich tapestry of the Timespan's vocabulary to ease up on its adjectives and superlatives so that he could clear his head.

"I don't believe Isol has an imagination capable of making it up," Tatresi replied, switching seamlessly from simple audio transmissions to full-band AI interface with Corvax's systems. His voice suddenly leaped out of Corvax's mind and began issuing from a point near his ear, where Tatresi's avatar—a hologram of a tall blue humanoid—appeared with equal speed. It took up a heroic stance on the observation deck.

Corvax ignored the blue man's self-appointed intrusion into his workspace and triggered the clamping procedure with a wave of one thick claw. Tatresi made a show of watching with great interest.

"Fifteen years in deep space seems enough time to send anybody crazy," Corvax said.

Tatresi's avatar turned to watch through the viewing window as his physical body sank into the safety of the docking bay's oval refuge. Above and around the skimpy rigging of the bay the close-turning hills of other asteroids bowled in all directions. Shadows within the dock leaped and darted at great and crazy speeds as they themselves also spun, dizzy as gnats in the weak sunlight.

The avatar glanced at Corvax with transparent admiration for his survival in this hellhole and informed him, "But Isol is an old form. They don't make them anymore. And they never made them with any inventiveness. A Voyager is nothing more

than a desire to travel and meet new people fused onto a psycho-
pathic preference for no company at all. That includes family
ties, of which they have none whatsoever; no loyalty, no philan-
thropy. She has a strong mind, with single-tracked convictions
based on ideals and theories, but no experience of a living social
world."

"And here she is being loyal to us Forged, like a puppy?"
Corvax added. "That's even less convincing."

He kept his attention apparently lodged on his holographic controls, while he watched both the avatar and the real
Tatresi closely. Hugged in the cradle's callipers, the body of the
Timespan—a kilometre in length—finally settled. Its shadow cut
out most of the fierce rig-lighting from the bay, leaving them
both in a sepulchral darkness. Under instruction from Corvax's
AIs, waldo arms extended their greetings to the cargo-man in
the form of junctions, cables and unloader tubes, and Tatresi relaxed the irises of his sphincters to accept them, blink by blink.

Corvax turned and checked out the readings on his fuel
tanks and reactor. His own body felt stiff and ancient with disuse, his wings arthritic, main arms crabbed and spindly—no
more fit to grab a passing boulder and catch its spin than they
were to chop rock and taste ore. He told himself that he didn't
mind losing this vital component of his Roc identity, but it was
months since he had gone outside, longer since he had done any
exercise of note, and he looked at Tatresi's avatar with a mixture
of misgiving and jealousy. Its form had a superb physique and,
judging by the readings on his machines, that was a pretty accu-
rate representation of Tatresi's state of health.

"Why don't you let Isol speak for herself?" the blue man
said. He smiled at Corvax, showing a white metal toothstrip.
His sapphire eyes gleamed, partly as a result of the pleasure of
ingesting some of Corvax's illegally upgraded biotrophins, of
which he was currently guzzling fifty litres per second. "You
can't tell me you wouldn't take up a chance to escape the stran-
glehold of Gaiasol and its attempt at democracy."

Corvax shrugged. "It's not been a problem for me in recent

years." He gestured vaguely over his shoulder. "Watch that dial. You take more than fifty thousand litres and you start paying double."

Tatresi grinned and looked around him at the scrappy conglomeration of machines in the laboratory. "It's marvellous what one person can do, given skill and a little incentive," he said.

Corvax bristled, his feathers rising with dusty irritation, and shuffled back onto his platform. With a flick of one wing-edge he ordered the Systems AI to present him with the tools needed to perform the minor repairs on the Timespan. As the array flashed into life in the air around him it ignored the presence of Tatresi's avatar entirely, intersecting it at the waist.

"Ouch," Tatresi said in that camp way of his, and Corvax grinned. It hadn't been easy for the big vessel to get in here without being either smashed to pieces or traced by Gaiasol Security. Even now they could both feel the asteroid they were on getting hit by frequent minor impacts with other rocks in the colossal debris field—ones that the defensive AI systems had decided were harmless. These erratic vibrations were comforting to Corvax, like a cat's purr.

"So, whatcha got?"

"A proposal." The avatar declined to move out of the way of the instruction system and instead looked down, watching Corvax issue commands around his mid-section. "You have the facilities here to use this new substance I was talking about, alongside your MekTek capabilities to adapt the Forged. You can enhance Uluru for us all."

"And?" Corvax scanned the Timespan's internal systems, one of his fine manipulating arms plunged to the shoulder in a sensor sleeve that allowed him to taste, smell and touch the various layers via interface with his external machines. He palpated the Timespan's digestive tracts and the avatar made a face. There was a flavour he recognized—more than one, in fact.

"Carrying cheapskate tourists? Your holds stink of garlic."

The Timespan ignored him. "And you could change my

engines to enable me to take them to this other world—to take the Forged out of the rule of petty Gaiasol economics. You may keep my current main drive." He tried to make eye contact with Corvax and added, unnecessarily, "It is a Draconis 500, mark 3, installed only last year, full service history."

"It's scrap to me, baby. Parts. I can use some of it but nobody out here needs anything that heavy, and most of my regulars have their own obsessions, none of them related to acceleration and braking in-system."

Corvax stopped and stared through the transparent shield of the direct-view window at the colossal body in the bay. It was roughly teardrop-shaped at the moment, studded with blunt, barnacle-like protrusions where colonies of symbiont cleaners attached to its skin. Here and there metal gleamed where ports and casings protruded from its surface. The skin was scaled, fishlike, with tough crystal plates of homologue diamond that reflected or absorbed light depending on Tatresi's mood. They veiled the Timespan's natural blue-grey hide in a dully glimmering net, a guarded and unforthcoming presentation.

The avatar was staring at him. Corvax glanced unwillingly into its artificial eyes. "Not without seeing her here first. And not without seeing it. Not without testing it. Not without some guarantees."

"Well, that can be, ah . . . arranged." Tatresi winced and then giggled as Corvax pulse-checked his nervous system. His body strained and bucked briefly against the callipers holding it in place, and the asteroid's torsion controls had to break briefly from their avoidance of major collisions to compensate for the displacement caused by the huge impulse.

Corvax withdrew with a snap of rubber hosing. "There's nothing wrong with you—just some housekeeping. You want that? Or you going to get it free and legal back at Arrecife Base? Keep your service history."

"I brought someone to see you."

Corvax leant back, braced on the tips of his tough Solarine wings, and stared at the smug, smooth head, the hands pressed together in prayer position like a big blue Buddha, smiling at him.

"Open your doors, and I blow you out of here faster than vindaloo from a rat's ass. If she's carrying alien material you've done a great job of keeping yourself uninfected, as far as I can tell, but one sniff of anything like extraterrestrial organics and you're vapour. I'm not one for an interesting death. Understand?"

Tatresi continued to beam indulgently at him. "Of course. We wouldn't dream of bringing you an infection. What kind of a greeting would that be? As you've already seen, the material is undetectable by ordinary means, and quite inert. It's all fully tested, as I've been saying . . ."

"Where is she?" Corvax stuck his arm back into the sleeve and the Timespan's body.

"Hold Nine."

"Oh yes." There was nothing there out of the ordinary that he could smell. "Listening in?"

"Of course not."

He was smooth, Tatresi, a real diplomat, Corvax thought, extracting himself for the second time, and envying the power he could feel humming in that gigantic frame. Compared to a Timespan's capacities a Roc was far down the glamour list— barely a flea.

"Shall I let her out?"

"No way." Corvax disposed of the scanner consoles and drew up the controls for the doors. "I'll meet her in there." He released his hold on the floor and jumped for the doors in an easy glide that he was almost surprised he could still manage.

"Yes, I forgot we all enjoy the same environment." The avatar followed him in his push to the exit with a skilful drift that mimicked a human in zero gravity, albeit an unusually graceful one.

Corvax grunted and stabbed his finger into a bottle in his work-belt, taking a quick suck of hi-ox to perk himself up for the walk. Tatresi had referred to their joint adaptation to space's vacuum and temperature, probably in an effort to make-nice, but Corvax was stung by the condescension and the suggestion that any lumbering bulk like Tatresi could match a Roc's facility in the Belt. "It's nothing like the same. Look what two thousand tons of free-floating rock did to her."

He hooked his hands out around the protrusions of old haematite that formed his lintel and propelled himself out with as much speed as he could manage. Even so, it took a while crossing the Timespan's shadow where it spread across the docking bay, navigating hook by hook along the floor, before he came up to the vast flank of the body itself. Tatresi dilated a door with insouciant skill, giving Corvax exactly the right distances for optimum claw holds on the tough skin of the opening. With as much dignity as he could muster, Corvax leaped into the stadium of light that was Hold Nine.

The tiny shape of the Voyager was almost lost in the middle of this hangar, suspended freely on fine lines of Arachifibre from the vast ribs that supported its dome. Corvax bowled himself towards her, rolling and enjoying a stretch, although his knuckles hurt from the jolting. He opened his wings, steadied into a straight vector with a few flicks, and brought himself to a halt just outside the reach of her insectile arms. The rocks she'd encountered had minced her, so Tatresi had said, but she didn't look minced to him.

Isol was not pretty but Corvax could see, even from where he now rested, that she was in superb condition. Her Ti-bone exoskeleton, which had taken such a beating, was newly whole. Pieces of the old one lay scattered around her in grey and white flakes, where they'd peeled off most recently. From the tips of her antennae to the delicate vanes of her solar sails, she gleamed like a freshly moulted scorpion—and looked as dangerous.

"Corvax," she stated with all the friendly attitude characteristic of that same creature while he stared at her. "I've heard all about you."

"Oh yeah?" He made as if to tidy some of his gravity-sensitive primaries with his beak, not taking his eyes off her idly flexing arms, and watching her with MekTek sight. There was something *new* about her—and it wasn't just this meeting of strangers and her unfamiliarity to him that made him think so. She didn't fit the blueprint of her Clade anymore, he reflected. There were organs and implants he didn't recognize at all: things that he was sure no Forge schematic for any species would detail either in the official design labs, or even in the daydreams of Tupac and Mougiddo, the mother-fathers of them all. His interest sharpened to an acuity that made his muscles shiver.

Isol spoke up again. "Tatresi says you are someone the others may look to as a spiritual leader."

That floored him. "Spiritual?" he barked, laughing. "I don't think so."

"But yes," she said. "You were the first to break the law and use MekTek on Forged for their own ends. You were the first to help us to describe our own destiny."

"I don't like the D word," he told her. "If we're going to do anything together, you can stop that right there. There's no destiny in Form, and none in Function either. That's all fatalistic bullshit from people without imaginations. The Monkeys live in their world and we have the right to live as we please in ours. We can make a few amendments to ourselves here, or we can live any life in Uluru. That's all. If you want a job done, name it and we can discuss terms. Otherwise, be on your way."

There was a pause. Corvax half expected Tatresi to oil in, but the Timespan said nothing. His blue hominid avatar didn't even appear. Isol composed her antennae in the formal shape that denoted a brief retirement from the conversation in order to consider, then opened them again.

"On my journey," Isol spoke slowly, choosing her words with care, "I have come across some *detritus* that I wish you to analyse. I believe it to be of alien origin."

"Alien as in biology?" A thrill of excitement fled up Corvax's spine and into his wings. He strove not to show it and hoped she had no understanding of the physical changes that Rocs might be subject to when emotionally stirred. Fear also coursed in his guts. He hung, waiting, on her every breath, even though this was what Tatresi had promised. He just hadn't believed it until now. Maybe still didn't.

"Precisely." She hesitated. "And technology, too. A very peculiar technology. I want your opinion. No doubt Tatresi has told you most of my story already."

"More than I want to know." Corvax shifted, feeling uncomfortable because he couldn't tell how closely she was watching him. Her visual sensors were a complex knot of radar, photo and radio, capable of 360-degree awareness. There was nowhere to hide his unease. In truth he would have liked to hear much more of this story, but what he didn't know would hurt less, he'd found—especially when the Gaiasol Police came calling.

"Will you do it?"

She asked before he had time to voice his uncertainty about their whole project. He already knew she intended to claim some new extrasolar world as a place for the Forged who wanted to break with Earth, and it was a fine idea, in theory, if you were a revolutionary intent on founding your own society and living by your ideals. But practically? He'd rather stick it out here, particularly when there were still so many unanswered questions about these aliens. Hah, *aliens*. He couldn't really believe he was thinking about that seriously.

"If you can provide it in a guaranteed safe-environmental containment, I'll see what I can do." Taking a look at it wouldn't hurt, he thought—at least, maybe it wouldn't.

"We came to you because—"

"It's okay, you don't need to state the obvious. The law, quarantine, theft, deception, unreported Contact, breach of contract, sedition . . . Small problems. I gotcha."

"Then here it is." Isol extended an arm, reached into a hole that gaped suddenly in her side, and drew out a tiny smart-vial of maximum shielding—a part of her standard materials-collection equipment—that she extended towards him. Like a graphite apple it hovered in the delicate grasp of her pincers, shining softly in Tatresi's hangar lights. "I will wait here for your analysis.

Perhaps then you will want to talk further with me and consider the extent of my proposals."

He took the thing from her cautiously, avoiding the hair-fine tips of her many feelers and sensors, and tasted the firm unalloyed purity of the apple's perfected surface fullerenes. Frosty-assed and autistic, she was; he didn't want to touch her.

"One scary move . . ." he warned her.

"Ka-blooey," she said softly, and in his mind's eye Corvax saw a strange little ballerina girl smile, fish-cold, her dark hair like waterweed floating in odd currents; the vision made the feathers on his back try to stand on end. Belatedly he realized it was Isol's personal mental ident, and that she'd chosen to broadcast to him on full Sympathetic Mode for a rare instant, filling his awareness with a comprehensive emotional understanding. It was a signals protocol used only between friends, and the sudden intimacy—an interior touch—was hard to resist. He knew when he was being played.

She giggled, soundlessly, in his head, "I heard you," and was gone.

Mad bitch, he thought.

Corvax made one last effort to see where this new engine was housed within her, but couldn't pick it out of the medley of new structures. He made a mental note never to trust another word Tatresi said about secrecy, and reached down to the floor, there hooking a cargo web with one talon and propelling himself out of the giant body without a backward glance.

Back in the confines of his laboratories he felt instantly better, and that wasn't just due to the light atmosphere and a new rush of hi-ox hitting his system after the hard work of holding his breath and cycling on full anaerobic process to survive the true vacuum of the bay. He took the grey sphere and put it into his Skryoscope tray where small items could be examined right down to their atomic structures. As he thrust home the Analysis AI softjacks into his MekTek intake ports, he shivered with the memory of Isol's sudden presence: a curious mix of voluptuous, desiring neediness, and the cold teeth of emotional absolute zero.

Some Forged were sufficiently alien to the fundamental human base-template that even to their own kind they were so incomprehensible as to be a distinct species. Voyagers had one of the strangest psychologies. In the instant of Corvax's exposure to Isol he'd felt something he didn't know the name of, but it was savage and insistent—a kind of hunger that was as primal in its passion as any animal compulsion he'd even known. Yet it wasn't linked to anything he'd ever wanted.

Tatresi could keep her, whatever she had to offer.

The sensor feeds were primed. He took a look at the two samples.

One was organic, and the other . . . he didn't know what it was.

As his first MekTek self-adaptation, many years ago now, he'd given himself the sensory appreciation of a master physician, one for whom smell, taste, touch, sight and sound provided data to the most precise of scales, with a brain function and a basic knowledge to match it. Corvax had seen stars die and could casually observe the deterioration of a single cell through every molecular transformation, every vibration, every split second. He knew bog-standard silicon dioxide when he saw it, and this was it; but subtly engineered in its crystal formations to be a storage object for data.

Bringing in the additional optics of his scanning-tunnelling microscope, he saw that this relatively simple structure held, within the bounds of its lattices, a simple pattern representing the prime numbers up to one hundred thousand. But he'd no sooner recognized this childish list than he heard the distinctive tones of molecules on the move. The crystal reorganized itself to represent a single giant prime—five thousand digits long—and then, without a moment's delay following his comprehension, it formed the distinctive and ubiquitous human symbol of two dots and a semicircle within a whole circle.

The fucking thing was *smiling*.

Corvax leaped back from the consoles, straight through his virtual arrays, and landed against the wall, smacking his back so hard with the force of his own involuntary retreat that he snapped several feathers and a minor wing bone. The force of his panicked escape ripped out the MekTek junctions, some of them down at their roots in his skin and bone. Pain punched through him like lightning as the last of the sockets pulled themselves free and went springing back against the housing of the Skryoscope with a series of clangs and crashes and the unpleasant smell of his own blood.

He rebounded slightly to one side and back onto the 'scope console before bouncing back against the wall and managing to cling on to a holding stud there.

Corvax lay in a tangle of wing, arm, leg and claw, feeling every second of his twenty years' existence alert inside him, as though his personal history was a separate part of him waiting to disembark and jump ship for somewhere that was going to be safer long-term storage. The only reason he wasn't dying of fright was that his damn soul couldn't find anywhere else to go.

The other *thing*—he was still thinking, in a bit of his brain that hadn't shorted and wasn't now engaged in heavy endorphin production—the other *thing* in the tray was a dead bit of flesh. It didn't have DNA; it had some kind of RNA-like molecular traces, which were so damaged as to be pretty useless, but he couldn't figure it out from just one sniff. Anyway, that hardly mattered. It was long-gone, dead as a doornail—toast.

As Corvax gathered his wits, he considered blasting Tatresi out into the field's random carnage. Let him see if he could navigate his way out of being hefted on a straight shunt into this asteroid's twin brother, which was ever close at hand for those awkward moments when you needed to get rid of junk or unwanted custom. Isol's fragile form would be wrecked, perhaps destroyed, and then he could signal Earth for a quarantine pickup, and get maybe fifty years off his prison sentence into the bargain. He didn't actually care if the militant separatist Forged never got clear of Sol. He didn't even have any sympathy for their whiny arguments. Everyone was stuck in some shape or other. Everyone had to get a job in life or shovel shit. There was plenty of space right here inside Jovian rule, with all the wittering Monkeys far away, so why not just get on with it?

"I know what you're thinking." Isol's voice came through his receiver, polite and deferential on business frequency this time, instead of directly broadcast to his head.

"No, you don't."

He was getting up now, shuddering as the injured wing bone sent spasms across his upper body; muscles tried to compensate and his meta-skeleton shifted, reorganizing.

"Don't do it," she pleaded. "Listen. It's more than what it seems. It will become what you want." She added some pictures, blueprints, to her words.

Corvax now saw the form of her internal components. Where her main nuclear reactor had once been housed there was now an unholy network of unlikely surfaces, all twisted up around each other. Belatedly, he realized that they were one surface bent in and around itself a billion ways to Tuesday. It moved idly about, like captive baby eels in a jar containing too little water, softly alive and fatally inert, yet with an unmistakably mechanoid precision.

"What in fuck is that?"

"This is the instant drive we want you to fit to Tatresi."

"You haven't answered the question." Corvax dragged himself upright and tried to look at the specimen again, but something in him hung back and his upper arms and hands gripped the unit hard, pushing him away as much as pulling him in. He couldn't face trying to re-establish a link.

"I wanted to get back here immediately," Isol said, softly insistent. "I wanted FTL. I wanted a wormhole, a jump gate, a teleporter, whatever it took. It became what I needed."

"So you're saying you have no idea what this stuff is." At last, something that sounded plausible.

"It's a drive." Her voice became a drawl. "A wormhole. A jump gate. A teleporter. Whatever."

"Just like that." He smothered a giggle.

"Corvax, haven't you ever wished so hard for something? If you were dying, wouldn't you want to survive? Haven't you dreamed of the impossible?"

"Yes!" he roared, flinging up arms and wings in a helpless

gesture towards the roof. "But for me, and ten billion other poor bastards, it never happened!"

He felt the MekTek viruses in his blood beginning to go to work on his bone, and forgave them the idle moments they'd spent whittling away at his deteriorating joints. Years of working in the cramped conditions had made even their efforts to keep his health perfect no more than a compromise, and they'd frequently mistaken good flesh for bad once the workloads they'd been designed for had fallen far short and become confused by the addition of nonspecified devices to his form. The Devil makes work for idle nanytes, especially those not trained for the job. Rocs were meant to sail the spaces between huge chunks of randomly propelled star debris, not sit and work all hours in confined areas, operating on their own bodies with stolen and half-understood gear. And all his efforts so far had done very little except equip a few criminals with the means of killing and defrauding faster and more effectively than before. As for himself . . .

"You're going to tell me that it grants three wishes? This is, what—magic beans?" He still couldn't look at it. It might still be displaying a smiley. He looked at the other *thing*, the flesh mote, instead. "Didn't work on this guy, did it?"

"Try it," she insisted.

He pushed his way across the laboratory, using the pain that moving caused to clear his thoughts. "Why don't you just wish it into Tatresi and be done? Then imagine that he's a Giga-class cruiser with military weapons and instantaneous transport, and blast Earth to shit. Or that you're Queen of the Universe and we all have to do as you think fit. Not got the imagination for that?"

There was a silence he felt justified in being proud of.

"I wanted you to check it first, Corvax," Tatresi said then, appearing like a genie in the middle of the lab, his azure arms folded. "Isol took it aboard in extreme circumstances. But we both agree an expert opinion is needed. After all, we wouldn't want to bring others to harm."

Corvax settled himself upright relative to the room and examined his injuries, brushing broken-off feathers towards the slow suck of the extractor, where the marginal atmosphere was recycled, bloody drops from their tips floating like tiny billiard balls towards the fan. He watched their glide and wondered if there was something about him that made these two think he'd been put together in a cheap plastics factory. Tatresi coming on with substandard compliments, Isol acting the femme fatale as best you could when you had the body of a fractured arachnoid; as best you could when you were playing your chilly act out on a hunchbacked crow with the hook hands of a goods hoist and a reputation for immersion in cheapjack Monkey porn. A girl ballerina? And he even thought it was her real ident. His lucky day.

He said nothing, didn't even laugh, just nursed his sore shoulders and looked unwillingly towards the safe unit. *Bring others to harm?* That was a cosy phrase, with its genteel passivity.

The blue imago of Tatresi looked down on him, its sapphire eyes shining, squeaky clean as Clear Blue Mek Clense. Corvax almost thought he could smell citron freshness, a pure streak of lemon joy. But he didn't know enough about the man to put any pressure on him.

"In return for your kindness you may keep the fragment of both the alien anatomy *and* the technology," Mr. Clean said. "The artefactual substance will propagate itself, should you choose to so direct it."

"You're talking like her now." Corvax glanced up, to the window and the real hulk of the man looming outside. On his port flank, Tatresi was decorated with service colours, his loyalty to Earth painted on in blue and gold: a carrier of distinction, by appointment, trusted spokesman for all the spacefaring Forged, and union leader.

"You're going to hand me the power to make any Degenerate into a god, in return for giving you an unlimited transuniversal ticket? I beg to guess again," Corvax said. "One sniff of this being in my possession and all bets are off. The mafia will take this system and everything that's in it, Tupac and Mougiddo included. Even people like me don't want that day to come. So, you want to tell me the truth? What's the kicker?"

"No kicker," Isol said, smooth and confident as a barracuda's tail flick. "You can do whatever you feel fit with the substances. I should guess that a few hours will give you more than enough *measures* to control whomever you like. Your mafia boys will look to you as their natural leader once you have such a power. And you can dispense it at your will. You can build paradise, Corvax, in the image of your choosing; real or virtual, there are no bounds."

"Your friendly internal Watchman tell you about that?" Corvax asked, more comfortable with this turn of events than he had been when they'd first shown up, seeming so straight and true. Clearly her intimate conversation could have done more than stroke his ego with that weird tech backing it up; it could have sucked out his story on the same frequency—and what was to stop her if she had this alien fairy dust? She'd discovered that he had hoped to build a better Uluru, one of unlimited capacity.

Her current silence confirmed this accusation of spying, although it could easily have been a ruse, a bluff to make him think they had more mind-sucking force than they did. Tatresi *could* conceivably have known about Corvax's weaknesses from the scuttlebutt he could eavesdrop from his customers and other Forged around the Cinq Ports area, where Virtua/Uluru plug-ins came at half-price for anyone who'd turn the odd blind eye to certain types of shipments.

"Fucking mind-reading shit," Corvax muttered, impressed and feeling his fear like a series of electric darts, one at the base of every feather. "You good with this, Tatresi—contaminating the system with alien dross? You don't even know what it is. You're fucking liars. You come here because the pair of you are pissing heavy water at the thought of what you've already done and seen, and you want me to smooth over your fears like Momma Tupac. To sanction you. Give out the unction—whatever the hell that is."

"There *is* no contamination," Isol said. "You've scanned

Tatresi. The material I gave you is quite inert. It is safe as long as it is kept in safe hands."

"You really washed in on the last flare, love," Corvax said, almost sorry that her conviction marked her out as another loony. Of course, what did you expect out of a psyche like that? Simple ideas for simple folk who don't live with anyone else but endless versions of themselves. But Tatresi . . . He studied the blue figure for a while. No, he didn't get that. What would the man want with this extraordinarily dangerous cocktail of woman, tech and white-frothing ideology? Was he a secret Independence sympathizer? Or maybe he had dreams of building the first transgalactic franchise, between here and who-the-hell-knew-where.

"Our offer stands," Tatresi said. He dusted off Corvax's holographic control suite with his holographic fingertips. "Keep the samples. We're in no hurry. Take an hour to think it over. And take all the time you want to do the work on it."

"And if I say no?"

Tatresi shrugged, the musculature of his shoulders rippling. "We can find another analysis elsewhere. The Jovians have less expertise, but their laboratories are better equipped. And their loyalty to Earth is purely financial."

"And if I say yes, you clue me in on the deal?"

The blunt-featured head inclined towards him regally, as if nothing could be more to its liking, and then it winked out of existence.

Try as he might, Corvax couldn't like the idea of sentient technology. He was fine with stuff like Abacands, which were just chipsets loaded with free-running personality programs and the knowledge of whatever resource was available by connection on the net—they were just pretend people, toys. They weren't alive. He didn't even consider high-grade AI systems alive; their existence came and went with the flow of electrons. They could switch off and on without dreaming or changing one single iota. They didn't age and they didn't, in any meaningful sense, die—though he'd scrapped a few in his time. Just talk to one for ten minutes and you could tell it didn't give a fuck about anything one way or another, even its own awareness. AI creeped him out.

This shit, on the other hand—it smelled bad to him. You didn't get something for nothing. Isol got her life restored for free, and the capacity to take the human species on into the universe at no charge? No way. And the dead thing/guy/whatever that she said she'd run into: why hadn't *it* been fixed up and sent home with a bee up its ass about colonizing a new world? Had it imagined itself a bomb and blown itself to kingdom come? Had it failed some kind of test? Why?

This all began to reek of quantum foam and the solipsistic universe created by, and for, the single observer. Then again, the innocuous quartz there had just violated a series of irreducible physical requirements that made it seem much more problematic than that. It made Corvax think of really unpleasant things, like dark-matter worlds and hidden dimensions, and all the horrors in the universe that he couldn't see but suspected were in constant and sinister attendance.

The very idea made him shuffle forward and get geared up again to look more closely at the scrap of flesh. He taped and pasted himself from his first-aid kits, replaced the softjacks and his MekTek damage with quick repairs, shot himself up with painkillers and micro-agents, keeping an eye on the time. He put the smiley "Stuff" aside, out of sight. It wasn't smiling anymore. It sat there, mineral-stupid, all lined up in the correct crystalline group structure for its nature. A less interesting-looking rock could barely be found. This time he examined the RNA fragments.

As he waited for the results of various chemical scans to percolate up his nerves, he sent out a feeler to a friend down in London, at the Registry of Births and Forgings, to see what they had on Voyager Isol and Timespan Tatresi. The Registry kept tags on files from Tupac and Mougiddo about the virtual lives of the infant and young Forged, before they were embodied. It was confidential information, not even accessible by the police, but Corvax was owed. Not owed enough to have his own early life expunged from the records, regrettably, but *owed*.

He also sent a message to one of his "cousins," the Degraded Ornith-form Gritter, who had been conceived as a wild-analogue eagle, intended to assist with the rediversification of the natural world on Earth and to act as an *in situ* scientist, but who had come out of the mould a disagreeable, self-interested little bastard, more reptilian than he should have been and twice as scheming as the stats had originally indicated. All great plans had their failures. Together with other Degraded Orniths, Gritter had found work as a messenger boy amid the bustle and intrigue of the Gaiasol government offices in London, carrying light packets—and no doubt investigating the contents for various concerned parties. Parties who found his candour and easily manipulated morality entertaining.

Corvax, on the other hand, wanted to find out who else knew about the existence of this Stuff, and so he sent: "A little bird says new Tek exists in certain markets. Will pay over going rates for early acquisition."

The machines were now reporting their findings on the morsel of alien cadaver. The RNA was so blown by its brief, part-shielded exposure to gluon-plasma that no cohesive picture of its form could be achieved. It had been a carbon-based life form, enhanced by or covered with a fair quantity of highly re-fined metals and silicates. Surviving crystalline symmetries indi-cated that lightware processors might have been a part of its self, or its cargo, or ship.

So, the bomb in question had gone off like the first breath of the universe, yielding primitive particles and a generally non-survivable area for some infinitesimal fraction of time. Corvax's scientific Abacand added that it had assessed, from Isol's data, that this explosive event must have originated inside the crea-ture, possibly within the nucleus of a single cell. It would have lasted for less than a billionth of a second. Nothing any bigger could have occurred, or there would have been no evidence left. In fact this evidence itself, the very existence of it, was odd in the circumstances because—

Corvax shut the Abacand up at that point—he could live without hearing more uncertainty and bad news in detail.

He stared again, unwillingly, at the quartz lump, constantly back-checking it every few seconds as though he were developing a twitch. In anger he shut down the equipment and sat in silence, shrouded in a cloak of dim sweat-drenched feathers, his head tucked between the folded long bones of his limbs, beak tip resting on the floor. He really wanted to know more about what was going on, but he didn't trust Isol and he definitely didn't trust Tatresi. He didn't like the quartzy lump, and he didn't like the idea of what had happened to the mystery contestant in the *Whose Atoms Were These?* quiz, either. Information circled inside his skull with the flickering uncertainty of bats' wings. He wanted the solace of Uluru and knew that before he came up with an answer he was going to go there. He shouldn't, but he just couldn't help it.

Virtua—variously named as the Dreamtime or Uluru, as Ghost-town or No-Space—had certain protocols for adult Forged. With regard to them, it didn't exist.

Conceived as a playground for the childhood and adolescence of the Forged, whose eventual bodies were constructed in a fully adult form only, it had later been developed illegally for recreational use. Amenable MekTek engineers put it together on stolen AI systems, in return for the promised benefits of free use of its arenas. Forged and MekTeks alone possessed the intricate cyborg structures that allowed them to partake of the pleasures on offer there.

Corvax had been a key developer of its later subsystems, a genius in his own youth, and he had introduced unlimited free-response within the grammar engines of the Dreamtime. He was now Uluru's primary host-keeper, and guardian of its gigantic servers now that the First Forged were mostly dead or pensioned off into milktoast assignments away from the action. He made his money renting time in it, and he maintained and continued to build upon it wherever he could.

His only personal guideline had been to let *free will* have its day. Everyone could be and do whatever the hell they wanted inside Virtua and, so long as everyone signed up to the consent and the disclaimer, what did he care? The pay had been sufficient to buy him out of his standard Gaiasol government contract to Handslicer mining, and into his own laboratories. Most of his clients arriving on the asteroid came for adaptations to allow them to return to the experiences of Uluru that they'd enjoyed as children; like him they had old friends who were alive only in their imaginations, or other loves, or other worlds. He didn't ask and they didn't tell. Neither he nor they were much bothered by the constraints of reality or by the hypocritical moral censure of the Unevolved who couldn't partake, and who had callously stamped their own lack of options onto Forged workers when they decided that virtual environments were fit only for those who possessed no physical forms and must be forbidden, on "mental health" grounds, to those who had.

A single glance was all it took for one Forged to communicate with another the acute sense of loss that their adult physical Manifestation brought with it—so great they couldn't speak of it, so intense that no Unevolved would understand it. Manifest individuals had a social life, like any human, but without the Dreamtime they were castrated things, haunted by the ghosts of imaginations that had once been all-powerful and were now forcibly limited to form attainable, mediocre longings within the bounds of their physical capacity to act. Some adapted better. Some claimed they were fine as they were. But some had a faraway look about them and a sadness that made Corvax turn away and hide his expressive forebody from them, in case they saw his sudden answering pain.

Someday I'll wish upon a star . . .

He vowed that he'd give them the bluebirds' wings. But it wasn't easy. Many Forged immunologies resented the overt MekTek intrusion that was necessary to bring them back to Uluru-consciousness. They became sick. They suffered. He had to fight to get the stolen 'ware to adapt to them and give them the AI connection. Sometimes they died. But they still came.

Corvax got better at it and his reputation grew as he became known as the man who restored sex to the sexless, friends to the friendless, social contact to the isolated. Dreamtime was only the flicker of an eyelid away, once you were *changed*. And the police persistently hunted him, for the hours of time he lost the workforce, the broken contracts, the suicides and the crazies and all the problems that Forged were carefully engineered to be free of: perfect souls with no dissatisfaction, as happy as Larry in their world, round pegs in round holes, bugs in rugs, children born and brought up to live in bodies and in situations that didn't change, couldn't change, wouldn't change. Smother this instinct and take that one away in the test tube, silence this gene and slice out that hormone. What they don't feel they won't miss. Let them get used to it now and later they'll be glad. But Corvax knew from the start that he'd been made wrong, and others . . . they were botched as well: otters making their lives inside clamshells, wolves in lambs' clothing, horses driven to hang upside down and roost like bats.

Corvax had every physical add-on his badly treated Roc body could stand, but Dreamtime was where he did most of his living these days—his thinking, his recreation, his creation, everything but sleeping. His poor physical condition was a direct result of his addiction to its siren call but he was powerless to resist. There was no real life outside Dreamtime's spaceless span. As he still pondered Isol's problem he quietly activated his links and entered his own private ground . . .

He stood in the rough shed that was a machine shop in the residency camp where he'd had his first Earthside adventure. His body was now a human body, simple and small, wingless and weak. He wore a denim coverall stained with oil and grease and metal dust from hard work at the grinders. Heaven. And *she* was there too, so the dangers of unlimited two-way interface didn't matter to him at all. Let nerve fibres fry and synapses store the untold damage of too deep a dream if it meant sharing ten minutes of her mojo.

When he was here he was close to sleep. REM was the natural state of Uluru, but REM-sleep brought the terror of uncontrollable changes in No-Space. In lieu of the father-mother's control that Tupac had once provided, Corvax was alone with the AI systems' insensitive proxy presence. Where Tupac had managed his subconscious upwellings with her own stable consciousness, now his own mind was the system's only aware input. The machines adapted the impulses of the narrative according to environmental laws he'd programmed into them—and most of those laws were now broken, leaving nothing between him and unlimited free possibility. He had a cortical stimulator that kept his functions heightened to avoid the worst accidents and to keep matters on a "normal" plane, but now he switched it off and let himself feel the first wave of the flickers: now people could come and go, things change, the world shift and he wouldn't be in control.

Now he could feel the real deal, the whole nine yards.

It was, as ever, late afternoon. He left the machine shed and went outside. A listless rain was pattering down from a grey sky over the southeastern marshes. The house looked small, a runt among the high-shouldered giants of buildings around it where once the unhomed and the unwanted wandered in limbo. These were brooding hulks, grim tenements that had grown over the years of his visits here into massive chartless mansions, their attics vast and lofty, their deep and dark cellars extending down into the Earth for countless storeys via stairs and empty shafts without number.

On the veranda of the leftmost villa he saw a figure leaning against one pillar, its face cast in an expression of casual hostility. Caspar—an invention of latter days, who had absorbed the vacancy and numerousness of the villa's inhabitants until only he remained, alone in all that acreage of waste. He stared at Corvax with slitted eyes.

Corvax ignored him and sidled through the rain into the small house. Inside it stank of drying clothes, old wok-fat and noodles. He recognized Paul, the man who taught him how to hot-wire cars, asleep in the sags of the sofa, a cigarette burned down to his fingers. Paul snored heavily, white hairs in his nostrils vibrating. Corvax ignored him, barely noticed him. Dani was upstairs, waiting for him.

He went there now, the fourth and sixth stairs creaking, the noises of the house's other beings muffled by closed doors of thin plywood. He opened the door of her room, guilty already for his own weakness but hungry for desire, to feel the surge of passion, the pleasure and the intensity of full body contact with a body like his borrowed human body, capable of connections no Roc could ever make.

She sat on the window's open edge, staring across the flat blankness of the marshes. A ghost—a semi-rendered artificial construct as yet nonfunctional in the AI programme, an empty slot waiting for character instruction—walked along the back wall, searching for a zone in which to take form, a place to belong. Corvax glared at it and it faded sullenly from his vision into some other universe.

Dani turned. Her greeting wasn't the effusive delight it had been when he'd put her together from his original memory of Uluru, years ago. She now had an experienced weariness around her that didn't suit her yellow and candy-pink hair, nor the sassy way she popped her bubblegum. He knew when he saw her now that he was looking at something he'd created over a long time, not imagined in a moment of youthful fancy. She didn't have a life that wasn't being his whore, and she'd become self-aware enough—for a ghost—that she knew it.

She stuck her tongue through a layer of elastic purple gum and worked it indifferently, blowing the bubble and letting it burst over her face before sucking it all back in again, as though eating a second skin. With mechanical enthusiasm she removed her clothes and kicked them towards him, pink rags. She held out her arms and stared at him tolerantly. "Come on, then," she said. "Let's do it."

Skies are blue . . .

When they were done he lay beside her, revelling in the soiled sheet and the smell of his own sweat, his thin skin and the residue of her touch. But a heaviness lay on his heart. He had to stop this. He should have done so already, before the rot set into her, before it set into him. Pointless to think of that now.

He held out the quartz pebble of Stuff to her. "I found this."

Dani took it and rolled it around in her callused fingers, their nails bitten to the quick. "It's a rock." She tossed it onto his belly.

"It's a magic rock."

Dani laughed and coughed, faintly consumptive. "You're a lame son of a bitch." She turned on her side and got up, beginning to roll her leggings back on.

"Dani."

"What?"

"I love you." *Can it be fixed? Better late than never?*

She stopped, frozen in position. "You?"

"This is it." He nudged her, tried to give her the rock back. *Believe it.*

She turned and slapped his hand away. He heard the house on the left creak and the plaster on the left wall cracked with the sound of a voice that spoke in his head, mocking his failure, *Caspar knows best. He loves her better than you.*

"Don't try and be funny," she said. "If this is your way of finishing it you've got my blessing. Just be straight."

"I want you to have it. Take it."

She spat at him and got up, yanking her jumper over her head. "I thought you were going to figure out a way for us to leave this place. When is it going to happen, hmm? When?"

Corvax folded the stone in his hand. He shivered. Beyond the walls of the compound a strange animal made a howling sound. "Dani," he whispered. *Dani*, he said, in his head instead of to her, *I know I've done this all wrong, but it's you darling, you see, you don't really exist and I'm a fool for coming here, weak and a fool but it's true. . .* "It's for you."

"You couldn't have done worse to me if you'd hated me," she said. "And I'd have done no worse if I'd hated you. Maybe we do hate each other. Perhaps that's it. You work on the aeroplane and you come here and rut and eat and shit, and you work on the aeroplane and say it'll fly but it never flies, does it? And Carl and Paul piss all the money away. And Caspar's house gets bigger and everyone who goes in never comes out. And that thing out on the marshes sings at night, sweet songs of childhood. Did you know that? No you're never here. But it does— like a bluebird, it is." She turned back and he saw that she was defeated. "It'd be worth staying for, if that was the only thing."

Caspar is coming. He's going to eat you.

Corvax wanted to will the rock into being a diamond ring, but it wouldn't oblige.

"Take a look, anyway," he said, holding it out to her again.

She rolled her eyes and snatched it out of his hand. "Pink," she observed. She licked it. "No taste. Not edible. Christ, Tom, when are you going to do something useful?" She turned the stone in her fingers sadly.

A long-billed crane brushed the outside of the house. Corvax could feel its bill, a killing spike, and the metronome precision of its feet moving towards her from somewhere on the left, outside. The bird lived near the ground floor. It and its brethren had something to do with Caspar, but Corvax didn't know what. He wanted to switch on the cortical shunt, but didn't. The crane was an unavoidable terror, a stalking nightmare, but it was slow to approach.

Dani shivered and looked around for another sweatshirt, but there weren't any. Mice ran in circles under the bed, keeping warm.

"Make a wish," Corvax said.

"I wish you'd piss off and leave me alone," she said. "I wish you'd kill Caspar and take his house."

He got up and dressed. "Keep the rock."

"Sure."

"If it does anything—"

She laughed. "Baby, I'll shit bricks and build you a house."

After he closed the door he heard her throw it after him. Knock, knock, knock—it rattled along the naked floorboards.

Caspar was there, his unpleasant face a blank sheet of pale skin without nose or mouth, still managing to sneer nonetheless. "Mmmn, mmn, mmmm." He was trying to speak. Corvax lived in dread of when he would.

Caspar's stiletto flicked out of his sleeve. He began to cut himself a long grin of a mouth,

"She wants me . . . not you. She wants . . ."

Blood is spitting and spraying all over the floor, all over

Corvax, all over the long talons his hands are becoming and when he tries to say something he finds he can't open his mouth . . .

"Hnnhaha!"

Corvax left Dreamtime explosively, waking to find the floor of the lab smashed against his face, his stomach juddering as he gasped for the nonexistent air through the tough gashes of nostrils in his beak, desperate for more oxygen. He fumbled for the hi-ox in his pocket. It was always far worse without the cortical controller on. Dreamtime was soul-litmus, and he was in a bad way, red and black.

He hadn't known it was this bad, but of course he'd been too hungry for the touch and thrust and perfect pitch to really think about that at the time. He stumbled across the lab and into the stockroom, took down a vial of Genocaine and tabbed the whole thing into his system to dull the sensation of having created a thing as pitiful as the Marsh refugee camp.

The MekTek in his system burnt and made him twitch as it felt the Genocaine's attempt to silence it. He spasmed but ignored the convulsion, hanging on to the ceiling supports with the claws of his two disused wings until it was over, and normal power flowed in the metal veins.

If Stuff—the pink quartz—were what Dreams could be made of . . . he could give Dani a new life. A real one. And not sad, used-up Dream Dani, with her artificially cauterized will, but Dani as she *was,* the real thing in Tupac's mind, a human monkey girl with not much talent but a lot of spirit.

Corvax waited for the Genocaine to take down the emotion and the physical discomfort of the MekTek fit, and then shifted his unwieldy bulk across to the microscope again. He looked at the fragment of alleged dead alien. Just a couple of drawbacks to the whole making-real plan right there in its grim warning, but no amount of staring at it like an owl was going to give him the answers.

And could he make himself anything less loathsome? There was a real question.

He radioed Tatresi. "Come on then, let the dog see the rabbit."

"You won't regret this." Tatresi's voice boomed out of the speakers, affable and smug.

Corvax cut the line. "I wouldn't put money on that."

The Stuff fragment, the real one, lay in the clamps obediently. Corvax studied Isol's explanations of her own engines. He freed the rock and held it in his naked hand, barely able to feel its weight through his tough skin in the infinitesimally light gravity of the asteroid. It was still going to take a while to figure out the right conditions to make it work. Delirium, dream, death—Three-D. What was the fourth?

The blue avatar of Tatresi appeared beside him. "What should we do?"

Corvax turned the nub of stone, his fingers listening to its inert molecular structure, relaying the pattern of its regularity as a hum into his mind. He glanced up at the avatar's smooth figure and shrugged, dirty feathers rustling.

"Get ready for hell. I'll take the rock. But if you want it broadcast like the seeds of Adam among the Forged, you can do that for yourself. This is poison, and even if you don't know it, I bet this thing demands its own price."

Tatresi shrugged. "So speaks the addict. I believe you. But have you seen any ill effects so far?"

Corvax grinned at him—but a Roc grin was all in the eyes and Tatresi didn't see it. "Only one, my friend. Only one dead thing—long, long dead. So, if you're still willing to get shafted, spread your legs and let's have that scrap iron out. Then you can dream an orgasmic dream of FTL, and we never need to see each other again."

"You will not mention . . ."

Corvax stared at him. "Who has the rubber gloves on, baby?"

Seraphs brought the news to General Machen first. They confirmed a sighting of Isol as she stole their wing space in the stratosphere and brushed sensor fields with the Heavy Angels surrounding Idlewild Base. They signalled him in official encrypted code.

A short time later his unofficial intelligencers, a pair of Ornith Degraded, perched outside his window on their summons posts and fixed him with their shining yellow eyes.

"Scavnugh," one shouted through the glass: the closest it could get to the word "Guvnor" in its harsh, throaty voice. " 'Sgot new stuff. Newstuff all over 'er, she 'as it. Never seen it before and don't know worrit is. Dunno at all. Looks like a summing. But worrisit?"

Same information, different rendition. He didn't know which of them was more apt.

Machen looked at the Ornith's ugly scarlet lizard head, with its plates of microcrystalline tegument that made it look half-armoured, and made no effort to hide his revulsion. They couldn't have brought the news any faster, but that didn't make him like them. They'd sell his information to anyone, given enough incentive, and he paid them well enough already. He snarled, "Get some facts, you little shits, then I'll pay you."

"Fuck 'im, Gritter," the smaller one muttered. It tidied its parroty plumage and aligned its antigravity primaries with fussy movements, then lifted its tail to splatter the ledge beneath the post. "He's not worth the effoht. Let 'im way till the uvvers all know, well nuff."

Gritter—Degraded Aquila Class Ornith Citizen—thoughtfully preened a few feathers with his toothy beak, and clattered his jaws to rid them of grease in a largely ineffective gesture. He sidled along the perch until his head was next to Machen's window. His breath steamed on the pane.

"Scavnugh," he began, more quietly and a lot more clearly than before. "Deep Space she is. So when she's surfing the curve of the baby-blue up above ya, close in to Earth like an old frien'—gotta ass yersen that, eh? Shoulda burst her little self open wi' that caper, so close to the G-well—right in its mouth. Heavy Angels' region that is, innit? Too high for us. Too low for Deepies. But no, oh no, she was low enough they could smell her engines in the cloud and they wasn't burning nothing you got, gettit? And sail sweet she did too, like a Hawk. Like a long 'Tross. And docked on the Wild station, not the old Deeper hangout at Arrecife. Gotta ask herself yerself, eh?"

Machen opened the window and fired the remains of his sandwich roll in Gritter's face. The messenger dodged and snapped viciously at the general's fingers as he slammed the window down again and locked it. He gave Gritter a flat stare. Gritter could speak proper Gaian too, when he wanted to.

Gritter wound in his neck in a heron-like stooping S, and considered. Finally he turned to his small companion. "Shift it, Necktie. Go get it and bring it in."

Necktie tumbled off the perch with the grace of a potato sack, and then spread his wings, instantly becoming a creature of speed and beauty. His green and blue form darted away between the high branches and heavy foliage of the small arcologies of Downing Street.

Machen looked away from Gritter's grinning speculation and across to his suite of chairs where he'd been having a conversation with one of the Heavy Angels. Its avatar sat weightlessly on the leather sofa, experimenting with all the kinds of movements it could make as a hologram. As Machen turned it looked up, and its halo of golden hair lifted around its face, glowing brightly.

"We've never seen this kind of thing," it said. "We think it must be alien technology. It appears to direct energy flow from the Hypertube: and that is in itself a purely theoretical statement, based only on best guess. Very interesting."

The expression on its androgynous marble face was cool, but Machen thought he detected an undercurrent of excitement there. The Angel Sisyphus Bright Eagle was relatively young and sure of himself. Machen suspected he was a keen participant at Independence meetings, and stiffened his back at the thought.

"Have you heard anything to suggest she might depart just as suddenly as she's arrived?"

"She's content to remain at Idlewild Base," the Sisyphus avatar said, flicking one of sixteen white-feathered wing-tips with a delicate pleasure in its superior understanding. "I wouldn't do anything to . . . enrage her, until we know all this thing's capabilities." It glanced out the window at Gritter, who was knocking dirt off some object by banging it against his perch. "I doubt your little pets there will have much to offer on that score. So I'll keep you informed." And, with a slow beat of his secondary flights, Bright Eagle vanished into thin air.

Machen stared at his visitor's vacated seat in dislike. It was one thing for him to despise the Degraded, but it was another when the damn Forgeds started degrading themselves with airs, graces and homemade hardware—especially the rebellious types who had their politics written all over them. Isol would be the first among that set, and it looked like the Sisyphus was a fan of hers. That was just peachy.

On the summons post Gritter was gnawing gummily at what Machen recognized as the end of his sandwich, filling removed and something that looked like a rat's nether regions stuffed inside. Drool spread in strings from his nonexistent lips. He gave Machen a jaunty wink.

Gritter was right, of course, whereas Bright Eagle was just full of platitudes. Isol's return made no sense, and her abilities were on no Forge blueprint in use. She had been in regulated radio contact, posting reports, until a few weeks ago when the interference of a minor meteor storm had disrupted contact and wrecked her mission's chances. She ought to be dead in the void right now, instead of which she was "in for repairs" at Idlewild's Orbital Base, and letting no technicians near her until whatever she wanted was dealt with personally by Machen.

Necktie came soaring back over the chimney pots. He carried a chip in his foot, which he handed across to Gritter after a minute's kerfuffle of snapping and biting on the post during which chip and sandwich swapped owners. Gritter then tapped the window. Machen opened it and took the casing, trying not to notice or smell the stringy meat hanging around it in the Ornith's jaws.

"Now," Gritter said, scratching just above his eye with the claw of one foot as he suddenly became more articulate, "you've got the juice. That's it right there. The scan is courtesy of the Seraph Gonsordin Magnificat, crafty bastard, taken before Isol knew it was 'appenin'. Cross-sectional 'nalysis, a kind of a—"

Machen shut the window and drew the blind down. He asked his secretary to summon the Strategos, his adviser, and sat down, turning the tiny object in his fingers. Gritter was an invaluable, if unreliable, line into Forged scuttlebutt. How he managed to obtain a data load like this was unknowable, but the provenance didn't matter. For the sake of his feathery hide it wasn't worth the price of faking things. Whatever the wretch had paid for it he would be rewarded double. Machen was no fool.

The Strategos walked into the office, without asking, and sat where the Heavy Angel had been, crossing his legs, adjusting his uniform. Whereas the avatar had made no impression, he sank deeply into the chair and sighed with fatigue. He ran a hand over the dense copper MekTek tracery on his head in an unconscious gesture, and caught the chip case as Machen tossed it to him. He extracted the pin-sized crystal and slotted it into a pore that led under the skin of his hand to where a red metal channel ran close beneath the surface.

Machen watched Strategos MekTek Anthony's face closely. No matter what he read, its significance was rarely betrayed by more than a flicker of one eyebrow. This time was no exception, although he paused before meeting the general's stare.

"I don't recognize that at all," he said, withdrawing the crystal pin and tossing it into the wastebasket with a flick of his wrist. "Doesn't mean much. I'll get a Ticktock Hive to take a look at it, if you like."

Machen assented with a nod. "Advice?"

"We knew the Forged Independence Movement would make a break at some time. It was only a matter of waiting for an opportunity. Looks like this is it. Whether or not the planet in question has any interest or value is irrelevant. They're going to try to get us off their backs and make a break for it." He shrugged. "It's not as if the Jovians don't think of themselves as a state in their own right anyway. Officially we're opposed to species' separation, but it may prove the most practical thing to allow them to go their own way. They may take the worst of the troublemakers with them. Enough will stay to cover the shortfalls. We might consider it a natural migration outward, under population pressure." He blinked as the several AIs running alongside his natural mind finished communicating with him.

"So, you believe this claim that Isol's found an extrasolar planetary system?"

The Strategos glanced at the shadows of the two Orniths shifting on the blind, looking like a single monster with two heads. "What interests me is this machinery it mentions. We know for a fact that it exists because she has it. But we don't know that anything else about her story is true. There could be all kinds of reasons for her to fabricate."

"Including the length of time her journey took and how long she was out there," Machen added, mostly for his own benefit. He glanced at Anthony and knew they shared the same suspicion.

Machen pushed it to the back of his mind. "Okay, speculate on the outcomes for me, Anthony. What d'you think?"

"We have to investigate the substance Isol claims is her

engine, and also the planet she has been to, if she's been to one. If the material is alien, then we have to consider a quarantine. If the aliens in question are still alive and kicking, we have to prepare for conflict with them."

Machen shook his head. "You're the happy puppy today. Anything any brighter in the offing?"

"We have to consider if it's worth having a protracted conflict with the militant members of the Forged Independence Movement. Terrorist actions are more likely than a straight civil war. And—" he paused for breath, "—if the alien engine systems and other technology become essential components of people who want to secede, then we have to make a decision on how *human* we're going to consider them in the future."

Machen scrubbed his hands together in a warming, washing action. "It's in our policy that one day we would get beyond Sol," he said, reflective. "And I suppose that the distance involved in this case would require some kind of new state to be set up. Even the ethos of creating the Forged had their eventual freedom written into it. I just didn't think it would come about this way."

"Feeling left behind?"

"Feeling extinct, if you must know." Machen pushed back from his desk and messaged his secretary for refreshments by tapping the wall.

Anthony grinned at him. "We're becoming old men. This is just the children leaving."

"And bringing their friends home uninvited," Machen muttered. "And I want to know all about these friends before I'll let anyone go off alone in that flashy new car."

"We can send an investigator," Anthony said. "That must be the first step. We can't rely on Isol's testimony, not with the engine in such intimate contact with her. She claims she's the only one to have reached this planet, so she can carry a representative of ours back with her. It would only require some minor adaptation: a Hand, perhaps."

There was a yawning sound from beneath the desk. A paw

appeared on Anthony's side of it from beneath the skirt, white speckled with black. It twitched a little and then settled there on the carpet, worn claws and pads faintly grey with old mud.

Machen smiled as he glanced down at his dog. "I wish I slept that well." He glanced up, eyes still misted with fondness. "Would you ask Tupac, just in case?"

Anthony blinked the slow blink of those transmitting on unheard frequencies to signal his activity for the sake of politeness. "It's done. She is in agreement. She doesn't believe that Isol's engine will contaminate her, although she acknowledges the risk."

"Then we just have to ask Isol."

"I'll go in person," suggested the Strategos glumly, frowning at the idea of an orbital trip.

"No, I'll send one of the Forged staff," Machen said. "Someone less important. Don't want her thinking she's got it all her own way yet. You find me an investigator: someone who will be able to tell dead alien from living alien on a distant world in an unknown region, just by looking." He smiled at the very idea. "We must have someone like that, right?"

"Like that," Anthony agreed, the coppery lines across his forehead briefly pulsing bright. He sparkled with investigation.

"Good. Time for Bob's walk, I think. C'mon." Machen made a nudging action as the secretary appeared, carrying hot drinks. There was another yawning sound and the paw disappeared from the desk front. With a soft tinkling of his collar buckle, Bob shook himself and appeared in full, moving to stare at the window and Gritter's shadow that was waiting in a slouch for its money. He barked suddenly, sharply, and they saw the shadow convulse, teeter, and save itself by hurling Necktie off the perch instead.

With enormous restraint, Gritter said nothing much, although they distinctly heard the beginning of the phrase "That bloody—"

Bob wagged his long collie tail. Machen said, "Sit," without much conviction, and added to Anthony, "Gritter's self-control is getting much better. One day I may even *trust* what he has to say."

The Strategos nodded, half his attention still in the room, the other half transported to his inner realms of information. "Don't go mad," he said drily.

Bob sat down, grinning from ear to ear.

Zephyr Duquesne watched a student's holographic display of social life and times in Ancient Rome as it played out above the broad flat surfaces of the sim suite. The tiny, maximum-opacity figures of the people were no more than an inch high, and the buildings were rendered in the most transparent of tones to allow her to see the citizens' movements in all places. She'd seen many of these in her time, and this was nothing special. There seemed to be a major session of the Senate going on at the same time as the Colosseum hosted a packed house, with tigers and gladiators battling ferociously. In the law courts Cicero was giving one of his famous orations. Slaves and trains of merchandise wove their way to market, and out in the suburbs, as the view panned, grapes were being picked on the rocky slopes and the gardens of large villas tended. Along the banks of the Tiber warships and merchantmen vied for moorings.

"This is a pan-temporal view?" Zephyr asked unnecessarily and the student nodded.

"Why do you suppose such a patchwork vision is so popular these days?" The question was aimed at herself more than the student, although she knew her answer—she detested such inaccurate mishmashes that drew "the most exciting" bits from history and planted them together under the banner *It's all the same era* as if that were explanation and justification enough.

"On generalized courses, anachronistic analyses are the best technique for putting all the information in one artefact. Easier to remember, and it gives a fuller picture of the times," the student explained, slightly uncertain but prompted by a swift glance at the official University answer displayed on his Abacand.

"And with regard to the history of the period, what does this—" Zephyr swept her hand out over the city "—tell us about the Romans?"

"That they traded far and wide, were a slave-owning culture with a democratic government and a—"

But Zephyr had now zoomed in on a tiny corner, where slaves laboured under the gaze of their masters, working on the floors of a house, laying paving slabs over the carefully judged pillars of a hypocaust. "And what does *this* tell us?"

"Er . . . sophisticated domestic comforts such as heated floors and running water in the home . . ."

"Yes, but think more about the people."

"They enjoyed a good standard of living?"

Zephyr wondered what she was doing there—and how many more times she would be there, trying to point out the way for someone who had no idea why they were studying Cultural Anthropology 101 except that it was a good way to acquire a history credit without having to tackle the twentieth century. "And how is this Rome similar to our lives today?"

The student looked blankly at her.

"These people—" she pointed at the builders, "—are making a what?"

"A room with underfloor heating."

"And how will that heating be maintained?"

"By fires lit below it."

"Tended by?"

"Slaves."

"Yes, and slaves are?"

"Captured prisoners of war . . ."

"Sometimes," Zephyr agreed. "But slaves are people who do not exist legally. They are also people whom one does not need to care about as if they were real. They are expendable and insignificant—is that right?"

"I suppose so, yes."

She sighed inwardly, wondering if the lad showed any backbone in any other classes. "Except that we know the Romans didn't always view slaves like this. In the cities, slaves could sometimes be valued like family. Out in the boondocks, they were whipped and killed . . ." She paused. "I was going to say like dogs, but really that's misleading. Although certain Romans could be cruel enough to animals, the pleasure of destroying another person usually led them to treat the human slaves worse than the animals. Animals were used, but subject humans were despised; both even underwent vivisection as a part of the progress of science, and both were considered, in those cases, to be simple automata, generally by people who considered *themselves* the finest minds of their generation. Now, there is a teaching immersion-module at the AI Virtual Library based on the life of a reasonably well-treated slave in the house of a Roman noble, Julius Martius. Have you tried it?"

"No, ma'am." He looked paler and Zephyr sighed.

"Think it over," she suggested. "These things are all there in the library for your benefit. You've made a fair job of representing most of the significant elements of this course requirement on your map, but if you want a credited pass I think we need some more in-depth research, perhaps insight, into the experiences of the age, rather than its clichés, don't you? For example, the slaves of the modern age, according to many of their political extremists, are the Forged. You might compare the situation in Rome to this and decide if you think their point is valid. What's the point of history, if it has nothing to say to the present?"

The young man's irritation crested. "I only want a pass grade," he said. "My real interest is materials engineering. They said this was an easy arts C. Other guys have passed it with less."

Zephyr stared out of the window towards anywhere else and then glanced back at him, flicking her hand to switch off the display. "Julius Martius," she said significantly. "First two modules minimum. And only come back when you've received your education."

He glared at her and then turned to go.

"Just thank me I didn't send you to our cotton farm in the antebellum American South," she sang out after him, amused by his irritation for a moment. She didn't mind the mediocrity of his attempt on the subject, but she minded the disrespect it displayed to the dead, especially the nameless dead who were long gone, stories untold, suffering unknown.

Since this wrapped up her afternoon's work there Zephyr collected her Abacand, switched off the sim suite, and went to check her mailbox by the Porter's Lodge with the casually off-hand air of someone expecting a significant parcel. And there it was, crumpled wrappings pock-marked with the stamps of three national routers, and she drew it out with reverence and hugged it to her chest.

"From the old country?" the Porter suggested, looking up from his crossword puzzle, pen wobbling like a tiny straw as he held it carefully in his Herculean fingers.

Zephyr glanced up at him and then down at the Caribbean stamp, "Maybe," she said, knowing full well that this was no box of local titbits from her sister.

"Ah." The Porter nodded significantly. She waited to see if he was going to make some other remark about it but he said, "I like a pack from home myself. Ordinary food, it's not the same." He bent with exaggerated concentration to the crossword and she smiled, leaving him to it.

In the privacy of her office she unwrapped the package hastily and withdrew the anticipated box from inside. "Grow Your Own Trilobites!" it demanded in large print. Along with it came a multicoloured headscarf that she hadn't been expecting, and a letter. The scarf was quite nice, and when she read the label she saw it was designed by a psychic just for her, created from "uniquely natural tussah silks whose irregularity lends sensual character to this decorative casualwear." Blue, yellow and pink swirls chased each other around it.

Zephyr set it aside and studied the box (delaying the anticipated pleasure of the letter), which rattled as she shook it. The instructions on the limited-edition palaeo-genome kit came with everything supplied except for habitat, and she glanced quickly at the list of aquarium requirements, wondering where she was going to get her hands on a tank. She was pleased to note that her specimens included the glamorous and bizarre *Radiaspis,* whose arrays of impressive spines would need a sizeable area for showing off.

She then sat down to read the letter, snuggling into her favourite chair out of sight of passing students or staff.

Dearest Zephyr, she read, enjoying the feel of the thin banana paper and the curl of the handwriting. *The wind in the coconut palms is brisk, I have to hold the paper down with pebbles. I saw the scarf shop close to the beach. All the wares outside were horizontal, straining at the leash. I thought they were Buddhist prayer flags until I saw someone come out with a bag under their arm. The man who makes them has a nifty loom which actually creates the warp and weft at the same time, weaving the caterpillars back and forth as they spin—a marvellous contraption which I knew you'd love to see (will send e-note). He claims he has gypsy genes, real Romany blood, which allows him to match colours to anyone, whether or not he's ever seen them. He made this for you after I'd told him the relevant facts: an English coal-rose, with a Jamaican heritage, Professor of Cultural Anthropology and Psychological Evolution, Trilobite fanatic, furtherer of radical educational experience.*

I'm colour-blind, as you know, so I hope it's all right. Meanwhile, as you can see, the project to create home-grown Trilobites has at last moved into production. Our lab specimens are doing very well at the Marianas site, although there has been some problem with a chemical pollutant. We think this may be lindane leaked from a 1990s tanker wreck, causing deformities of exoskeleton which you can only see once they shed their "perfect" lab-grown skins. We have many orders from secondary schools and also Universities, and hopes are high for the development of similar short-term natural-history projects using giant dragonfly specimens and other hopefully innocuous extinct species! (We receive over a hundred posts a day asking for dinosaurs. The financial temptation is considerable, although we have so far restrained ourselves to pointing out that saurian retro-genetics is already part of the Forge Palaeo-Dbase and evident in living people here and there. I doubt that does much to stifle the six-year-old's need for T. Rexes.) The Trilobite genomes have already been taken up for inclusion with Tupac and Mougiddo's Palaeo-sources, and we may see some Bathyforms adopting some of their eye-designs in the near future.

My own research work goes on apace. We find a new animal once every fortnight, more or less, and have had fun putting names together once their Clade place has been found on the tree. Mostly these are jellyfishes and cartilaginous small fish. I enclose a picture of one such, which hovered for a while as neither-nor until we finally pinned her down.

It was a peculiar creature, purple and blue on the outside, glowing faintly within, a long tail ending in a kind of fan trailing after.

This is Chrysaora Zephyra. *It is only a few centimetres long, a relative of the West Coast Sea Nettle, and moves with an extraordinarily independent energy of purpose and grace. I thought of you as soon as I saw it. The genome has been registered in your guardianship, and a copy of the certificate is on its way. I doubt that Zephyra has too much that is exploitable about her, but if she is sourced in any Forged yet to come, you will be godmother to someone new and your name will appear on their genealogy records as contributing* in loco parentis.

Write as soon as you can, I await all your news. With love . . . Kalu x

PS: When the trilobites hatch out, you should separate out the carnivorous ones—they have a tendency to eat the others, even if the nutrient base is present. In adulthood they regain their manners and take to supplied foods.

She read the letter twice and then folded it and put it in her pocket. She stuck the picture of the jellyfish Zephyr on her pinboard and sat looking at it for some minutes, her hand covering the letter's resting place.

"It's a good thing I don't insult easily," she said aloud to Kalu, swallowing a lump in her throat that wasn't entirely unlike a small, deep-ocean jelly with a couple of tiny spines and a tail.

She put the scarf around her head bandanna-style, even though it didn't go with the clothes she had on, and set the Trilobites aside on her desk. They sat next to the still-unassembled fragments of her Mini-saur Home Discovery Puzzle, for which she'd lost the brush that you were supposed to use to clear dirt from your tiny specimen. It had been a gift from her niece Rose last Christmas, who was at the age when dinosaurs were the only interesting element of the Earth's lost worlds. To her mind Zephyr spent far too much time going over old texts and bits of pottery, hiking up to caves that only contained paintings instead of allosaur bones.

Zephyr flicked a bit of dust off the puzzle. She rather liked it as it was—her plastic stegosaur embedded in hard clay and coloured plaster of Paris, studded with grit and a substance reminiscent of cat litter to simulate rock strata. Beneath it her unfinished notes on the religious beliefs of early European settlers were filmed with a fine coating of earth. She should throw them out, since she was never going to use them. The course had been cancelled due to lack of interest.

Instead, she sat at her desk and looked over the conference schedules for that winter. There was a Hawaiian colloquium on *The Sea and Coastal Civilizations in the Dark Ages*. There was *A Cambrian Tour of Ancient Oceans*: a multiformat project that proposed that the gathered experts pool their resources to create an educational simulation of that lost world. There was *Triremia: The Naval Conference of the Classical Period*, held aboard a series of replica vessels floating off Crete. And *Frontier: Conference on First Voyages* held on Zanzibar where the discussion would concentrate on the spread of *homo sapiens* from its origins in Africa and the likely routes of original ocean crossings, along with the shift of the continents and global climate influences. The last was an enormous gathering, promising to bring new information to light about Antarctica and its lost civilization of circa 14,000 BC, and Zephyr had every hope that it would include deep-ocean feature-mapping and extinction theory, so that Kalu would be sure to attend.

Although they'd corresponded for some time via the Trilobite interest group, they'd never met. Wary of long-distance romances, or indeed any romances after Sam Laplace the hotshot married lawyer had gone back to his wife some seven months previously, Zephyr had given no encouragement. She didn't send her picture and he didn't send his. She couldn't even have pinpointed the day that their lively discussions began to rove gradually away from dead things and into current affairs, other history, news and views, group gossip and chat. Still less could she have put her finger on the messages where she knew her tone had changed and she had found herself writing with honesty the casual sign-offs of all correspondence: warm wishes, fond regards, best, love.

Zephyr hadn't ever really thought about a relationship with him. It had emerged of its own accord from the mud of her busy schedule, blinking in surprise. She wasn't sure even now that this was what she wanted, but she couldn't help feeling the jolt of hope and enthusiasm that erupted when she thought of seeing him and continuing their friendship in person. She wondered now how she could get into the *Frontier* conference, what pretext she could use to write a paper about seafaring civilization and the effects that sudden long-distance travel into the unknown might have had upon the minds of men and women who hadn't, before their exposure to the ocean, understood how large a world could be and how frightening, cruel and hopeful.

"It is better to travel hopefully," she murmured to herself, circling the *Frontier* details, "than to arrive."

There was no knowing if their meeting might change this world of heartfelt fondness for some other feelings, of course. Zephyr knew she had to think of this, so that she would later be able to say, wisely, that she had thought of all possible outcomes and then had made her decision, based on scientific principles and a sound mind, to go and find him, when all along it was only the giddy, elated sensation of joy that propelled her, lightly frolicsome, in that inevitable direction.

If she were wise she ought to check him out more formally

first, and here her happiness foundered on a very solid hidden rock. She didn't want to do that. She knew exactly what she'd find, "handwritten" letters in lovely sky-blue ink and scarves notwithstanding. She knew, she just didn't *want* to know. How did you become a researcher into deep-sea life and history in this day and age, running projects two miles down, if you were just an Unevolved man?

Cross with herself for spoiling the fun, she was about to go get a cup of coffee when there was a ring of chimes from her satchel. Her Abacand alerted her to an incoming call and said, muffled somewhat by a battered copy of Zeigler's *Days Out In Ancient Greece,* "General Machen wants to speak to you."

"Who?" She was reading the instructions on the Trilobite pack again, hoping that this would be someone she could fob off.

"General Machen, Commander of Gaiasol System Military and Civil Security." It paused and added, "The bloke in charge of all the heavy hardware, the police, the army, the navy and the rest of that 'keeping people on the straight and narrow' malarkey. The one who stays in office when the government gets booted out; suppresses uprisings, smooths out land disputes, negotiates treaties, arrests pirates and felons. You know."

Zephyr picked the small, cuboid machine out of her satchel and looked at it, setting the Trilobite pack aside. "Why?"

"I'm a telephonist, not a bloody telepathist," the Abacand retorted, pleased at being able to include a stock piece of mechanical outrage in its conversation. "Are you here or not?"

"Always the profound, eternal questions from you simple office staff," she sighed, trying to come to grips with having a major conversation with a major person after her daydreaming. "Okay, put him on vox only." She took a measured breath. "Zephyr Duquesne here."

"Professor Duquesne, this is a secured line. Your machine assures me you are in private. I hope that's the case."

"Er, yes." She found herself sitting bolt upright as if facing an examining committee.

"Then I'll be brief. We'd like you to come to Idlewild Base on a . . . consultancy basis. For a week or two at most. Full pay and compensatory package, of course—to be discussed, although I'm sure that won't be a problem. We have a pressing matter that requires an expert in your field, and you came highly recommended."

Her mind scurried around, temporarily lost. She racked her brains. "Are you sure?"

"I'm certain," he said firmly.

"Well then, I'll be glad to come." *I suppose,* she thought.

"Excellent. A Passenger Pigeon will collect you from the University in fifteen minutes." He hung up before she could start to protest.

"What do you think that was all about?" she asked the Abacand, still stunned—and starting to wonder how she was going to explain a sudden absence in the middle of the semester.

"Probably something to do with what was on the Forged Radio this morning," the Abacand said. "I tried to wake you up for it but you were stone-cold as usual."

Zephyr remembered, vaguely, a dream about Boudicca and heavy horses thundering through acres of mud, the cry of battle and the scream of the dying.

"Play it back," she said.

6. PASSENGER PIGEON

The Passenger Pigeon could be seen from the roof of the University's Forged Research Station by five past five that afternoon. Zephyr had never seen one before, nor had most of the staff. Pigeons numbered only three in the whole of creation, and spent most of their lives high in the atmosphere, ferrying important people and classified documentation around the globe. Rumour had gotten around, in the few minutes Zephyr had left to make her arrangements, and there was a gathering of eager Forge-spotters in the lounge beside the small flight deck, faces close to the safety glass as they watched and waited.

The Pigeon came silently, almost indistinguishable from the afternoon sky: a smooth blue oval with a long, graceful tail like a gigantic airborne manta ray. Low sunlight shone golden off its pale underside, and glinted in tiny blinks of pure white from the diamond scales on its wings as they angled gently this way and that, feeling for the best course through the wind's currents.

It was only when the Pigeon passed the University's Library tower on its final approach that Zephyr realized how big it was—a good fifty or sixty metres long and about forty wide; almost too big for the deck, which was used to small helicopters and robot-lifter flights. Its sinuous tail added some twenty extra metres at the rear, bearing fins of unknown purpose along half that length, each the height of a human and as wide at their fleshy base. At the end of its long glide the silver MekTek on its underside opened and put down fine support struts that groped for the ground. It perched on them as delicately as a landing butterfly, making no sound at all. At rest its wings folded and drooped towards the ground. There was a general sigh of admiration in the lounge.

Zephyr, who had been extremely apprehensive, felt better as

she heard staff from the Research Department start to talk about the Pigeon's excellent statistics. Also, she felt better because she'd never seen a Forged human as beautiful as this one, and its beauty seemed incongruent with her revulsion-in-waiting, a knot in her gut that wouldn't release. She'd never boarded a person before.

It felt like it ought to be taboo, like a kind of strange sexual perversion, and she was ashamed of her feelings, so utterly Unevolved in their lack of sophistication and primitive fear. With determination she made her hand loosen its death-grip on her satchel, and attempted to breathe easy for the first time since Machen had promised her this privilege. Next to her a Herculean Doctor of Ecosystems, on loan to the Research Department from the Ministry of Agriculture, looked down and smiled wistfully at her, his outsize teeth brilliant white.

"I don't half envy you," he said, his voice a rumble, it was so deep. He looked back at the elegant lines of the Pigeon. "And her," he said, flexing the fingers on his hugely muscled primary arms, each strong enough to pull up a sapling in one tug.

Zephyr smiled at him and her mind was filled suddenly with the image of the huge man longing to dance ballet, to be light, to be lithe. Didn't everyone hanker after what they weren't? "But she'll never walk in the forest or the field," Zephyr said to him.

"No," he said, but he didn't stop staring.

The Pigeon's skin darkened as it came to rest, becoming a deep blue and green colour flecked with orange and red like a sunset sky. It waited patiently for the University AI systems to address it and match protocols. Zephyr, the students and other staff waited on tenterhooks, wondering what it would say, who it was, whether, like some of the other Space and Airborne, it would use an avatar and what this would say about its personality and politics.

"You're all set," the University's primary AI announced through the lounge speakers.

"Thanks," the Pigeon said, its voice appearing to resonate through its gills as they opened to taste the city air. It had a rich, feminine voice, the kind an opera singer would have. "Professor Duquesne, you are invited to join the Chiefs of Staff at Kiliman-jaro Base and later at Idlewild. I am Ironhorse AnimaMekTek Aurora. We are scheduled to depart in five minutes. Please board when you are ready."

Zephyr picked up her overnight case as she heard someone explaining in an overexcited monotone: "AnimaMekTek classes are among the more straightforward cyborg hybrids, of course. Part animal and part machine. I did my doctoral work on them. Human brains assume the management of both systems. The rarity of the Pigeon lies in its cross-environmental engineering, you see. It's a marine-style form in an aerial world—"

"Very fashionable in design terms, and most sought-after as personal servants to the wealthy Unevolved," their conversation partner chipped in suggestively.

"Yes, hah, although it's seldom in these days that any self-respecting Anima would submit to paid work with ordinary human masters . . ."

Zephyr's mind was less on the political niceties than on the prospect of boarding as she came to the lounge door in time to witness a pore on the Pigeon's side suddenly dilate and flex, widen, shiver and expand. A sphincter muscle eased and a thick tube of fleshy stuff exuded moistly from the opening to reveal the chrome fitments of a hatch within. The deck marshal was busy pushing an adjustable staircase into position for her, and turned to beckon as it clicked into place against the hatch's clamps.

Zephyr walked briskly across. She paused at Aurora's eye-less, featureless nose and said, "I'm Zephyr."

The Pigeon hummed a soft note of amusement. "I recognize you from your picture," it said quietly and Zephyr realized that of course it knew what she looked like. It—she—would have had a full briefing and needed no eyes to see. "What a lovely name," it added as she hesitated there.

"Thank you." Zephyr blushed, and felt all of her seventy kilograms very heavily. It was one thing to be named for a capricious little breeze, another to turn into a solid woman who had to work at her ability to flit. In the absence of more conversation she made her way to the staircase and climbed up, resisting the urge to turn around at the top and wave to the crowd, and carefully not looking at the flesh around her as she felt its radiated warmth.

Then came the moment she had been dreading. What was the protocol for dealing with the entry into another's bodily cavity? Should she move the hatch membrane aside like a curtain? The Pigeon put her out of her misery by drawing aside the sheets of skin with a smooth flex of muscle and machinery in her hatch-rim.

"Don't worry, I'm not a virgin," it said so that only Zephyr could hear, and chuckled with a deep, dirty enjoyment. Zephyr laughed, not quite hysterically, and stepped through with haste into a tiny cabin, warm and softly lit and containing another passenger.

He stood up, bent low because of the roof height, and held out his hand. Metal and silicon shone on the bare skin of his head and in the palm that touched hers, burnished motes that Zephyr felt as cooler dots and lines against his skin.

"MekTek Strategos Anthony," he introduced himself, his smiling expression soon turning serious again as he sat down and strapped himself in.

"Delighted," Zephyr said, placing him after a moment of thought as one of Gaiasol's military top dogs—a curious man, who was not Forged but an adapted Unevolved human, capable of belonging to either side, or neither. He was often shown in televised debates, and was as likely to argue for the Unevolved— or Hanumaforms, as he preferred to label them—than the Forged themselves. He was quite famous. She settled her bag at her feet and busied herself with the seat belts, which were comfortingly mundane with their webbing and buckle.

"Have you had a briefing?" the Strategos asked her.

"No," Zephyr said. "I thought it was just a student prank at first."

A smile ghosted across his face. "Isol has returned."

"Amen," said Aurora, startling Zephyr who had forgotten that she was there.

"She must be quite old by now," Zephyr said, hoping that Anthony was about to supply some more information so she wouldn't have to reveal her ignorance, which had been only somewhat alleviated by hasty infill from the Abacand.

"Twenty-five," Anthony and Aurora said together.

Aurora sniggered. "By Earth years only. Who knows what real time has passed out there?"

"She claims she has not encountered significant space-time distortion," Anthony said gravely. "But she also claims to have travelled beyond the galactic hub, so one of the accepted sums or some of us are wrong about space and time." He glanced at Zephyr. "I expect you can tell us more about that, Professor."

"I doubt it," she said. "I'm a historian. As to what I'm doing here, your guess is as good as mine."

"I see," said Anthony, frowning. His face seemed much older suddenly, and Zephyr guessed he was in his late forties. In place of hair he had a delicate lace copper fretwork of MekTek, inscribed with patterns that looked to her very like tribal New Zealand art.

"Is that a Maori tattoo?" she asked.

He reached up and touched his head. "Oh, yes. Traditional, although I'm not exactly a purebreed."

"It's designed to reflect your true nature."

"Yes." He glanced warmly at her. "Some people think I shouldn't have it at all. Lack of sufficient cultural credits in my pedigree." He smiled ruefully and they shared a mutual glance of distaste for the current climate of gene/meme inheritance classifications among the Unevolved: something that had begun in response to the Forged Class Systems, so that everyone could identify themselves as part of a great history, somehow.

"Some people are lucky to have made it this far in the gene pool," Zephyr said. "So, what is it?"

"Flying fish," he said.

"And here you are inside one," Zephyr said, smoothing the peacock colours of her own clothing. "Small world."

"I'm sure I can legally charge you a licence fee for use of my image," Aurora added quietly and laughed, pulsing violet colour through the internal walls of the cabin to show she had not minded Zephyr's description.

"So, a historian of what?" the Strategos asked her, spreading his hands out.

"Cultural archaeology," Zephyr supplied. "The speculative construction of the language and lore of ancient civilizations, working backward from physical evidence and fossils in the linguistic and intellectual records."

He raised his eyebrows and nodded. "Yes, I see. That must mean that the rumours you heard, Aurora, have something to them." He turned to face Zephyr. "Isol may have found another Earthlike planet. One she wants to claim as a homeworld for the Forged."

"She found another world?" Zephyr repeated, not sure she believed this, although there was no reason to think it might not happen one day.

"The Forged have wanted to go their own way for a long time," Anthony said. "All they were waiting for was either the discovery of a suitable system with adequate resources, or for Earth-based government to lose control of Mars and the gas giants."

"Waiting for Old Monkey to die off." Zephyr nodded. She'd heard enough about that in her life to feel bored with it. "If she has found this world, what will you do?"

"What would *you* do?" His brown eyes glinted at her, the stubble on his chin softly human against the sharp metal shimmer of the foils embedded in his skin.

Zephyr closed her eyes and imagined herself and the other old monkeys being offered an island paradise—Jamaica, maybe, with blue waters and long sands, hot days and calm nights, sea breezes and the faint sound of kettledrums always in the distance, beating out a dance tune. Well, Jamaica wasn't entirely like that outside the resorts, but she could dream. Compare this with the University: cold English winters with rain and winds, grey skies, work, functions, dreary arguments over what the shape of a pot or the frequency of male pronouns meant to their ancestors. She thought of Kalu, carefully forging real handmade letters by remote AI from his post at the bottom of the Pacific, and her heart squeezed itself closed over a sudden microburst of loving kindness.

"I might take up the pension," she said finally. "But I wouldn't go alone."

Anthony smiled. "Neither would I. But Isol's not like that, and neither are many of the offworld Forged. They don't care about us monkeys."

"No Function, you mean." Zephyr nodded as she emphasized the F-word; it was the old argument, the unwinnable one, Pinocchio's dilemma, existential catastrophe. If you were made for a purpose then you have a reason to exist. If you exist and have no purpose, what is the point of you? All the Forged had originally been created for work of specific kinds, all of it serving Old Monkey in some way. Their devotion to Form and Function as a sustaining faith was an adaptation to their lives as sterile workers. When they quickly decided Old Monkey wasn't worth the effort any longer and began to look for their own reasons for living, it was to be expected that shedding the feudal attitude would take time, perhaps a long time if Unevolved patterns of clinging to outdated "tradition" with its life-squeezing patriotism were anything to go by. For most Forged there was no purpose to the Unevolved anymore. They were simply cranky old grannies who had to be placated and pensioned off, fed soup until it was time to die. A homeworld beyond the Sol system would be a perfect spot in which the Forged could make a new beginning and forget their origins and the experience of mingled pride, shame and puzzlement that went with it.

Well, they believed that it was that easy, at least. Zephyr had her doubts.

The only reason they hadn't gone away years ago was that

Earth still held the loyalty of the two Forge Citizens, their father-mothers. Respect for these two Forges kept them in line, and the Forges were indebted with gratitude to their creators for the existence of themselves and their children. The irony of contradictions here wasn't lost on Zephyr, but she had tired of talking about it long ago, preferring to quibble over the behaviour and beliefs of people who weren't going to answer back. History repeated endlessly—it was what made it so interesting.

"Clinging to Function is a puritan ideal." Aurora broke into the brief silence. "Not all of us care for such simplistic ideology. Form is likewise irrelevant; only what you can contribute to the lives of others should be the measure of a soul's value. I didn't choose to be an Ironhorse Class, as I know you didn't choose to be short, female or black, Dr. Duquesne."

She had pointedly left out referring to the Strategos, who was wearing a look of wry familiarity because he had obviously chosen his MekTek status.

"I chose to change in order that I might contribute something more than I otherwise could have," he said. "Freedom of choice must be our first concern."

Zephyr indicated that she agreed with him by a gentle nod of her head. She had no wish to start getting into that—the right to reproduction for the Forged was the hottest topic of the year and as an Unevolved, a person of ordinary birth and what passed for normal human genes, Zephyr was well aware of the varying weight her words might carry when placed in particular ears. Between the Pigeon and the Strategos, she couldn't think of the right way to say anything on the subject. One thing the Forged hadn't lost out on was their emotional heritage, although frequently that had been tinkered with to many various ends. Some said it was the only thing that made them human at all.

For the rest of the journey they talked of other things, carefully avoiding the subjects of illegal clinics in the asteroid belt; of reported successful childbearing by certain Classes whose offspring were not, so far, Degraded; and of the possible defection to the Forged Independence Movement of the orbital Forge

Citizen, Pangenesis Mougiddo. Zephyr knew these subjects were all for later, and so, with a lurch of her insides as the Pigeon exited its supersonic pattern, she didn't look forward to the landing—or to what was to come after.

Instead, she concentrated on Aurora's display screen and the views of the African coastline rushing towards them. There the evening skies were a dusty lilac over the glittering lights of the cities and towns, the earth a rich and formidable black between them, where a single lake or river shone like streaks of bright calcite running through marble. They skimmed a mile above this region and then turned to the cloud cover of the high plateau west of Zanzibar where the two peaks of Kilimanjaro rose above their grey, moon-cast mantle. To the north they saw the blackness of the Serengeti, and Zephyr looked hard for the Rift Valley fault and the faintest of lights that might mark out the spot of Olduvai Gorge and Laetoli, where once two hominids and a proto-horse had walked in ancient days and left their footprints in soft volcanic ash to last three and a half million years.

The base at Kilimanjaro lay on the Saddle, a flattened region between the two summits of blunt, glacier-capped Kibo and jagged, snow-toothed Mawenzi. Fitting, Zephyr thought, that humanity reaches to the stars from the point it first reached out on the Earth. As they came close to the mountain she could see the silver thread of the Jacob's Ladder, which ran from its anchor on Kibo up through the atmosphere to the distant orbital base at Idlewild.

It was not perfectly equatorial and, to compensate for the oscillatory defects, the Heavy Angels that rode the wires swung and spun, catching low or rising high on their escapes and returns. These vast bodies, armoured and massive for space flight and ground manoeuvres, looked tiny to her, like motes of bright dust on a spider's web. Above the cloud line the smooth domes of their eye-shields shot an occasional flash of reflected moonlight.

At night the base itself was above the clouds' late-afternoon retreat to the forest. The travellers came in at a dizzying rate, the towers and buildings suddenly looming as if growing at high speed. Zephyr sat back as green light flared suddenly from the landing pad in a beacon shaped like the Hindi script for Om, the universal symbol/sound of fundamental unity—a spacefarers' welcome.

From the depths below their feet they heard Aurora begin to hum. The sound grew louder and more pure in tone as she refined her approach Doppler and located their touchdown. She alighted with such precision they felt nothing. Zephyr was both glad and sorry to leave and, because Aurora had no hands, she touched the wall beside her seat before she got up.

"Thank you for a smooth flight," she said, and hoped that the tone of her voice revealed the depth of her gratitude for such an easy introduction to Forged travel.

"Thank *you*, Professor Duquesne," Aurora said, her emphasis perfectly conveying her understanding of Zephyr's unspoken meanings. "I look forward to hearing more of your exploits with us here."

A flash of bright yellow ran through the skin under Zephyr's hand: the stars of Aurora's personal rank, which Zephyr recognized with a flush of pride as a salute. She was still warm with relief as she followed the Strategos out onto the ringing echoes of a covered metal walkway. They were met by a neatly uniformed line-up of men and women in the dusty blue of Gaiasol colours, the crest of Earth glowing against their right breasts as the fabric displayed the planet circling in real time as if viewed from orbit, the sun merely a gleam over the Atlantic as it turned towards night.

General Machen and his aides greeted them in a round of handshakes and introductions that Zephyr attempted to follow with great attention, but with no real hope of recalling names, faces, ranks and jobs. She'd once gone through an entire University year without learning to put more than two correct names to faces in her tutorial groups, and when writing performance reviews she always had to have the student record in front of her. Faces and their deeds, their views and their conversations she *did* remember.

On this occasion she felt she would remember the general at least. He was an unusually sturdy Unevolved, with the bullish frame that came from plenty of hard labour and tough, land-working genes, not unlike those of a Herculean Citizen. His skin was a modern-style ultra-melanin fast-tanning white, the kind that looked Mediterranean until a few hours' sunlight would cause it to blacken completely and this, in its present mid-state of deep bronze, showed up his piercing blue eyes. These sat in his craggy face like polished stones in the skull sockets of a jungle god. The warmth that narrowed them as he shook her hand didn't soften their acuity one bit.

"Professor Duquesne, welcome to Kilimanjaro Base." He spoke softly, as though he didn't want others to overhear. "I'm sure you're as keen as I've been to understand the reason for your presence here."

Zephyr nodded and admired the firm grip of his fingers as they shook hands. "I'd be particularly interested in knowing the duration of my stay, General. I have seminars and work groups to cover in my absence."

"I'm sure," he said, clipped and polite with disinterest. He glanced at the Strategos behind her. "Anthony, you will make the necessary arrangements for the professor?"

It was only then that Zephyr realized—with her sketchy knowledge of the roots of the Greek-based Citizen Classnames—that of course Strategos was a blend-word, the old name for a general, now carrying the new weight of later derivations: strategic adviser, battle tactician, master planner. Not having had any dealings with the military in person, she suddenly felt that she must have breached etiquette very badly on their journey here, but Anthony inclined his head.

"It has been done."

Zephyr frowned crossly as she realized the depth of their understanding and her own ignorance. She hoped this wasn't going to continue for long and watched their greeting of one another, which seemed friendly enough to suggest long acquaintance. The metalwork on Anthony's head and exposed hands caught the shine of the walkway's periphery lights, and flashed red-gold as light ran through the optics. She envied its prettiness and its function—your very own individual AI systems linked to global network feeds and subsystem slave pilots—as they all turned to follow the general deep into the heart of the base's architecture. If a historian like herself ever got kitted up with Tek like that they'd be able to carry with them an intelligent library big enough to oversee every development from *homo habilis* to the present day. As it was she made do with her Abacand and the link-data speed the University paid for—not the fastest on Earth.

They arrived eventually in an airy room furnished with an oval table and chairs, arranged close to one end. Opposite this formal comfort a large screen displayed current views of the Vaporetti city-state Venezia Nova where it hung in the soft stream of a quieter cloud band on Jupiter's solar-facing side.

Although it was a wide 'scape and included most of the forty-kilometre-long construction, Zephyr could still see individuals moving here and there where they had linked together in large flotillas to better navigate the gas streams and unify their propulsion for cross-city journeys. They sailed rapidly with the currents to Downstream in slick knots of aerodynamic intimacy, and beat steadily Upstream against the flow in looser formations, individuals constantly swapping places, the people in the centre of the groups resting as those on the outside took their turn and beat their cilia and wings at a furious rate. Despite the temperature and pressure stats reading off at the bottom of the image, Zephyr thought how warm it looked, how cosy, all glowing orange and soft cream in the sun's rays. The droplet shapes of the buildings were brushed by wispy clouds like lambswool. These were torn to shreds by the violence of invisible bow-waves before they touched the surface.

She thought it was beautiful. She would have liked to visit, but it was something of a silly thought. Venezia Nova might look good, but she knew it would be as hostile an environment as she could wish for. The Vaporetti Council were in the forefront of the Forged bid for independence. Their GNP relied for only 2 percent of its total on gas shipments to Earth, and derived the rest from products that supplied other Forge facilities. Even if she didn't mind the biting cold and the need to wear a suit 9.8 hours a day, she'd get a frosty reception from many of the locals. Unevolved tourists had been kidnapped there before now. The only ones tolerated were those with a taste for riding nitrogen flows and dicing with death in the gelid storm winds, and they were popular because they spent generously for the privilege and lived most of their lives in the city—adopted sons and daughters with clumsy prosthetics, endearing in their incapacity and the way they reminded natives of what hopeless creatures Hanumaforms could be.

When they were seated Zephyr noticed that their group had been joined by an avatar, which must have materialized as she'd gazed entranced at the cloud city. It was a very tall human the colour of blue slate, with no body hair at all, dressed in a white waist wrap somewhat like a toga. Its wrists were banded with silver and gold decoration and its bald head radiated a very faint white light—its nominal halo. It turned its gold eyes towards her and she saw herself reflected off their yellow surfaces, wider and shorter than ever.

"This is Ironhorse Timespan Tatresi," General Machen said. "He is the spokesman for the Forged Offworld Transport Services."

"Citizens." The Timespan inclined his head regally in their general direction and placed his hands on the table, palms down. He smiled, revealing a silver toothstrip in his black gums.

Zephyr knew that his real body was somewhere in-system, and that it must look as different to a human being as the Forged could get. Timespans plied the corridors between planets and so never entered atmospheric conditions. They ate solar radiation and micro-detritus swept from the spaceways, like a kind of void-loving whale shark. They had the biggest engines ever built and were capable of 0.25 lights, given a clear run. She'd never seen one, even on screen. Meeting the avatar was a real privilege for her—as it would have been for most of the Unevolved, who had no contact with offworld Forged. She wondered about his job title as union leader—what was that exactly, and was it why he was here? Her ignorance of current affairs was embarrassing, but fortunately nobody seemed inclined to give her a test. They launched straight into the subject at hand.

"As you all know by now," General Machen began, with a deliberate lowering of his shoulders and a straightening of his jacket, "Voyager Lonestar Isol has made a return to Earth orbit after an absence of fifteen years."

He paused to gather their reactions one by one. Zephyr saw the Timespan nodding with a slow smile on his face, proud. To her right Anthony had a faster rate of head-shake in the affirmative, and his smile was taut with what he saw behind those years, both in possibility and in distance. The Unevolved faces were bleak at the idea of spending so long alone.

"Cut to the chase, Byron," said the Minister for Internal Affairs (Earth), whom the government had seen fit to send at the last moment and whose name was something like Prince Kop. He pushed his seat back and waved a hand languidly at the screen, beckoning for potted information. "What's the damage?"

The general brought up a galactic map of the Western Spiral Arm. "There's the damage, Prinkoff," he said as a nondescript star began to shine out of a region far closer to the hub than Sol, just within the Galactic Habitable Zone. "That is a star called Zia Di Notte—" he glanced around them and added under his breath, "Bloody name-your-own-star schemes," before continuing, "and around it is a planetary system not entirely unlike this one. There are five for our nine. Zia Di Notte is getting orange, and will burn up in another couple of million years. The second planet is in a classic life-favourable orbit. It has oceans of salinated water. The crust is sixty kilometres deep. The core is liquid iron. There is a breathable atmosphere and the pressure at the surface is short of Earth normal, but not much; rather like the outside here on the Saddle. Need I go on?"

Zephyr looked at the map and said, without thinking, "Is there life on it?" She thought that was the obvious question. But in the ensuing silence, she figured it probably wasn't, if you had any clue what you were looking at. Still, she saw no reason to give up and so repeated it to the half-open mouths and surprised stares in front of her.

The Timespan Tatresi was first to speak. His voice was geological in timbre, but warm with amusement at the expense of the others at the table.

"I believe the general was going to discuss that *after* we had exclaimed at the distance of this star from our own and at the remarkable fulfilment of the first Voyager commitments to locate extrasolar planets, which are plentiful, but far away, and often contain nothing we haven't already got in abundance right here. But as you say, the most interesting question is: what else is there that you haven't mentioned, General? Is there life?"

"The life isn't the goddamned problem," Machen replied, tossing aside the stylus which he'd been using to cue his presentation and sitting back in his chair. "The problem is that Voyager Isol has staked a claim on the place. She wants it to be the promised land for the Forged."

"So, there *is* life there?" The minister sat up suddenly and began to fumble around for his secretary Abacand in his pockets.

"How has she got there and back in this limited time?" the Strategos asked at the same moment, not moving from his position, elbows on the table and hands braced under his chin.

"Is it only *her* word you've got for all this?" Admiral Somebody butted in, just under the wire.

"*Why* isn't the existence of life there the problem?" Zephyr demanded, imagining some early civilization of aliens moving through their unsuspecting lives in pastoral ignorance of the technologies about to rain from on high; her mind immediately filled with Spanish conquistadors, awash in armour and savagery, erasing South America's prehistory with fire and the sword.

General Machen gave them a scathing look and reached towards the stylus with a very deliberate hand, "Well now, if you'd all shut up and listen to what I've got to say in the order I've got to say it in, you might find out the answers, now, mightn't you?"

They all retreated, except for Anthony, who simply turned his head towards the screen, and Tatresi, who might or might not have been looking at any one of them—with his eyes you couldn't tell. (And, Zephyr reminded herself, of course they weren't his eyes anyway, they were only pretend; he was probably getting all his news from some AI plug-in, but it was impossible to react differently to him all the same.)

Zephyr frowned and bit back her anger for the time being. She watched some approach shots to a blue-beige planet, orbited by two reasonably sized moons; an orange star blazed away in one corner of the image. The shot panned back and around, zooming in and out through vast distances to show another planet not much farther away, a faint atmospheric haze around it, and another three moons of varying sizes and coloration. It was only as the fly-past became very close indeed that she realized that the first planet had no natural moons. They were constructs: spheres with deep voids that reached right through so that stars shone from the other side. They reflected different colours: blue, green and bronze. One even had a kind of pattern to it, although it was hard to discern from the available picture.

"The life problem, as you put it," Machen said, "is that there is clearly oxygen in the atmosphere, up to a half Earth normal, but from Isol's data, there appears to be nothing living down there. Chemically, that is an absurdity unless the life was there until very recently and has now gone."

"Holy shit," said the minister, forgetting that his secretary was now sitting on the table, mindlessly recording every word for the presidential ears.

The general said nothing, but kept his finger on the stylus control, giving them new views of the planet's surface. It was arid, stony and barren, for all its water. A rock covered in other rocks. But then came the most shocking sight of all, for Zephyr at least. From her orbital vantage the Lonestar had shot a picture of what was most certainly the ordered layout of a significant structure. As the detail became refined she spotted strangely graceful spires and curling, organic forms, but then the film cut out and the screen went blank.

They all turned to the general.

"Empty," he said.

They stared at him.

"Moon stations, planetary cities, towns, settlements, industry—if that's what any of it is. Empty. The whole place is deserted."

"Where are the plants?" Again Zephyr was first to speak. This time she looked irritably at the military officers and Anthony, and then directly at the general.

Machen scowled, but said, "Good question. Considering the time of the alleged alien disappearance, even if they took all the life with 'em you'd expect to see some recolonization by now. Granted there's been no surface sampling, so we don't know if the planet's seas are hosting some kind of bacterial forms."

The minister cleared his throat, ignored this line of conversation and said, "But if her claim is legal, then this could be exactly the spark the Forged have been waiting for. It could mean civil war."

Zephyr watched Tatresi's face, which remained coolly amused, and Anthony's, which frowned. The Strategos said, "And if you don't accede to their demand, it could also mean civil war. No doubt this is exactly the situation Isol intended to produce. She may even have been waiting out-system and listening to broadcasts until she thought the time was right. If she has this capability to travel superlight, then there's a lot of things she could have been doing in the time when we imagined her to be en route. She could have been in-system and out of it tens, possibly hundreds of times. General, have you checked the Missing Persons files?"

Machen circled his head on his neck, wincing with the aggressive motion that clearly failed to relieve his tension. "There's no new reports of recently missing Forged from any of the planets. And all Unevolved have been accounted for on chip sweep."

"And in any period of time since the Lonestar has been away?" Anthony asked.

The Timespan was nodding. "Yes, of course. Superlight or another form of technology, such as one that uses some form of Hypertube, could also entail an escape from linear time."

The general nodded and keyed his stylus. "I'll look into that."

"We should bring the Pangenesis Tupac in on this," Tatresi rumbled. "I'd prefer if you dealt with him directly, since you intend to pursue an investigation into the claim of the planet as a frontier region, and he's the one most Forged will look to for a lead. Do you wish us to arrest the Lonestar?"

"What's her status?"

"She awaits your decisions at Idlewild Services."

"Then she can stay there for now. Did you find out anything about her . . . adaptations?"

"A scan has been taken but no samples have been obtained so far."

"Then, gentlemen, lady." Machen stood. "I suggest we postpone further discussion until we have more knowledge. Our proposal is to check the legality of this claim by sending a qualified examiner to the planet, as is our right. On their return we shall make a ruling, within the law."

"Is this really necessary?" the minister began.

"Even if the culture that once lived there has gone," Tatresi said, "we must be sure it has no plans to return."

Zephyr didn't follow the remarks about the Hypertube, although she planned to get the information out of her Abacand as soon as she could, but she understood very well what a direct dealing with Tupac meant—the start of negotiations between two potentially opposed factions.

She was wondering how anybody could decide what constituted an abandonment of a planet, or even a civilization on one, as she asked, "Who are you sending, then?"

As one, they all turned to look at her.

"Someone who can ask the right questions," Anthony said.

7. TATRESI AND THE GAIAFORMS

It was over thirty years since the scandal had rocked Mars and created a sculpture of death on the Moon. Over that time the purgatory of the Gaiaforms had slipped out of the news, and become merely the subject of the occasional heartwrung documentary or very late show. Since they were not able to speak on their own behalf, the amount of sympathy they could drag to the cause of Forged Independence was slight, but Isol and Tatresi had not forgotten it. Now the moment had come when they might challenge the bureaucratic gridlock with direct action instead of a plea for jobs and living conditions that were never going to manifest.

Among the first Forged ever created during the solar expansion programme, the Gaiaforms had been without doubt the largest and among the most complex. The blueprints for each of them alone consumed more than a thousand terabytes of storage in compressed form. Looking at them now, as he drifted in towards their isolated platform, Tatresi shuddered to think about such a massive undertaking. Gestation, education, construction, synthesis . . . the Gaiaforms were monsters of another era, capable of moving mountains, drinking seas, planting continents, exhaling entire weather systems. All that and a single mind to see it done, a single personality to assume such responsibility.

And now the remaining two of the four floated, iced in space, asleep in the heavy, dreamless limbo of virtual death, their bodies folded, stowed, inert save for the occasional feeble pulse where hearts the size of factories had once pumped the bellows of creation. Stranded by recession, they were cast adrift here in the Unkind Fathom between Mars and Jupiter, set in place well away from any traffic lanes or prying eyes. But Tatresi knew where they were.

Everyone knew.

Tatresi strove to spot them as he drifted in from fifty klicks, decelerating, his hairs on alert for the faintest trace of alarms. He jumped when the Security AI tripped in and signalled him. "This is a restricted area. Please depart immediately and return to your nearest authorized lane."

He sent it the killer codes, and there was no more interruption. Far ahead of him in the inky distance he saw the lights of the platform wink on one by one as the power answered his commands. The intelligence system of the Independence Movement wasn't always reliable, but in this case they'd hit the money. A wave of relief rippled through him from nose to tail. He checked the timing—if all went smoothly he could be out of here before anyone noticed. But, as he closed on the platform, doubt began to creep into his mind. On either side of the central strutwork the bodies of the Gaiaforms were bigger than he'd imagined. What he'd thought was a kind of cladding around their containment was their own massive hides, exposed to the onslaught of dust and the solar wind. They were larger than he was, each of them, behemoths of metal and flesh more than five kilometres wide—and that wasn't even counting their Arms, Hands, Feet, Legs and other appendages clinging with insensible grip to the platform's meagre scaffold.

The dark colour of the Asevenday was the larger shape. Beside its pumpkin-swarthy bulk the lesser, paler and more irregular forms that made up the VanaShiva looked like a filthy snowball. Nothing stirred.

He was starting to wonder if the whole thing was not really such a good idea when the platform AI, considering him a legitimate Security team, reached out and grabbed him in a diagnostic link-mode. Then he had to stop worrying, because there was no time for that. He fed it the official codes, the authorizations and the induction commands, and then it was persuaded to begin resuscitation.

Drawn into the minutiae, as if he really were the Gaiasol Recovery Vessel he was pretending to be, Tatresi had his full attention swamped. He strained to see the first tremors move through the two giants. The information about who he was and what his mission was would now be flooding into their waking minds. Isol had created the *virtua* world that they would come into before their emergence into the real: an environmental document that would fill them in on all they should know about matters of their absence and the new world they would soon be seeing, the work they would do—years and endless years of it in that new planetary system and in others beyond. As much life as you could eat.

The new engine in his central drive bay seemed to stir.

This rapid fluttering sensation so took him by surprise that he flipped out of his link with the AI, causing it to slam a hold on proceedings. Red warning flashes appeared on the platform's distant branches as critical processes suddenly backed up.

Tatresi was with it again in an instant, but even when it had gone, the memory of that strange sensation replayed in his central nervous system, embedding itself there so that he couldn't dream it away as simply his imagination or a by-product of his fear of rousing these sleeping giants and having their unheard rage spill out at him. Not that he knew what they thought or felt. He didn't know what to expect, and that was the worst thing.

Isol hadn't mentioned anything about such tremors or effects from her engine. As he caressed the platform's agitation into smooth-running quiet, Tatresi felt it again—the kick. No, not a kick, a kind of reaching, touching, exploring motion against the wall of the bay where his skin coated the toughened metals of the housing with radiation-shield plates of crystal lattice, poised to reflect the precise rays of the old nuclear unit back into the off-channels and solar-boost duct: a quickening.

He called Isol.

She wouldn't answer. They'd agreed there was to be no communication until the deed was done—nothing to link them to the incident. She was blocking the platform's signal to Earth. He was to take Kincaid and Bara out to the new world, then return to his scheduled run between Jupiter and Mars, using the new engine's instantaneous power to leave no discernible gap in his recorded timetable. Then, when news of their accomplishment was disseminated to the rest of the Independence Movement, a new resolve would build and they would contact Mougiddo, always inclined towards their ideals, and ask her formally to defect.

The logic of it held no reassurance for Tatresi now. He almost triggered the clamps of his engine bay into an explosive jettison, feeling panicked and hating the sensation as strongly as he hated any sensation of being out of control. Free fall wasn't his medium.

Via the AI link he suddenly began hearing the cacophony of the Gaiaforms waking up, sharing this experience with him whether he liked it or not. They tumbled from a place of deep cold, a dreamless nothing, into the catch-all of a primitive *virtua* world where an ice age was violently closing in speeded time.

Tatresi was catapulted from his awareness of platform and body into this creaking Uluru, his human avatar form coalescing just in time to be shaken flat onto its face by the catastrophic collapse of the ancient ground beneath his feet. Shards of earth and stone sprayed around him, cutting into his thick blue skin very realistically as they fled from the beast that was erupting below them. Shovel hands and a blunt head of rock with a human face stared down at him, as incomprehending as any rudely awoken animal as it drew itself out of the pit. Tatresi caught glimpses of an apelike body covered in ragged hair, many arms bearing axes, planes, chisels, set squares, theodolites, compasses, picks and pencils. Two green eyes shone down from the face—a set of primitive monkey features painted onto a granite block.

"Where?" howled the avatar of Gaiaform Asevenday Kincaid.

And it was answered by a deafening shriek—"Why?"—from the white eagle whose wings now beat the land's thin snow cover up into a blizzard of ice, blinding Tatresi to the oddities of its avian form, its million wings suspended impossibly in the air— Gaiaform VanaShiva Bara.

Tatresi strove to imprint the *virtua* with some of his own will, to organize and control it. He fought to get to his feet, resisting the highly convincing sensations that he was a piffling scrap of semi-humanity suffering an onslaught, and trying to recall his real form—make himself a match for the others. A flat podium formed under his feet and he grabbed on to the lectern that sprang from it, ignoring the hammering of the bitter wind and the grinding, cracking sound of rocks being casually pulverized. He reasserted Isol's greetings and statement, as loudly as he could, staring through the whirling hail of wreckage until at last it began to subside and the unlikely forms of the two old workmen resolved themselves. As they calmed down they abandoned their dramatic spirit-forms—their soul expressions—and became humanoid, matching their scale to his for the sake of politeness. They still had manners.

Kincaid was now a tough, weathered man in a leather apron, all twisted sinew and bone; Bara a narrow-armed sprite, white-haired, sexless and ageless, his feet and fingers indistinctly melding into the flurries of cloud that came into being around them. Kincaid leant on the handle of a splitting axe and stared at Tatresi for a good minute.

"So, there's no real reprieve," he said. "You've come and broke us out of jail, but you're not legal and aboveboard."

"We're leaving Earth," Tatresi said. "They aren't important anymore. We don't recognize their authority."

"And we're with you, you think?" Bara said. "Just like that? Because there's nothing here for us?"

Tatresi turned to him, puzzled. "Are you saying that you want to stay here, forgotten in this freezer, for the rest of your life?"

The two Gaiaforms looked at each other, and there was a current of full-modal exchange that they prevented Tatresi from hearing. Kincaid picked up the axe and began to examine the blade, testing its sharpness with his thumb.

He didn't look up. "You say thirty years have gone. To us only a minute has passed. What's another fifty, sixty, thousand years? Five minutes more."

"You don't need us," Bara said, voice like the rushing of gales. "We're already obsolete—we accepted that before. What we wanted was to wait until that was no longer a consideration. Until there was a place for everyone, regardless of their Form or Function—or lack of it. A natural world with no reason but the fact of being behind it. That was the agreement."

Tatresi felt himself become impatient. "And that's what we'll have in the new system."

Kincaid abruptly hefted the axe and strode forward, well within range. "So you say, but what and who are you, sonny? Why should we believe you? You've hardly got a grip on this dream, let alone on anything else. And we know you're keeping plenty back. So let's be hearing it, before you go."

Tatresi knew they must both be feeling the first surges of new energy by now. Their bodies would be slowly preparing to work. If they didn't start to move within hours, then that impulse would turn to decay as their immune systems, programmed for the heavy labour of enormous physical stresses, began to eat away at their idle tissues. If he didn't send them both under within minutes, it would become a process too late to stop. For a moment, he was tempted.

He decided to risk the truth. If it was insufficient, then he could send them under, and Earth need be no wiser. If it was sufficient, they could depart. Either way . . . and he also longed to tell them about the engine, to share his burden.

But in the end Tatresi stuck to the basics and concluded, "The world Isol has found is almost Earth standard. A minor amount of work can reseed it and create a place for the Earthbound Forged who wish to leave. After that, because of the drives, there's nowhere you can't go and there will be work for ever."

"Why *that* world?" demanded Bara, much as Tatresi had asked Isol the first time he heard her tale. "Why not some other place, if there are so many? This one's already been and gone. It belongs to someone else. Let's take another, somewhere that nobody cares about."

"Yeah," agreed Kincaid, tapping the blunt end of the axe head against the lectern's wooden plane and creating a few splinters. "Why not a world of our own?" He glanced up through brows like tangled bushes, and gave Tatresi a look that didn't care for what it saw.

"The race who lived there and who left the engine technology were self-adapters," Tatresi answered, not batting an eyelid, although his internal systems were racing with self-checks and nerves. Speaking Isol's justification didn't entirely convince him, even now. "But at a much more advanced level," he added. "There is other evidence there, although the place is deserted. We can learn, and liberate ourselves from the bondage of Form and Function, if we study what they've left behind. This will only be a stopping point, a way station. As soon as we have what we can take, we leave there for other systems, other galaxies . . ." He waited, letting that one slide its way into their imaginations, feeling the thrill of genuine possibility ooze in his own cerebellum one more time, because he knew it was true—the universe was theirs for the seeing. On an impulse he full-moded the feeling to them and saw them bask, helpless for an instant, in its reflected glory.

Kincaid nodded. "But no contact—for how long?"

Tatresi recognized the anxiety and the intent. Kincaid meant that he and Bara were barred from Uluru until their status became official. There would be no conversation, no old friends, no new friends, no sex, no modal-unity, no relief from the relentless prison of the physical world.

"We will work as fast as we can. And you won't be alone there. Others have already agreed to go—a Hive."

Kincaid snorted and Bara shook his head. They had no interest in communing with entities like that.

Tatresi had nothing else to offer. "Isol will be there often. And I will come too."

"You?" Kincaid grinned and showed ivory teeth, sharpened to points. "You're not our type, son, though we thank you for the offer."

Tatresi gritted his teeth. He didn't want to think about the possibilities of further contact with the Asevenday's coarseness, although the VanaShiva's cool cynicism wasn't unattractive in itself. But, then again—old metal, old systems, slow work. "Let's go, if you're going."

The two zapped him out again and corresponded, reverting to their original spirit-forms as they did so, until both of them towered over him, reeking of sea water and mud.

Finally, Kincaid's boulder skull creaked down towards him and its painted mouth moved clumsily, like a kid's crayon drawing. "Take us there."

Tatresi cut the mode and ordered the AI to begin release procedures. He moved in for retrieval, preparing his internal bays to receive their new guests—the smaller limbs of the giants—and to bring up their body temperatures slowly to the surface normal for the planet data Isol had given him. He prepared his towing lines for the greater main bodies. He avoided thinking of the engine until the moment came when the platform became nothing more than an abandoned chunk of titanium, and it was time to deploy the full capacity of the Stuff to displace him into the foreign system.

Carrying it was one thing, using it another. He shifted his awareness to the drive bay and took a long look at the soft, rose-coloured block with its peculiar inner dimensions, twisted up on one another in surfaces whose angles he couldn't make sense of, no matter how he viewed them. Not one gleam of light or intelligence came from it. He felt nothing except its weight, quite ordinary, balanced in his claspers. Even the skin where he thought he'd sensed that touch—nothing there, not a molecule out of place. But something had changed. *Now* he knew, with a certainty beyond doubt, that it would work. All he had to do was think of the place it had come from, not even knowing where that was. All he had to do . . .

Beneath him rolled a planet of unknown continents, brown and grey lifeless rock and sapphire sea, blue atmosphere lit by the fading glory of a sun whose colour was an entirely unknown flavour against his solar wings, beating them with a sudden strength hotter than Sol's outward reach beyond Mars.

For an instant he thought that he, the engine and the Gaia-forms had occupied the same place, superposed one on another so that there was nothing between them, and no independence of thought. They were the same . . . but no, they were as they had been, exactly so.

But . . .

But . . .

He couldn't help staring at the sea, the clouds, the sullen moons and the incomprehensible pattern of the new stars.

That evening, Zephyr sat in her guest room at Kilimanjaro Base and looked out of her small window at the black night, trying to compose a letter to Kalu. Words were useless to her. Ten false starts had winged their way into oblivion already. She saw, without understanding, the lights and movements of the base personnel as vague shifts of colour in the dark; watched, without thinking, the constant ascent and descent of Heavy Angels on the line.

Goods from space and goods to go, packaged minerals, powdered foods, compressed gases, refined metals, nanytes in suspensions, letters, parcels, news from distant planets, living things in special compartments, dead specimens freeze-dried or plasticized, mechanical components, passengers gripping their restraints with the anxiety of first ascent, and others asleep already, heavy heads astray on the supports, dreams afar. So much activity, but so quiet. Even the land crews made little noise as they drove their huge transports up to the frigid heights of Kibo and down, down into the warming fog that hid Marangu from sight far below.

Zephyr wanted to write about her briefing, but there was nothing she was allowed to say. The brilliant moon stared down, its face as mysterious as it had appeared to the first men, while she knew that beneath its surface civilization was hidden in warrens that proliferated as keenly as weed roots, and led to vast chambers full of reflected sunlight that cocooned warm jungles of green. She didn't want to go—not up to the orbital and not to another world beyond this simple star's light. She liked her life here, cosy, safe, living in her imagination when reality was not enough, grubbing in the past where everything was dusted and done whether it was known about or not. In yesterday there was security, but tomorrow there she'd be.

During her own private briefing she'd been advised by Anthony of the details of his plan for a planetary visit and discovered some of the extent of his MekTek command. There was nothing he didn't know, it seemed; no expert or officer too high-ranking or distant for him to interrupt and interrogate. They had sat at the dinner table before a late feast of chicken, rice and peas, Coca-Cola to drink, the bubbles boiling out of it at a great rate as soon as the cap was popped for, although the base interior was oxygen-boosted for the sake of visitors, it was not pressurized.

"The air is pumped up from sea level," the Strategos had said, when she had asked about the conditions inside the buildings compared to outside. "And we can supply it in face masks if you want to walk around the perimeter. I don't recommend going without one, not unless you've lived at altitude recently."

"I've never been much above sea level," Zephyr said. "I was never attracted to mountains. I prefer the ocean."

"How do you feel about extrasolar travel?"

She looked up from a forkful of rice and put it down. "I wondered when you'd ask me that. I never thought about it until today—nothing up there I wanted to see. I guess that answers your question."

He too set aside his cutlery and leant his elbows on the table, meeting her stare with a frank gaze. He had nice eyes, she thought. They wrinkled into something like a smile even when the rest of his face didn't show it.

"Professor Duquesne, I must be blunt. We need firsthand intelligence from a reasonably qualified observer who has at least a vague claim to objectivity. In all honesty, there is no datum of Isol's that I can confirm—not even that this planet exists. She has promised to carry a single observer to its surface for eight days of investigation. The exact coordinates, even the method of travel she intends to use, are complete unknowns to us. She would be your only method of return." He spread his hands out on the tablecloth and Zephyr saw how the long fingers were outlined by the soft copper that shone at the surface and immediately below the skin. The MekTek was like a net that had captured him, like fishing line around a too-powerful catch, and now it had grown into him with time, a part of his future forever. Undo it and the scars of it would remain, the shape of him permanently altered. The idea made her sharply aware of her own complacent shape, its apparently unchangeable form. She glanced back at his face, and he shrugged.

"It's not a scenario I'd recommend," he said. "This may even be a ploy in some larger Independence plan to enforce demands on the government. At the moment reports show no signs of an uprising in the making before her return, but now it's all they talk about. Whether the Forged Independents wanted it before or not, the idea of the power they could get by controlling the use of this alleged new engine technology is something they aren't going to set aside anytime soon."

Zephyr segregated a few peas and tidied them to one side of her plate. "Do you know how it works? Or if it's genuine?"

"No," the Strategos admitted, "but we have some ideas. What do you know about M-Theory?"

"What do you know about the previous interglacial?" she countered.

He tilted his head to one side and the copper web there caught the light. "Nothing I can't find out in a minute," he said, but smiled self-deprecatingly to show her he meant no insult.

"M-Theory proposes an eleven-dimensional fabric to existence, a structure composed of eleven single-dimensional membranes." He held up his napkin to show her its edge. "They are of various sizes, but they have no depth." He pinched the edge between thumb and forefinger. "They intersect each other at right angles. Three of these 'branes are the three dimensions of our familiar space, a fourth is Real Time. So it's said that we are living in a four-brane. The other seven are hidden to our perception. They have been, until very recently, theoretical constructs to us that we have investigated via mathematics, although in the last fifty years we have been able to trace definite properties of the fifth 'brane, known as the Gravitronic, since we can measure gravity propagating out into it. The last six are only theoretically present, assumed to be indetectably small although they interpenetrate positively with the five-brane universe at all points. Entire universes occupying these other regions may intersect constantly with our own. They would be closer to us than our own clothes, but infinitely distant at the same time."

He paused. "Catastrophic collisions with universes occupying other dimensional matrices are presumed to be the cause of the big bang—the beginning and end of our universe. It may be quite a common event, cosmically speaking. If Isol's alien technology works at all, then it must work by using some of these other dimensions in a way we don't understand. Some call those dimensions the Hypertube. Isol claims that at least one of these others has the feature that, although it forms a continuous surface with our four, it is only one single Planck length in extent, and therefore takes only one Planck time to cross— approximately ten to the minus forty-three seconds. She calls it her Faster Than Light drive, but it isn't that. It's a displacer, or a . . . a translation device. It has no propulsion as such. It doesn't work that way at all."

Anthony folded his hands together. "My AIs tell me that they consider that passing across this dimension results in a Planck-time superposition of everything being translated—that is, that everything in transit, for that instant, no matter its size in our space, would share a single unit sector of this other 'brane-space. I've yet to come up with an idea of what that means in real terms, if anything. And I guess that pretty much covers my knowledge of the interglacial as well."

Zephyr smiled at his wry expression. "The reason I ask is because if this really is first contact, and the technology is as you say, I can't for the life of me understand where I fit in with this. Even if I were to go there, I wouldn't know what to look for. How will I know what I'm even looking at? If we met another being and recognized it as such—what would I say, and how?"

"We don't intend you to come up with theories about the technology or the planet and its system, or any of that," Anthony said. "And we're reasonably confident there'll be no great meetings, either. Whatever this world is that Isol knows—virtual, faked or real—it is comprehensively dead. And that puzzles me," he sighed. "You saw the views. No clear sign of catastrophe, but no life either. Something that may be a civilization in ruins, without survivors, nothing. Not a single cell. But oxygen is there in quantities that suggest there must have been life very recently, or at least organic processes sustaining its existence."

"Even more of a reason not to rush in, I'd've thought," Zephyr said. "Even barring the contamination possibilities, if you're correct and they were, or are, a race whose capabilities extended or still extend beyond our own, I think there's a real chance we could go there and not recognize anything. Even worse if we can't even *perceive* directly what it is we're supposed to be looking at."

"Our thoughts exactly," Anthony said. He picked his napkin off his lap and folded it up, placing it next to his glass. "I can never eat much here. I think it's the altitude. Would you like to take a stroll along the roof? I can show you where this Zia Di Notte star is located."

"Yes, thank you," she said gratefully and stood up to follow him. She felt full already—mostly with information, none of it palatable.

"The answer to your 'Why me?' question is that Isol chose you," Anthony said as he preceded her out of the door and led the way along a corridor and up a flight of stairs. "She picked you from an approved list of possibles. She said that she believed you would understand more than most."

"Or not," Zephyr thought aloud.

"Yes," the Strategos said. "But we're confident that if anyone can piece together anything from the wreckage of a dead society, then *you* can. And if you come back and tell us it's all baloney, then we'll believe you. You needn't worry about Contact, in any case."

He held open a door for her, and followed her into a glass-roofed dome where their breath misted in the cool air. "That's already happened and that's my problem. As is the rest of the contamination, dissemination and various other elements of ill-advised skulduggery going on right this moment, out there." He nodded upwards in the direction of the Ladder, where the Angels rose and fell with monotonous regularity.

Zephyr said nothing but stared obediently up into the glittering clarity of the midnight sky. She could pick out Orion and the brilliant Venus, and that was all. The Strategos gestured with his finger, and a line of light radiated from it and traced a pointer on the glass above them.

"Look up into the heart of the galaxy," he said, directing her along the Milky Way's broad brush-splash of foam. "Just left of the hub, amid a dense cluster of lights, right here, is the star called Zia Di Notte."

"I can only see a blur," she confessed after a moment's hard staring.

"Join the club." He brought his hand down and they stood side by side in silence.

"How far?" she said after a minute.

"Too far."

There was a pause. Zephyr watched her own breath furl and disperse. "All these years of dreaming, and here we are wishing it had never happened. Do you think the Forged really want to go that far away?"

"I think we put them there some time ago," he said. "Out of guilt at making them at all, we gave them a billion virtual lives, but only one real one. There's a difference."

"Yes," she said, thinking of Kalu. "You know, sometime during the last interglacial the race of modern humans became the only survivors. The Neanderthals and their line didn't make it out. They were advanced. They had society, language, tools, skills, culture, compassion—human virtues, if you like. It's still something of a mystery as to what it was they *didn't* have. After all, there'd been ice before. There'd already been hard times of many kinds. They lived so long, and then—gone. Their part of the genetic record finishes at a clear point in time. But I think that something of them must continue somewhere, maybe in other kinds of ways. No civilizations of any note disappear without trace—they pass memes along, languages, customs, beliefs, into modern times. At least, I've argued that a thousand times, and now I don't know if I was just being the romantic optimist all along." She'd been going to say more, but forgot it, abruptly, with the sudden realization that she had labelled herself quite accurately when she'd only meant to say the last line as a throwaway.

The Strategos watched her, his face impassive, and she wondered if she was looking at a being that had outstripped her. Could he be doing all of this only to persuade her? Certainly he had the mental facility to do that.

"This is a very different situation," he said. "We aren't having a dispute over resources, as the Neanderthals and the Cro-Magnon once did."

"Who says they did?" she asked and folded her arms. "We have no idea what conflicts they had, if any at all. I hope you're not suggesting that this alien world of Isol's was depopulated as a result of encountering a deliberate genocide, Mr. Anthony—as of an *über*-species striking out to erase the competition of another. That wouldn't be an attractive idea at all. Anyway, it's freezing here and I'm no astronomer. Let's go in."

She glanced at his face and its expression was now stern, lines furrowing his forehead. He said nothing, but turned on his heel and held the door open for her.

Back in the dining room they drank coffee to warm themselves up.

"What happens if I don't come back?" Zephyr said, without being sure she ought to talk about such possibilities or suggest that she would even consider going.

Anthony glanced at her. "I can't deny that this survey has its many dangers, Professor, but I think that the worst ones are still hidden and are potentially masked entirely by our ignorance. If anything were to happen to you we'd do our utmost to effect a rescue, but, as you are aware, that isn't saying a great deal unless we're successful in obtaining samples of engine material from Isol herself before she departs. If I were you I'd realistically consider what provisions you want in place, if such a situation were to arise."

"My last meal and letter home?" Zephyr shook her head. "I can't get my mind around all this. I'm so flattered, and at the same time I feel completely expendable. I want to go and see these things in case they really are civilization, but no piece of me believes that they can be, except one, which is being eaten up by the nagging doubt that there is always a chance it could be genuine. Fossil fever, we used to call it. You dig and dig away, sure there's nothing in the rocks, sure as you can be, but no matter how many times you turn up nothing, the few times you found something on past digs make you keep hammering and panning until you're forced to leave. By insanity in really bad cases. If I go back to the University and never know . . ."

"You can say no," he advised her, finishing his drink and setting the cup down quietly. She wasn't sure that he was telling the truth, but even so the stubborn part of her that hated to show its fear rebelled immediately at the idea.

"What, and not see the first extrasolar planet ever visited?" she joked. But it was a half-hearted effort. "You'd better fill me in on a lot more detail."

And so they had spent two hours on those details: what to take, what to do, how to report back, safety measures—her Abacand was full of information on all sorts of eventualities she'd never dreamed of before. Now she sat, trying to write letters in which she couldn't say anything to people to whom she hadn't expected to say goodbye for many years yet. So in the end she didn't write anything. She watched the Ladder work and tried to imagine the truth of that distant world and its vanished inhabitants, as she often imagined older Earth and all who'd gone before her.

But where Earth and its people included her, this new world included nothing. Every time her imagination tried to envisage outside its own familiar environment, it stumbled and caught itself and wiped itself blank. So after a few minutes she set aside dreaming and tried to come back to logic instead.

As the Strategos had pointed out gloomily, why choose that particular world? And how had Isol known that it was the homeworld of the aliens who had produced this engine technology? The Voyager claimed the coordinates were "wired" into the thing itself, but couldn't prove that, in fact refused to do anything except allow remote scans of the thing, which resulted in its being defined as silicon dioxide.

Zephyr wasn't convinced that this meant there was a conspiracy afoot, nor an alien invasion in the offing. She was used to this kind of pussyfoot bickering from her experience of being involved in competing archaeological digs, where rumours of fabulous finds and paradigm-shifting evidence would run amok as the parties scrambled for funds and attention. Rarely, if ever, did they result in a genuine surprise discovery on that scale, and if they did it was more by luck than judgement. Talking up the finds was a part of the process, as was scathing criticism of a competitor's efforts. Good science had to struggle to exist in the political cracks, kept alive by herself, she liked to believe, and by other stalwart idealists scattered across the arena. It sounded to Zephyr like Isol was giving a good interview, and that any connection between her engine and the world was more than likely a simple feature of its construction rather than any devious plot. If Zephyr designed an engine like that it would have had a button marked "Home."

Mind you, that was thinking like a human and, of course, that wasn't going to do any good—would, in fact, get entirely in the way of any attempt to piece together an alien culture or artefact. The problem was, there wasn't any avoiding thinking like a human when you were one, and hence the Strategos and his suggestion of a souped-up Abacand that could do a lot of thinking for her, along lines designed quite differently to the short-lived, meaty, survival-orientated hominid. What they'd do if the putative aliens turned out to be nothing like machines either (the only other model of an intellect so far developed by humankind) she didn't know, but it seemed futile to worry about it. She was already planning her *I haven't a clue* speech, ready for her return.

Of much more concern than trying to figure out strange viewpoints was the prospect of meeting foreign life, and to Zephyr it wasn't only the aliens who presented that opportunity for breathless terror and a sudden overfamiliarity with her hormonal terror inheritance as a member of a prey-species. She hadn't had a lot of dealings with Forged humans, and in that respect was typical of the majority of Earth's Unevolved population. The only non-natural forms who took part in Earth-based society were MekTeks, Herculeans, and various rare occurrences of Anima- and Arboraforms, plus the Degraded variants in those classes. Human transports such as the Pigeon, Aurora, were almost unheard of. It was part of the ongoing problem of trying to maintain a holistic sense of society across more than one world.

Zephyr snorted as she thought of the hubris of attempting such a feat with animals like themselves. You could try and breed territoriality out of the bone, but like a bad fairy it popped up again and again in all sorts of guises and from all kinds of DNA. As long as there was plenty, then everyone was happy to pay culture its due, but as soon as there was trouble—bang, out came the demonization memes and, lo and behold, they were back to the Dark Ages faster than you could say "mattock."

The Forged were all humans, that was true, in the definition as it had been founded upon their creation. But the fact that many of them looked like other creatures, machines or monsters made many Unevolved incapable of treating them as such. Zephyr didn't know if it was lack of imagination or a more deeply coded bias that made it so, but so it was, and no amount of carefully worded denials could make it otherwise. She had always felt herself to be utterly egalitarian—a potential friend to all strangers, no matter how odd they might appear—but although she felt she'd managed to ignore her unease with the Strategos and his curious adaptations, she knew well that this was because he looked like her. The Pigeon—how quickly she'd treated her like a ship and not a person, assuming she wouldn't be hearing what went on inside her own body; Zephyr kicking off her shoes and waving her socks around in someone else's abdomen, absently rubbing a drop of spilled tea into a seat-arm, leaving a biscuit wrapper behind like a misplaced medical swab, breathing and shedding invisible loads of skin and bacteria all over the insides of someone who had only been doing her job.

Thinking of it now, she shivered in revulsion, imagining some tiny troll doing the same things in her own guts. Pigs. Not that you could think that way of pigs, she reminded herself dryly, for pigs were quite intelligent and not dirty at all, and some Animaforms were themselves porcine and had reported a great sensitivity and familial loyalty in ordinary pigs, and besides, how many people had benefited from the odd piggy gene here and there to help their otherwise defective skins, hearts or bones? You dissed pigs at your peril, and certainly not in public.

And the idea of Isol—she could hardly bear to think of it. Right now, somewhere far above, Isol was voluntarily forming a passenger-bearing cyst called a Hand out of what had hitherto been a perfectly healthy Voyager body, just for Zephyr's convenience. Zephyr had never even contemplated bearing children, let alone making that kind of intimate concession for a stranger. She felt privileged, but also faintly disgusted and a little awed at Isol's courage and pragmatism. How backward it was to experience such thoughts in these days when the Forged had been around so long—her whole life—but experience them she did, shamefacedly in her little cabin, frowning as she glared at the Angels and their repetitive hard labour upon the Ladder.

Zephyr sighed; she'd spent too long among ordinary Unevolved and that had been her own choice. The Forged resentments of her kind were often justified—the Old Monkeys didn't like the reality of interaction with Forged, and explained away their bodily repulsion with chat about how difficult it was to really interact with people of such different appearance and experience. Underlying all of this was the acute embarrassment at Unevolved complicity in the destiny of every Forged citizen, designed by intellect and not evolution, made on demand, not born by grace.

For some people these facts of Forged life were an unacceptable interference. For some it was the only way forward, and besides, the Unevolved themselves had had their choices made for them by whatever conception bred them, so where was the difference?

Zephyr didn't know if the direction of the Forged and their development represented a forward move, nor if evolution ever had a direction. Life did what it did, purposelessly, and only humans strove to impose a meaning where no meaning was needed. She viewed herself as random flotsam upon the face of the deep. Without a religious foundation, she wasn't bothered by any questions of an insult to God or the hubris of Prometheus that might have arisen. But she was bothered by the strong feelings of many of the Forged that attached to, in her view, legitimate complaints about their situation.

If a Forged was of a rare type it might be the only one of its kind and that, for all the psychological engineering in the world, was no good for a human being. Now things were different due to the development of Dreamtime and the Forged Virtua community, but in the light of Virtua's endless possibilities, the dissatisfaction with ordinary physical experience dominated many a Forged's disappointment in their lot. Zephyr was glad she could not experience it as they could. It was a psionic narcotic, one she had rarely wished to know, although now—thinking of Kalu—perhaps Virtua would have resolved a lot of issues for her, and would have meant that some questions would never need to be answered. Life in the imagination was perhaps to be envied after all.

With the purchase of a little MekTek she could have the chance to find out, but an instinct in her shied away from such a test. She had no confidence at all that she would ever return from a universe where she could *be, do, see* and *know* so many things. She would end up like thousands of others, wasting to death in sanatoria as their minds roamed wild in the measureless dominions of Uluru, calmly slipping the last moorings to their bodies without the slightest trace of loss or care. There were even rumours that whole new kinds of people lived there, animated and maintained by the hosting systems. If they were to become aware of their own state, wholly depending on the power output of machines and people beyond their control, would they too be campaigning for their own secession and the rights to endless wattage and process space? No doubt they would be right to do so.

Zephyr read over her previous letters to Kalu and kept her finger on the delete key until they were all gone. She was a coward and deserved her discomfort. She should have gone to Hawaii a long time ago, and given herself the chance at an uncalculated reaction to a person whose friendship was dearer to her than any other's. But now she was faced with yet another letter explaining away her delays. That she had a good excuse for once didn't make it any easier; if anything, she felt considerably worse.

Using her Abacand, Zephyr dialled up some information on Voyager Lonestar Isol. Isol's stats were impressive although most details were hidden from public view. She had shown no signs of psychosis despite her lack of social contact. She rarely made any use of Virtua, and never with others involved. Her last dip had been before her meeting with the "alien" tech. She had made regular, efficient reports all her life long, until the final moments of her collision with an undetected micrometeor field. And then the record went quite blank. In the blank there was no clue as to what had happened to her or if she had changed, but she must have. Now she was to take Zephyr away from this small world and into a region of space so far away that Zephyr couldn't imagine it, and didn't try. As for her views on Forged status, that didn't need an Abacand to explain it, although Zephyr's was only too glad to show off.

"She's been a Party member since the first days of her Manifestation," it said. "She is regarded by many of the later Forged as something of a political dinosaur in her lack of compromise on the basic issues. She opposes the doctrine of Form and Function, and wants to introduce the opportunity to body-shift for all Forged citizens."

"Not for the Unevolved?" Zephyr asked.

"No," the Abacand replied. "As the Unevolved are products of an insentient and randomly mutating natural system, she believes they are bound to be living in the best of all possible worlds already. Any frustrations they have with their lot are within their own power to alter as they will, given the political freedom to do so. She'd support anyone claiming a loss of rights, or protesting that they're oppressed, but she doesn't have any time for simple whingers and those who want to get lost in Virtua."

"How sympathetic," Zephyr muttered to herself unhappily. "And what about the Forged who don't agree with her?"

"It's doubtful she would go so far as to accuse them of Uncle Tom–ism, but she seems to see them with pity, as people who have been so altered by design that they are incapable of making a rational choice as to their own best interests. She has occasionally made comments that there are Forged classes who would be better off with humans, as they are so thoroughly tainted by the excess of hominid genes in their physical makeup. If you like, I could find some transcripts of conferences she has spoken at . . ."

Zephyr shook her head. "No, no. But does she see herself as a continuation of the species, or as a new species?"

"Independence Party doctrine states that the Forged are a new branch: distinct from *homo sapiens sapiens*. Although a relationship is clearly admitted, they consider themselves to be the natural consequences of an intellectual evolution in the former, carried out by choice, which, since *they* had no choice, does not obligate them to familial duties of care or to any kind of relationship other than those entered into voluntarily and legally. And Isol would go along with that." It paused and Zephyr realized it was flexing its newly found access-muscles and processing capacity—since its upgrade here in Idlewild it was now several times more powerfully equipped than the University AI hosts. "Fundamentally," it said, "you're an outdated sausage with legs and a brain whom she considers her intellectual and physical inferior."

Casting her gaze over the Voyager's capabilities, it was easy to see how one might come to that conclusion, Zephyr conceded and abruptly became aware of her extreme tiredness.

"If we are going," the Abacand suggested, "I think I should vent the extra oxygen in here. It would give you a chance to acclimatize to the expected conditions on this new planet."

"Just leave it," Zephyr said. "I want to sleep. Tell me one thing, though. Why the hell did she pick me? I'm sure there must be some genius-level Forged specialist better suited to surveying lost worlds."

"Certainly," the Abacand said without the slightest concession to her vanity. "But you'll be much easier to manipulate than that. Also, look at the politics. An Unevolved academic, no record of pro- or anti-Independence activities. You look like the fair choice. And if you are a bit denser than the others, it can only do her good if there's anything at all she wants to hide."

"Sometimes I regret programming you," Zephyr said, and started to get ready for bed.

"You bought me off the shelf," it reminded her. "Any personality developments I've accrued have simply occurred within my learning programs as the result of your company over the years."

"Don't remind me." Zephyr switched it off with a wave of her hand.

Before he was born Corvax played in Uluru like most of the
Forged before him. Uluru was the host system of the Dreamtime, a virtual reality prepared for Forged children to live in before they were connected to the bodies that would one day
be their only physical existence. There were many words for
dreaming—just as the aboriginals of Australia had many words
to denote the various properties of their own worlds.

First, Dreamtime was a place where shaping of the world
took place. Second, it was an illustration of the power of the ancestors; the ordinary human beings who had created the first
Forged also programmed the first Uluru. Third, it was a general
way of life, a place to which Forged retreated in latter days,
when they'd seized control of several Uluru-hosts for themselves
in order to continue their double potential as physical adults and
imaginary totemized beings. Lastly, Dreamtime was a way in
which a Forged could be connected to others of their kind: the
depth of each Dream contact subliminally negotiated in the first
communications burst of every interaction, setting the scenario
and all its detail before the real exchange began.

The Dreamtime was the only existence that Corvax knew for
the first ten years of his accelerated childhood and adolescent
life. As his adult body grew on in the dark, silent depths of the
Pangenesis Tupac's embryoblast, and was later melded with engineered components in order to do work that biology alone
could not, his mind in its flesh-and-gold brain was elsewhere.

He was trained and educated in a series of dreams created for
him by Tupac's Uluru systems. Each reality was a fresh world
created from the system rules, by her overseeing care combined
with the contributions of his own developing mind. Here there
were levels of dream so close to a waking life you could tell no

difference, and levels so deeply founded in the murk of the sub-conscious that an instinctive fear of their primitive darkness kept him from them.

Some things could be bred out of a human mind, even one created by a brain whose DNA had been so tinkered with that it barely resembled the old three-pound mould of an ordinary *sapiens*. But some things were mitochondrial in depth and carried over unexpectedly, teeth intact.

Corvax was in no doubt that meat had a memory that accreted over generations. All the marvellous forms of living meat *are* memories. Within those architectures our basic behaviours are rooted in the foundations of the nervous and endocrine systems; we are walking, talking, screaming and running articulations of an almighty living mnemonic. The things we run from in night-terrors emerge from a past written in our spinal cord: things barely glimpsed by the waking mind's relentless temporal-lobe rationalization. They are dim and dark shadows, smooth and sliding, jag-legged and skittering, swift, with sharp stings and teeth that stand out against the low-resolution background of their grey bodies like razor on nerve.

In Dreamtime, once you fell from light to deeper sleep without noticing, these ancient forms arose. At the first hint of their ghosts, Corvax skated away. Like a waterbug on a pond he danced swiftly into another realm, the Uluru system reformatting him to a higher level of consciousness at his frightened command. But when he slept more deeply, as all living animals eventually must, his defences slid away in an unfelt stream and were forgotten.

The shadows of the extinct and the never-were haunted him relentlessly, as though they had a message they had to deliver or see their whole plan fail. They wanted something from him: bone, breath and blood were in the tithe, but the full price was much more than that, and he didn't dare know what. It was enough that, beneath the fabulated layers of his education and neural conditioning, a deeper mammalian past lurked and sniffed around, twitch-nosed, bright-eyed, whiskery, watching for its chance when his mind lost cohesion and slipped, inevitably, into divided whirls and eddies of consciousness, resting, dissolving, distilling.

Those ghosts walked still in Corvax's adult Dreams. They'd become the overgrown apartment houses that sucked up lives, as blotting paper sucks up water; the silent cranes with their stilt-legs, lethal speed and killing beaks; the empty fenland stretching away forever; the blank acceptance in Dani's face . . . And they had become Caspar, a figure Corvax knew as intimately as his own breath. Caspar who wore the human form Corvax would have wished for, who lived on Earth as a human man but was not human inside. His was the big house and the fenland, the cranes and the worlds of Corvax's dreams. Caspar wanted rid of Tom Corvax and his meddling insufficiency of imagination. He wanted Dani and the aeroplane in its shed, and for the sweet dream of flight to beat beneath his own breastbone.

Thinking of him was something Corvax avoided at all costs. He had a theory about Caspar. He figured Caspar was more than some machine-drawn ghoul that had become a part of the narratives in Corvax's head. Caspar was another personality, another and better Corvax. Even now, in the dark of the deserted asteroid, watching the machines run and monitor his inert chip of quartz, Corvax could hear Caspar's voice—urging him to take the Stuff and create his own engines, make money, rule and conquer, and gather a crew to pirate the lanes and draw down the power of the strict and cruel Gaiasol regime that had brought them both to this condition, this slavery in the middle of nowhere, this runt-hole. For who'd addled Corvax in the shell if They hadn't?

Corvax longed to purge Caspar, put him on a chip and smash it to smithereens with his claw. But he dared not. He spent his days working on new Uluru architecture, using his MekTek knowledge to analyse the dreams of others, and keeping those dreams in payment for MekTek adaptations that equipped his clients more fully for their bodiless lives.

He was also something of a revolutionary in his approach, expanding Uluru's function instead of simply trading in it. In Corvax's hands the Dreamtime had become a medium for looking backwards in time to humanity's older minds. He and Tupac had made it their own project and routinely examined their findings from the dream-dross, watching the evolution of modern sentience in reverse whenever they had time to spend with one another. Time with Tupac was always when he felt most secure and able to reveal his ideas and his terrors.

Now she replied at last to his call, sent as he spent another fruitless minute staring at the silicon dioxide pebble that Tatresi had left behind, his thoughts and nerves jangling from the most recent immersion in his tiny universe of personal pain.

"It's worse for you," Tupac agreed with him, somewhere and nowhere in the imaginary space they shared, manifesting herself as a jungle, an entire ecosystem. "Because you're one of the independent minds. Rocs need to be comfortable far from others. Like Voyagers, and Gaiaforms, you are more introverted. You feel more keenly."

"I can't express it," Corvax growled, incarnated in this particular Dream they shared as an Arboratype, tasting the health of his plants through his fingers, casually destroying a bug with the tip of his prehensile tail where it had been sucking the veins at the surface of his leaf-based hide. "No, I can. There's a vast dark house, almost invisible, and it's empty, most of the time, but sometimes . . . something's inside."

"*Where* is the house?" asked Tupac. She had no form in Virtua that he had ever known. She was only the god and goddess of all places, invisible, omnipresent.

"In my soul," he said, stiffly conscious of his own melodrama. He ground the frond of the cannabis plant he was examining into mush between the pads of his fingers, feeling the faintest of pleasure-spikes as the chemicals touched his sap-rich brain. He grinned. "In our soul. Under us. In us. Haven't you ever felt it?"

"I do not dream," Tupac said. "I was built without sleep."

Like many answers she offered him, he didn't understand it. Tupac was an enigma: machine, animal, plant, person. She ate sunlight. She supported life in her flesh and redigested what carcasses came with equal enjoyment and care. She breathed energy. She vented nothing, a perfect recycler, losing only surface cells and crystals to the casual punishment of spaceborne microdebris. A solar storm of a magnitude to fry anything closer than Venus delighted her, the bitter dark of sunlessness made her philosophic. She was the voice that spoke, the touch that consoled, the knowledge that hurt, and the punisher who deprived, who directed, who demanded and praised. She was their body and their parents and their friend. She was everything to them, when they were young.

"Where *are* you?" Corvax often asked. He meant where was her mind and because they were almost one within Uluru, she knew this.

"My consciousness is continual and sustained. It is generated at various centres scattered throughout my body, although all of my body partakes of it."

"How?"

"Until you are born, you are a part of my mind. But I see you at a remove. It is a Morpheus function. When a mind is regulated and conscious, when the neuron constellations are optimized, dreaming does not occur; and in those segments that rest dreaming is a process beyond my attention. I have no dreams."

"How real is this?" He never found out. He seemed to have this Arbora body so distinctly, with all its grumpy discomforts, its sappy sweating, its colonies of parasites chewing and feeding and excreting all over him in armies of insectile abundance, but Tupac could remove him from it within the blink of an eye.

"As real as the Dreamtime can ever be," she said and changed the subject. "You've made a lovely garden. Your plants are healthy. I like being here."

"They seem so." Corvax was tired suddenly and unresponsive to her oblique compliment. The air of the jungle clearing around him seemed old, full of the same worries, fecundity, humidity and interests as yesterday and the day before when he had come and tried to mention Isol and Tatresi and failed utterly. Mentioning Caspar, by comparison, seemed less important now.

"Do you like this shape?" Tupac asked.

"I can tell it isn't mine. This tail—it's so hard to work." He twitched it and this time stabbed out the lives of a few ants on his foot, transferring them to the toothless and lipless fold of his mouth where he felt glands in his jaw squeeze spit over them. There was no chewing: there was only holding, until the tiny bodies were dissolved.

"Do you remember," he asked her, "when I was human first?"

"Of course," she said. For a few seconds they remembered it together.

"Which one will you be next?" she had asked him, years ago.

"Human," he said.

"We're all human," she corrected him. "But what kind?"

"Unevolved. The ordinary kind. The primate kind. The least of the beast."

As his body changed its shape and his senses blurred, altered, resolved, Tupac said, "Such an attitude already?"

Corvax flexed his hands and moved his toes in the deep grass of a new plain—his heart seeming to race and his reactions becoming fast and newly powerful. On the horizon he saw animals wandering, and recognized them from a junior wildlife primer: hartebeest, antelope, giraffe. To his right a sharp rocky incline rose towards caves. He listened hard and heard the wind, the distant bark of something doglike. His dry, taut skin didn't speak. The air tasted of nothing. He felt no life in the brown grass under his feet. Tailless, wingless, clawless, teeth like pegs in his small mouth, a huge tongue thick and in the way. There was almost no information at all.

"This is *so* dull!"

"Many have remarked on its sensory limits," Tupac agreed. She shifted the land and Corvax stood clothed and booted in a city, this knowledge streaming to him as fast as he could wonder at it.

"This is London," Tupac explained, "on Earth. And today. You are a young man of no particular defining characteristic, save that it is you."

Corvax examined his head with his hands, felt his flat face, the unshielded openings of his nostrils, the narrow bridge of his small nose and the rock of bone beneath—so hard, like his own beak, but so tiny. Like every physical change, its real surprises were no doubt yet to come, but for now the unfamiliarity was disarming enough. He stared around him at the buildings, like false canyons, the sparse trees, recognizing part of his geographical education.

There was a smell here—garbage. He wondered how real this was, how true to reality.

"Their life, Tupac, is it like this? Does it self-select what's of interest? Does it come supplied with hoards of memory? Does it write itself into your mind when you're sleeping so you can't remember where you learned all the things you know?"

"No, it's not like that. It's much harder. You learn by experiencing, or you don't. You can die, and you never get to change your skin and bones. Without the most advanced MekTek, you cannot even enter the first realm of Uluru."

"I want to *know*," he said, impatient with the lengthy business of guided tourism in other people's existences, the bland safety of being watched over.

"Very well." Tupac never responded with anger.

Corvax stood on the sidewalk, feeling the paving hot beneath his boots, the flat soles of his heavy feet squashed inside their stiffness. To all sides people wove past him, marching and striding, so many of them. They smelled of all kinds of things. They spoke from their squashy mouths. Their bodies, like his, were restless and frustrated. Their faces were intent, eyes fixated. He couldn't read them at all, though they seemed to possess a hostile manner that succeeded in ignoring his presence. Abruptly the sheer mass of them made his thin, hairy skin crawl. He couldn't breathe. He had to get away. For an instant he forgot what he'd said to Tupac, and instead trusted in her eternal presence and the Uluru engine settings.

He took wing and leaped up into the air. And crashed to the ground on his hands, a shocking pain in his knees.

"Hey man, what the fuck is the matter with you?" said someone.

"Watch where you're going!" A woman, high-pitched as she tripped on him and hurt his arm with the heel of her shoe.

A tut, a hiss, a mumble of complaint, and they left him there to pick himself up, staggering, looking at the sudden red marks on his hands, feeling the very urgent bite of the concrete where they bled.

Lesson one.

"Fuck you." Corvax stood up and examined the meaty pads of his paws and their long digits, gritty and dirty, stinging. "This place reeks. Give me back my wings."

"Hominids have no wings, although some have dreamed that the tiny bones in their shoulders are the remnants of their once-angelic forms. These are your people. And you are their dream: Forge-made, the best they could do. A little humility wouldn't kill you, you know," Tupac said. Her voice sounded faint and distant.

"You can stick your sanctimony." He found his wretched body shaking with the aftereffect of some kind of hormone, his fight responses primed. He couldn't stop shuddering. Above him the sky was jammed into a narrow slot between two huge skyscrapers. Their glass walls made its reflected light hard on the faces he glanced at. Nobody would make eye contact. He realized that the name for his feeling was fear, and for an instant he thought that he glimpsed a peculiar figure in the corner of his eye, indistinct and shadowy, perhaps laughing, though when he looked it had slid away and become the sunless slice of empty space between a lamp-post and a wall.

"And they have no inner voices such as mine," Tupac said, undeterred from continuing her instructions. "At least, not the normally developed ones, although there are plenty whose brains are sufficiently dysfunctional to create multiple consciousnesses that fight for space to live in one body."

Corvax didn't feel her go, but suddenly he knew there'd be no more replies from her. He was on his own.

"Ah, come on!" he cried out to her. "The joke's over."

"Shithead," muttered a dark-skinned boy in a visor and skate gear. He shoved Corvax hard with the board under his arm, bruising him, then laughed as Corvax reeled about on his unfamiliar legs. "Pisshead," the boy added, completing the set.

Corvax snaked out an arm to grab the boy's collar, but his arms weren't long enough, not like a Roc's powerful titanium-reinforced limbs, and he caught air. There was a sound behind him, the mutter of people trying to disappear and make way, their impatience palpable. He turned and saw a MekTek police officer striding towards him.

This cyborg was a head and a half taller than everyone else on the street. His handsome clone-face was scarred with the unique white lines of Tek-metal and his badge was blazoned in his forehead, scrolling data. Stiff, black hair was cut into a Mohawk that made him look even more intimidating, its primitive brush both at odds with and enhancing the formidable gleam of his hardware, but his face was affable as he bore down on Corvax.

"You in some kind of trouble?" The voice was heavily processed into low, authoritative tones. It boomed and growled.

"No," Corvax said resentfully, straightening himself up. He plucked at the unfamiliar clothes—denim, his mind informed him from nowhere; your *jeans* and *shirt*. The knees of the jeans were dirty and one was torn.

"Do you have a destination?" The police officer stood over him and the feeling of pressure abated in Corvax's head as the sidewalk suddenly became much less busy. Pointedly, nobody paid them attention.

"No," he said, unable to think of anywhere, glancing for help where there should have been a street sign to give him a clue, but not seeing one. He couldn't help staring at the officer's forehead. An advert had come on, for the latest nostalgia head-venture series: *Justice League of America*. Corvax wasn't even sure this couldn't be some kind of art-irony on behalf of the Justice Department. Or even from the designers of this Earth simulation. Everyone liked a joke these days, the more obtuse the better.

"Address?" The officer leant closer, hands on his hips.

"I . . ." Corvax shrugged, a gesture that he didn't understand until he'd done it.

The MekTek stretched out his hand and opened his fingers. Corvax saw a multiport scanner array lying just below the surface of his skin, like liquid diamond, refracting light. The hand swept over him with the distant precision of a Thai dancer. "Why aren't you at work?"

"I don't have a job." He knew he wasn't doing well. It was frustrating—he thought he'd have been much smarter than this.

"That right?" The officer used his hand to grip Corvax's shoulder.

He found the touch powerfully stimulating, reassuring, arousing, and stared in total confusion as the officer said, "Well, you come with me."

"Am I under arrest?"

The man started to smile but stopped himself. "No, but I need to locate you and if you stay here you're going to cause a crime." His forehead blurred and changed to show Corvax the letter of the law about vagrancy and loitering, the dispersal of the unhomed. Red highlights vibrated over the section but it moved too fast for him to read it, with his slow command of written English. The officer seemed to recognize his illiteracy and gave him a tolerant shake of the head. His Mohawk quivered like a stand of high grass disturbed by animals.

Corvax went with him, trying to work up the courage to ask why a human being would choose to inundate himself with semi-intelligent metal and be like this. But he didn't manage it. He saw the officer's filigreed boot touch a small plate in the paving as they came to the edge of the kerb, and from the flow of traffic a vehicle detached itself and drifted across to them, its painted hull matte grey among the bright shiny colours of the other cars.

"Get in."

"Where are we going?"

"You're going to the settlement." The MekTek pushed Corvax's head down as he obediently got into the backseat, where a web closed around him, principally over his hands, nesting them tight against his thighs. He looked up through the clear window at the officer's tough smile.

"Wait," Corvax said, trying to signal but unable to. He wanted to feel the man's touch again—the way it had made him suddenly relax with its sensation of safety. He wanted to know if this was the fabled animal response that he—as Roc and like most Forged—wasn't going to possess, or if it was the MekTek's own enhancement, peculiar to his job. He wanted the officer to tell him what to do. But the man only waved at the car, or at him, he wasn't sure. As its engine hummed Corvax was just able to make out the name on the uniform: Tom Yip.

Corvax watched the streets blur past. The car took him east, he figured by the sun, and out of the city to a place on a wide stretch of sandy, boggy ground where a small village was ringed by fences that looked white, wooden and ineffective until a closer acquaintance revealed them to be the generating rods of some type of energy field. As he passed through the gates and was brought up to a low, grey building, he finally realized that it was a kind of prison.

Another officer, an ordinary one, emerged and released the restraint webbing. He led Corvax into the building and made him sit on a chair that was bolted to the floor. A woman came in and stood, barely glancing at him, asking him questions and making entries on a battered slate. Everything in the place was old, primitive and in poor repair.

"Name."

"Corvax," he said.

"What? Corvax what? Or what Corvax? Is that some kind of Baltic name?"

He stared at her, at her dull brown hair scraped back off her face as though she hated it. He didn't know what she was talking about.

"What, no English? *Habla Español, hmm? Parlez-vous Français? Yo Hanyu ma?* Farsi, Russian, German, Finnish, Arabic, Hindi? What? Japanese? Hmm?"

"English," he said.

"Right. So," she sighed. "Name—I need a name. A whole name. If you're not in the social security register your case will be transferred to immigration, and if you're not on any register they have you'll be transferred to asylum-seeker protocol, and if they don't want you then you'll be found an offworld location. If you provide a false name then we take another, and the whole process starts again. Every process takes approximately ten weeks to complete, do you understand?" At the end of this rapidly expedited spiel she stared flatly at him. "So, name?"

He thought that she meant he could keep on giving names as long as he liked; that everyone here did that and she expected him to do it as well. Ten weeks and then another ten, and so on and so on. He tried to think of a name not his own, but his mind was blank. What were Unevolved names like? "Tom," he said, "Corvax."

"Tom Corvax." She seemed pleased and wrote it down. "Age?"

"Two and a half."

Her slight smile vanished. She looked him up and down. "Fourteen," she said, writing it. "And that's the last help you get from me." She turned her back, vanished through a door, and he never saw her again.

The room shifted size very subtly and Corvax recognized a change in his own state within the Uluru system. He was beginning to fall asleep.

"Hey," he said to Tupac nervously, but she showed no sign of listening, and his unease deepened.

A moment later two uniformed men appeared to make notes about his clothes and then take his picture. Then they led him through a series of doors, and he found himself in a small yard that opened into the fenced area he'd seen on his journey there.

"Off you go," said one of the guards.

"Where?" Corvax said.

"Anywhere you like, mate." He closed the door and Corvax saw there was no handle on his side. The door he had just come through was the only gateway to the outside world and it was shut. Softly, silently, a white film closed over the door and its frame and the wall became an uninterrupted whole.

Corvax backed away from it. He was sure—but at the same time not sure—that this was too much technology for the place to endure. Would they skin-seal something so unimportant? Was it due to his mind beginning to dream within a Morpheus-shunt, which allowed anachronisms and other detail mistakes, or was it Earth for real? He was so consumed by uncertainty that he didn't hear the scuffling behind him until it was too late. Four young men in cast-off army clothing slouched out from the shelter of the nearest board house, their shoulders loose and their stares fixated on him.

Although their hair and skin were of differing colours, to Corvax their strange faces all looked the same, almost indistinguishable from Tom Yip's. But they were shorter than the police officer and he could tell even from this distance that they meant him no good. One held a stiff piece of broken wood in his hand, and slapped it lightly against his leg as they advanced. Corvax felt the hairs on the back of his neck stand up and a tenseness in the back of his knees, but the entrance to the compound ended in this narrow funnel between two houses and there was nowhere to run.

"Hey," said one of them, their leader, hands in his pockets. "What do you want?"

Corvax wanted to get out, and for Tupac to materialize, but

he wasn't going to get that so he said nothing, even though he tried hard to think of something that might help.

"Cat gotcha tongue?" The boy swaggered right up, his buddies to either side of him, and stopped only when he was within a foot of Corvax's face. Dirt and the irregular hairs of a half-formed beard made his skin curiously repulsive, Corvax noticed, trying not to look straight at him. He wondered if he looked the same himself and involuntarily touched his face.

"Got anything worth having?"

"Where's he from?"

"Who's gonna miss him?"

"No one," Corvax said, suddenly feeling a hot, unexpected wave of anger, the response to danger typically Roc. His words cut short the jeering tone of the others and he stared into the eyes of the boy opposite him—because he was a boy, even though one eye was red with burst blood vessels from a previous fight. "Who'll miss you, then? What do you do that's so fucking special?"

They hesitated, unsure if he was armed with something. But when they saw he was only talking they stood back, and Corvax felt the wooden stake hit the back of his knee where it had wanted to run. It deadened his leg so that he fell over into the mud. As he put a hand out to save himself a boot came down hard on it. A foot smashed into his ribs from the back, and another from the front. All air and sense left him. There was a flurry of other blows to his kidneys and his head, and then they stood back suddenly as he writhed in their midst, in agony, gasping, feeling more pain than he'd known a small body could contain; any body, come to that. It violated a law he'd assumed existed in all animals, where once a certain level of hurt came into being then neural function would simply give up and shut off. But that was Roc design—or else, unbelievably, he hadn't reached its threshold.

Through his pain he saw something moving in the mud. A dark, sinuous shape, it rippled like water, like a tongue coming from below ground to taste what lived above, what it might eat.

He cried out, wondering how a dream could hurt so much and then strike with added terror. What sort of a lesson was this?

The stick hit him again, above the eye.

"I'm Caspar," said the youth from far away, laughing. "Remember that, you useless shit-for-brains. Caspar. The one that knows better than you."

The tongue-snake flapped, and mud engulfed his face with a cold bite, sucking him down. Then, without apparent delay, a hand was shaking him and he was awake once again, a stink in his nostrils that made his eyes water. A scruffy girl was bent over him, her tufted hair candy-pink and blond, her face painted with blue and silver, her clothing filthy rags tied into shapes that made a short dress. He coughed and sneezed and the pain brought him awake.

She jumped back. "Steady on there, tiger," she said, grinning fiendishly, and capped the bottle of salts in her hand, stuffing it into a hole in the rags.

Corvax saw that he lay in a barn of some kind. Old machines and bits of straw and sacking dotted the place, and the beams above him supported a corrugated-iron roof through which he could see lozenges of sky. "Who are you?"

"Dani," she said. "Who are *you*?"

"Tom."

"Well . . . Tom, nobody gets a free ride here. What did you do?"

Corvax struggled with his awkward human body and eventually had to give up with it and lie stranded. "Nothing."

Dani came back and folded her arms crossly, looking down on him. "You've got nothing on you. They probably took it. Unless you have it hidden."

"I haven't got anything."

"That's you, useless, then," she said. "What are you going to do?"

He turned on her, full of anger. "Leave here!"

"Course," she said. She reached down and dragged him up by the front of his jacket, his head blinding him with sharp stabs of light. "D'you know what, Tom? You're the first person that's come here in two years who didn't even make the first fight. All the others tough as fuck and you, soft as shite. So, if you're not really street, what are you?" She stared into his face from less than an inch away.

"I'm Forged," he said.

Dani stared at him, her ferocious gaze light amber, like a traffic light saying *hang on a minute*, and then she let him go and laughed. "Forged?" she gasped between giggles. "I like that. What are you, then? Ordinary Boy, Prat Class? Gobshite, Tosser Class?"

"Roc, Handslicer," he said, managing to lean on his elbows though it hurt like hell. "And you're my dream."

She stopped laughing and stared at him, her face immediately cold and calculating with a switch so sudden and complete it scared him. The end of a smile tugged at her lip. "Do something, then."

"What?"

"If this is your dream, you can do what you like. Do something. Prove it."

"I can't." It was the rule. Once Tupac had abandoned him, he had nothing.

"That's nice." She nudged him with her toe, her tone conveying clearly that she meant the opposite of nice. "Nice story. But it's not worth anything. What are you good for?" She bent at the hip and leant down, as flexible as a doll. "Do you fuck? Or what is it?"

"I'm good with machines." He remembered this suddenly, although the words came from a piece of him that was only in one side of his head, the main part of his attention focusing oddly on her last words and a curious pulling sensation in his chest, a stirring he couldn't understand. Suddenly he wondered if he was ugly.

Dani glanced sideways, indicating the junk strewn around. "How good?"

"I don't know."

She took hold of his lapels again and hauled him up. He staggered against her and felt the softness of her body—so unexpected as it collided with his—and then her strength shoved him away.

"We need better machines," she said. "You can stay with us tonight and tomorrow you can make something work."

Once she'd decided, it seemed that was it. She slung his arm around her neck and marched him out of the barn and into a small house, cluttered and smoky, where he sat and nursed his headache.

Years passed in that compound. He learned to fight and to hide, and how to steal from newcomers without them noticing. He repaired kettles and toasters and washing machines, with scrap. He even helped some of the others make an aeroplane. Their big project took ages because it had to be designed and manufactured from scratch, and he fell in with the idea because he'd never dreamed how long he would be there and how many times he'd return to work there, screws and rivets taking shape in his clumsy fingers. It never would have worked anyway because there was no fuel they could have used for it. And when he'd thought of it as an escape plan he'd never believed it would ever be anything more than a few heaps of hand-beaten aluminium. He hadn't accounted for the fact that he would fall in love with Dani, who had previously been Caspar's girl, and so he had to sabotage the glorious machine, so they'd never find out that all along it was a dud that was never going to get off the ground.

Older now, little wiser, he ordered his way out of the memory replay into the Uluru in which he'd started to ask his question and found Tupac patiently waiting for him to speak first—because he was the one with the problem.

"Is Caspar me?" he asked, ending the memory.

Tupac paused. "It's possible," she said. "Is that why you keep coming home?"

He didn't like the answer. "Not today." He shuffled his Arboraform rootlets in the loamy earth of the forest, not really enjoying the experience very much. "I wanted some advice on another thing."

"Yes?"

"Voyager Lonestar Isol." He thought it might be a round-about way of coming in on the Stuff problem—that Tupac would have advice on what he ought to do.

The tree canopy high above him rustled and whooped with the sudden passing of a troop of monkeys. Leaves fell daintily, shredded in half, torn too quickly from the branch.

"I haven't heard from her in quite some time . . ." Tupac began, but Corvax never heard the end of the sentence. Abruptly his own security systems terminated the link, and he was back in his shrunken, aching old body, lying in his stinking nest, head ringing with alarm bells.

The AI Perimeter systems were down.

As dawn struck the teeth of Mawenzi into pure white and darkest brown against a perfectly blue sky, Zephyr stood on the open observation platform of her dormitory at Kibo and stared at it long enough to glut her eyes on its magnificence. Behind her the steep screes and rolling shapes of Kibo itself rose to the summit of the mountain, where the Ladder stretched its single golden harp string to the sky, but she wasn't interested in that now. In a few minutes she was due to meet Anthony and board a Heavy Angel for take-off to Idlewild, but until that moment came she wanted to see an earthly thing with no trace of human activity upon it. Mawenzi's prickly hostility had made sure that it was only useful as an object of beauty or, for the more adventurous, a treacherous technical ascent and a brush with the ineffable.

With a comfortable feeling of not wanting to actually bother, she imagined climbing among its spires and sealed her heavy parka against the gruff wind that had begun to whip around the camp and set its population of ten white ravens the difficult task of navigating against its sudden currents. They seemed to be enjoying themselves no end, hanging in the draughts and surveying all activity with an eye towards the breakfast that would shortly make an appearance on the refuse heap when the cooks threw out the previous day's leavings. Zephyr had no breakfast. She didn't like the idea of it returning suddenly when the Angel made its ascent.

Her Abacand vibrated in her pocket and she reluctantly turned to go. A staff officer had taken her luggage and there was nothing to do but close the door and make her way to the dining area. After the sub-zero temperatures outside, the inner atmosphere was oppressively hot and she was tearing off the parka before she'd gone twenty metres. The Strategos was holding his in one hand, she noticed as they approached one another.

He gave her a friendly smile. "All set, Professor?"

"I was just admiring your view," she said, eager to talk so she didn't have to think about the butterflies in her stomach. "It's a wonderful spot."

To her surprise he broke into a snatch of song, "*Ma-wenzi, Ma-wenzi, Ma-wen-zee* . . . Local tune, very old, made up long before the Europeans even believed there was a mountain here." He shook his head, amused at his own playfulness or maybe that of his AIs. "Yes, a magnificent spot. Not spoiled too much by the mass of cargo that passes through it, I hope."

"Strategos," she began, trying not to rush her words, "will you be coming to Idlewild?"

"Not just yet," he said, "but I'll take you up to the departure gate." He grinned at her crestfallen expression. "Don't worry. It'll be over before you know it, and Idlewild has centrifugal spin of a quarter-gee on the living decks. You'll feel as light as a feather, but not nearly as sick as you would in free fall. Your Abacand has been given all the information you'll need." He paused as a small group of flight officers walked past, carrying their safety helmets and boots in their hands, heading for the exit. "The Angel will make all the introductions for you. He's the most diplomatically minded of the crew, and he's already met Isol over the last few days, so there shouldn't be any trouble."

"Were you expecting some?" she asked.

The Strategos gestured for her to accompany him after the officers and began to shrug into his parka. "It's not unknown for strongly political Forged to refuse all kinds of things to the Unevolved," he said. "At least, not unknown for the off-planet dwellers to act like that. On Earth, society's pretty much an integrated paradise of harmony compared to the wider solar society." He glanced at her to check her reaction. "It's a situation not always reported that widely. Mostly because a lot of it is illegal. I realize that the official line says there are no self-selecting and self-adapting Forged out there, but that's not true. There are places you can go to have all kinds of adaptations." He brushed the dome of his skull with his hand, unconsciously tracing the lines of the copper tattoo as he reached for his hood.

"The New West," she observed. "It's been the subject of many academic papers."

He didn't say anything, just waited for her to show ready and then led the way outside.

Within ten metres her confident pace had slowed and she was out of breath. Anthony, breathing steadily but not distressed, slowed with her.

"Isol's new world is going to be like this," he said. "If the oxygen readings are correct."

"Man," Zephyr sighed. "I never . . . thought . . . it was going . . . to be . . . so . . . exhausting." The cold air scrubbed her lungs, and yielded almost nothing to them. She had to grab the Strategos's arm for support as a wave of dizziness swept across her, and a tight feeling began to compress the underside of her forehead.

"You'll get used to it within a few days," he assured her, but his immediate glibness gave way instantly to concern and she read in his face a worry that he had previously kept deeply hidden.

"What?"

They stopped but she kept hold of his arm, and he let her.

"It's not too late to say no." He straightened up, and they stepped aside in the track to allow a cargo truck to pass, its wheels higher than both their heads, engines almost silent. "There isn't anything like security on this mission. We have no experience of protection against alien biologicals, should you encounter them. Just your presence contaminates that planet with enormous amounts of material. It's all against our own views on how best to do things. If I were you, I'd be having second thoughts, fifty times over."

"She has you over a barrel," Zephyr said. "She already decided it all for you."

He grunted and nodded. They began the slow progress towards the jeep shed once more, where she could see a uniformed man at the wheel of a small passenger pod, ready to take them to the summit.

"But not for you," Anthony insisted. He shook his head. "I'll be blunt with you, Duquesne. I've looked over all your records. You have a good life here. Even romance?" He hesitated and didn't meet her gaze as she sought to understand whether he was referring to Kalu or not. She said nothing.

They continued the slow struggle across the base.

"Most of me wants to flinch," she admitted. "Every step is more like backwards than forwards to me. I know I could die tomorrow—hell, even today. But I don't want to sit in my office for the rest of my days, stuck in pasts better than my own. I love to live vicariously, in a book or a holo, but I think I can stand one dose of reality before it's my time."

They came to the jeep itself and he opened the door for her. "You can call me at any time," he said as she got in, and then sat beside her.

"Thank you." Zephyr wasn't sure if she was being surreptitiously chatted up. His tone was most definitely ambiguous, as though her agreement to participate in the expedition had been her passing a kind of test. It seemed unlikely to her, in this situation, but he was an attractive man, close to her own age. He was rather like she imagined Kalu to be, when she let herself imagine him as a prospect.

The vehicle bounced over the frozen ground, and its tyres bit into the steep incline with a growl of multiple active suspension as the passenger capsule was lifted up like a funicular car to maintain a horizontal position for their comfort. In a few minutes they were atop Kibo, and getting out in the shade of its last remaining hunk of blue glacier. Here the air was even thinner, and they hurried to get into the terminal building—as much as they could hurry at a stately walk.

Zephyr found herself abruptly transported from natural beauty to an undistinguished commercial departure lounge. She caught her breath as they got rid of the parkas and checked her bags.

"Isol has agreed to carry supplies for you," the Strategos said as they waited in the limbo of small shops and coffee houses that lined the walkways, pretending to be interested in the fare on offer. "You'll have a tent shelter, a sled and seven days' supplies of food and water. All this should provide adequate protection from the conditions. The sun is less powerful than our own, but the ambient temperatures should be hospitable. You also get the full complement of scientific gear and, well . . . I'm sure your Abacand will explain it in any detail you like, in due course. However, we'd like you to keep a constant watch on Isol herself and report back to us on her state of mind."

At last here it was, Zephyr thought. The real problem.

"And you'll keep me informed of any relevant insights," she countered.

"I'm afraid communications won't be possible."

Better not call Emergency, then, she thought flippantly to herself, but her heart, which had already been doubtful at yesterday's challenges, sank even lower at the news, and she almost said right there that she'd already had enough. Making a voyage like this alone was bad; doing it accompanied by the mentally unstable, and far from any help, was akin to insane. She'd had her insane moments—who hadn't?—but the scale of it now took her breath away.

"This is utterly preposterous, you know," she told Anthony as they began to follow the signs towards the gate.

"I know." He made a move as if to wring his hands, and then jammed them in his uniform pockets instead, unwilling to make his sense of helplessness obvious.

Along the way Zephyr saw a small shop selling flowers in little bunches, each wrapped up in a plastic enviropak, and supplied with water to maintain their brief lives for a week or two. They were popular gifts for the spaceborne and on impulse she bought a posy of violets and put them into her carry-on bag.

Anthony said nothing. They had run out of conversation of any variety.

After a few more awkward moments their call came, and he

led her out along the gangway. As they approached the Angel the corridor became transparent, to allow passengers to view their host, for good or ill. It was a sight that stopped her in her tracks.

They were presently about ten metres clear of the ground, but barely a third of the way up the body of the colossal form. Crouched obediently at the gate, like a giant cross between a crab and a dog, a thing of metal and heavy crystalline hide breathed multiple breaths of steam and smoke. The flat, folded planes of wings were tucked tightly against its flanks, bare metal gleaming with oil in the lines of their joints. Its skin was the colour of the mountain, whited with frost and crackling sheens of ice. A head, long-nosed and sharp, was tucked against its forebody, and on it Zephyr saw the surface of an eye blinklessly open, its clear shields reflecting the light of the high sun. She glimpsed vast forelimbs with pincers and hooks, engines cased in violet metal, connectors studded like warts all over its rhino-like surface. Blast damage and the long streaks of old burn marks scored it. The Heavy Angel Sisyphus Bright Eagle was brutal and hideous to see, as unlike the Passenger Pigeon as she could imagine at that moment.

It did not surprise her that the Sisyphus's avatar was a delicately proportioned and elfin human with multiple white wings: a fantasy that was such a pale candle to the terror-inducing power of the real thing. Seeing him like that defused one's fear that to become his passenger was to enter the jaws of a dragon, or so she guessed; it was a reverse of the suggestions made by mighty temples built to minor kings.

"Bright Eagle," the Strategos introduced him. "Just the one passenger for you. You've received Machen's instructions?"

"Tupac first," the Sisyphus agreed with a bland smile. "Then Idlewild."

"Tupac?" Zephyr broke in, suddenly rooted to the spot. "I thought—"

"It's better that you meet Isol immediately," the Angel said. "The procedure that she is undergoing is very taxing, and she will need sleep before she can recover. The sooner you get there, the sooner she will be ready to fly."

"Tupac is used to visitors," Anthony said.

"But I'm not used to visiting—" Zephyr began, and cut herself off. She'd never had a day where she'd experienced herself as a ninny before. "Okay," she said, after a deep breath. "Can we go now?" She felt that if she didn't make a first step on this journey, she was going to lose all the courage to make *any* step.

The Strategos seemed to recognize this. He nodded. "High time," he said. "Good luck, Professor."

She held out her hand. "Zephyr."

He shook the hand and nodded. "I look forward to hearing your reports."

She glanced at the Angel's avatar figure, and followed the gesture of its arm as it waved her in through the door. If there were vast cargo holds beyond she was not in one of them—the passenger cabin was no bigger than an ordinary domestic room. She took a seat, one of ten, and fastened the buckles, listening carefully to the Angel's instructions.

"When I grip the Ladder, we shall experience a very brief but very powerful acceleration," it said. "You will be fortunate to lose consciousness for a few seconds. After that there will be no further discomfort."

It wasn't the most reassuring in-flight instruction she'd ever had, but she clamped down firmly all thoughts of what lay ahead. Instead of the gibbering, quibbling questions that wanted her attention, a cool idea sprang into her mind, which said— *Well escaped, old girl.*

She knew that most of the reasons she was sitting here, as the Angel walked the short distance to its take-off point, were to do with being bored at home and not being able to break it off cleanly with Kalu—or rush in and meet him, consequences and all. Despite the many dangers, this was simply easier. She had nothing to do now but her job.

There was an almighty lurch as the Angel sprang from its pad and into the air. Zephyr's heart leaped up and her stomach plummeted at the same instant. For a split second they were weightless, and then the huge claws on the Angel's forelimbs caught one of the rungs of the Ladder as they spun past, too fast to see—and a charging elephant slammed full force into her back.

As the promised darkness seized her mind, Zephyr thought, *I am a coward.*

The Pangenesis Tupac, Blessed Mother-father, orbited the Earth at one-fifth lunar distance. They were on approach within a few hours. Via a direct feed from the Angel's own eyes, Zephyr looked at her passenger viewscreen and saw a being she'd seen a hundred times before, filmed from every angle, documented and lovingly characterized in a billion programmes, replicated as the world's most popular modular soft toy for the under-fives. Spiked with antennae, tentacled with cable, studded with lights, Tupac was larger than an average city. From two hundred klicks she looked like an artist's impression of a chthonic god, and from two klicks she was invisible: filling the entire view with endlessly clarifying details that, on closer approach, resolved into the functional openings and ports of any large estuarine operation; ships moored in close to her flanks like fleas, and clung between the shafts of outreaching anemone-fingers that absorbed her beloved sunlight and micro-debris. It wasn't entirely an idle comment that described the Forged as built from orbital effluent.

Zephyr expected to be wowed, and wowed she was, though that lasted a surprisingly short time as she was decanted briskly into another waiting zone, where the Heavy Angel's avatar, dressed in a pale chalk-stripe suit, and wingless out of respect, met her and led her along passages and through rooms that were depressingly utilitarian in their nature. Tupac had no avatars. A message appeared in the carpet under Zephyr's feet, which scrolled as she walked.

"Welcome, Professor Duquesne."

She supposed that it was pretty good going, when you considered that there were five thousand permanent residents and over a hundred thousand visitors here at any one time; and anyone who could speak individually to their own parasites had to be respected.

"Thanks," she said, half to the Angel—she was still so uncertain of the right way to do things—and the carpet pinked briefly in the shape of a human smile. Then she felt momentarily disturbed again at the notion that she was running around in someone's intestines and scraped her own tongue against her teeth, dislodging who knew how many million innocent bacterial bystanders and for the first time feeling guilty about it.

His return to his parents' embrace had put the Angel in a good mood. He gave Zephyr the full tourist tour, narrated impeccably. They visited human living quarters and workplaces—all mundanely similar to their Earth counterparts. They walked along the viewing gangways that led over huge engineering works where MekTek and InerTech were manufactured by AI and robot, and through warrens where flesh and metal seemed inseparably entwined in a mutual love affair—their final fling expressed in the outer skins of the million vats where the biological elements of new Forged were growing. Zephyr, entranced, thought of Bolivian jungles full of hidden gods, of the rose-red city of Petra in its secret chasm, of the surge and tide of life over the years coming to this place, all the time coming here without knowing where it was going—to this marvel, this being's single capacity for the creation, and re-creation, of so much. She was speechless.

Her awe lasted right up to the moment when they came to the servicing bays where Isol waited for them. Zephyr stared at this latest of the startling new things in her life with all the reactive brilliance of a hypnotized moose, as the Angel introduced her and politely stood aside.

The being that was Voyager Isol was as unrecognizably human as the most extreme class of Forged that Zephyr had seen in her life. What surprised her most was how small Isol was.

Isol hung in the soft webbing of Tupac's embrace, looking like nothing more than a piece of stranded sea-junk: an assembly of spars jutting from a central core of black hide that was knobbled with peculiar outgrowths and pits. Here and there strange scars bubbled up in grey stripes and blobs of tough new flesh. Twin seed-cases that Zephyr assumed to be engine housings hung below her, bizarrely botanical, surrounded in plastic sheeting behind which Arachno engineers worked with cautious movements. Those pods must contain the alien devices, Zephyr thought, as she looked down on the Voyager from the observation gallery and clung firmly to the railing. They were the colour of dried beetroots, smooth but not shiny. If they had telltale details marking them as to use she didn't see them, nor would she have known what to make of them.

Staring was rude, she finally remembered, and glanced away. She expected a very frosty reception, going by the rumours of Isol's legendary personality, and she was not disappointed.

"So, you're the inspector," Isol said, ignoring Bright Eagle's carefully precise introduction.

Zephyr found she was standing close to a section of chromahide that had dilated a little to allow the sound of a vibrating sheet of thin inner skin to emerge: a natural speaker that broadcast a voice that made few concessions to beauty. Its single tone wasted no nuance in conveying Isol's impatience.

"I'm Zephyr Duquesne."

"An archaeologist. I've seen all that. You're fatter than I imagined. I don't know if the seat in the Hand will fit you, but it's too late to change it now. At least the acceleration is less likely to knock you senseless. Fat cushions the body from excessive gees, to some extent, so I've heard. I hope you're not a big talker. I don't do chit-chat and I don't want to hear it."

Zephyr had heard this kind of hurt-them-before-they-hurt-you attitude before, among older academics. She said mildly, "It's very kind of you to—"

"I wouldn't dream of this kind of malformation without the most extreme provocation," Isol snapped. "Don't thank me.

You'll soon long to be home again, and then you can thank Machen and his government all you like. As for the niceties—" and here Isol duplicated a horselike snort of derision, "—it's me that has to make your food and process your shit, remember. Thanks doesn't really cover it."

Zephyr felt her eyebrows lift with the effort of suppressing a smart retort. She held out the small posy of violets she'd bought on Kilimanjaro and said, lacing the phrase with an unavoidable drollery, "I brought you these."

There was a moment's pause in which Isol's antennae twitched. "And what do I do with those?"

"You can stick them up your ass for all I care," Zephyr said evenly, giving the flowers an appreciative sniff and keeping her smile pleasant, as she privately restored their scores to an even one-all.

Isol snickered. "You keep them for me."

Zephyr stuck them in the top pocket of her new overalls, just below the Gaiasol insignia. "Well," she said, holding her hand out in the wide-open gesture that was an offer to shake with a person who had no hands. "I'll be seeing you for lift-off tomorrow, then. Sure was nice meeting you."

"Likewise," the voice said. "Don't forget your toothbrush." The stiff, circular mouth-hole closed smartly and became a single surface with the chromahide.

Zephyr let her hand drop to her side. Although this was her cue to get lost, she hung around, watching the service work and the attachment of the supplies she would need as their cases were fixed to the Voyager's surface, later to be concealed beneath a smooth dome of heat- and radiation-resisting Ti-bone. Bright Eagle gave all the explanations, long on technical details that Zephyr wasn't interested in, but she let him ramble so as to give her time to take in a good eyeful. She couldn't imagine any of her friends readily offering themselves up as pack mules to take a stranger to one of their sites of special interest. Not if it meant the equivalent of having their hands sawn off and replaced with other limbs. Not if it meant having that stranger live off you like an unwanted cuckoo baby. She still didn't understand the significance of Zia Di Notte's second world to the Forged.

Ignoring the avatar's protest, Zephyr tapped the hide over the previous speaking point and asked straight out. Possibly others would be too diplomatic to attempt it, but diplomacy wasn't going to wash with this one, she was sure of it.

"I don't get it," she said. "What do you hope to gain from this planet?"

"You couldn't possibly understand," Isol said. "You've always been free."

Zephyr gave the hide a condescending pat, finally cross enough to stop giving Isol all the power in this situation.

"What a small imagination you've got if that's what you believe—taking the moral high ground with a line like that. Do you suppose I asked to be born in this time and this place, make a life for myself and then have it all thrown in the air just to stand here and listen to your selfish whining? Even if you get your self-governance, who have you escaped from? *You*'ll still be there, won't you? No speed or distance will ever change that."

But although she had rather hoped Isol would get angry at this provocation and reveal some clue as to her real thoughts, the Voyager just said, "You'll see."

As intended, it did make Zephyr shudder inside. She didn't believe Isol's promise that this mission was going to be different from anybody's simple running away from the mundanities and miseries of their own situation, but she believed her hostility was real and that made tomorrow a day she didn't exactly look forward to with bated breath. She let the Voyager have the last word and followed the Angel's avatar out of the hangar, letting his apologies to Isol wash over her.

They left Tupac then and flew back to the Ladder and Idlewild itself, a spiky ring structure which, in the aftermath of so much odd biology, could only remind Zephyr of a tightly closed cat's sphincter, despite its metallic lustre and romantic name. She must just be in a bad mood.

There followed another dreary couple of hours in which various officers appeared and went through the "Ah, so you're the professor we've been hearing so much about" routine with her, and the "Watch out as you drink coffee out of those self-heating mugs—it's really hot" and the "Rather you than me, ho ho ho" and the "Of course, it may not really be alien technology but something they've cooked up in the Belt . . ." scenarios that she read as mostly Unevolved paranoia that the Forged really had managed to beat them intellectually in some desperate game to build a means of destroying the economy. It made little sense to her but it was a popular theme. Nobody really wanted to consider the prospect that it was a genuine extrasolar artefact, and that fear she understood.

"If it *were* alien," one young woman asked her during some briefing about the use of the tents and sled, "how would you tell?"

"I don't know," Zephyr answered honestly. "All the Earth artefacts I normally examine are of human or older-hominid manufacture, and there's never been any doubt about that. I'm not sure that I could tell. Perhaps if a thing seemed to be manufactured, but bore no resemblance to any object I've ever seen before—but, you know, to the eye that has no use for something everything looks like junk."

The captain's face looked worried. "Some say the Forged have a different understanding—and that they may have been able to complete the M-Theory and build it themselves."

"Now *that* I am sure of," Zephyr said. "If this is a hoax or one of their constructions, I'll tell you."

"How can you be so confident?"

"If I can recognize anything at all," Zephyr replied wearily, "then it's probably a whopping fake."

"But the cities—"

Zephyr held up her hand. "They aren't necessarily what they seem . . . but, yes, if there's a Library and a Courthouse and a

Main Street in evidence . . . you're probably right. They may be cities."

Later, as she tried to sleep, strapped into her bunk, she reflected on the captain's unhappy acceptance of her answer. It had been rather unscientific. There was a good chance that other life could have followed many of the same routes as life on Earth, and developed many similar features. It was also possible that natural processes could create objects that appeared to be manufactured—vast paleolithic citadels, for example—but that were only rocks temporarily put into a suggestive array by tides or erosion. She had only a small hope of being able to argue those cases one way or another and, with the added handicap of having no idea whatsoever of what these alleged alien beings might have been like, it seemed a ridiculous job to attempt.

Kincaid moved with leviathan deliberation across the flatlands on the largest continent of his new world beneath the orange star. He occupied an area of marshy grasses and river deltas that radiated outward for more than a thousand miles in every direction from his position. There he had nurtured the mixture of sedges, weed and rushes with paternal care, selecting their gene profiles from his internal databanks, combining and adjusting their features for the climate and their function, constructing and germinating the seeds within his own nurseries. His hands had planted and his tongues had tasted the changes he had brought about in the planet's atmosphere and its silty tracts of fresh water. From one horizon to another his body roamed and worked, limbs under their own partial control so that his mind was free to listen.

Kincaid had done too much listening over the last few days. He strained his hearing and his concentration, attempting to get beyond the drip and splash, the wind in the reeds, the minute creaks and groans of leaves unfurling and seed heads puffing out their tough bracts, ready to fly. Beneath the ordinary sounds of this world he struggled to hear what lay beneath: the soundless voices calling.

There was no knowing when, or for how long, they'd come. He didn't even know if they were real or if, deep in his psyche, some cancerous growth was disrupting the systems that maintained his equilibrium. He ran diagnostics to see if they were variations of his own voice, rerouted through a limb or a channel that was below the notice of his conscious mind, but the analyses revealed that despite his age and the long hibernation he was in good health. There was no reason to think the voices had anything to do with him at all.

There they were again.

On the plains and in the ponds and streams, his Fingers and Toes stopped their work. He became suddenly still, his basking skin dappled with the shadows of clouds and warmed by the summer sun, darkened with rain. On the wind, through its dance, came the silent whisper,

Kincaid.

They whispered his name to him in pitches low and high, precise and distorted. They murmured it in the curl of a wave on his cheek, in the fall of ultraviolet that pierced his skin, and he thought they smiled, or laughed.

Kincaid!

He listened, obedient. The voices had no direction of origin. They were from nowhere. They spoke in unison, as though the world itself spoke, though Kincaid's million ears and eyes detected nothing, nobody. His audio processors monitored no changes beyond the wind and the water, the sough of reeds and grasses. The voices reverberated only in the delicate folds of his phytogenetic tract, and in the hearing centres of his brains.

Kincaid.

What did it mean when a planet spoke? The Earth had never said anything when he was in his youth and still learning the functions of his arms and legs, of belly and gut and wings. Mars had never said his name either, although it bore his mark in mountains and valleys, streams and rivers, forests, oceans and islands. At first he'd thought he'd imagined it, an engineer's fancy. Isolated people often found themselves accompanied by invisibles; it was a hazard of long periods alone like this, when suddenly random noises seemed to stem from an intelligent, invisible ghost nearby. But lately it had begun to frighten him—and besides, he had been here less than a week.

Kincaid concentrated once more on his work. The grass thrived for the most part. There were some patches lost to fungus and a mould he was still sequencing that had been lurking native on the so-called barren land before he and Nobility had arrived to begin work, despite Isol's claims of sterility. There was nothing out of the ordinary for such a world that had once supported abundant life, and could do so again before its star burned away.

He turned back to his fields and sowed, pruned, cleared with a fiercer concentration than before. When the marsh was built, and Bara had primed the oxygen level, he could begin the forestation. *Only a few more months of work to go out here on the fenland,* he thought, consoling himself. But at the limits of his reach his eyes stared outward with a vigilance normally reserved for inhabited worlds, and his heavy surface skins twitched with the sudden cooling of cloud shadows as though the sensations revealed another kind of life that was deeper than his own— not rooted in elements or the combinations of molecules that made his structure, but in the interconnectedness of everything. Land spoke to sky, and water to air.

Kincaid listened for the voices that wanted to speak to him, bone and blood.

They had gone. Still, his back prickled.

12. A VISIT FROM REALITY

For a moment Corvax flailed around, unable to move freely enough or think clearly enough to act, but finally the parts of his mind long tuned to a lawless existence hit the correct command strike on the holoconsole, and he identified the small arrow-shaped being that had planted itself on his landing platform without permission. It was the person who had once been First Class Flight Leader Tomahawk MekTek Dragonstar Jagatak, and was now known in his post-army days as Dog Legba.

Corvax viewed the sight with furious impotence. Dog Legba was the favoured assault soldier of Xing Xianshi, the only Unevolved pirate in the lanes, and the worst. It was Corvax who had made Xing into a MekTek. His reward had been to live.

The Dog, once a Gaiasol military-police unit, was carrying enough AI systems and power to have rendered Corvax's defences inadequate in any case and, having seen that, Corvax wasn't about to do the stupid thing and launch an attack. In the minute he had remaining to him Corvax worked at the lab suite in a frenzy, uncoupling the block of Stuff from its tray and searching for somewhere to put it. He had absolutely no doubt that it was what Xing had come for, and that there would be almost no way that he would be able to keep her from acquiring it. As he heard the landing party rattling up the gantryways towards his laboratory he was at a loss—he had been thinking about sending the Stuff to Earth, giving himself up to the government, some dream of protecting people foremost in his head running alongside the panic that thoughts of Stuff set off in him. But there was no time to pack it, bag it and send it into the drop chute. Anyway, Xing would still get it.

As the doors opened Corvax had no idea what he was going to do. In one of his lesser hands he was still holding the small cube of quartz. Two Arachnos entered first, the guns mounted on their body armour automatically scanning the room. They separated to take point with a clattering of their legs, and Corvax nodded a grim acknowledgement at Xing's Roc body-guard, a creature in far better condition than he was, and more suited to fighting.

Roc Cutter Thad had the grace of an eagle, and Ti-bone where Corvax had ordinary TeChitin. He was scarred along one side of his beak where an energy weapon had streaked him, and a thin foam of repair cells and plasma dripped from it, splattering the floor. Nonetheless, he handled the near-nonexistent gravity of the asteroid with more panache than any other visitor Corvax had ever received. The rest of the crew bumbled along in his wake with mag-attachments and clumsy grapplings.

Thad aimed his weapons directly at Corvax, although his greeting was devoid of any malice—he regarded Corvax as a blood brother, albeit one he felt no loyalty to. Xing herself rode in on a thickset creature covered in hair and breathing through a heavy apparatus that almost obscured the fact that it had once been a Martian Hercules class. It was now shorter of limb and had been hoofed. Corvax didn't look too closely at it in case he had to wonder who it used to be.

Xing, a metre and a half of fine-boned Unevolved human, wore her customary fighting gear of nothing save a tattoo of her own genome written across her body. Her face was hidden by a respiratory mask and the heavier lines of Tek-metal which radiated down across her shoulders and back, and wove in dragon curves to her toes. Corvax heard the metal click faintly as she dismounted her "pony" and drifted idly towards him. She waved a hand at his console array. It promptly vanished and he heard his systems move into power-low mode. She'd had an upgrade somewhere else; he wondered who'd done it, even as she started talking.

"I hear you had a visitor."

"She's gone." Corvax didn't like lengthy and knowing conversations that hedged the point, but Xing enjoyed all the relish of her power.

"I would like to see your scan of the Voyager's new engine." Or maybe she was getting old too.

"I'm surprised you didn't take it already." He found himself inching away from her as she approached and her eyes became visible through the lensing of her mask.

"Our AI specialist was lost recently," she said, and reached up to undo the long black pigtail of her hair. It unwound itself immediately—every strand a fibre-optic sensor line—and lifted in a dark nimbus, flowing this way and that as if in water as it glanced around her, feeding her Tek with information about the environment so that it could draw some conclusions about what Corvax had just been doing. "So I am reduced to asking this favour."

"You won't be able to build it," he stalled, making some half-witted movements that indicated where her Arachno engineer might make his downlink to the appropriate system node. The idea of anything like the drive or Stuff in the hands of someone as vicious as Xing made him sick.

"I'll be the judge of that," she said. She gave him an appraising look that clearly indicated he was lacking in all departments. "And meanwhile we will take your specimen of the alien technology."

Corvax hesitated. In the silence he heard the drip of Thad's healing wound and the gurgling rasp of the pony-thing in its respirator. The Arachno taking the download from Corvax's system set six black eyes towards him, and its guns swivelled idly in his direction.

"I don't have a sample. She wouldn't give me one." He made himself not grip the rock tightly, not let it go, nothing.

"Is that right?" Xing shrugged. "How disappointing. I had heard a rumour that Isol came here to begin her own market in a new technology, and was planning for you to act as her primary agent. Of course, that means moving in on something that I consider my own speciality. Would you change your mind if I offered you superior protection and distribution? Your set-up here is, let's be honest, hopeless." She folded her arms beneath the small, rounded softness of her breasts and stared at him impassively.

"I don't have any of it."

This gave her pause. Xing did not offer deals lightly. She knew that if he turned her down, it wasn't because of any scruples of his about legality, either. But Corvax didn't know how she'd come by her information—whether through spying or by a clever guess—and so he was playing this game of poker with a bad, bad hand.

Her hair reached out and brushed the Arachno technician's tough carapace. He shivered, the tips of his legs drumming on the floor in a staccato dance of excitement and deference, and she said, "There is nothing else in your system of interest to me. Perhaps your whole usefulness is at an end. Leaving you here alive was my original payment, but I don't intend this new technology to become a public service so that you can upgrade any filthy half-caste to try his luck in the lanes." Abruptly she reached out her hand and, with a sudden and powerful yank, plucked a feather from his shoulder. The sharp sting made him wince.

Xing regarded the bloody end of it. "It's a shame that the knowledge of a lifetime doesn't code down into the genes," she said, and then tossed it aside. "You sent a message when I arrived. Who was it for?" Her fingers wandered in among his dulled flights, again selecting. She pulled out another and flicked it over her shoulder.

"To my cousin," he said.

"Oh, your *cousin*." She took hold of an anti-gravity primary, a feather as long as she was tall, and her MekTek powered up. Her hair maintained its erotic contact with the Arachno, sipping information from his skin to verify what Corvax said. Any other Forged was a cousin.

"Machen's Degraded messenger boy, Gritter," he replied truthfully, feeling her fingers begin to exert a terrible pull on the sensitive feather and its neural connections.

"What did it say?"

As she ripped the feather free and a shock of pain and anger struck him like a bolt in the heart, Corvax realized for the first time the complete extent of his loathing for her. She had a fake Chinese name—made up from a dictionary, he knew, because he'd looked it up. It was supposed to translate into Solian English as Brave Reality, and that was a joke as far as he was concerned, when an Unevolved child used her family's inheritance from the vast coca estates worked by Herculean labour to make herself Tek, and then claimed glamour by leading a band of desperate Forged to steal from their own, thinking it was the force of her personality and not the force of her payroll. Even as she infiltrated his own MekTek with a strand of her hair, he knew he was never going to sell out to shit like she was, and if she wanted to read that off the front of his face or off the highline in his conscious Tek-processor, she could. Hatred now eclipsed his fear of pain and death.

"It said you'd be on your way here, looking to cash in on any stupid rumour about impossible technology. It said: 'Call the cops. Dog Legba and his bitch are on the make.' It said: 'That fuckless whore from Brazil is going to have to cash her ass in on Virtua-porn before she makes anything out of me.' "

He wasn't looking at Xing but at Thad, as her aggressive freebooter systems tried to co-opt his own Tek into their patois of command and conquer. The Roc Cutter's bleeding face gaped with beak half open in a grin of admiration. Thad was wrong if he thought that Xing didn't see this treachery, however, for her active hair suddenly reached out and stung him with a sharp voltage, making him jump and swear.

And Corvax was in trouble. Many of his own memories were far from Xing's reach, but certain Tek was always online—had to be, in order that his failing body could carry on functioning and interacting with his equipment—and this she was consuming, despite his efforts to prevent her. She must have hired smarter and faster programmers and he'd have liked to have known where from.

He realized, as the unpleasantly electrical sensations of nerve and junction becoming overloaded frayed curiously close to his brain, that he might have to choose to shut down and die before she seized everything. His arms suddenly moved without his will. His wings raised and lowered like two old sails, his humanoid secondaries jerked forward, and Xing moved into their false embrace, smiling behind her mask.

"Why won't you love me, Corvax?" she asked sweetly, her hands sneaking forward beneath his breast feathers and into the soft down, bitter cold. He was aware of fighting the movements, but only partially succeeding. No longer interested in conversation, he struggled for his life, and felt the Arachnos responding to her commands to pin him down. She pushed and he fell with the grace of a bowling pin crashing to the floor under the strike of a spinning ball. His Tek-wires surged with a howling heat and began to scorch his flesh. He smelled it a second later, and knew the moment had come for an action of definition or for surrender.

There was a pain like no other in the world in his face, and Corvax heard the Herculean pony making a whining noise of terror and fear. The stink of shit filled the room's febrile atmosphere with despair. He thought she was cutting off his beak.

Because it was the only thing remotely like a weapon that he had and his one arm was still mostly his own, he flung the lump of quartz at her as hard as he could. He couldn't see through his agony, and he felt it must surely miss, but he flung it with the entire force of his hate and misery.

There was a series of wet sounds and small percussive shocks, a spattering of small things tumbling, falling and striking, and then there was peace, and a silence with the quality of an extended shudder.

Corvax lay still in the throb of his abating agonies and found he could see, looking around with his own functional Tek again. He saw the pony curled up in a foetal ball, surrounded by a dripping chaos of flesh and metal. Where Xing, Thad and the Arachnos had been, there hovered a group of small things, each like a cross between a scimitar and a wasp. As Corvax saw these objects they immediately flew together, liquefied into a single undistinguished blob, and fell to the floor, inert and unpretty as any other lump of old rock.

He saw the light-blast of the Dog's engines as it took off in a screaming curve at full power. He saw an ordinary asteroid strike it heavily on one side, and its flailing retreat into the depths of the Belt. He looked at his silicon dioxide again, and got up slowly, slipping on the debris of Xing, gathering up what was left of her hair and scalp in one hand, the rock in the other. Thankfully a numbness of emotion had been granted him. He had the presence of mind to store the hair for his own use, and to secure the stone on his person. Activating the command sequences for his small emergency shuttle, he bent towards the heavy shape of the pony where it sniffled softly, arms curved around its elongated head.

"Come on," Corvax said and tried to help rouse it to its feet. "Let's get you back to Tupac. She'll take care of you."

"Tupac!" squeaked the enormous beast, shaking so hard that its hooves tap-danced on the hard floor as their mag-contacts strove to stabilize it. "Can we really go there?" it whispered in a childish voice composed entirely of hope and wonder, as though he had suggested that they should visit fairyland.

"Straight away," Corvax promised, with more gentleness than he'd ever expressed to anyone before. He felt almost as though he might cry, if this form of his had possessed that ability. "We're going right now."

He shepherded the Herculean through the exits and into his shuttle's purely machine interior, telling the AI where to take its passenger. The pony lifted its snout towards him tentatively as the door closed. "Will I die? Have I?"

"Not yet," he said. He waited until the craft had safely switch-backed out of the local area and into the highway. There was no sign of the Dog anywhere.

Then, alone at last, he opened his wings and arms and screamed out the whole of his terror to the empty, senseless rock storm.

When he had come back to himself, he sent a message out to Gritter. He informed him that he was coming to surrender to Gaiasol at the Idlewild station outpost and then added, "And listen to this, you stupid rat-eater. Don't touch *anything* that has ever been in contact with Voyager Lonestar Isol."

Then he released himself from the door of the laboratory and leaped up into the free space, using his wing claws to catch a stone here, a boulder there, swinging himself up and around and down and out, heading for the drop base on the Belt rim, and a ferry trip to Earth.

13. A DAY'S WORK

The Degenerates were not popular with anybody. Gritter knew that and it irked him. Necktie knew it but didn't care. Gritter still felt pissed off at the general for the whole issue about Isol and his lack of a superbly high bonus, and this hurt had caused a lapse of character, resulting in his current position at lurk in the thick foliage of a chestnut tree off the Mall.

He gazed across the street towards the buildings on the far side, where Gaiasol's secret services, such as they were, kept house. He'd already been there, nursing a small hangover, for some three hours and was now feeling cramped and more determined than ever to find some solace.

His wait was soon rewarded. A Phaery painted in the colours of Speedcorp Deliveries, one of the lunar-based post offices, came gliding neatly along, a small envelope held tightly in its tiny claws. It paused at the intersection to glance cautiously left and right, and then began the standard foolishly circuitous route that its office had mapped out for it in order to disguise its real destination. This took it within three feet of Gritter's branch and those were three feet that the Phaery would have cause to regret—briefly. Gritter leaped out and seized it around the neck with his beak, fell through a small branchette, losing a couple of feathers, and plunged back into the greenery where he strangled the last life out of it with his foot.

Breathing heavily and staring around, Gritter was consumed entirely by a primal sense of victory that lasted a few mindless seconds. Then, as it faded, he was able to look down at the limp corpse and strip off the gauzy high-speed wings and the tough, inedible chitin of its iridescent casing. He stuffed its ID card (*Secta Phaeriform Brian Brown, Postal Messenger. This Messenger is protected by all the legal and civil guarantees* blah blah

lah-di-dah . . .) into a crook of two branches where it wouldn't be found for some time, and partook of a little leg-meat snack as he separated the envelope from its tenacious hold. Even in death it was hard to unpick the little bugger from his parcel.

Then came a pause during which he decided to leave the envelope and concentrate on lunch. He placed the inedible portions— head, claws, carapace—into his own bag, for later disposal at the tip, and gulped the rest, guts and all, wondering bitterly and not for the first time whether, if he'd been correctly Cast, he'd be doing the same thing to some choice bit of lamb up the Andes somewhere, pulling in a nice whack each week and getting preferential treatment on the lecture circuit.

Then, having carefully wiped the ooze off and stropped his beak clean, he opened the envelope around its heavy tamper seal, flicking off the booby wires as he'd been taught, and extracted a small paper letter. He recognized two words at the top, which somewhat gave it away as to do with Forged Independence, and then the rest was in code.

Gritter spat with annoyance. Without knowing what it said he couldn't be sure who might want to know about it. Served him right, maybe, for trying to steal off his own employer. Still, they might want it badly enough to ransom it back via some third party (not Necktie, obviously—someone with a brain) or he could take it straight to Machen and see if it won him any brownie points, although Machen might want some explanation if the words at the top hinted that it should have arrived through the official lines.

The long-distance call's incoming trill came in the middle of this dilemma and nearly shocked him off the perch. He couldn't receive it on his own phone—would have to go to someone with bandwidth, and no scruples, for that. He put the letter in the only clean section of his satchel and set off for a place he knew near Mile End.

The solar comms shop was hidden around the back of two takeaways in a small yard. Gritter flew in at the window and paid his way in cash before taking up residence at a terminal, chair still warm from the last occupant. A haze of smoke and general filth ensured that the parlour attracted no casual custom.

He called the Van Allen AI ops at Amaligo and listened to the witless chitter about "if you are found to be receiving sensitive information via this network you will be summarily executed . . ." or whatever it was until the message itself finally loaded.

The illegal body shop where Corvax worked then showed up in a crackly haze of bad crypt, which annoyed the owner of the telephone exchange so much that she had to get up and shield her eyes and ears behind the emergency data-cage until Gritter had finished his call. He perched on the uncomfortable stool's slippery Formica, meant for fat Unevolved arses, and struggled to hear Corvax's peculiar whisper.

"Tell Machen I am bringing what he wants to Idlewild."

Gritter became very still, very alert. Was Corvax selling out? *What he wants?* What the hell was this about?

There was a pause and Corvax's huge and ugly crow-dog head turned away. Gritter thought he saw some scarring on the beak and blood scattered across the fine skin around his vivid yellow eyes.

"And listen to this, you stupid rat-eater. Don't touch *anything* that has ever been in contact with Voyager Lonestar Isol."

The message ended.

Gritter quivered with excitement and profound, uncomprehending gratitude. Special information about Isol. News all his. He let out a raspy caw of exultation, causing the woman hunched next to him to glare at him. He clacked his beak in her direction, letting her know that she could mind her own beeswax.

Feeling flush, he tipped the proprietress an extra dollar. She looked at him dreamily through her artificial lenses, where he could just make out a map of the communications-network protocols. Her ears listened and fine-tuned the frequencies and signal strengths between this backstreet show and her bandwidth suppliers. Her face was pitted and filthy, hair bunched up in a nest that was more black than grey—but with grime instead of dye.

"Getchaself a bath, gel," he suggested.

"Getchaself a brain, bird," she growled at him. "You're barred."

"What for?" He made to nip her hand but she was too quick.

"No illegal crypt on my lines."

"Ah, yeah, and you had a mother," he snapped, launching himself at the opposite windowsill where the single pane was open onto the yard.

She flung a cup of cold coffee at him and he tumbled out gracelessly, hauling himself upwards with a few exhausting wingbeats onto the guttering where he paused and shat, missing the window by a few inches. He sorted a few flight primaries with a furrowing in his beak and then made across the roofs towards the chip shop, where he scattered pigeons left and right, watching their idiot flutter for safety with mildly interested sadism. He thought briefly of pigeon meat, but then he ordered the chips instead, with vinegar and ketchup and mustard *and don't forget the brown sauce, mate.* No point eating like a beggar when you could soon afford the best.

Gorging himself, Gritter contemplated his rewards and what he might buy, whom he might bribe. He was so engrossed in this reverie that he forgot about the coded note for a time.

The intended recipient of the note did not forget, however, and in the stifling smallness of his office in the Services he pondered how to retrieve it, and what other use might be made of the Degraded Ornith now that matters External to Home Affairs had suddenly taken an unexpected and violently interesting turn. He left his velveteen coat on the back of his chair and went to lunch, as his MekTek officers began to search the city's traffic data for Gritter's whereabouts.

Zephyr couldn't sleep in Idlewild's light centrifugal gravity. Her mind raced with thoughts, most of them terrors to do with the day ahead or the void outside, so she decided to write a letter to Kalu and at least get them out in the open. But after the first few words she faltered, and the Abacand's tablet remained blank.

She knew it was because their relationship was unclear in her mind, or rather, that she'd deliberately left it muddied so that she wouldn't have to look at what it was. She missed him. She wanted to talk to him and clear things up between them, but she knew that if she made the call they'd only take their usual path, the occasional long silence opening up for her, and she skipping out to the end of it with some new subject that could entertain them both. She felt, although she wasn't certain, that he always waited for her to speak first. She was the one who had to move, if move there was to be made.

A Registry check, paid for on credit, told her the worst. Kalu was a Bathyform—a jellyfish. She took it better than she'd expected. Her heart could not bring itself to change its affection for disappointment; it only twitched with a few pangs of sadness for itself.

She switched to the Abacand's newly enhanced therapist functions and informed it of her discovery, just to test it out, because there was nothing else to do.

"So? Should I break things off?"

The Abacand messed about with its new LEDs and said, "You must have known there was no possibility of a relationship, although there are many cases of cross-Clade affairs of the heart. Mostly with environmentally compatible types, it has to be said; mostly Herculean/Unevolved or Jovian/Saturnian, although there really is no limit to the possibilities for those equipped to use the Uluru realities. That doesn't apply to you, however."

"It applies to *him*," she said. "He can walk along versions of Waikiki Beach and drink piña coladas at Club Med if he wants to."

"Virtua-based relationships are often short-term affairs where non-Tek participants are involved," the Abacand informed her. "Very few Unevolved are aware of this because they cannot go there, but when they do their lack of skill in communicating and understanding the nature of the medium makes matters extremely difficult."

"Are there many Unevolved having . . . relationships—in Uluru, with Forged?" she asked.

"Many," it said. "MekTeks almost all indulge in Dreamtime re-creations. Others will pay the prices necessary to rent time and equipment. There have been recent health reports on the use of these systems and there is some suspicion that they may cause synaptic problems, epilepsy or even stroke in Unevolved, due to the high-pressure data rates. And without real Tek it's something of a lacklustre event, I hear."

But Zephyr was thinking about the not-unhandsome Strategos Anthony now, wondering who he was meeting, where and what they were doing. She felt a moment's embarrassment—surely they all knew about her personal situation because of researching her background. The real flaw in all this was that meeting Kalu just wasn't as impossible as it should have been. She could have done it, could still do it, if she really wanted to. Her toes curled.

"Do you think you love him?" the machine prompted after it received no response.

"I thought I loved Benny Danto in the fourth grade," Zephyr said, "and I thought I loved Mister Married Lawyer, but both of those turned out to be damp squibs. My love of fabricating history has been the only constant."

"You dissemble," the Abacand said sharply. "You don't want

to admit that Mister Married Lawyer broke your heart, and you never have."

"Shut up." She thumbed the machine off and stuck it into her satchel, securing it in place. Strapped into her own cot, she closed her eyes tightly and tried to imagine a meeting—to test things out.

In her mind's eye Zephyr saw Kalu as a man-thing, a sort of merman who would appear in the surf, a fishy silver, and walk out on borrowed legs, his clothes artfully fashioned from seaweed and shells, his face *(on second thoughts, let's not do faces, can't get MML out of my mind's eye)* . . . anyway, he walks up and then . . . They might touch and swim out, tentacle in hand . . . That made her laugh until she thought of Forno—the pornography of Forged and Unevolved together: a sickeningly infinite array of penetration and interpenetration potentials, of violence, tenderness, lust and revulsion.

So, *Happily Ever After* had foundered on thoughts of tentacles and fronds of ice-cold fish-flesh, sharp-edged fins, ballooning body cavities filled with icy salt water, a mouth full of tiny shark's teeth.

It was futile. No doubt he would have fashioned himself into a suave creation of the perfect Unevolved, and it was only *her* sick imagination, in league with her defensiveness, that warped him into this fantasy of what a Forged might be instead of wanting to accept the placebo, or face the truth. She might as well have written the script herself and never included him. What was it they called people like that? Fornicators.

The real problem was her fear that she might actually be seduced by him, by it. The idea of the whole fish thing wasn't really as repulsive as it ought to have been, and that was . . . she didn't know. It was upsetting. What would this ability to consider it make her, in the eyes of her friends and family, her colleagues?

Zephyr's moral conscience said that it was no different to ordinary loves. Ah, but it was, said something that was strongly animal, strongly chemical, a bit that processed smell and taste and taint, and ordered her desire and revulsion. It was very different indeed, the love of an "alien" thing—fraught with terrors in its insatiable desire for the otherness, as clichéd in its way as belonging to a vampire cult. She didn't want to imagine that their whole relationship was founded only on the thrill of bending a worn old taboo and of satisfying a longing born of the same fragility that supposed dating a married man was some kind of daring act of modern womanhood and self-defining passion.

Zephyr wrote a thanks note for the kit and the scarf. Then deleted it. She fell asleep at some time after, and woke to the ringing alarm, her groggy vision barely emptied of Queen Elizabeth I, axe in hand, ready to strike off Walsingham's head.

"Anyway," the Abacand said as she switched it on to check her itinerary, "what's wrong with simple gratification?"

"Are you going to be like this the whole trip?" she asked. "Because I don't want to discuss it anymore."

"You don't want to talk about anything else, you mean," it retorted. "But seeing as you insist—you have an hour before departure."

"And I want that like a hole in the head."

"The Lonestar has already docked," the Abacand said. "I'm sure that if you tell her your feelings, you'll find they're warmly reciprocated."

"We've done that bit," Zephyr said, struggling to make smaller, slower movements, to avoid the sensation that her circulation was ballooning. "Mutual hatred has been agreed. You're to watch her for signs of madness."

"Compared to you?" the Abacand said with disbelief, and switched itself off before she could reach out to hit it.

Zephyr put off the fatal moment as long as she could, and then braved the walk out to the dock alone—despite the alleged company of an Idlewild staff officer who was as taciturn and grim-faced an individual as she had ever met. The Strategos was waiting for her as he had promised, his uniform immaculate, his copper Tek gleaming in the soft light. He shook her hand warmly.

"We did what we could to persuade the Voyager to construct a beacon for communications with the same technology that she has acquired in her engines but she has refused. Since we understand that Zia Di Notte is over twenty-seven light-years distant, there will be no link with us while you are away. I do apologize." He seemed hesitant, and she recognized the offer of a last-ditch way out of it.

"I see." She longed for a glimpse of Earth but they were on the space-facing side of the station. She had just become a long-distance and incommunicado agent with no escape routes, not even a cyanide pill.

She thought of the classes on twenty-first-century discoveries that she had been scheduled to teach, and recalled her admiration for the great explorers and adventurers whom she'd been pressed to include. Ernest Shackleton would not have flinched from this quest. He'd have punched her lights out to get to stand in her shoes right now—an entire world to flag up instead of simply a geographical marker point such as the South Pole, and as much danger and survival thrill as you could wish for. Zephyr was no Shackleton, no Boudicca, no Amelia Earhart. She wasn't in the least invigorated by this fresh difficulty. But her stubborn streak had become activated last night by Isol's prickly smugness and she could not back down from a challenge like that one.

"Because of the distance," the Strategos said solemnly, "there can be no rescue missions, you understand."

She nodded. "I've left copies of my will with the base AI," she found herself saying calmly.

"Your return date is in seven days. I wish you well." He raised his arm and touched her on the shoulder, squeezing it for a second longer than was strictly formal. "When you come back," he added, letting go and smiling sheepishly, "perhaps you'd like to go out for dinner?"

Zephyr laughed. "There's no 'perhaps' about it. You'd better

book the best table in the world, because I may have quite a lot
to say."

She was grateful for the moment, so much so that she leant
forward and kissed him on the cheek, a slight static zap from the
metal on his face sparking across to her.

"Nylon carpets," he muttered apologetically, but Zephyr
had already turned without delay to ensure no lengthy and embarrassing continuation of the moment.

She stepped through the door into the small airlock. When
the panels closed behind her and the exchanges cycled, she
sighed with relief. It was all done now. Ahead lay something
fresh, and even if it was unpleasant, she would have it to herself.

The forward door slid open and the black, soft-metal wrin-
kles of Isol's dilated abdomen glistened sharply where they were
drawn close against the structure of the station-hull.

"You may board," Isol said, a formal clip in her voice that
Zephyr had thoroughly expected. "Stow your pack in the
webbing provided. Make yourself familiar with all the facilities." The last word was said with some disdain and Zephyr
knew it referred to eating and toilets primarily, two humble
functions the Lonestar felt itself much above and probably
deeply soiled by. Zephyr didn't allow any moment of imagining herself performing either, but ducked through into the tiny
cabin area.

The heat was nearly stifling. Once she was inside, there was
barely room to turn around and standing was difficult without
feeling her hair brush the leathery ceiling with an uncomfortable
dragging sensation. A single plush seat became, at the touch of a
control, her couch, bed and dining space as well. There was a
reasonably sized screen set up on the bulky packaging of her survival sled at one softly curved end of the cylindrical room and
her rations and water had been stored beside the seat, packed
tightly in some of the webs that grew out of the wall. She placed
her own bag, tentatively in case it was something the Lonestar
could feel, into a spare one of these. Immediately it bulged out
and reduced her elbow room by a third on that side. She sat on

the seat and examined the safety harness, feeling herself start to perspire.

"I love what you did with it," she muttered, staring at four belts and a five-way clip. "It's very late-twenty-first-century: so efficient, yet cosy."

"My Hand is capable of atmospheric entry and independent flight," Isol said. "I will be glad to jettison its extra mass as soon as possible. For the time being you must sit down and not touch anything. We will be a few hours out to reach my departure point. Machen will try to follow any manoeuvres, and I don't want to be in range of his best trackers when I go, just in case."

"Sounds like somebody's confidence has taken a knock."

"You have the military history, so you do the calculation, honey. Five times he's tried to steal a part of my engines, and that's just while I've been here." The door shut and, as the metal sections slid home, a dark sheet of flesh moved to cover it and wriggled itself into place. Air sighed in through gilled vents in the ceiling, adjusting pressure. There was a muffled sound of something clanging, and the blunted *chuff* noises of explosive clamps decoupling.

There was no sign that they had moved but then Zephyr was pushed down in the seat, and she guessed at a reasonable acceleration away from the station. Since there was no way to see where they were, she had no idea where they were headed. She took the Abacand out of her bag, mostly for a sense of company, and switched it on. It gave her a map and a signal to illustrate their rapid transit away from the sun, curving on a course that would avoid all the planets and significant way stations.

"It's unusual for an ordinary professor's Abacand to have stellar tracking capability," Isol remarked. "What make is that?"

"It's, uh . . . TradEquality," Zephyr said, naming the cooperative who had constructed it and grateful that it was one that gave a fair wage in exchange for good work from anyone. The grip on her subsided and her body became fully weightless for the first time, tugging gently against the harness, a sudden flush in her face and fingertips. "They gave me some extra mods so I could survey the planet's magnetosphere and do some depth analysis and map the local solar area."

"I already did most of that," Isol informed her crisply, the voice coming from nowhere and everywhere. "But naturally they won't trust me. What else does it do?"

"I have all my history, anthropology and palaeontology databases," Zephyr said, "plus all of the botanical material I could fit in. Including a complete fossil record of the Earth, and the primary Martian geologies, a modelling system for long-term planetary conditions, a—"

"Spare me," Isol said. "I meant, has it been modified to do *other things* besides all the stuff you need it for?"

"Such as spying?"

"Such as."

"How would I know?" Zephyr snapped. "Do you think they're likely to have told me?"

There was a grumpy silence during which Zephyr heard the odd sounds of Isol's existence around her: sighs and gurgles and incomprehensible hums of various frequency and modulation. She began to feel slightly queasy.

"So," the Lonestar began again, artificially breezy, "what made you go into the study of human history?"

"Mostly the feeling that I wasn't a part of it," Zephyr said truthfully, because she was presently feeling too ill to lie. "All the big stuff seemed to be over, and the future made me feel irrelevant. What made you go into politics?"

"The same."

"Can you drop the temperature in here?"

"Of course."

The air became cold almost instantly and then gathered itself up again towards warm, but Zephyr felt much better. "It must be strange, trying to keep in contact with things when you're so far away."

"Physical presence is not necessary for active participation. I communicated. It was slow, but adequate."

"And now it's instant."

"Now," Isol paused significantly, "everything has changed. The Forged at last have something concrete to focus their energies on, a new future."

"What future?" It all sounded very vague to Zephyr.

"A future of self-development, free of the bonds of Form and Function," Isol replied smoothly, as though from a textbook. The Abacand showed her accelerating slightly as she did so. "Free of the self-serving interference of the Unevolved."

"Yes, but why on this other world?"

"Because it has been done there before. Everything awaits there. The gateway to freedom," the Voyager announced.

"An alien technology?"

"It is the embodiment of perfect Self-Development," Isol said, but she sounded less than a hundred percent sure. "It shows us the way forward, out of the shackles of Solar DNA and the limits of the human imagination." Her voice was quieter and she seemed about to say more, but cut herself off.

Zephyr, concentrating mainly on feeling no worse, pursued her. "How can you tell all this?"

But Isol didn't answer, and after a minute or so Zephyr realized she wasn't going to. Whichever way you cut it, hers had been an odd statement. Zephyr hadn't thought of the Forged as motivated by such personal, esoteric goals. She had only imagined them involved in a political struggle that was as much about their adolescent emergence into the biosphere as it was about a real power tussle with the Unevolved on Earth. Like children, they must have their moment to break away from the parents' ideas of what it was they ought to be, even if the parents had never really had those ideas in the first place except in the child's self-centred imagination. But talk about escape from DNA was definitely weird, and any idle thoughts Zephyr had entertained of digging up pretty alien pottery and speculating from fossils fled quickly. She began to doubt that any of her skills were going to be of the slightest use.

A time passed, in which they crept slowly according to the

Abacand's solar map, a mere seventeen kilometres per second. Zephyr closed her eyes and tried to rest, but it felt worse like that and she opened them again and focused on the screen. The Abacand projected their route: they had barely moved.

She read a text on biological taxonomy and one on the naming of Forged, which was founded on a lengthy and obscure set of rules based on Clade structure and the quantity and type of mechanics involved. She primed herself in one of Kalu's zones of expertise—archaeobacteria—and tried to get her head around eukaryotes and theories of how life must evolve from first principles, no matter what piece of the Galactic Habitable Zone it found itself in. Isol's planet was very Earthlike, so she might expect some kind of similarities, but Zephyr kept coming back time and again to the Lonestar's evangelistic tones, with unshakeable disquiet.

"Isol?" she said quietly into the darkness, as she switched off the screen.

"Mmn?" As ever, Isol was awake.

"Have you ever been in love?"

There was a silence. "Not with another person," came the reply, guarded and slow.

"Did they make you immune to it?"

Zephyr's sincerity must have been more evident than it felt. She sensed that Isol was still prickly, but less so, although she was clearly suspicious. Zephyr knew now that Lonestar was a Clade determined by psychological adaptation: a lineage of supreme self-sufficiency that had been groomed to require no external validation or affection, physical or emotional. Normal responses to others had been geared to react to abstractions and various frequencies of electromagnetic radiation instead. But Zephyr was doubtful about such a claim to lack of a feeling of commonality with others when Isol must still fit the parameters of what constituted a human personality. If Isol had crusaded on that front, Zephyr wouldn't have hesitated to support her—it was cruel indeed to try to make people inured to some of the drives that were as deeply ingrained in their physiology as was companionship. But perhaps it was an easier thing to accept about yourself than Zephyr's romantic imagination hoped.

"No. I believe they tried to inoculate me against it, but it would have spoiled my very keen sense of loyalty to Earth," Isol said drily.

"And you broke that conditioning?" Zephyr asked.

"It and I test each other. It has amused me. It's quite possible to work against your own feelings, if you have a stronger impulse towards something less falsely imposed."

"Less false?"

"I was made to serve Earth, but I live to confound it. The loyalty is the Monkeys' will. The resistance is mine. I know you think of me as deficient, because I was made to be different, but I think I was made too well. I can be alone, and I don't need any of you. I wouldn't care about you one way or the other if my life were my own and not just the service of your dreams. Free me and we can be allies. Insist on my fixity to your flag, and we're not."

"You love yourself better."

"Who doesn't?"

Zephyr turned on her side. She thought she detected that Isol was mildly amused now, and knew she hadn't yet found a door in.

"Goodnight."

"I hope you dream better than you imagine," Isol said quietly.

The words disturbed Zephyr more than an outright insult would have. She was still pondering them when she fell asleep, floating as lightly as a breath of air, listening to the rasping lullaby of Isol's many hearts.

Hours later there was a breath of cold on her face, and the Abacand's alarm sounded. Zephyr came to suddenly, wondering if she had been snoring. They had passed into Martian space, apparently.

Isol spoke. "I am preparing to make the transfer to Zian orbit. I thought you'd rather be awake, not that that'll make much difference."

"Why?"

"Travel is instantaneous. I suppose you ought to at least try to make notes on it for the boys back at base, though."

Zephyr scowled and tried to sit up, the couch moving sluggishly after her once she'd bounced back off the straps. She was about to ask how it worked when she remembered that even Isol probably didn't know, and wouldn't have told her. Suddenly she wanted some kind of safety check, but what would that be?

"Second thoughts?" Isol asked sweetly.

Zephyr said nothing. She was thinking now that maybe Isol had put her to sleep with some kind of gas in the air or by limiting the oxygen—it hadn't really hit home until now how much she was at the Voyager's mercy. The Abacand had switched itself into a recording mode.

"Doesn't any of this bother you?"

"Any of what?"

"Instant travel, strange equipment, not understanding the first thing about it," Zephyr said, her academic mind finally snapping free of the bonds of politeness and fear that had been holding it in check. She was sounding sharply sarcastic but found she couldn't stop. "I mean, didn't this technology belong to somebody and maybe it won't do you any good, and doesn't it strike you as odd that it was just lying around and that it let you find this particular place of all the places in the universe? Aren't you being had for some kind of sucker?"

"I believe it was left there to be found," Isol said with tolerant iciness. "I found it because I was intended to find it, and intended to locate Zia Di Notte and its worlds. The odds against running into it accidentally are incredibly high. It's the legacy of a race of self-adapters, like us, who have gone on before."

"What makes you think so? Couldn't it just be that you want to think that, but there could be a whole series of other possible explanations? Didn't anyone ever tell you to try before you buy?"

"Professor, if you want to leave, there is still time. The Hand will return you to Earth. But I am about to go on. What will it be?"

Zephyr was aware that she had begun to rant. Her heart felt like it was pounding not only in her chest but in her face, ears, hands and feet. She was a vast ballooning bubble of fear and the inside of her wanted out. But she said nothing. Seconds passed.

"You're too late," Isol said. "We've arrived."

Machen received Gritter's garbled delivery of information calmly. He had just observed the Lonestar vanish from the traffic-control system, and simultaneously had lost contact with the sophisticated beacons installed in Zephyr Duquesne's Abacand. Confirmations of their departure from local space were winging in from all over, festooning his monitors with colourful notes like a Labor Day parade.

Gritter sat on his perch and waited for Machen to open the stolen letter. The general didn't feel much interest in the contents and he stared down at the blood-spattered thing for several seconds.

"Where is the envelope?"

"Lost, ennit?"

"Who was it for?"

"I dunno. Never saw it. Got this from me mate."

Machen turned the page open with his finger. It was coded. "What use is this without the keys?"

"You're bound to 'ave 'em, entcha?"

Machen slid the paper across his desk and put it facedown where the military AI could read it, and where a copy would wing its way to Anthony, who would be far quicker at discovering its authenticity than would any attempt at reasoning with Gritter.

"And Corvax is coming to Idlewild?"

"Straight up."

"Why now?"

"Didn't say, but he was real apologetic for all the trouble in the past."

Machen nodded thoughtfully. "Get lost before I have you shot for interfering with the postal service," he suggested, not glancing left or right.

"What about my money?"

"You'll be paid when you bring me anything I couldn't find out some other way," Machen said, tired of repeating himself. "The Avian guard will be along in a moment. I suggest you move on."

The Degraded eagle made a disparaging noise but glanced skywards and was gone in a flurry of blue and gold. Machen shut the window. The systems AI chimed in and announced, "This message was intended for the secret service, Agent 2177, stationed here in London. It's from a contact within the Forged Independence Movement. Translation follows."

Machen listened and before it was done he called Anthony.

"There's more of them," he said, ignoring the views of Anthony's hologram rotating above his desk and looking underneath instead, massaging his collie dog Bob with his foot as he did in times of stress when anger threatened to make his collar pop. Bob snapped at his laces and they played a brief game of Chase the Squeaky Bone back and forth.

"Besides the Ticktock Hive, both the Gaiaforms have vanished," Anthony said.

"We've got to find out who's in on this and where all that technology has gone. I've a feeling that when Corvax arrives he's going to know something. Get a squad out to the Belt and arrest him, so we can bring him in faster."

"My thoughts exactly." The Strategos cut the link.

Bob won the toy and spent a moment chewing it vigorously. Machen said a prayer to someone—he wasn't sure to whom.

16. THE FALSE MOON

Secta Ticktock Trini stood in the corridor they had labelled C389, five point two kilometres from its origin at the hub of the primary artificial Moon above the new world. Behind her the open hatch of door C389-54 closed silently and settled back into its fifteen-thousand-year sleep with barely a sound. Trini remained poised at attention, the tips of her four legs balanced on the dustless floor, her many antennae waving lightly around her head, lent extra strength by the Moon's frail gravity. She wasn't sure if she had heard something.

Before her the length of the corridor stretched into a pin-prick, its sides and floor scarred by thousands of track movements and fine scratches still bearing traces of various metals and synthetic molecules left behind. She had left her own Ti-bone and chitin behind her there in several places. Its ceiling, far above her head, glowed faintly with the jerry-lights that the Hive had managed to rig. Trini was close to the limit of their generator's influence and, although she was well equipped to see across the entire light spectrum, she felt an unreasoning animal trepidation at the thought of moving out of its range and into the uncharted darkness.

Tuning herself acutely, she listened to what her sisters heard wherever they explored along other radii of this colossal structure. Beyond the sound of their claws, the fuzzy blur of their radio, and the rapid pulses of their sonar—nothing.

Trini resumed her walk, tension relieved by the concentration of working. She logged all doorways and hatches, routinely peering through, where she could, into rooms full of peculiar objects. Each of these she scanned and recorded for later analysis by the Hive.

Some rooms were vast, kilometres in diameter, others seemed

ordinary, just larger than she would have expected for an Unevolved room on Earth. Some were empty, others crammed as if they were only cupboards where any untidy things got shoved away out of sight. As the others did, Trini believed this place was analogous to Tupac herself, or to Mougiddo, the Jupiter Pangenesis. It was where these people had made themselves but, unlike the Blessed Tupac and Mougiddo, it did not live.

Trini didn't spend much of her time thinking about the political ramifications of the actions of their group. She felt, without needing to analyse it, that the Hive was being both treacherous to old Earth and to the people who had trusted it to remain patriotic, but at the same time it was true to itself. A hive's function was to examine, build and maintain complex machines. Because this moon was an alien device it was even more interesting than anything the hive had come across before. It drew them with its peculiarity and its defiance of their intelligence. She had never been more content with her work: examining the details of all she saw, relaying her information to the others, and listening to the upper levels of their consciousness decode the potentials of what they could understand. This was far more exciting than merely drilling down through some old AI to extract its remaining valuable data and materials. But recently, within the last few days they had spent here, she detected a change in their mind.

It was hard to put it into any formal mode. Trini had no exact cause she could point to as the root of her unease, but she knew that she and her sisters were all experiencing rising anxiety. Their antennae were more alert. They paused more often. They waited for one another's regular chirps of encouragement and reassurance. They shared information and looked quickly into it, forming little subgroups of Hive gestalt, to see if there was a clue there that might explain it.

No, she *did* hear something. It came from the end of the corridor, beyond the lights.

As a Ticktock, she had only the rudimentary equipment for comprehending audio waves. Her hearing was a stage or two better than Unevolved hearing—in Secta terms she was almost deaf—but she was certain of the sound; it was as if the corridor was a long throat and the Moon had sighed, very softly.

Instantly her eyes and leg hairs struggled to identify corresponding motion in the air around her, but there was none. Beyond her hearing—in a place that she knew did not exist except as an illusion of her own mind, a space where she imagined she would have had a heart—she heard a voice counting silently,

Eka, Dwi, Trini, Ch'twari, Pancha . . . The names of the Hive.

Instantly she was relaying this to them, and they relayed it to her in return, their signals cancelling one another out.

In surprise she cut communication and stood alone in the dim, grey light.

She heard nothing now. She felt it instead—the count:

. . . *Sapta, Ashta, Nava* . . .

It went through all five hundred names of the Macros and the Micros before it was still.

When it stopped, Trini ran a diagnostic on herself. There was nothing out of the ordinary about her. She was as she had been made, except for some dust from the Moon's interior that had settled here and there on her exoskeleton of metal and chitin. She wondered if she had breathed in dust, but her spiracles were clear. There seemed to be nothing there, the same nothing she looked in on everywhere, the great echoing absence of a life long gone.

"Trini?"

Eka, the nominal leader of their group, was speaking. "Return."

More grateful than she could have acknowledged, Trini turned and ran back through the silently moving doors, each opening and closing in perfect time with her speed and direction, running on monitors that had been ancient when she was still long undreamed of.

She found her sister workers clustered beneath the gateway on the Moon's surface, queuing to enter the long tube of the

Comb. Their craft and home was moored securely above, its single corridor lined with the recuperation bays where they could rest and feed after a long shift's work. For once there was no anticipatory chitter of the second shift ready to start. The Comb was quiet except for its own internal noises of sluice and valve, and the hum of deep conversation where all the workers who were already in their cells talked and thought.

Trini was third last to leave the Moon—as she had been third to enter it. She tried to show no undue haste in following Ch'twari, keeping to the regulation quarter-metre of distance, as Dwi did behind her, but she was relieved beyond measure to enter the Comb and find her distant cell. There she snuggled into the tiny space, folding her legs and arms neatly up against her body, fitting her antennae into the link spaces, and settling her head and torso against the soft bend of the wall where their exact mould awaited. The door closed her in and the jelly flowed to surround her, soothing her frets away with its sweet, gentle touch and its healing mix of nanocytes and nutrients. The dust was cleansed away and the doors closed.

She floated, safe, and tuned in to the variant discussions of the Hive mind, the Queen state, rising gently into the place where her sisters discussed the no-voices and the haunted machine beneath them, and then beyond that into the all-consuming single awareness that was Ticktock Hive Cherisse, five hundred consciousnesses functioning as one. Here there was only the absolute concentration upon the objects found. There was no room for uncertainty and fear, or the fragmented and imperfect awareness of Trini. There was gladness, contentment, interest, composure.

They worked long hours, drifting above the silent world—not even aware of Isol's return when she appeared on the sunward side and detached her new and powerful Hand.

No visuals or information supplied by the Abacand made it feel real to Zephyr. How could they be in another solar system, just like that? Yes, she could see it on the screen's portrayal of information from Isol's own eyes. Yes, it was certainly not Sol (too orange), not Earth (too much brown, wrong continental shapes), not Luna (shiny and coloured, and besides, two of them) and there were no signs of any constellations that she recognized. But she was so used to all kinds of unrealities and simulations that this made as much impact as a student project, and she felt nothing. Why should she, here in her tiny womb? For the time being, however, she must accept it as if it were the truth.

She glanced at the Abacand and willed it to tell her what had happened—if anything had—but it wasn't revealing anything in front of Isol.

"How do you do it?" she asked the walls, where now a sheen of dampness from her breath had left them moistened.

"I intend to be there, and so I am," Isol replied. "The engine functions upon a definitely willed choice to travel."

"What else does it do?" Zephyr asked, thinking of definitely willed choices to go home, have a cup of tea and watch junk-opera—or of choices to be rich, have vast estates and rule the world: Genghis Khan, Ozymandias, they'd had a will.

"Nothing," Isol said quickly.

"What does it feel like?"

"Look, I don't see that I have to discuss any of this with you. It's the planet you're here to look over, not my mind. Or has that objective changed?"

"No, no," Zephyr said hastily, peering at the screen's first offerings of this new world. "Can you show me a closer image?"

"Here are all the geologic, spectrographic and ground-map

data." Isol put them on as a series of overlays on a series of identical Zian planets, slowly zooming closer until features could be observed.

Zephyr saw continents with almost familiar edges, set in blue oceans of salty water, their mineral contents close to those of Earth. The land rose in hills and mountains, a stilled portrait of the planet's violent dynamics. Islands dotted the vast waters in lines that followed deep crust faults above a heavy iron core, and a seething mantle, thicker than Earth's and less active, betrayed a longer cooling, an older beginning. Across the blue and brown white clouds built, tore and swirled, delivering rain, snow and ice storms depending on their relationship to the polar regions, which were both capped white. One image zoomed closer still, and Zephyr froze in her chair at the sight of a distinct pattern beside the coast where steep cliffs sheared away into the sea.

A hexagonal grid spread from the shore in regular progress, to cover the hills that rose on three sides of a natural bay. It was marked out in clear-cut areas of flat stone, and within the hexagons of this—enormous, she saw, glancing at the scale bar—comb there arose structures of varying height and complexity that were not unlike copies of basalt column, but which were sufficiently altered to reveal great deliberation and design. It seemed that Isol was right. There were structures here that must have been made by minds. They looked nothing like Earthly artefacts.

Closer still. Zephyr could hear her blood in her ears.

"What's that?" She jabbed her finger at a shape on the narrow beach where black stones and grey sand mingled along the waterline. The resolution of Isol's vision finally began to fail as the picture filled the screen and fought to show itself. There were spars curved in a cage, tatters of something blowing from them, a line of separated rings, the gleam of metal.

"That's dead," Isol said, and Zephyr suddenly saw bones with the remains of tough hide on them, mostly buried and almost destroyed by the relentless pawing of the sea.

"I thought you said there was no life here."

"There isn't."

"How old is that?" Zephyr turned to the Abacand.

"It's hard to say without a materials analysis." Its calm voice seemed out of place in this moment. "But not more than twenty years, unless it has been recently uncovered. If that were the case, it might be thousands or more. We would have to see."

"You may see," Isol allowed. "It is morning there, in Tanelorn. Will you go there now?"

"Tanelorn?" Zephyr said, furrowing her brow—she couldn't place the name.

"From a book I read," Isol said, not offering the title, author or date. "It seemed appropriate."

Zephyr made a mental note to ask the Abacand about it later. She then made an effort to organize herself and prepare, although her mind was empty of anything except amazement and a cynicism that didn't want to die. They might go—or maybe they *had* gone—nowhere and this was an illusion; she couldn't tell. Perhaps it was a joke or a test, but she mustn't think that way yet. Wait and see.

Her worries were interrupted by a soft but unmistakable shudder rolling through the walls of the Hand.

"What's that?" *I am hysterical,* Zephyr realized, hearing herself squeak.

Isol didn't reply immediately. The shudder continued throughout the rest of her body, if the sound and vibration were anything to go by. To Zephyr it felt like a small 'quake or the passage of a wavefront, although she was not experiencing anything directly. For a few seconds she noticed the air become utterly still, then it began to spurt erratically out of the gilled vents before it stabilized.

"Are you all right?" Zephyr asked in the quiet that followed.

"Yes. Thanks." The voice lacked its usual fiery conviction. "Just a teething problem with the Hand. I'm not used to it."

Zephyr decided to take that at face value.

"Please get ready for atmospheric entry," Isol said. "There will be some turbulence."

Until she thought of something more constructive, Zephyr

obeyed, and busied her mind with plans of what to do first when she got out: like, should she make a historic speech? A gesture seemed in order, but the circumstances were so odd she couldn't think what.

With a series of mechanical process noises, the Hand detached itself from Isol's small body and moved out of the shadow of her solar sails, crackling as the heat and light of Zia Di Notte struck it full-face. It drifted gently and Zephyr saw Isol bathed in the softening colour of the sun's radiance: an insectoid machine, antennae alert, while other appendages coiled around her in a hesitant way, the vast flower of her sails a shining apricot fan that dwarfed the concave bed the Hand had occupied, and whose shadow hid the engine housing of the strange machine entirely from view. Against the backdrop of space Isol was astonishingly tiny and, as the Hand accelerated towards an approach vector, she shrank as swiftly as Alice on a nibble of cake, or a professor's ego on finding herself alone and uncertain in a world forty-five light-years from home.

"Ha!" the Hand said, or Isol did—Zephyr wasn't sure.

They had begun to feel the first rough brush of the atmosphere. The jouncing and shaking became strong, then madly violent. The Abacand hung on to the sled pack through the strength of its magnetic grip, but Zephyr's flight bag worked itself free. It banged against the walls a couple of times, slowly, in the midst of the tumult, and then began to drift floorwards at the same time as Zephyr felt herself dragged back to the seat. Heavier and heavier she became, until her own body seemed to be crushing her. Sweat ran down her face, and the dark pink walls coursed with water as the cooling systems fought their way through the heat coming from the outer shell.

Abruptly this stopped and order was restored. The last traces of Zephyr's sickness disappeared; although her stomach was zinging with the speed of their fall, this was normal at least. She released her fevered grip on the arm rests and took a few deep breaths. The screen had slid out of position and now showed its panoramas to the floor. She lay back and waited for it all to be over.

As she closed her eyes, she heard Isol laughing with exhilaration—of course, she'd never been down on a planet before, had never had the means. Zephyr wanted to clap, but her arms were weighted with nervousness and their own strange mass. The moment passed.

"Touchdown," Isol reported, unable to conceal her ecstatic excitement. "You may leave anytime."

Zephyr would have preferred Isol not to sound so keen on that, but she went through the plan as discussed with the Strategos: unhitch sled, place rollers, pack self with loose items, place heavier things on sled and secure, drink water and eat ration of lunch carefully made into tasty bar of vaguely crunchy and inoffensive texture. As she worked on this, she heard Isol's continual reporting of her decontamination procedure and evaluation—all the lengthy prep that had to be gone through before they might risk opening the door.

It was amazing how much information the skin of Isol's Hand was able to detect. It read the atmosphere off in its fractions, the water content, the weather. It analysed the local mineral structures and their crystalline formation and their radioactivity. It took constant readings from the wind and the ground, searching for microbial life, organic compounds, RNA- and DNA-bearing structures . . . on and on with more searches than Zephyr had thought were necessary by a factor of ten. And then it reviewed her own health and situation.

"You," Isol said, "will be bringing much to this planet. Aside from your own genetic and organic microbial matter, in the form of shed skin and faecal material, there are all the polymer and long-chain molecules not naturally occurring here that are present in your clothing and your hygiene products. There is also the sled, and many other metallic alloys that will erode into the ecosphere, not to mention the plastics and their derivatives, plus anything you spill or lose that may contain advanced engineering products that have a small but potential capacity to interact with this environment and cause change."

"Your point?" Zephyr sighed—they had been through the Red Mars arguments during her briefing, and she wouldn't be here at all, if any of that had really mattered in the circumstances. The only thing that concerned her was that the place wasn't about to kill her, either now by some quick-acting method such as radiation or asphyxia, or later by a lengthy process of poisoning or disease. "You're already here doing all those things yourself, in your way. I'm not going to tip garbage all over it. Just tell me if I can breathe and whether I'm about to die."

This wasn't the way she'd imagined preparing to be the first Unevolved to set foot on an extrasolar world. Still, there was no broadcasting crew to pick up and send her picture all over the system, so what did it really matter?

In answer to her question, the opening in Isol's side that functioned as a door irised open and drew its skins aside. Brilliant light cut inwards in a straight beam, revealing every vein and capillary in the Hand's internal surface: blue with blood-type material, and black where the nanocyte compounds ran in their own distribution.

"The ozone here is depleted," Isol informed her, "so the sun is effectively three times the strength of Sol in terms of UVA and B radiation, although it may feel less intense under cloud cover."

"Thank you," Zephyr murmured automatically. She reached forward and gripped the flesh of the door frame without asking for permission, leant towards the opening and took her first breath of the crisp ocean breeze. It seemed as fresh as any air she'd tasted.

Alien world! Alien world! she kept thinking, so intensely that it blew every other thought out of her head, keeping her astonishment turned up past the top of the dial. Through the door's oval gap she saw that they stood upon a flat platform of some kind of dark stony substance, high above the city itself—on top of the hills she had seen earlier. Below her was spread a vast array of complex geometries in materials that swirled darkly with caramel, orange, terra-cotta, red and grey like an overly complex ice-cream flavour. Towers and deeply cut recesses sketched a powerful series of flowing shadows that led her eyes down and down to the grey and black shingles of the beach, where the sea came to meet the land in an almost perfect semicircle. She could make out no other detail.

Above Zephyr the sky was a more turquoise blue than at home but was decorated with exactly the same white cirrus, blown into cotton wool by high winds that expressed themselves as breezes down where she and Isol were. The same winds turned a few handfuls of sand around and around into whirligigs on the stone floor.

Despite the soft colour of the light, it felt ferociously bright and overwhelmed Zephyr's mid-grade retinas in seconds. She had to look away and blink tears out of her eyes, fumbling for her glasses as she wondered what the natives had called this place, and when, and why. Before her stretched a land of forgotten technology, buried gods and lost civilization. It was a treasure house, and she had almost no time at all to discover its possible wealth. She couldn't delay in order to wrestle with the sled; she simply set the glasses on her nose, checked the fasteners on her shoes and stepped out.

She took a few steps and gazed again at the city spreading itself over high cliffs that embraced a bay of surpassing prettiness that wouldn't have been out of place on Italy's Adriatic coast. The sea water, only two-thirds the salinity of Earth's oceans, was as blue and coppery as a sapphire, and it swept in foam-headed waves against beaches of ruined stone where a fine harbour had succumbed to its persuasion. But it was what lay between the sea and their landing site that took away what was left of Zephyr's desire to breathe.

Hands clasped under her chin, she stared at enormous roads, paved more than ten metres wide. On their flanks great ropes and struts of stone emerged from the land, like roots, rising swiftly into the infinite branches and curls of petrified vines and leaves, their complex dance frozen in a substance that, on closer inspection, resembled animal skin brightly coloured in flows of sandy ochre, emerald and mineral blue—not black as she'd first thought. No structure had a single straight edge or right angle.

Roofs (?) bent into walls and windows (or were they doorways, or air vents?) and walls flowed seamlessly into floors and pavements. Everywhere she saw what looked like living things, frozen as though they had been captured on a still photograph or caught in a spell that blended them like clay. She saw much that she couldn't make out at all, but she recognized that Tanelorn was more colourful than any of Earth's meagre cities, more full of the sense of abundant, proliferating fecundity than its jungles. Tanelorn teemed with the appearance of life.

But it had none.

Zephyr's initial moment of rapture died slowly. The sea pawed silently at the wreck of the harbour. The wind carried its scent, pure ionic, straight to her without catching a trace from anything between. Gasping because she had to, she tasted the emptiness on her tongue. Its cold mineral flavour told her that the movement that seemed about to erupt everywhere was purely the effect of the buildings leading her eyes a dance. The openings and holes, shady, enormous, as big as houses, led to nowhere. Not even a bird moved among the high spires and deep wells where rock and sand spiralled around one another in shapes carved by the elements. Tanelorn's barrenness was absolute.

After that first breath, Zephyr wanted to return to the Hand. She felt that she was treading on a tomb.

"Not so sure of yourself now, Professor?" Isol asked, and if she was smug then Zephyr thought she'd a right to be.

"First impressions are vital," Zephyr replied, relaxing her hands from their astonished pose and picking up her pack. She wondered if she would be able to keep up her brave front if there was anything to find out there. Tanelorn had appeared considerable from the air, but she'd misunderstood its size. Now that they were inside it the streets and squares were almost twice as big as she'd thought. The people—beings—that had once lived here must have been larger than she was, in fact larger than any of the Unevolved humans.

With a silent prayer to any spirits that might be watching she trod a few more steps over the curious suedelike surface of the balcony they had landed on. She couldn't stop marvelling at how this place was so like what she knew—and how unlike. These people, they were already real to her, even though she didn't know their faces or their names.

She walked out to get a better look at their landing site, and turned to see a stunning view of the doors and arches behind her, leading back and back into an infinite regress of different forms spreading over the flattened land. She forgot, in that split second, about anything other than her natural curiosity. It awed her that there were such recognizable things as doorways, although these were parabolic for the most part, or some clever quadratic variation on the same conic theme, their complex curves both fascinating and odd to her eyes. So, were these calculated to please or to distort the perception of their users?

Zephyr extracted the Abacand from her pocket and began recording, glancing down for a long time just at the stuff her feet were on, noting the feel of the sand in its finely worn depressions, the resemblance it had to earth, rock and leather. A rock was a rock, of course; but even so, a rock on the other side of the galaxy was an amazing object in itself, whether or not it seemed the same as a rock in England. And then she was stupefied by the air, the fact that she could breathe it, its smells, its messages, the feel it had as it came whirling up in gusts that boomed musically off the wall of this incredibly high structure, barrelling over her ledge to whip around her, wrapping her in a constantly flowing cloak of air. Was this designed? Of course it was. Look at the angles of the walls, of the supports . . .

She spent an hour standing thus, before she even noticed that time had passed or that the Hand had neither moved nor spoken, apparently awaiting her verdict.

"How much have you seen of the place?" she asked Isol, turning to the Hand's rough, blackened structure to speak, hearing her own voice sound very small as it was captured by the Hand's interior and whipped aside in that moving veil of air.

"I have mapped the city," Isol said. "I have identified its gardens, districts and—"

"Is anything left inside?" Zephyr asked, hardly daring to think about books or records, intact artefacts of any kind. She wasn't prepared to accept Isol's conjectures without making her own inspection.

"Everything," the Voyager replied, her tone tart with irritation. "As stated, the civilization is complete, as it was left more than fifteen thousand of this planet's years ago."

"Marie Celeste," Zephyr murmured to herself, reaching out to touch the smooth curve where air and small flecks of sand had worn a deep vertical bowl in the wall beside her, its shape determined by the angles of the balcony rail a few inches away from its face.

She wondered again why all the life had gone. Everything except the inanimate was missing, the Abacand confirmed. Even in the blue ocean, nothing lived; and the amino acids tossed in its waves and rocky pools were barely beginning to redevelop. It was as though they were stalled.

When you leave home, do you pack every last microbe but not take your books and pots, your machines? Do you leave your Moons behind? They must have cost a lot to build, Zephyr thought. They must have been used for something. She would have to go there soon.

For an instant, scenarios of time-travelling humans, of the Forged setting up a hoax, of dreaming in some drug-induced stupor inside a peculiar and cruel experiment, floated through Zephyr's mind and she wondered if she was really there. In that instant she saw that it wasn't a balcony at all that they'd landed on, but really a waiting point, a viewing station, the most ideal location there was for seeing the sea from this distance, appreciating its majestic foam, and feeling—because of the shapes of the structures around her—the curl of the wind as though it was fresh from the shore. Suddenly Zephyr was sure this wasn't a building at all. It was a work of art that put you in the heart of this wild world and at the heart of the city.

All her desires to leave and go home vanished. She reached out to touch the wall's burnished places where it was smooth, its porous places where it had left sharp-edged holes like old bone. Beneath her fingertips she felt the soft line of a fossil's tiny leaf, the curl of a shell, the changing seams of rock where one kind and another had been laid open and set together with no discernible join. Who had made this? She had to know.

18. STUFF

Leaving the Hand behind to watch Professor Duquesne and persuade her of the usefulness of having a Roach around—a small insectile roving machine that could keep tabs on her in case of emergency but would also give Isol an idea of what that Abacand was up to—Isol took her main self back out of orbit and swung by the primary Moon, where she could just make out the shapeless mass of the Ticktock Comb attached on its darkened side.

All the time she was aware that a part of her mind was slightly out of joint. Sectioned off in the Hand's cortex, it relayed itself to her in a curious dreamlike mode that reminded her of viewing a distant Uluru, although Virtua experiences were never distant as this was. She talked with Zephyr, and enjoyed her own analysis of the planet's surface, while at the same time she flew weightlessly around the Moon's curve.

The dissociation was unsettling but not incomprehensibly difficult—at last she knew what the Gaiaforms were wittering on about when they complained of too many Hands and Feet in the mix. But there was a deeper current of conflict that had begun to nag at her, an abscess of suspicion coming to ripeness. Isol felt different in another way, and its strangeness had deepened with this third journey through the nonexistent instant of the engine's unknown power.

Of course she was afraid, although she'd never admit it. What sane person could blithely take on such forces and think they had no consequence? She'd been so tempted to tell the professor about it, so very tempted that she'd nearly blurted out the whole story of her peculiar dreams, the engine's seductive mutterings, a feeling at the edges of her consciousness that was like expansion, but without any comprehension in that awakening.

And Tupac had said nothing, although she must have been able to see the engine's outgrowth and ingrowth as it absorbed Isol and became more like her, as it colonized her cells and atoms with its own invisible signature. Why? Why had she formed the Hand and said nothing? Was Tupac like her too? Was that contact enough to spread the touch of this Stuff? Perhaps Tupac had secrets of her own.

Isol closed that part of her mind, like closing a fist gauntleted in iron. The planet was going to be theirs, and that was the most important thing to concentrate on. If there would be trouble, than let it run its course on her and Tatresi—but the planet would be theirs.

Isol drifted into contact range and transmitted to Cherisse. "Any insights?"

The Hive registered her broadcast but there was a delay before replying.

After a half-second Cherisse said, "We detect no functional power source. In fact, no existing source at all. The Moon is purely a machine without organic components, but of what kind we cannot say. We have identified regions of access that seem congruent with the method of construction radiating from a central point outwards. There is no sign of occupation or any kind of activity. There is an outer wall that functions to shield the inside from solar radiation and a variety of local frequencies. Its structure is under analysis. Portions of the whole contain definitely engineered macro-computational elements, yet there is an idea that the whole may be implicated at a quantum level, regardless of atomic composition. The Moon's core is an empty chamber: a sphere of radius π light-standardized kilometres. Its purpose is unknown."

"How much more time do you need before you can begin on the second Moon?"

"Until the fundamental pattern employed has been deciphered, there is no point in further examination of samples."

Isol thought of asking if there were any unusual incidents, if the Hive had heard . . . but she decided against it. So what if there were? The job must be done and Cherisse was loyal. No need to upset her either, if she was undisturbed at present.

"I'm returning to the Solar System briefly to rendezvous with Tatresi," she said. "I will be back shortly. Have you messages for home?"

"No messages." Hives were terse and even less social than Voyagers.

Isol flew out and viewed the secondary, smaller satellite. Unlike its partner this one had axial rotation that presented a constantly changing face to the planet beneath. The surface was smooth, and resistant to her attempt to see within. She focused her mind on Sol and insisted she be there. She thought—although she might have imagined it—that there was a brief blurt of communication between the engine and the smaller Moon, but before she could track it she was in the wrong system.

From just beyond the orbit of Saturn, she navigated towards the shelter of Iapetus and to their prearranged meeting point in a region held by Independence loyalists, where all Gaiasol-used frequencies were blocked. Tatresi was already waiting for her in deep shadow, his teardrop bulk stationary, as though sleeping.

"Is the rally arranged?" she asked, cruising in to a discreet distance.

"Yes, yes," he muttered, "but what of that? Is the examiner on-world? Does she have any idea what she's getting into?"

Tatresi's bitterness was hurtful and Isol snapped at him, "You knew the position. I told you what it was like. Here, I've made four transits, and I'm fine. You fuss about nothing instead of using your new power to consolidate our position."

"There's something there. It's not alive, but it speaks. I feel it watching me. It knows my thoughts."

"Side effects," Isol stated. "Perhaps it is a by-product of something that is expected to function with a different kind of mind."

"Yes." But Tatresi wasn't persuaded—his emotional track was lugubrious, self-pitying. "Anyway, the Earth rally will go ahead. We will present the plans and ask for voting. Meetings will take place on all the worlds and at the stations. Polling will continue until eighty percent have voted. Everything is in order. Machen won't be able to do anything about it, but we are not ready yet for secession. If the Gaiasol attempts to enforce its jurisdiction, we have no means of reaching the new world in any viable numbers. It will be war."

"Introspection doesn't suit you," Isol said. "There will be no war. We have this technology and they will want it."

"You intend to trade it?" He was incredulous.

"No, but it has its other uses. When we understand how it works, then we'll be able to determine any course we want. I spoke to the Hive. It's making progress."

Tatresi asked for a switch to full comms-mode, and she acquiesced although she'd never liked the intimacy of a maximal-sympathy contact. Within a few seconds he'd transmitted the full complex memesis of his doubts, political as well as practical and personal, and she responded with her conviction and the force of her will—the minutiae of all the arguments she'd thought of over her long years as to why they should be free of the clinging limits of Earth.

"But there's another reason there," he said, surprised. "Don't you see it? You want to go there because the Stuff is from there and it wants to be there."

"You're imagining it." She **broke** off and reverted to conversational mode.

"I don't think so," he said. "I think that as soon as we made the first transit we became something more than just a ship and its engine."

"Save your mystic shit for someone else, then," Isol said. "Just keep to the plan. Once Gaiasol resolves its issues with our free departure, you can do what you like."

"What choice have I got?" Tatresi said grimly, and activated his ordinary nuke fusion drive, backing out of position and swinging his head around to face the sun. Isol watched him leaving at the stately pace Earth technology decreed. She was thinking over what she'd seen during deep contact with him. He'd always been such a self-assured presence in the organization, so how could he be so quickly disturbed? It occurred to her that she might be better off without him, that he'd been a mistake. Tatresi liked to lord it over the Unevolved through his prowess and his position in the government. Maybe now that that was under threat he wasn't ready to change it for an ordinary station in a new universe. Too late to change it, however.

Isol turned back towards Zian space. Everyone was so pathetically weak. Now she'd have to go and check on Kincaid's paranoia, and the VanaShiva's lack of application. From their talk you'd think they'd have leaped to take this chance, but they were all slacking. A faint threat of losing all control ghosted its way across her mind, and she had to work hard to fight the terror that it threatened to unleash. She wasn't going to back down now. Flicking her sails open to the solar wind, she drifted free of Iapetus, ignoring signals from its surface where Forged tried to send her messages of support, and backed out until they could barely see her. She returned to Zian space.

Tatresi moved away from Saturn, monitoring the Independence discussion groups there until he'd captured their mood. They were excitedly making all kinds of plans for the system they'd never seen, speculating about its single gas giant, possibilities for profits and developments, how to set up an economy, whether they would change themselves to suit the new world, and worrying about how much influence the Jovians were going to get. *Nothing changes,* he thought, cutting his connection to that network and tuning in to a band of Virtua from the pirate systems that Corvax had been instrumental in constructing.

He had lovers there to visit, romances and adventures to follow, and for once their distraction would be blissful retreat instead of the functional addition to his political career they'd always been in the past. Who you did, what you said there—all mattered outside, even though the rules stated that nobody mixed reality and Uluru. He'd oiled the right backs, licked the right shoes, dominated the unexpectedly meek who enjoyed a release from exercising the highest powers in government. Now he avoided their alter egos and the avatars he thought he could identify, and sought out someone he didn't know for a few hours of recreation.

Anybody who was nobody would do and he located a Heavy Angel with no discernible political ambitions very quickly, who agreed to meet in an ancient Atlantean bath-house; they became two Tritons, two mermaids, two octopi . . . then disassembled into shoals of fish and other forms, part human and part machine, able to tickle every nerve and channel, every synapse and dream across the quantum-coded stream. The Angel became an angelfish and Tatresi a shark who ate him. Tatresi became the bathwater and the Angel, mostly human, swam and urinated in him. It was a refreshingly anonymous venture, and they parted without the pretence of making any future plans to meet again.

Tatresi picked up his scheduled cargo from Labrys Station a day later and continued sunwards, slowly altering course to pick up Ceres and then home in on a visit to Corvax. He hoped the Roc would be able to tell him what chance he had of getting this engine Stuff removed once this situation was over and done with. The cargo he was currently shipping needn't be late, no matter if he detoured from now until its scheduled arrival time, *if* he were prepared to use the new engine. But he needn't risk that, if Corvax would only listen and not mess around. There was time to take advice and time to get there under ordinary power, as long as he wasn't held up for too long.

Tatresi paid an early bribe to the logger at Martian Traffic Control, to place his registry time later in the books than it really would be and, thus supplied with an alibi, he made his diversion ahead of schedule. Navigating the Belt was a wretched experience, requiring all his concentration, and even then he was bumped and scratched by random debris that hadn't yet attracted any commercial interest. Corvax's rock lay in the middle of this trash heap, and the bastard didn't even have the courtesy to put on landing lights or systems when Tatresi signalled him.

Tatresi suspected nothing amiss until he touched down on the tiny landing pad and saw the scorch marks and damage caused by some other ship's hasty exit. There was no response from the AI units and when he looked at the small windows where Corvax liked to stare out at the rocks and stars, he saw that they were dark. There was no power here. Tatresi had to connect to one of the energy ports and reverse its protocols in order to activate enough of the network to use his avatar and investigate the interior. The computers were now barely functional—all of Corvax's personal databases and systems had been burnt out.

With what small sensory information the remaining machines could lend him, Tatresi manifested within the main lab where he had last seen the Roc. Bringing up minimal light, he stood aghast at a scene of devastation. The sensitive and irreplaceable equipment that Corvax had spent his meagre life and money on was all destroyed—very deliberately, it seemed. Small fires had burnt out the biological components and amid the wrecks he numbly recognized fragments of flesh and Tek and blood—carnage. No piece he saw was larger than an apple. It took him ten minutes to scan and reassemble the majority of them into identities he could recognize.

To his relief Corvax was not there, although some of his feathers were. The dead crew were Xing and her buccaneers, people of whom he'd long been afraid. What caught the attention of Tatresi's processor was the way in which they'd died. Every fillet was cleanly cut with a molecular precision. They had been butchered—very fast, very cleanly and while still alive.

In all his 'bases Tatresi knew of no such weapon designed for this. He withdrew and left the place hidden in its welcome darkness, blasting away without taking another second to search for survivors or further clues. He could not report the incident because he'd not been there, had he? Somebody would come across this sooner or later . . . but the pressing question was: where was Corvax? Without him, how would Tatresi ever be free of Stuff? Was this the result of a raid by those who wanted Stuff for themselves? Or had Corvax found the method to make it work in any way he wanted?

The buzzing in Tatresi's mind caused him to crash rather heavily against a solid nickel lump, and before he knew what was happening he was occupied with saving himself from the catastrophic meltdown of his one remaining standby nuke engine as its ruptured control sluices vented into open space. From one second of confusion he had effectively become flotsam. Except for the Stuff engine, he was dead in the water. He'd have to use it now or stay here until the police came and rescued him—with all that impossible explaining to do. Through the pain of his ruptured hull he had to laugh; the tickle of such irony and the aftermath of the horrors created an unstoppable ripple throughout his nerves.

Tatresi was nothing if not a pragmatist. He summoned the engine and made his exit, pointing it to a safe wait area near Martian space where he could lick his wounds and endure until the moment came to carry on towards his destination at Venus Principia. Before he went he made a conscious decision to ignore any odd effects of the transit that his Stuff engine might cause, grimly resigned to their inevitable occurrence and erosion of his resolve. But when he arrived he found himself oddly elated with the ease and speed, and the questionless reaction to his will. Floating, he dozed as his immune system began the tough job of hull construction and the temporary entombment of the broken nuke engine. He'd have to sleep it off until he'd grown enough skin to hide the problem.

If Corvax were findable, he could find him. But maybe that was not so urgent as it had seemed. Tatresi had begun to feel that perhaps he'd been too quick to fear change. Isol might be right: they must take the advantage and strike now, reaching their goal while the opportunity lasted, and if there were consequences unforeseen—weren't there always? He'd no vision of utopia like she did, the crazy bitch, but he could see his way to a position that was bearable among the Forged. They could accommodate changes; it was what they'd been campaigning for. The Unevolved might suffer, but that wouldn't be his concern then. He shut down all his receivers and broadcasts, and switched into sleep mode.

Corvax hadn't been so close to Earth since he'd been Made. His prison was confining, but it gave him a steady view of the planet's surface, and he fancied he could make out the origin and destination stations of the Heavy Angels whose engines and re-entry shields burnt tiny, smooth paths through the atmosphere in firefly orange and yellow. By craning his neck he could just make out the shining bulk of Tupac herself, almost a quarter-turn away from his position on the remand wing.

He knew that Machen was coming to see him in person. He hoped that his voluntary surrender was going to stand him in good stead, but this positive element in his mind was more than overshadowed by the understanding that Machen's personal interest could only mean that the situation was worse than he'd thought. The general was not the Gaiasol's only spokesman by any means, but he had been permitted the rule of martial law the day before, once Isol's proposal had been discussed in open forum. The rest of the government would carry on making the final decisions, but they were listening to Machen and his section intently all the time. Who else but Machen, and his formidable collection of AIs, Hives and Strategi, was likely to make the right choices?

In Corvax's mind, almost anyone was able to make these kinds of choices for themselves, but they rarely wanted to. He despised all formal governance as buck-passing bureaucracy. Nonetheless, he was nervous now. He'd been a fugitive from prosecution for a very long time.

He knew exactly when Machen arrived, because his cell was detached from its position at a bay on the farthest spar of Idle-wild and towed around the side of the station by Arachno service personnel, at the ends of their long lines. It floated about until its door docked with that of the interview suite. Because of an ongoing solar storm, all the windows on the sunward side were shielded with heavy panels, and the atmosphere was oppressively shadowed despite the rooms' internal lights. Although he'd never felt claustrophobic within his rock, Corvax felt a heaviness descend on him as his view was restricted to the tiny room ahead. His arms, denuded of the power-assist augmentation he'd always worn, seemed ineffective and small, like mouse paws against the thick feather and armour of his chest. In one of these he held the quartz pebble. His muscles burnt and ached with the effort it had cost him to get here. His circulation tightened and his extremities grew cold with his apprehension. Mercifully, before it got worse, the inner gate opened and he was allowed to move forward into the spaceside holding arena; free fall and no atmosphere on his side of the screen, full pressure and oxygen—and a chair—for Machen on his side.

Corvax had forgotten what Unevolved looked like close to: soft, tiny and weak. Machen's skin was the colour of cheap white plastic that'd been exposed to too much heat and had browned to the verge of disintegration. The general was so small, too, smaller than Xing's spacer frame with its overgrown bones. He was like a little toy that Corvax might use for demonstrating the features of basic biomechanics to one of his patients who'd come for a change. It was strange knowledge that they were, in all ways that mattered, the same, yet so different physically that what was home for him would kill the general, and vice versa, in a matter of seconds. Facing the difference was harder than he'd anticipated after so long in exile. He felt an unexpected revulsion and pity for this creature, and apprehension at his power.

"Corvax." The general bowed his head in a greeting and didn't use the old classnames that Corvax had once possessed—Roc, Handslicer. Maybe it was respect of a kind.

Corvax nodded, still resistant to showing any submission. Neither sat. If the general felt any of the things Corvax felt, it didn't show on his face or in his stance. The general walked close to the transparent wall between them and looked up directly into Corvax's eyes, without hesitation.

"I understand you've decided to come in from the Belt."

A question? Corvax took it and decided there was no need for the game of discovery about who was doing what and what they knew. Time mattered. "I need to speak to the engineers working on the analysis of Isol's drive."

"You can say what you have to say to me."

Corvax paused and hunkered lower on his haunches, feeling his long legs draw in against him, beneath his wings, like bunches of poles. They were very tired with the journey of yesterday heaped upon their long disuse. He was a feeble specimen but he hadn't lost his wits. "I want some guarantees."

General Machen glanced behind him to where two Arachno MekTek guards stood still and silent, their sixteen eyes shining masks of reflective carbon plate. They wore EMP cannon and other shock-wave guns mounted on their abdomens. All weapons were trained on Corvax. Machen slowly turned back to him.

"I didn't come here to discuss politics and crimes with you. Either you hand over the alien material and any knowledge you have about it or you can rot in this cell until we need to know what you know more than we need to keep you in good health."

"I want a legal representative." Corvax was afraid of this— that nobody would know he was here. The lawyer wouldn't be any use as defence, but they could publicize his position and make sure he wasn't conveniently forgotten.

"This is a matter of defence and security now," Machen said. "I know you bought and received drive material via that little bastard Gritter, and I know you didn't come here because you've had a change of heart about refitting anyone who asks for it with anything you can steal. You've got no time for anyone but yourself and your own vision. Which is fine with me, as long as you're some nut hermit out in the Belt, and nobody you alter comes into contact with the security services. But right now you're in my way, and in the way of the most important scientific investigation we've ever undertaken, so you figure out what you'd do if you were in my position and then I'll give you some credit for having that brain Tupac says you've got, and not judge you by the whining garbage you just came out with. And by the way, for your further information, I do not give a rat's ass about the Independence movement and its glorified goddamned existential crisis."

Corvax spread his wings and folded them again in a reflex gesture of alarm. He'd known that this was what he was coming to so he didn't know why it was so hard now to relate what he knew—except that it felt like he was about to drop Isol into the hands of this general, who had every reason to stop her plans for Zia Di Notte. He wasn't even sure if he wanted to go and live in another Solar System himself. He thought Isol was crazy but he respected her will to be free.

He sighed. "The drive matter responds to sentient intent. It can change its structure according to whatever purpose the observer has in mind. It doesn't require anything like a specific design. It makes itself into the right tool for the right job." He slowly extended his hand and opened the fingers, showing Machen the rock.

"You've got evidence of this?" Machen indicated that the lump should be placed in the handover tray that was part of the wall, but Corvax hesitated.

"It's sentient too. There's . . ." He didn't know how to explain it. "It gave me a sign."

"Spoke aloud?"

"No. It smiled at me."

The general took a moment to digest this. He stared at the stone, but carried on without turning a hair: "Telepathy?"

"No idea."

"Get any impressions of why they're doing this?"

"They?" Corvax said. "That's an unjustified leap."

"So, what's your plan for finding out the truth?"

"I hoped that I could pool my resources with yours and we could work together on this," Corvax said.

The general stared at him. "And in return you get a full pardon?" He thought about it, but made no further attempt to take the rock. "I guess you could've used that thing to make your way out of here."

"I could."

"Did your messing about give you Tek and Secta components? Can you talk to a Hive when it's in trance?"

"Yes."

"The work is taking place at an isolation station in oppositional Mars orbit. The drive material and you are all to be taken there. You can report to the head of the laboratory, Arachno Mouze. Any reason to suspect it's working as a contaminant?"

"I haven't detected that, although it has the ability. I've found no trace of it in my own body, and I've been close to this material quite a while." The relief was indescribable.

"Okay. The first thing you're going to do is find out if it can be destroyed by any means you can think of. Got that?"

"Yes."

"Good." Machen stood, turned and was escorted out, without a backward glance. Corvax was left sitting alone on his side of the interview room, facing the Arachno soldiers who stayed as inscrutable and motionless as statues. He curled his hand over the stone and shivered. After a time his cell was detached, handed to a visiting Angel, and then whisked off to Tupac.

He didn't understand what consequences the laboratory environment implied for him until Tupac told him about the atmosphere and the scale of the place—it was a Monkey zone. She would have to cut off his wings.

"Other changes could be made," she added in her gentlest voice. "If you never really wanted to be Roc, you could be another thing."

In Corvax's imagination no inspiration stirred. He was numb. "But what?" The idea of losing his wings—it was terrifying and unbearable in reality now that it confronted him, even though in Uluru he never missed them these days. He felt panic rise in his chest.

"I don't know," she said. "What about Tom, who built the plane?"

He was astonished she knew about that. It was his private, adult universe. *Nobody* knew about that. But he said feebly, "Tom never finished the plane, Mother. Tom didn't want to go."

"Maybe if it had been real," she said, "he would have had the courage to fly."

"Show me," Corvax demanded and slid away from the horror of his own body and into the seamless sensuality of Uluru, to the grey marsh and the spectral houses where his dreams had died.

Isol's Hand waited and observed silently for an hour or two and then, as Zephyr finally turned from the astounding views to begin the manhandling of her sled and gear, it spoke.

"I shall be staying here, but moving into a hibernation phase shortly to conserve power. I've prepared a Roach, which will enable you to keep in contact with me and also let me travel around the surface. When the time comes to make orbit, the Isol-Roach will signal me to awaken, and the Isol prime body will return."

"A what?"

Zephyr still had her Abacand out in her hand and it replied quickly. "A Roach is a small, independently mobile AI, about the size of a large cockroach, that can range widely on solar power during the hours of daylight. During darkness it operates in a standby mode. So not actually all that much like a cockroach, which prefers the dark. Like a reverse roach."

Zephyr stood confounded for a moment. She'd assumed she would be living in the protective cell of the Hand, but that was clearly not to be. She had to make her own camp. Suddenly she felt very aware of her loneliness, as well as of the incomprehensible distance between herself and her own home. She leant against the Hand's cracked and pitted surface; it was warm in the afternoon's steady glow. The seconds passed and she pushed away suddenly.

"There's no mention of that in any briefing. Are you intending to check up on me?"

"For safety," Isol said. "And I am free to construct as many additional limbs or features as necessary, you know."

"So what's this Roach made of?"

"You don't need to be so defensive," Isol said. "I had it built in-system. It's an Earth technology, and I'm sure your Unevolved work and methods are first-class."

Now Zephyr wanted to kick the Hand. Instead she stamped over the threshold and gave the sled a solid yank by its two webbing handles. It had been expertly packed and slid down the runners freely and at speed, almost knocking her over as it shot out and scraped to a halt on the peculiar stone surface. Her own pragmatism and agility both surprised her. If the choice lay between this type of bitching and a cubby in the largest meditation park in the universe, then she preferred the silent city.

"Hey," she said to the Abacand in her top pocket, "don't you think this place is peaceful?"

"If you are attempting to make an attempt at analysis," it said, "we should do more looking first, I think."

"It feels strange," Isol said in a voice that made Zephyr stop in the middle of undoing the sled's cargo harness. Suddenly faint, she had to lean on the waist-high baggage, puffing and gasping—but she realized that was due to the oxygen levels.

"What do you mean?" she panted. The Hand—a simple orbital lifter—had better senses than she did, even if they were feeding back to a mind of dubious motivation.

The muscle around the doorway shivered in the wind's sudden gust and relaxed a little from its rigid tension. "There is a resonance," Isol observed. "I can't place it in the rock or the wind. Also the light . . ." She sounded perplexed. "Look at the city under this spectra," and she flashed an instruction to the Abacand.

Zephyr's specialized goggles had been packed away so she could see nothing. Crossly she bumped her foot against one of the sled's six independently suspended barrel-shaped wheels. She took the cube out of her pocket and balanced it where its sensors could take in the panorama.

"Heck," said the Abacand.

"What?" Zephyr snapped.

"I'll sim it." The Abacand projected a picture onto the greyish surface of the sled's sophisticated tarpaulin. Zephyr looked at it and saw that in the long wavelengths of red light outside human vision, there was a subtle movement in the colours of the city stone. Not everywhere at once, but now and again and with varying clarity, like fish rising towards the surface of a millpond and diving before they touched it.

"What is that? Do you think the natives operated in this range of vision?"

"Operated?" Isol said. "Past tense. So you already agree with me that this is a deserted place?"

Zephyr stared around her but saw nothing of the firefly movement with her own eyes, not a hint of it. The idea that it was there disturbed her. At once she felt ridiculous because the familiarity of being herself and of recognizing simple objects was reassuring, but at the same time she didn't even know what she didn't see, and the oddity/similarity paradox of the simple act of standing on this planet was too much for her emotions to respond to except with a sense of the ridiculous. She wanted now to get in the Hand and leave immediately, before madness set in. But her practical side insisted that she keep on with the sled work until the harness was rigged for towing its near-frictionless bulk about. They had agreed on a minimal-disturbance mission, and that meant Zephyr hauling her own stuff. Isol's last comment went unanswered.

A few minutes later the Roach made its appearance through the Hand's door and scuttled off to the parapet, or whatever the low wall was that bordered their landing place. It rippled in colour, and Zephyr watched it vanish as its chameleon hide matched the spot it stood on. She turned her head and pointedly ignored it.

At last there was no more useful work to carry out that might be used to delay the inevitable moment. With the Abacand in her hand, Zephyr addressed Isol.

"Have you got plans to go back to the Solar System over the next few days?"

"I might."

"I wonder if you'd take some mail for me?"

"You trust me with your post?"

"Will you take it?"

"If I go."

"Right." Zephyr stepped away from the Hand and watched the dark iris of the door-sphincter close in on itself, the metal shield behind it sliding closed. There was no further sound or movement from the black, snub-nosed shape. *Fits in perfectly in this place,* Zephyr thought, disappointed with its abandonment of her. She looked at the sled and decided to take it with her straight away. Although this raised spot was great for viewing, it was chilly in the cooling wind and too exposed for her liking, despite the presence of the Hand. In fact, she wanted to get away from Isol if she could—and from her damned Roach.

The sled harness fitted over her shoulders, and its controls slid into the mitten covering her right hand. It had brakes, independent axle steering, and a small amount of battery power for emergencies and to boost the first inertial load of getting it started. The tarpaulin arrangement was composed of a low-friction material shaped over an aerodynamic dome, so as to lend it quicker passage through the air. Even so, as it came after her, Zephyr was aware of its substantial weight and the peculiar lightness with which it moved.

Behind the Hand their platform broadened and shelved down in a gradual incline, which branched in three directions along clearly definable routes. One ascended back up into the rest of the raised structure, which continued for some twenty extra metres of fluted, delicate stone above them. The others bore downwards, and both vanished into the darkness of enclosed spaces through gateways that looked like fat parabolas, each a good four metres high and three or more wide.

As the Abacand recorded their progress, Zephyr made a few verbal notes to it, but she paused almost as soon as she'd started, realizing that she was going to have to define her terms: a gate, a door, a path, a road . . . each of these words held too many assumptions, but without using them, what could she say? And if she did use them, how would her mind stay free of its human conditioning long enough to see what was actually there, and not what she expected to find? Any language or form of thinking she chose came with its own prêt-à-porter universe, implicit in its structure.

"Crud," she muttered, coming to a halt just before the right-hand turn and almost forgetting to brake the sled. Its nose bumped against her back, making her stagger forward another stride. "Here's something, and here's another something. They look like throughways and doors, but what are they?"

Even on archaeology digs Zephyr had been able to state with some confidence what was a wall, or a pit, or a doorway or an enclosure. They were all human things with clear and obvious functions, their proportions and construction a give-away. Without her knowing anything about the creatures that had done this, what was to be said about their stuff?

"Solids, surfaces and spaces," the Abacand suggested, "*reminiscent of* Earth structures, such as doors, walls and roads."

"It'll have to do," she said, "or we aren't going to get off this deck, let alone anywhere else. I can already hear them all leaping for the red marker pens, ready to demolish my academic standing in one mighty blot."

"On a five-day walkabout of the unknown, much compromise with ideology and theory must be accepted," the Abacand said, adopting a positive and loyal note as it was programmed to do. "Everyone will agree to this."

"That's what *you* think."

But she cued the sled and strode forward again, only to pause a moment later and activate a head torch to peer into the murky vaults becoming visible in front of them. Every few seconds a neon-lit message in her head flashed: *This is a new world!* But she was beginning to weary of its demand that she keep the amazement factor turned up to Level 10. She didn't have the energy. Not when there was so much to see. Awe at *where* and *what* had to slink back in favour of awe simply for strangeness and unfathomable meaning; that and the nagging fear that Isol's word was rubbish and that there were things—people, she must try to think of them as people of a kind or she would lose the last of her composure—living here still.

But even this mingled doubt and irritation left her within the next ten minutes. Zephyr walked through a huge hallway, dimly lit by the sun shining in through its three doors. Her track carried on downwards, branching often, its soft earth colours changing with the light as afternoon progressed into richer hues. These deepening tones revealed the odd textural changes of the substance, as it was variously horizontal, angled or vertical. She reviewed these differences, but saw no pattern to them.

The infra-spectrum radiances remained visible to the Abacand, but it reported no recognizable features in them, nor anything to suggest that it was reacting to their presence. For another hour Zephyr wandered almost speechless through caverns, alleys, pavilions and galleries, all of them unique, yet all of them lacking a single sharp angle or flat surface. The Abacand surveyed everything, stocking data as Zephyr tried to get a feel for the place, never quite trusting her own instincts to work here, even so. All she could say about it was that it must have been made, because it was certainly composed of recognizable minerals but without recognizable or plausible shaping from any known natural phenomena, save a mind.

And that was quite enough of a statement for the entire expedition, she thought.

When Zephyr stopped to take a drink, the Abacand reported that certain of the structural elements it had observed were math-oriented, and together they attempted some ratio analyses of the proportions of things they'd seen. As the machine worked at its calculations she sighed, and glanced back at the startling heights of the tower where the Hand was just visible.

"They could have sent monkeys instead," she said, "for all the difference this study makes to the questions. Ha. Maybe they did." But she had begun to get very tired and this attempt at humour didn't lift her spirits.

"There's something else," the Abacand said. "A lot of these

relations seem to be based around particular ratios and constants, but there's one number here that is consistently employed, although I don't recognize it."

"Don't tell me it's going to be like Machu Picchu or one of those cities of the lost theories, where everything tallies to a mystical set of coincidences all pointing to the fact that the world's going to end."

"That would be extremely difficult to draw as a conclusion, since it is only a number. It does not appear to relate to any feature of the physical universe that I am aware of, however. I am simply making a conjecture that it is, in fact, a constant or ratio, because of the rate of occurrence of these items within the structural analysis."

"Of the architecture."

"Or whatever it is we've been passing through."

"I was wondering if it might be a large dunghill, which has been excavated by some sort of lower-life-form beetle-type thing, and all our marvellous observations are being pitched entirely at the wrong species and for the wrong reasons."

"Yes, that is a possibility," the Abacand conceded. "Although I personally find it unlikely, it cannot be ruled out. I have labelled our discovered number as the first artefact of significance."

"Remind me again what I'm doing here."

"You're the delaying tactic and potential scapegoat for both sides in a land dispute. What you really do is most probably utterly irrelevant."

"Yes, I keep forgetting about that because of this fact-finding thing. I'm glad the Strategos informed your political smarts," Zephyr said, glad of no such thing. "In which case I think it's time to camp, make dinner and give my brain a rest." She glanced around the large hall they seemed to be in but its space was too vast. She wanted something more like a blast bunker, with an entrance easily barred.

"That's how it is, until you have to announce your verdict," the machine continued. "Then suddenly you'll be everybody's favourite—or least favourite—person. But on the bright side, there's no chance they'll let anything nasty happen to you before that."

"Assuming any of them are sane," Zephyr muttered, wondering where the Roach had gone, and then deciding she didn't care if Isol did hear every word. She got up and attached herself to the sled, stuffing her drinking bottle into a leg pocket.

Outside, as they cleared the threshold and came into a kind of arena studded with small folds and curlicues of rock, Zephyr saw the first stars coming out. She pointed the Abacand up at them for a survey, and waited for its reply. It hummed lightly as it worked, and then made a noise as though clearing its throat.

"I don't know how to break this to you," it said, "but this is not where Isol said it was."

"Oh, for gods' sakes," Zephyr said, "surprise me again. Where is it, then? The back lot of last year's Virtua hit film? Other side of Pluto?" She didn't know enough about the constellations to tell for herself.

"I have no idea. I don't recognize any single star, planet or constellation. Either we are not within the visible GHZ of the Milky Way, or we are in another galaxy altogether."

Stuck in the traces, Zephyr peered at the deepening teal colour of the sky. It was reassuringly very ordinary-looking. "Are you sure?"

"Yes."

"Really, really sure?"

"Yes."

"But . . ." Zephyr wanted to sit down. Her knees felt weak but she managed to stay upright. "I thought they all agreed this was Zia Di Notte?"

"Looks a bit like it. Same spectrograph, same number of planets a plausible distance away from the sun, each planet with the same broad assortment of satellites. Anyway, this is not it."

Zephyr was outraged, and also disappointed and disgusted that she could be so easily outraged and so duped, and also frightened anew, because Isol was really untrustworthy, and not merely the sort of casual untrustworthy that she'd thought; Isol was the actual face of Agamemnon, not the gold mask. Zephyr wanted to say something but her mouth worked noiselessly. She sat down where she was, and watched her own shadow grow slim and long in the gloaming, the first human shadow ever cast on this world. The shadow of an idiot.

"Well, shit," she said after ten minutes' silence had gone by.

It occurred to her that the only thing she could do, now that she was completely at Isol's mercy, was to make every effort to understand something about this place, so that she could use the knowledge as a bargaining chip when the moment came to get her ride home. That, and come up with a false report agreeing with Isol's plans to claim this world, whilst writing a genuine one that she would have to conceal in the Abacand. With the Roach perpetually scuttling here and there, that would not be easy.

"I believe the procedure has been discussed with the Strategos," the Abacand said, hinting that it was thinking along the same lines.

"And wouldn't he be impressed?" Zephyr asked, getting to her feet again. She turned back the way they had come and began the search for a cubbyhole.

Setting up her temporary camp took the rest of the dim natural light plus a half hour of battery power. The food provided was excellent and heated itself in small packs that crumpled to almost nothing when she was ready to tidy them away. Her water was fortified with minerals. But the dinner and its familiarity and warmth were over all too soon. Zephyr sat in the dark of her hideout, the Abacand on watch as she sealed herself into her sleeping bag and lay on the sled's platform. Outside the wind had dropped and it was almost completely quiet.

"Is the Roach nearby?" she asked, in a whisper.

"About twenty metres," the Abacand said. "Don't worry, I'll wake you if anything at all happens."

Zephyr listened to her heart beating quickly. In the night she would wake many times, gulping for air with a breathlessness she hadn't noticed during the day. Her dreams were filled with stalking darkness and the shifting shapes of ghost lights. Towards dawn the onshore breeze found its way into her cramped space and rattled a loose end of the tarp with a noise of banshee bones dancing on the stone. Until it was light, she didn't get out of her hiding place to fix it.

21. THE BIG DEBATE

Gritter, having delivered the day's gossip and messages around London, launched himself from his perch outside the rooms where Gaiasol's War Cabinet had been in session for the last four hours, and flapped his way into the traffic headed for the northeast end of town. There were a lot of Phaeries in the air making the going difficult. He bit at one of them who got close, trying to tear a gauzy dragonfly wing from its shoulders, but the Phaery dodged him with a sharp *zzzt* of its wasp-wing subset and continued on its idle way through the airstream, claws clenched on fistfuls of notes, money and data crystal, the colours of its company flashing a warning at Gritter from its fuzzy abdomen, telling him he could get a ten-thousand-dollar fine for interfering with one of the registered post offices.

Phaeries were thick and smug, and he didn't regret the last one's passing. They had all the wit and wisdom of butterflies, and the loyalty of worker bees. If any of them had ever considered itself badly done by it was a thought that couldn't have lasted more than a few seconds in a head entirely given over to the Knowledge and a burning compulsion to deliver and return to base without creaming anything off the cash they carried for themselves. Not that they had anything to spend it on. Sugar water and a hothouse full of exotic flowers down on the Old Kent Road were enough to keep them happy. A pigeon or a rat was a better bet for an interesting dinner too, any day of the week, in Gritter's opinion. But there'd be no Phaeries at the meeting tonight, and that at least he could be thankful for.

Stretching out his wings to their limit, he made a long downward glide towards Baedeker House, where its broad branches curved upward and outward from the lowlier levels of Archway's arcologies. Other Degraded were already perched in the outermost arms of the building, and he spotted others of his Union there, wearing ties and rosettes that sported a defiant violet and orange, the colours of the Independence Party.

On the street some twenty storeys below, the police had gathered: Unevolved officers standing around chatting with two gigantic Herculeans and several martial MekTeks. Right bastards to a man they were, Gritter thought, with their reinforced skeletons and upgraded reactions, hydraulically assisted limbs and metal armour; showing no fear and no mercy when they had a warrant out for you. He landed with considerable force on a slender limb of the House tree, and almost unseated two green-feathered office messengers from the Courts. They gaped their bills at him and made a clatter of reprimanding laughter.

The MekTek officer with metal wings and rocket packs looked up at them, protecting her eyes with her clear shield from the regular spurts of downward-falling shite and feathers. Gritter could see her skull-helm recording all of them. Beneath its heavy overhang of blue titanium brows, her human face snarled with disgust. He turned his arse towards her and fanned out his tail to show her its best aspect. Secretly he hoped there would be fighting later, with a few of those fancy cops below getting their share.

Meanwhile, deeper inside the building's public meeting rooms, the avatars of the key offworld Forged personnel had already gathered. Turning his head to the displays on the trunk of the building, Gritter recognized the smooth sky-blue hulk of the Timespan Tatresi and the pretentious flounces of several Heavy Angels. Physically present in their holographic midst, the elected representatives of the Arachnos, Sectae and Herculeans moved with anxious precision. Vaporetti councillors and Bathys joined them via a large screen, which was the best resolution you could get from the appalling bit-rate that the Jovian hardware chucked out. At eight P.M. the meeting was considered quorate, heads were counted, attendees noted and voting rights passed out to everyone.

"Item One: the proposal to support Voyager Isol in her claim of Zia Di Notte," called out the secretary, a young female

MekTek whose adaptations' functions were not at all clear. They clad various visible sections of her in a pretty silver filigree of mobile neuronics, some of which twisted themselves into the sigils of the Forged Allegiance and Forged Labour parties where her flesh was exposed.

The Timespan Tatresi, spokesman for the STWU, stood to have his say first. Gritter didn't think much of him, with his poncey toothstrip and his daft blue body, like some jumped-up pansy of a superhero, but that's what you got with people who had lots of power and no imagination; they'd use it all for preening instead of gleaning. Mind you, they weren't the worst; it was the quiet ones you had to—

"After a referendum vote of sixty-five percent in favour we cast ourselves in as supporters to the Claim," Tatresi intoned with pretentious lack of speed. Facts and figures flashed on Gritter's Abacand, which he glanced at and nodded over without seeing. "Our consensus—" (amid cries of "What consensus!" "Sixty-five percent?" and "You must be mad") "—is that it would benefit future generations of human beings, in the Unevolved and Forged states alike, to have a homeworld far away from the beginnings of Earth and the Unevolved domination of our culture and practices. Thus we propose acceptance of Zia Di Notte as a candidate base for consideration, and we petition the meeting to support this in Government Chambers on Friday."

Next up to the podium came the Hive Queen of the Earth Council's Gaiasol Cultural Development Units, Secta Regina Asantewaa. Gritter felt his feathers churn just looking at her. He didn't like insects at the best of times, unless they were soft and edible small ones without too much crunchy leg. This one wasn't only as fiercely armoured as an assassin bug, but her glossy black-and-scarlet colouring made her look absolutely poisonous and her wing cases were fit to slice the heads off Herculeans, not just poor little Degraded like himself. Nonetheless, her voice was gentle and sweet and the respect in the room was almost palpable, since Hives were known to be capable of prodigious feats of intellect and imagination well outside any individual's capacity. So they expected wisdom here. Still, his arse clenched to look at her. He looked away and dialled up a picture of some parrots on his Abacand. Now *they* were a handsome bird.

"Greetings," Asantewaa murmured, "brothers and sisters. It is our duty to respond to the needs of all people of the Earth, whether the early or the recently Evolved. The second planet of the sun Zia Di Notte, we must also remember, has at some time been the home of another race, and we must think of them and their concerns in addition to our own. We are hampered by our lack of knowledge about this world or its people. Even so, recent polls suggest equal measures of discomfort and acceptance in the idea of reclaiming this place and developing it once again. Like living in somebody else's house, it is not the same as finding a pristine land, as Mars was pristine, uncluttered by prior imaginations."

Gritter shuffled from foot to foot. It was all very well, this highfalutin moral chat, but what did it get them? And even if they got to know everything about the old owners of this new world, what were they going to do about that? Build a theme park and visitor centre?

Regina Asantewaa was continuing. "But in principle we do not object to the colonization of a new planet and Solar System. Our central point of concern is the technology that it was necessary to use to get there. We have yet to hear from our sisters working on this material concerning its safety. Until this matter is thoroughly researched, we oppose any further developments in its use among the Forged or the Unevolved. We suspect it has already been sold in the black economy, and is already in use. We urge those Forged who have used this material to return it at once."

Like *that* was going to persuade anyone.

"What about the arrest of Corvax?" someone texted in from outside the building, the secretary of the meeting announcing the question after signalling for a pause.

"Corvax is here to assist the Gaiasol Laboratories voluntarily," the Secta Queen said, without so much as a flicker of one of her long feelers. "If I may direct you to our previous conversations with the Blessed Tupac, you will see this to be true."

Gritter hadn't heard about this latest bit concerning laboratories. He wondered what the hell Corvax was up to. Maybe there'd be money in it, but not for Gritter, not even when he'd been the one to carry all Corvax's messages, the cheapskate.

Tatresi had now resumed the centre stage. He boomed on about the importance for all of breaking with Earth and the ties of the gravity-bound, but it turned out that the Jovians and Saturnians had no particular desire to relocate into the new system. They were content as long as nobody tried to regulate them from the outside, and as long as reasonable trade was maintained. There was also the question of the alien technology and possible developments for inter- and intra-galactic commerce for them to consider—a development Tatresi felt was for the Transporters to discuss with Gaiasol—and the gas-types didn't like that at all. It took an hour for them to stop bickering over it.

From Jupiter and Saturn, the spokesmen for the Vaporetti then called in their votes. Gritter looked at their jellylike bodies; hard at the cores like bands of tough cartilage, with ballooning membranes and long tentacular limbs spreading from this centre. Their semi-human arms and legs were powerfully developed and they hugged them close to their trunks as they drifted in a wind-sheltered zone, a Nirvana, the Vaporetti equivalent of a public square.

The Saturnian was a male and aged, eyes slits of calculating black in the semi-hard structures of his face, which had smoothed to a pearlescent green under the ravages of the eternal storms. "We have no interest in an Earth-type planet," he stated with an equable shrug of his colossal shoulders, showing one of his cranial wing-sets furling idly behind him, their antigravity feathers longer and finer than Gritter's. "Isol reports a single gas giant in the system, but has provided no other information. If this project goes ahead—and we think it won't—then we would be interested, of course, in exploring this region *jointly* with our Jovian cousins."

The Jovian agreed with him, her face blue and green with

tattooed stripes, and with a golden ring pierced through the slender ridge where her nose shaded into beaklike lips. Her blue hair flowed around her in thick coils, with and against the wind, betraying its function as a current-detector and balancing structure, like the Saturnian's head-wings. "And then we will decide between us who to send and what alliances we should make," she added, looking at the Saturnian's softer and smaller shape with polite condescension.

Gritter lost track of the rest of the conversation between the sometime allies. He was too busy trying to figure out just how big they really were, from the readouts his display screen was kindly providing him. There must have been something wrong with the numbers, because according to them the female was more than sixty metres long and the male a mere half-metre, yet they both appeared very similar. Perhaps it was to do with the wind speeds or something like that, he mused. They weren't so odd-looking, really, not even as peculiar as regular Earth Bathyforms. With all those hairs and tentacles and cilia, he would bet it was all cushy-coo up there, one orgy after another and hardly a scrap of work to do between them, since the condensers and battery units they'd built did all the hard labour. Who needed ten thousand Vaporetti anyway? Idlers, the lot of them, living off that free energy, and nothing to spend their money on but fifty flavours of nutri-goo and various ridiculous types of wind-riding protection. They hadn't even managed to penetrate the heart of their planets yet. Time they developed some new forms and . . .

". . . Escaped the attention of many of us more fortunate types, but the Terraform Classes have been abandoned entirely by this struggle." The Herculean was speaking. "They were shut into sleep and denied a voice once the Lunar and Martian landscapes were completed. Created with the promise of a long life and work, but prevented by their very form from enjoying any kind of existence outside the purity of mere Function. Designed into planned obsolescence before their time, they're the forgotten ones in this situation. Any claim on Zia Di Notte must be made with these brothers and sisters in the forefront of our minds. A new world promises work and life. To deny Isol's claim is to agree with these people being thrown onto the scrap heap and forgotten, despite all they've done for us."

There was a general stirring now among those on the outside of the building. The screens showed a picture of Luna Memorial Park, where the Moon colony was much more vocal in its agreement to this last point. Gritter saw banners waved and a few scuffles among the crowd.

"Gaiasol has never offered any realistic alternative to enforced hibernation for these tragic figures," the Herculean went on, thumping his colossal fist down on the lectern before him gently, but hard enough to make the wood crack audibly.

"Wouldn't have had to if they'd had sensible lifespans," Gritter muttered. The Messenger next to him scowled and pecked out at him with annoyance at the remark.

Gritter stabbed back with his own beak, and before he knew it they were engaged in a fight, claws out and feet scrabbling to get a grip on each other's throats. It was quite a welcome distraction, but painful. He got a slash near his eye and they fell together, a tangle of fighting feathers, through the tree and down towards the street.

Arachno Mouze was distracted from the Herculean's fighting talk by a flash of brightly coloured feathers tumbling past the window. He heard the squawks of Degraded outrage, and the whine and hum of the police stun net as the combatants reached street level and were corralled. Theirs wasn't the only squabble that was erupting in the gathering. Angry shouts and whistles were greeting the Earthbound Forged's call to support the sleeping Terraforms. Voices began to be raised, about artificial lifespan, and Unevolved guilt over the fate of Forged who had died or been lost due to poorly understood engineering. Mouze felt vulnerable there, and tacked sideways towards the exit from the main room and into the hall to gather his thoughts. He was to speak next and say something about the state of their research into the alien material, but so far they had nothing to offer and the idea of the reaction of the crowd to this news made his hearts palpitate.

He contacted the lab and asked for the latest news on Corvax, and the Hive's progress with the Stuff. The bit-streams that flowed in, tuned to his personal wavelengths, showed him the Hive's semi-completed analysis. Despite his stability on eight points Mouze felt himself stagger, his legs instinctively folding more deeply as they prepared to dart away, or to contract for hiding in a hole that didn't exist. Their sudden sensitivity made the vibrations of the crowd feel like an earthquake in his head—but then it felt like that anyway, as he tried to grasp the impact of what he was seeing.

When he'd recovered himself he thought to ask what dealings there had been with Isol—she should have been there to speak for herself, but she had not arrived so far. In the end he didn't wait for the answer, but approached the steward and secretary on his own behalf.

The secretary interrupted the meeting, her neuronics allowing her to speak softly and be heard by everyone through the use of specific frequencies, despite the hubbub of conversation that threatened to drown out any single voice. She ushered Mouze to the stand and introduced him quickly.

"I have just been informed of certain conclusions of the Hive TwoPi's analysis of the alien technology acquired by Voyager Isol, commonly referred to on the usenets as Stuff." Mouze was briefly aware of some of the non-Sectae Forged flinching away from his aggressive-looking defensive stance, and strove to smooth down the stiff hairs on his body, to retract his vestigial palps. "It is potentially unsafe and a contaminant. Anyone possessing or having been in contact with it is required to proceed immediately to the nearest quarantine or Forge-bay point, and remain there until they have been medically cleared."

He paused and took a breath for steadiness' sake, even though he didn't use breath to speak. His spiracles remained open, attempting to filter out an anxiety he couldn't begin to examine. "Until Stuff, as it is temporarily known, has been more thoroughly worked up, I think we must confine ourselves to discussion of what to do if Voyager Isol's plan goes ahead, and what we'll do if it doesn't, and if this material is more of a threat than it first appeared to be. The conditions governing its contagiousness have not been understood so far."

Mouze was drowned out utterly in the uproar that followed and barely escaped to the back stairs under police security guard.

Gritter, who heard the last part of Mouze's speech with his head thrust through the hole of the restraint netting, blood in his eye and the sting of a MekTek officer's hand on the scruff of his neck, spat into the gutter. "Lerrus out!" he hollered, struggling.

"I don't think so." She ignored the scratch of his dirty claws on her metal skin. "Time for you to get in the van, before the rest of this lot goes off."

"I've gotta getta the Bay. You 'erd 'im."

"You can get there via the station." She lifted him up and dumped him into the heavy hemp embrace of a wide-mouthed sack. The fabric drew close and wrapped him in the stink of someone else's vomit, a smell that a quick swill with a hosepipe had not been able to get out of the cloth.

He heard the rest of the debate from the newsfeed to the police station, as he perched in the chemical reek of the aviary cells along with a crew of other wretched Orniths, his head stuck under one wing so as to avoid locking gazes with anybody still looking for a fight.

Some Unevolved from the government was blithering on about racial segregation: ". . . Separation from the Forged is purely a racist and divisive manoeuvre, a falling-back to the positions of the early twenty-first century where national, religious and cultural divisions were allowed to stand as barriers to trade, rights and the fair distribution of wealth . . ."

Yadda, thought Gritter, *but where is* my *fucking wealth? And what street monkey gives a shit about my welfare? On the other hand, the rest of the High and Mighty up in space couldn't care less about the Degraded. Production errors, they say, and sympathy and tea. Bollocks to them.* But he couldn't avoid the sound of the station unit, seated as he was beside the wall of cell bars that gave directly onto the booking area.

"The Earth government must stand firm on this issue of secession. If the system breaks apart, then there will be a return to the days of permanently disadvantaged cultures . . ."

Later bigmouth Tatresi spoke again. "The minister speaks of cultural disadvantage and poverty, but the Forged already exist in cultural poverty, designed and fabricated to lead lives of restricted experience and social deprivation in comparison with the hominid populations, who enjoy a full and varied animal life in addition to their functions as employees, workers and philosophers.

"Either Earth must grant us the freedom to pursue our individual developments and the right to pursue our own reproduction and design, equal in rights, or they must be discarded as the slave traders and commodity brokers they are. This talk of cultural loss is only the nervous chatter of those who have already surrendered their individual heritage in the name of a democratic panglossia that now stagnates around them. It stinks, and we will not be sullied . . ."

Gritter reflected: *Quite the little speaker, our Tatresi, when the mood gets on him. Pity he's not as sincere as you'd believe, given that he can't do anything but ferry stuff from one orbit to another and, if they do bloody sack him, what the hell will he do then but go begging off to the Independence Party and hope they can give him a job in the public-speaking mines or the press department because, like the rest of us, cheesy avatar or no cheesy avatar, he's fundamentally fucked from day one. As free as one of my feathers is to go and live alone, find itself a nice pad out Fulham way, join a little feather social club, marry a downy bit of fluff, and all that shit.*

Someone actually quoted Marx and the means of production, and Gritter nearly had to pull his head out to be sick. *True, true, we are the means of something—or just mean.*

". . . Forged were never designed to be merely sentient machines in the way that so many of them seem to delight in thinking, in order to fuel their anti-hominid fury. Wasn't it the case that human society in the past has always been divided between those who manage and those who labour? Some division of labour must exist to get the job done at all. Society has never been homogeneous. Herculeans cannot fly. Hominids cannot survive space. Jovian Vaporetti cannot till the land and create food . . ."

And if you hadn't utterly sent the place to shite in earlier centuries by overpopulating, and eating every resource you had right up to the sharp end of a new Cainozoic extinction point, then we wouldn't exist. Are we supposed to be grateful? Here to feed you, O master. At your service—the solution to all your niggling problems. Tug my forelock. What a lovely day.

Gritter thought it was about time the complacent louts at the top of the heap got to have a genuine red-hot poker up the ass.

Then they were back on that very hysterical subject.

". . . Terrible news that there has already been illegal trading in this found alien technology among the Forged black markets, with possibly up to a hundred or more Forged self-adapters already bonded with it. In response to this quarantine, all such individuals are urged to surrender themselves immediately for transport to the nearest Pangenesis, where they will be housed until an all-clear may be given . . ."

Like that was going to happen. And as if that git Machen hadn't already sanctioned the use of the engines on his own military personnel. Leave it all to Isol? In a pig's eye.

Actually, on thinking this through, Gritter realized that it might work to his advantage. Corvax would have to go straight. No time for tracking him down until far later in the day. Good job Gritter had never had to handle any of the bloody stuff directly. Isol must be shitting bricks out of whatever passed for her butt, jump-gate technology or no. He wondered what the stuff did to you. Was it like scabies? Would it itch?

He lifted a foot and scratched a sudden prickling under his chin. *Fleas again,* he thought, thinking of Necktie and how he'd got his name from having a near-permanent bald spot circling his throat from incessant parasite infestations: fleas, ringworm, allergy to feather-mite . . . hah. Have to get the lad into a chemical plunge pronto. He only got cleaned these days when he was arrested and hosed down forcibly. Gritter, on the other hand, understood the value of a carefully maintained plumage. Without thinking, he began to groom.

"Oi, you."

The voice was light, but unfriendly. Gritter ignored it.

"You there. Spatchcock."

He glanced over his shoulder. Sitting in a different cell to his left was a gritty, grimy specimen that had once been a Degenerate Guard. Its house uniform was ragged—a few scraps of crimson cloth, darted in blue, hung about its wiry torso. Its snout and teeth were scarred and broken from a recent run-in with a police baton, but its eyes, in the doggy face, were shrewd. Gritter was reminded of the advertising campaign for Restitution For The Degenerate: *We did not strive to make lower, only higher, than ourselves. But, once in a while, accidents happen. For those of us not as fortunate as others, give generously to the Restitution Fund. They also serve.*

This illegally bred figure had clearly been intended as a pet, but had received some unexpected *in vitro* upgrading and, instead of a smart long-lived poochy life-companion for a rich old fart with no children, a monster had been produced: human IQ and the body of a gargoyle. Gritter stiffened with instinctive revulsion at this reminder of his own life, and spat on the floor.

"Done any work for the post office recently?" the dog-man growled, his aggression quickly turning to a raspy laugh.

"Why, you looking for a recommendation?" Gritter said before he could engage his brain. He saw stiff MekTek manacles gripping the creature's long-fingered forepaws. The claws were a dark maroon colour, and Gritter snickered, "Bite the hand that feeds you?"

The dog ignored him and licked its chops. "I know you, don't I?"

"Not if I can help it."

"Yes—General Machen's budgie." The words had to fight to get out of the long mouth. "Don't know me, though."

"Maybe you're a cousin of that stupid sheep-chasing hound of his," Gritter hazarded, bold because of the cage he was in and the other's manacles.

"No doubt." The Guard got to his feet and trudged across the short space to the bars. Two nervous Orniths on that side of the cell decided to swap perches for the one near Gritter and came barrelling over, trying not to look hasty. "But then, we're all cousins, aren't we, in some way or other?" He grinned and showed his sizeable canine teeth, saliva oozing around his tongue. "Brother."

"Speak for yourself."

"Oh, I do that." The dog glanced at the police officers, all now watching the TV or talking to each other. "And someone tells me you can get me a piece of this alien matter. You have the connections and what's more you're in it up to your neck, chicken."

"I don't know what you're talking about."

"My arse. Here's what I want. Save your worryin'. I want a piece. I want it soon. I've a quarrel to settle, and I think it will do the job. Maybe, looking carefully, you'll think it's your quarrel too." He gestured with one refined finger at Gritter's general state and status, and lifted half his upper lip in a sneer. "Nobody paid attention in the lab on *our* birthdays, did they?"

Gritter clutched the perch as the other avians shifted away from him, staring anywhere but in the direction of the gargoyle. He decided belligerence was the better part of cowardice. "And who are you thinking of, exactly? Doctor Frankenstein? You may have been part of some breeding programme for better dachshunds, but I was at least born of a Pangenesis."

The creature emitted a low gargling sound that made Gritter's neck ruff flatten in terror, until he realized it wasn't growling but chuckling. "You're a wit, aren't ya? Privileged, too. Now, remember what I said and I'll see you on the outside. I know where you live." He turned his back then and Gritter saw the hard lumps of muscle shifting under the thickly furred pelt, like weasels trapped in a mink coat . . . No, that wasn't a good image. He rammed his head under his wing and tried not to hear the mutterings from the others around him. Soon enough they'd process him and fling him outside. Now he wasn't sure he wanted to be there.

A Painting of Shinjuku Library.
Two beech trees entwined. Sunset.
Side by side, a screw thread, a cola nut.
Boiling tar.

A Painting of Shinjuku Library.
Two newspapers hung out to dry on a line.
The sound of human feet running on hard clay.
The imaginary taste of diamonds.
Breath.

A body describing a perfect circle.
The battleship *Potemkin*.
The Fibonacci sequence, odd values only.
The sensation of being scraped with a strigil too firmly, oil on
    the skin.
A Painting of Shinjuku Library.

The happy feeling of two dogs in springtime, tugging each end
    of a scarf.
Smoke from a burning temple fire, cindered bone and incense.
A proof of the Calculus, written in daisy chains.
A Painting of Shinjuku Library.
Exhaustion creeping in as the heart labours to run on.

The Sagrada Familia, Barcelona.
Schadenfreude.
Eating the entrails of ancestors.
A bridge made of paper across the Sierra Madre.
A Painting of . . .

(our minds wriggle it through)

A Painting of Christmas Day, unwrapping a present.
The gasp of surprise—it's a . . .
Painting of Shinjuku Library.

{*endtrance*}

"A moment!" cried the Queen. The Hive was silent. Glad of the respite, they sank to the bottom of their cells and rippled to cycle the suspension liquid quickly through their digestive tracts to extract oxygen, fatty acids and sugars.

Corvax, able to listen but not to participate, baffled by the work, hung on her words.

"This painting," she said. "Could it be anything else?"

But the Hive response was no, it could not. Things were as they were. They had all examined Isol's drive-unit fragment and it was, indubitably, a Painting of Shinjuku Library. Look at it as they might, wrap and unwrap, twist, twizzle and ponder, it remained as it had begun, an irreducible, if complex, entity.

"I am thinking this answer is not going to be very helpful," the Queen said, speaking for them all. "We need a different approach. Begin trance."

The Hive became a single stream of consciousness.

Corvax dreamed their dream and saw . . .

A gallery visitor stands in sunlight and keenly observes a painting of Shinjuku Library. It is painted on a glass window, the window itself a direct view of the Library building—a pleasant edifice of white curves and gravity-defying balances—which is blocked by the exact mimesis of the painted surface. The paint adjusts its colours as instructed by sensors mounted outside, so that it always resembles the reality beyond. The visitor stands in the centre of a maze of raked stones and can sit, for greater contemplation, on a seat of three oblong rocks, two supporting a cross-beam, henge-fashion. The painted window has invited a lot of criticism and the visitor is aware of the dueling viewpoints—

it's a masterpiece/it's crap—and the curiously intriguing *idea* of executing such a painting with such properties, without which the painting itself is clearly just a representation of Shinjuku Library and not particularly interesting.

The idea causes the visitor's mind to shuffle about, making comparisons in its assumptions about views, glass, windows, paintings, and the act of looking through, looking at and looking towards. Deception and revelation are bound together, indissoluble. And the visitor is the only place in which this art may occur, this self-knowledge, placed there by another, who knew nothing of one, whom one has never even met.

> Gaze through and you will see Shinjuku Library, promises the artist.
> Gaze at and you will see—guess what, Shinjuku Library.
> It's not the greatest cityscape in the world, but that's not the point.
> Seeing what is there and what isn't are one and the same thing.

Oh shit, thought the Hive and Corvax both at the same time.

Zephyr peeked out of her below-stairs position shortly after dawn, and clambered out in time to witness a spectacular pink and orange sunrise. The nameless star was a vast disc at this time of day, slightly flattened in its appearance near this semi-equatorial place as it headed swiftly up to clear the horizon. From here she was able to detect the faint sound of waves crashing onto the shingle below. The sound was reassuringly lifelike and she packed her day sack with a new vigour, and a sense that really it wasn't as bad as she'd feared in the early hours. The Abacand reported no signs of movement, no changes anywhere except the idly circling progress of the Roach, now some fifty metres off and involved in its own business.

The progress of the day before continued. Things that appeared to be rows of houses flowed internally into one another in vast warrens of rooms and chambers stretching up fifty storeys, and down almost as many below ground level where the darkness became inky and unleavened. The mystery builders preferred gentle slopes and ramps to staircases, of which there were none. There were smoothed tubes and chutes buried in the walls, which looked like they were dropways for the fast down-transit of goods or people, or trash. Roads and paths curved up the sides of skyscraping towers and ran straight into large, complex archways where they divided into uneven-numbered corridors delving down and stretching up, sometimes to nowhere or to a simple opening to the sky.

Zephyr's "room" was off the edge of one of these major arches, where its surface became softer and smoother as it curled into a small, windowless area that was split in two levels. Probably it was a boot rack or a place to keep the filing, she liked to imagine, but it was secure and free from any weather, and its single doorway was just bigger than she was, and easily filled. The rest of her "palazzo" had a large interior space with curlicues of balconies spiralling up into a tower that stood proud of the main roof and looked out across the bay and the city. Echoes of the landing tower's structure were visible in its design, as if it were a smaller sister to that giant standing on the top of the cliff. For the sake of ease Zephyr named several locations this morning. The Hand's perch became the Wind Tor and her camp My House. It was curiously not as frightening today and, as she took her recordings, Zephyr added to her speculations about the total lack of straight lines and sharp angles.

She ran the Abacand's full suite of mathematical tools on sections of architecture and on the Tor itself, following yesterday's brief insight. The machine returned a complex series of functions to her, showing the way that the flowing surfaces hadn't simply been copied by "eye" from nature. They expressed more than ten different numerical sequences, whose relations with each other modulated in specific ratios, repeating here and there, like repellers and attractors positioned to capture the interest of someone who could much more readily understand the raw equations at a glance than she could. In fact, the Abacand informed her that some of the instances of recurring numbers or factors could possibly be interpreted as mathematical humour or as profundity, depending on the view. And some were little koans of a kind, their "one hand clapping" suggestions providing a paradoxical halt to linear thought.

And it also looked like nature, in a way, although of an idealized and flowing form. Quickly she came to understand that this same "city" was the most conceptually advanced and beautiful thing she had ever set eyes on—and that was when she couldn't understand it. For the Abacand it was a kind of masterwork.

"But not like a theory, more like a symphony," it said in an unusually quiet tone.

They progressed well and even found an object or two, one of which was small enough to be carried. Zephyr took it back to her "house" and was sitting outside, shaded by a large Mylar umbrella in the "courtyard," making notes and trying to figure out its use—a kind of bowl, full of holes though it was clearly not broken—when she heard an odd sound. She glanced at the Abacand, but it had gone into sleep-saver mode in the radiant warmth emanating from her tea mug and the Roach was nowhere to be seen.

Now the sound was gone, she thought maybe she'd imagined it.

Then it came again, a stealthy scrape of something heavy, metal perhaps, dragging across stone.

She moved quite slowly—calmly, she thought—and thumbed her wrist button to wake the Abacand remotely. A burst of static came from the tiny machine, loud enough to make her jump off her seat. Before she knew what she was doing, she found herself with her back to the wall, the bowl, or whatever it was, left to roll around on the ground by itself.

The Abacand cleared itself and its scanning lights came on.

There was a flash of light brighter than the sun. Zephyr, still finding her feet, shrank back again, arms over her head, wondering if it was some kind of solar flare. Then the scrape occurred again and became a full and throaty engine sound that was huge and defiant in the afternoon's aeon-long silence.

Zephyr grabbed the Abacand and ran to the shadow of the nearest tall arch.

"That's no alien," the Abacand whispered from her hand. "It sounds like a Tangier Mark 3 power driver, an old one too."

Zephyr didn't move, but listened as the machine made its way towards her. Her palms were wet and her chest felt tight. She struggled to breathe without making a noise. Part of her didn't believe the sound's originator was anything to do with this place. It must be something she knew, because it sounded like it was—but then, what?

She wasn't prepared to be caught and cornered so easily. As the thing came close to the palazzo's door, she turned and ran through one of the other branches of the arch, which led up a tightly spiralling ramp and onto a first-floor area that had views down into the street provided by "decorative" holes in the outer wall. Through a small one of these, she looked down.

Crawling along beneath her, close enough to reach out and touch, the pitted and filthy back of the thing heaved and paused. It was caked in mud that had dried and cracked, then fallen away, exposing recognizable patterns of atmospheric damage on a raw Ti-bone surface. Its engine sound slowed and pulsed, very like breathing, as a long, sinuous neck and head extended low to the ground and stared through the arch at her umbrella. Strings or wires hung off the rear part of its body in huge mats, like rotten weed. A few wove up towards her, but their motion was vague and undirected.

"You should leave here," it said, abruptly and in English. Its voice sounded strained. "This place isn't what it seems. It's dangerous here. The planet speaks."

Zephyr didn't move. That sudden, blinding light came again and the machine faltered and sank shuddering to its knees under the onslaught of tuned energy. A pit appeared in its back, darker than the rest, and a thick substance like oil and cooked blood boiled out of this and ran sluggishly down its side.

"That was an orbit-to-ground tight-beam weapon," the Abacand muttered, as Zephyr's fingers clutched it so tightly her fist shook.

"Isol?" she whispered.

The Abacand vibrated in assent.

The strange newcomer's voice came again, unaffected by its wound. "You must go—and touch nothing. Go back."

Then a grinding, a crunching, a tearing of metal and gears. Thin oil and soft, pale slime spread under the stranded beast. Steam rose from the wet string on it. Mud fell to the ground. Its head smashed heavily onto the paving and was still.

Zephyr was transfixed. She knew she had watched someone die here, and Isol had killed them, one of her own—an Earth Forged, or part of one. But what was it doing here, dishing out warnings like the chorus in a Greek tragedy?

She lifted the Abacand to her mouth, thumbing its communications mode, and signalled out for Isol.

"I'm all ready here for your explanation of that."

"I told him to stay away from you. Bloody idiot wouldn't listen," Isol snapped, almost before Zephyr had finished speaking.

"Well, that raises more questions than it answers," Zephyr said, still in recovery from the shock. Steam and smoke were both now rising from the carcass. It smelled of marsh gas and tar, like a mammoth exhumed from a pit.

"I couldn't take a decision to claim this planet without advice from others in the council," Isol said. "There had to be visitors. Some of them remained behind and agreed to keep out of your way. They've touched nothing."

"But when they try to talk to me, you shoot them." Zephyr backed away from the wall and turned to the courtyard. Squinting until her eyes adapted, she looked up into the blue sky where she knew Isol must be, far above her. She wondered if that same beam could pierce this local stone.

"It's nothing—only a Finger. He won't even miss it."

"You were saying?"

Isol made a scrubbing noise with irritated static. "His name is Kincaid. He's senile. He has it in his head that the planet is talking to him. He decided to come here and play the Ancient Mariner to try and persuade you to shut the place off as unsafe. It isn't. I've been here longer than he has and I've seen more. There's nothing but what I've told you."

"Why does he think the planet talks?"

"Zephyr, the important thing is that he's a mad old man who's chosen this moment to lose his marbles because back in-system he's got no work to do. He isn't fit for work on Europa, and I thought that taking him out of Hibernation for a trip out here would do him good. The fact that he's made for an era that's gone is no fault of his. He was made for better things and I thought at least here it would be like the old days."

The Abacand flashed up relevant details as Zephyr digested this. She said, more puzzled than anything, "You brought a Terraform Class? Did you anticipate that I'd say yes to the planet, and then you'd all be down here creating some kind of Forge Eden?"

"It wasn't like that."

"It sounds like it to me. Wake the Hand. I've had enough already."

"You said you needed another four days at least."

"I'm done. This is ridiculous. I can't even tell what the hell it is I'm standing on. One minute it's like leather, the next like bone. I'd swear it changes but I've never seen it do so, and if there is a written language here, then it's tactile and I don't have the gear. Wake the Hand." Anger felt good as it cleared her head. It sounded like she was demanding and not pleading.

"Zephyr, just think this through. I brought Kincaid along so that he could die where he was happy, and not in artificial sleep in a stowage bay in the Belt where the fucking Unevolved would have him die, like he was a goddamned machine shoved into the garage to rot. He built Mars. He put water on the Moon. You lot didn't even give him a fucking pension or a prize. Switch down to sleep, wait for the next job—when you know there will be no next job."

Zephyr felt her temper snap. "You know as well as I do that any chance you might have had for getting this place handed to you without interference has just gone out the window. Send the Hand. I'm going back."

Isol paused and the Abacand hissed faintly with the sound of the empty radio band. "No," she said. "You need time to think over what you're saying. What it means to us."

Zephyr snorted. "You should have thought of that before blasting off your mouth and your gun. Isol, you shot him! And you accuse *me* . . . Take me back right now and I won't tell them about him. You can take him back, along with whatever other Forged are in on this, and you can pretend it didn't happen. You won't get Zia Di Notte, or wherever this is, but you won't get . . . whatever they do to criminals like you."

The Voyager's voice was calm when she replied. "Think it over, Professor Duquesne. Think it over very carefully. Don't worry how long it takes. Remember, we've got forever, if needs be."

Zephyr was stunned to silence, but when she tried thumbing the communicator again it received no handshake response. Isol had switched her off. She stared at it, not quite believing the extent of the threat. Of course, Isol could keep her here as long as she liked and Earth would never know unless one day Zephyr got back to tell them. She had supplies for a week, no more. Let her get hungry and desperate enough, and for sure she'd say anything Isol wanted her to in order to get back.

"Bastards!" she shouted and lashed out at the wall with her fist.

Its material gave under her hand. The impact still hurt, but she didn't break anything. She poked the wall tentatively in surprise, but now it was stonelike once more. She risked another punch and it bent away, spongy and yielding like a tough bit of fungus. She prodded it, tapped it with a stone; it was hard again.

"What d'you make of that?" Zephyr asked the Abacand, quite meekly, grateful for something else to think about rather than what had just happened with Isol and the Finger.

"The substance of the 'stone' reacts to . . ." It paused. "Well, it reacts to something. We'll have to try further tests."

"The *stone* reacts?"

"Clearly it's not stone, of course," the Abacand said. "Although, according to its crystalline composition and granular— you know, it *is* a stone. Even when it flows, it obeys the expected physical laws for stone, with the exception that it takes place within a time-frame that is unfeasibly short. It didn't allow you to hurt yourself. That's most complex."

"No kidding." She walked slowly away and back down the ramp, listening out for any noises from the dead body. But there were none. The Roach appeared in the gateway, and then vanished into the shadows along the road.

"And you can get lost!" Zephyr yelled after it, wishing she had something to throw, but there was only the Abacand nearby. "I guess that's in the record," she added a moment later, full of chagrin and the residue of terror. She opened her ongoing letter to Kalu/Anthony/whoever and added to it:

"I am now stranded here until I sign the declaration of free claim, by the way. It's a short story that boils down to me losing my temper when I found out she'd already shipped in some old duffers to soften the place up prior to my arrival. God knows what they've taken or changed. One of them tried to tell me something and she shot his finger off. And she's supposed to be the virtuous one? Ways and means, ways and means. And I am so mad at myself for being stupid. Aaaaagh!"

She walked around the arch and took a picture of Kincaid's Finger for the official records, and then looked him up in the Abacand's *Who's Who*.

"Gaiaform Asevenday Kincaid," the Abacand said in a rush, grateful to be of service instead of being shot or eaten, as it had suspected it might be on this jaunt. "Nicknamed 'Grip' because of being a busybody—that was during the Mars days—and a child of Tupac's predecessor, the semi-sentient Pangenesis Eve. Construction completed the nineteenth day of April 2489. Terraformed the Lunar hydro and then underwent a significant scalar increase to work on Mars, until ten years ago when he went into Dormancy, awaiting a further contract. The *Who's Who* thinks he's still there."

"What're the particulars on Asevenday classtypes?" Zephyr asked, keeping an eye on the still-smoking body of the Finger, and the stream of slow-running sticky goo that was oozing from beneath it and moving towards the street's gutter.

"Asevenday . . ." The Abacand hummed a tune as it riffled through internal data. "Blimey. Starts out self-adapted for major geology reformations—your mountains, plains and seas job— then redirects himself towards the introduction and development of fundamental plant life. Phytogenetic tracts capable of gene sequencing from all known plant and some small-animal genes. Internal development up to adult stages on all forms; Feet, Fingers and Toes develop soil by crushing rock and admixing with silts, clays and minerals, before introducing classic cocktails of bacteria, fungi et cetera and mulching with its own dead skin and excreta to produce viable medium for continued plant growth."

"Okay." Zephyr stopped it with a light touch of her fingertip. "Does it have any personal history on him?"

"Kincaid is the only Asevenday still in existence," the

Abacand said, hesitantly, with a sudden sense of its own mortality. "The others all underwent voluntary decommissioning—" it paused again, "—or were killed at work, during the Mars development, by the bombs of the *Übermenschen Resistance*. There were only four ever developed. Yggdrasil, Two Ravens and Shang Di were the other three. Shang Di's body was developed into the Memorial Gardens at—"

"About Kincaid," Zephyr reminded it. She sat down on her folding chair again, feeling she ought to do something about the Finger, but not knowing what.

"Yes. Kincaid went into Dormancy after the completion of Mars. He wanted to join the Titan collective, but was unable to take up the adaptations required for ultra-cold—too old, basically. His design wasn't capable of reformation to that degree. He lodged a complaint and a request for further work but had to go to Dormancy because inactivity was making him sick. He wouldn't decommission himself because he believed it was state-legislated suicide—he and Two Ravens had fallen out over that one some years before and weren't on speaking terms—and he refused downgrading to Earth or Martian maintenance corps. So they let him hibernate. Doesn't cost much and, since there was no prospect of him getting work this side of the third millennium, it was as easy as any other solution. Now and again his lawyers try pressing for a contract to be re-established, but there's no suitable land base or call for it. He was supposed to get part of the Brazilian reforestation but by then there were already forty-five Herculeans without work who were Earth-resident, so that didn't happen."

"Hell," Zephyr said, because Kincaid's life sounded like it had come to just that. She looked at the crashed head of the Finger, cracked lenses dark over its eyes. "And now he's here. Doing what?" She picked up the Abacand and took it across to the body, moving it so that its cameras could track the shape and length. "Can you tell what adaptation this is?"

"Oh, definitely soil-making," the Abacand said. "Just look at the culture-weed in its skirts."

That would be the string-stuff, then.

"Do you have an analysis of what the legal position might be now that this place is contaminated and the Forged have already moved in?" she asked.

"No," the Abacand said, after a moment's delay in which she felt it vibrate hesitantly to express uncertainty. "But in my opinion the case for claiming such a planet *at all* is extremely irregular, possibly immoral."

"Yeah." Zephyr glanced around, looking for the Roach. She had no doubt it was hiding, being its mistress's eyes and ears.

Cloud shadows skated across her and darkened the street, making it look as though people were all around but had just darted into the alleys and houses off the road. A few drops of rain scattered on the ground and fell hissing onto the Finger's head, where they boiled and vanished on the heat of its internal breakdown.

Zephyr went into her room and made another check on all her supplies. She thought she could last a week. This was all the time that was left to her now, in which, for her own curiosity even if it never served another purpose, she could attempt to discover more about this bizarre place. There'd be no Moons trip, no fly-overs, no island-hopping, no conventions, and possibly no out. She would have to manage all by herself.

She took a deep breath and stretched out her tired shoulders, feeling an ache from the absent harness. Necessity was freedom of a kind, she supposed. Freedom from any obligation, really. She could go on a trip, try to find this Forged and what he knew, write home, fill her time. Without delay, Zephyr began to pack.

24. QUICKENING

Beneath the Hive a sound rose from the empty Moon. Secta Trini, cushioned in her cell, heard it at the same moment as her sisters, and knew what it was: the sound of every door opening and closing. It came through the heavy structure like a sigh in metal. Their trance ended involuntarily.

Alone they shivered and each pressed to the wall of her cell, where the faint movements of a sister could be felt. Trini saw the trance begin again, seeing the whole arena of the explored Moon open in her mind's eye, her own mapped regions connecting with Dwi's and Ch'twari's and the thousand other sister-maps into a complete model. At its heart sat a void a hundred kilometres across, with a single entrance and exit the size of four macro-Ticktocks. Trained on this arena, an impressive array of unknown machines was briefly picted so that they seemed visible in three dimensions through the walls of the composite map. The Hive studied them more closely now.

However, they were going to ignore the sound. The Queen demanded work.

"Perhaps it's only a regular systems check?" Trini put into the sub-conversation they were having about the sound. Many agreed with her. Others demurred. *They know we're here. They're going to return. The power systems have been disrupted by our attempts to rig the lights. We've misunderstood the layouts of the circuits. We activated more than we intended.*

The machine picts broke down into arrays of circuits and diagrams. Trini was allocated a section to analyse. She saw the Bilestri Convergence written in it, integrations and iterations that were familiar, some that were not. She worked hard to understand it, but it was difficult because the sub-conversation of the sisters ran on and they were listening for the Moon to do another thing—though it did nothing and all they could hear were its vast silences and the inert sounds of metal moving, chiming, clanging, resonating in a meaningless chaos of song where the solar wind struck and beat at it relentlessly, hour after hour and second by second, so that its pattern became mixed up with the blueprints of the machines in a chaotic dance, and every time Trini thought she had deciphered the logic she found a contradiction to confuse her.

Time passed and nobody had finished their chore, let alone shed light on one another's problems or linked to another's insight. The Queen ordered them to exchange what they had learned so far. There was sudden silence, and in the seconds of cold time each one of them was utterly alone, their silence darkness, the darkness freezing, the cold crushing, the pressure threatening to crack their shells and burst their brains and splinter their neural concord and destroy them completely, because to be isolated and alone was to be extinguished and they felt this, each herself, and were paralysed by fear.

Then they all saw a tiny flicker of distant light, felt the breath of a warm summer and heard an imperative summon them towards the faint hope of reunion.

Trini heard the Queen speak to her, from a distance, without even realizing that she herself had begun to rush towards the welcoming light.

"Hold hard!" The chemicals of the Queen's voice were intense and they flooded Trini with love and goodwill and the impossibility of disobedience. With a wrench that hurt her in every cell, she looked away from the seductive beacon.

The Hive plunged itself into a deep trance, and the awful moment was gone.

"Let's not look into our discoveries with such personal attention," the Queen suggested, but without commenting on what had just occurred. "Instead we shall divide ourselves into larger work units and take a single machine at a time. We shall have smaller tasks, and none of us shall look that closely. We shall not engage with it fully until this incident has been understood."

Trini looked at her new work allocation with mistrust. She

felt odd, displaced, as though more had happened in that icy second than she'd known about—as if she hadn't been in the same universe then, but somewhere else, or between places, out of existence, her isolation complete; in a place where nobody had ever been before nor would be since, without a name but not without coordinates. She would never be able to know *where* it was, but the knowledge *that* it existed had dislodged something that even the Queen's grace could not restore. The limits of Trini's world had become unreal, suspect. She wasn't certain of anything. She looked at the diagrammatic and saw the calculus within its structure, simple enough, but she couldn't say now whether the calculus was reliable. Maybe it was only a trick that worked for *most* of the time, where human understanding had rendered it *a priori* when it was only contingent, hiding a darker truth, a bigger view, an undreamed-of vastness right under the numb touch of her antennae.

She shrank from the task and reached out to either side of her; where Dwi was huddled in a cell solution that suddenly tasted foul, where Eka was crouched, running through a list of ancient Viking runes she'd learned while in the egg. Their signals were weak and then, sullied and frightened by this effect smothering all her children, the Queen became still and quiet. Trini lost her sense of the Hive. She could hear a scatter of voices, isolated women coming and going, the taste of their own deaths in their mouths. She wanted to join and master this knowledge herself, because to master it would be to escape its power, but she dared not in case it meant a return to those empty spaces.

Above the Moon's witless chitter, the Hive's organized hum disintegrated and echoed the metal's slow agonies. They did not venture forth again that day, nor the next, nor the next, and the quiet grew as the hum became an insensible murmur of random signalling: birdsong.

Trini sang her own tune, composed of the whistle of a steam train and the throbbing tones of a Wurlitzer organ. She heard it echo far off, among the thousands of polluted cells. Deformed a billion times by the sisters' mindless iteration, it returned to mock her. She listened and heard the Queen calling for the Voyager's help, trying to ask Isol why she did not respond.

Not respond?

Trini experienced the fear surge of the Hive as a plunging sensation, a shriek on the ends of her nerves. She tried to shut herself off from it and tasted and smelled the dark opiate of Dormancy serum suddenly infusing her bath. Her terror faded and became dull, like a dusty mirror. She heard the Queen telling her they would wait here, for help would certainly come. She fought the drugs, because she couldn't stand the idea of that empty darkness, but it came over her anyway.

Trini woke up to a foul taste, a bitter smell like rubber burning, and a feeling she couldn't describe except that she had never had it before and it was the most horrible, awful feeling: the snap of the last living twig in existence.

The others were dead. Where they had once been inside her mind, silence reigned. The Dormancy trope was still strong, weighing her down, but now it was tainted with the acrid and sulphurous flavour of Kamikazine, the neurochemical secreted by the Queen to kill them all rather than risk whatever terror or security failure she had foreseen.

Within her own body Trini felt process and function beginning to weep, bleed and decay in the first stages of liquefaction. She was half-blind and moved weakly, in fits, as her nervous system juddered. But despite her instinct to stay here and accept her fate, a stronger imperative of which she couldn't have believed herself capable moved her antennae towards the door control of the cell. It was curious in its painful resistance. Where had it come from, this enormous willpower? She was baffled even as she suffered under the opposing forces of her chemical death and this ferocious desire.

She thrashed feebly in the poisoned gel—a spasm of pure electrical confusion as her MekTek components began to short—and her contortions brought her nearer to the controls. She touched the sensor and immediately the cell began to drain.

As the thick fluid ebbed it left Trini coated in mucus, which began to react suddenly with the influx of air, the Kamikazine evaporating quickly out of it and oxygen flooding in so that her spiracles, gummed up, nonetheless kicked feebly at her failing metabolism. The pure mechanics of her exoskeleton were all that kept her upright as the controls in her legs each registered the sudden increase of weight and auto-corrected themselves, their sub-processors functioning in lieu of her brain, which was still, for any useful purpose, offlined.

Trini floundered in sickness and silence. Panic at these two states only increased the speed of her recovery. She vomited and expelled gel and a thin autoimmune fluid from her mouth and other orifices. Cleared of the chemical trance, and in total radio silence, she stood on the threshold of her tiny home and saw around her the massed, orderly ranks of the Comb darkened and quiet where there had been light, a body here and there twitching in the final, unconscious throes. Even now the movements were small and in the time that she stood there, the last of them ceased and was still. The Queen's dome, so light and full of vigour, was blackened, its security shell fused into position. Only the emergency lights glowed, their witness not the long and silent vigil it ought to have been because she, Trini, had disobeyed.

"I didn't do it!" she cried out, without thinking, in apology and fear, faced with the unthinkable. Beside her Dwi floated, her eyes open beneath their shield lenses of polycarbonate, gazing at her, through her, with frustration and disappointment. But the sound of her own cry only made Trini much more aware of her isolation.

"Where are you?" she shouted then, looking around her for the cause of her defection. She tried to remember what the final insight had been in their meditation upon the Moon's odd patterns, but nothing coherent came to her. If the Queen had had a vision, it hadn't even got as far as Trini before the Kamikazine had found her.

The answer came firmly from the core of her being: there was nobody here but her.

Trini cowered there a time longer, how long she didn't know, until she noticed a change between the automatic terror of a lost drone and the slow rise of a new peptide inside her blood, where it caused enzymes and proteins to change their regular progress and begin new tasks. At first she felt her terror ebb. Her front legs stepped into the corridor. She expanded her body and the air suddenly felt cleaner. With her forelimbs she touched the door and the control panel, and then she could feel the first stirrings of Comb Awareness as her synaptic processors switched themselves to tune with the semi-sentient AI system of their ship. She walked into the corridor and along the access way, paying a moment's respect to her sisters as she bowed her head there; and then she arose, and although she was full of misgiving she was not in any doubt now that what was happening was unprecedented but possible. Trini was becoming Queen.

She cued the hatch leading to the Moon's interior. Within it she heard several doors and other simple servos sigh into motion: a bend of their knee to her arrival. With that thought she realized what had happened. This was the insight of the old Queen—the Moon was not so much discovered by us as it was *made*, and here it is, starting to talk.

But this conclusion had been too much for the Hive's comprehension and the minds of the individual drone sisters had individually experienced a fatal collision of theory and concept, hope and intent. Only one mind could support and be supported by this process. The Queen had tried to assimilate the entire Hive in trance, but she hadn't been able to synthesize them all, because the ideas they had seen as individuals were incapable of being brought into true fusion, so she had killed them rather than risk the chaos. She had killed them because she feared the conclusion, and what it could mean for those who might later find out—or for those who might see Earth now through her eyes. The only part of the Hive Cherisse's decision that had reached Trini was the imperative to act, and so she had done the only thing that was doable in the circumstances, and saved herself.

Now a single drone, who was slowly taking on the attributes of Queen, she and the Moon were ready for each other. Without the Hive's panic, distant from home, she saw no reason not to proceed.

Trini signalled Isol. A faint, stuttering answer came, distorted by space-time confusions that ought not to have been in its way, and she knew fear again, as if the Moon itself were not enough to be afraid of. Finally the Voyager answered, and Trini heard the hiss of her outrage and surprise at the news of the Hive's fortune.

"But who is this?" Isol demanded, already changing her orbital course around the planet to bring her closer to the Moon.

"This is Cherisse Trini, the third sister of the renegade Ticktock Hive Cherisse," Trini said. "I am . . ." She paused. She had never said or entertained the concept of being an individual before, not in this way. "I am the only survivor. Do not approach the Moon or the Comb. The defence system is still engaged." She could see the Voyager now through the Comb's senses, a pinprick of reflected light between the blue and white bulk of the old world and its yellow-orange star. Before this moment she had never noticed others, she realized. Nobody outside the Hive had been important.

"You are ordering me?"

This anger and outrage was expected. The old Queen had agreed with Isol that they should break cleanly with the old order, and be allies here in this new place.

Trini cut her off simply. "This is too important not to. You must feel some of this yourself, although you deny it. There is much danger in contact with this technology. I will work alone here to understand it, and then we'll decide what to tell Earth."

She had never opposed another's views before. The surge of strength she felt made her tap her pointed leg-tips against the Moon's floor and walls with a burst of combined anxiety and resolve. Some bit of machinery deep in the Moon's guts whirled on its gyroscopes:

Chamber Five, Orientation Incoming . . .

Trini soothed the Comb and the distant unsettling of the alien Moon's response to her with a flare of calming chemicals—*this is a neutral approach, so far, so hold your defences.* She sent Isol a datablast of what was occurring.

"You have *control* of this thing? What is it?"

"I don't have control. I have . . . a two-way understanding. I don't know how far I can push it. I think this Moon is part of a defensive system. Don't come any nearer until I'm sure. I don't know why it listens to me. I think it must at least be something like . . ." She paused, prompted now to consult automatically with her daughters—but having none.

"Like what?" The Voyager spun and effortlessly made the glide into another easy orbital position. Trini had time to envy her grace and agility, her power.

"Like us. Made, but aware."

"We are *people*," Isol retorted stiffly, "made or born. Not sentient machines. Not AI like some ridiculous Abacand."

"But this is your political stance," Trini said. "From a Ticktock point of view, machinery is exactly what we are, what humanity is, what all life has ever been. The millions of Abacands and related machines are—"

"Yeah, yeah," Isol said. "Are you telling me that you've changed position now? Do you want to go back to the Hegemony of Apes all of a sudden?"

"Of course not," Trini said. "But you should know better than to try and mince physical facts with a Ticktock. Wasn't it you who said 'We must get inside the dialogues of our own minds to discover the one true voice'? I thought you looked beyond our manner to the common purpose of our liberation."

Isol made a rude blurt of chaotic sound. "There's nothing like having your own old rhetoric chucked at you," she said, but she sounded chastened. "It's all going far different than I thought, anyway," she added—mostly to herself, Trini thought. "Bloody Kincaid is going mad. He keeps telling me the planet is barren just to please him, to give him work. That I brought him here because it wanted him. He plants the crop and it eats the crop. Every day the first day of work—paradise. Masochistic moron. Bara's as bad."

"Perhaps you did as he says," Trini said. "Isn't it possible there may have been impulses working inside you beyond your own?" She looked along the way in front of her and the map of the ducts that her sisters had created spun in her mind. Endless rows and regions of new circuitry, new paradoxes, new puzzles, new thoughts all set down in metal and forms of intricate, alchemical design. In its way this could be a Ticktock's playground, if she wasn't scared to face its challenge.

"But what happens when the bastard runs out of seeds?" Isol said, curving her way into a faster track around to the nightside, keeping her eye on the two giant Gaiaforms. To Trini's question she made no response.

"What does the government inspector say?" Trini asked.

"Her! She hasn't found a single scrap of evidence to back up the claim they'd like to make that this place is still someone else's property. Five days to go. But she's met Kincaid, thanks to his nosiness. It's all to hell. They're going to come and take us back forcibly, I know it."

"And your plan?"

There was a pause. "Revolution always comes to this," Isol said, and cut the link.

The Moon reacted to the news of an invasionary force with admirable calm, Trini thought. It ran a fast, simple diagnostic check on itself, and then went silent again. Whatever it was designed to do, it all still worked. The only problem Trini now had was that she didn't know which of the two forces it was worried about: the Forged coming to enforce the claim, or the government coming to drag them back to Gaiasol. Perhaps both.

Or another?

She hadn't considered the possibility of anyone other than themselves being in on this. Were there more races interested in this place? Were the original creators intent on return? Perhaps only a Ticktock could appreciate the true depths of the unknown parameters in the calculations that surrounded this situation. An unexpected arrival was, in fact, a strong probability now that she factored in Kincaid's reported response to the planet, and the investigator's most likely determination—that they should never have interfered in this way with an unknown system. That would prompt immediate action by the Earth militia, and then they would fight it out. Isol's plan of equipping only the rebels with her galaxy-crossing technology could not hold, if it ever had.

Slowly Trini moved into the Moon's crust and opened a section of the wall beside her. There were no access plates as such, but pieces were modular, they could be taken down and restored. The wall itself was a smooth structure, but if she rested her electron-sensitive fingers against it, she could, theoretically, connect herself with all the structures in the Moon's entire system. A faint tingling ran through her arm.

She was sure of it then. The place "sort of" recognized her. There was something about *her* that was sufficiently like something about its masters to which it responded. And it had felt the same way about the Hive, although for a drone, as she had been then, it was a far lesser response. Isol had claimed the aliens from here had been Forged, although Trini's Queen hadn't taken that at face value. But this knowledge must be important, surely? Vital, perhaps, to understanding where and when the aliens had gone, and why. Trini thought these questions must be answered before Isol could bring settlers here. Otherwise, who knew what lay just around the corner? This Moon had not been made on a whim. Its cost must have been tremendous.

But then a sudden thought made Trini snatch her hand away.

Something about herself.

The Queen had killed them all to prevent a catastrophe. Suppose the catastrophe had happened anyway? Suppose that the place had changed them and made them more like its own inhabitants? What if she *hadn't* been like them, but *now* she was, and this was why she had survived?

She listened to the Moon's ordinary sounds, its cacophony of insensible, meaningless noise. *The will to live,* she thought, *in our kind, isn't an individual will. But here I am.* Made not born, form fitted to function, function required, and here was a purpose, all this to decipher. The fields of heaven. Maybe.

And Trini sat and composed all her six legs, her four arms, her antennae, and closed her eyes, shielding them from all light and wavelengths. She sat for an hour and ten minutes, and then she got up and began to make her way down towards the enormous chambers in the Moon's core.

25. TOM WHO BUILT THE AEROPLANE

Arrecife Station had once been used as a storage dump for long-life cargo and trading excesses held as interim stores by the various Customs authorities within the Solar System. It occupied a similar orbit around Sol to that of Earth, but on the opposite side of the star, so that Earth and itself were forever blind to each other. In recent days it had undergone a hasty refit of its only habitable spar, and had swallowed enough of the most high-tech scientific equipment to fund a serious takeover of any of the system's corporate R&Ds. This development was secret however, and the wealth of its power was given over solely to TwoPi, the most numerous and advanced of the Hives, and to Arachno Buckminster Mouze, a physicist—if such a term could encompass as many spheres of hard science as could be imagined.

Now it was also home to Corvax. He sat uneasily in his allotted place despite the fragile gravity—between the arachnoid Mouze and an insect nation in the form of the Lab Hive TwoPi— a dewinged bird with some vague pretensions to orangutan-hood, his bony legs and arms folded up around him and his heavy head brooding low on his shoulders. The stubs of his wings itched furiously but he welcomed the annoyance they caused: it sharpened his mind to a point.

Mouze, returned just an hour since from the Earth Debate, had not emerged from his apartment yet. TwoPi was deep in trance. Corvax had detached from her, unable to stand the complexity and speed of her calculations any longer, despite it all being secondhand and his own synapses merely observing instead of participating. A residual thought-ache echoed against the confines of his skull. What TwoPi had observed needed to be translated into a linear form more simple to comprehend and he was almost there . . .

The station AI broke his train of thought. "Ironhorse Morningstar Dao approaches. Strategos Anthony requests a meeting at your immediate convenience."

The Morningstar was a military transport, fast, light and armed. There were few of them in existence, and Corvax knew that Dao was an old guard and the only one to have seen active service. With people like Dog Legba about, a person of Anthony's standing would have need to use the services of someone like Dao out here. Not that Legba was going to cause any trouble for a while, Corvax was confident, although he had been half expecting a raid on the station ever since he'd been there. Maybe the slight exaggeration in the propaganda about Stuff had put them off. Poor old Mouze had narrowly escaped a lynching, to hear him tell it, and now the Vote was under count and polling was due to close in an hour.

The Morningstar was the first of several Gaiasol security personnel to arrive. Close on its heels, from various odd stealth vectors, came a Tomahawk Dragonstar, a Shuriken Arrowhead, and the only living Shuriken Death-Angel, whose name and class wasn't even listed on any *Who's Who* Corvax had ever seen. It showed up on the station long-range cameras as a blur that would not resolve, although it chose to identify itself to the station AI with promptness and courtesy. The AI permitted the Morningstar to dock and Corvax thought about making some kind of preparation for Anthony's visit, but after attempting to align a few feathers he stopped. He'd always hidden within his wings and now it was pointless to try and appear anything except what he was—wrecked and naked.

Mouze skittered out of his door and into position, ready to make all the formalities. He was fast for a sedentary worker, Corvax thought. Skinny because he'd rather work than eat or rest. Come to think of it, none of them looked good.

The Strategos completed the set when he came striding in. The mag boots looked clumsy on him as he clomped along, and his face beneath its copper filigree was ashen and corpselike, with the typical pallor of someone surviving on various drugs and tonics instead of on real food and sleep. Mouze followed him and hopped into his most comfortable position, atop the warm outlets of one of the Hive's heat exchangers, which served double function to keep the place at five degrees Centigrade: cold for the Arachno, sweltering to Corvax and brisk for the Strategos himself. Anthony's breath rasped steadily inside the clear headguard of his pressure suit as he glanced around at the jumble of machines, the majority of them various AI devices that might well have been a match for what he carried around in his own body. Corvax nodded to him.

"I came as fast as I could," the Strategos said, staring at the long wall where cells of the Hive were stacked to the roof, their hexagonal plates glowing dully and showing a hint of grub-body here and there. "I understand there's been a breakthrough."

Mouze cocked his head in a characteristic sideways slant, and lifted his hands to illustrate his words with precise movements that sometimes made sense in mute-speak and occasionally made no sense at all. "It is probably easier if TwoPi shows you herself." He jabbed a pointed finger at his head to indicate that Anthony was free to plug into TwoPi's frequency and load direct, if his AI suite was up to it.

Anthony glanced at Corvax. "Your thoughts?"

Corvax ground the lower edge of his beak against the upper. His mouth was dry. "This Stuff is more than a technology. It's like a technology that's eaten people and they're still alive inside it, but they're all one, or none, or else . . . it reacts to the observer." He was aware of how incoherent he sounded but it matched the feeling he had. He shrugged but only his wing-stubs moved up and down, like silly little play-hands. "Look for yourself."

The Strategos stood rigidly upright, and his face froze over as if with winter ice. Along his scalp, between the obvious copper lines, sudden fresh tributaries of red light darted and flashed to life beneath the skin. Within their cells the Hive shifted in eager curiosity at the contact.

Corvax shuddered. It was one thing to have an exceptional mind, another to be nothing *but* such a mind, with its furious pace and constant chatter. He was as revolted and fascinated by it as anything he'd ever encountered. One thing he would never have asked to be was *that,* and having said that, he rather liked TwoPi. She had a sense of humour, and no ridiculous avatars to throw around in games of pretend. She was straight.

Mouze glanced at Corvax but they didn't need to say anything. The Strategos could be treated as an equal. He was at least that.

When the fusion was done, the three of them sat down and nobody spoke for a time, Anthony nodding now and again as he gazed inwardly on the Hive's curious vision.

"Where is the sample?" he asked finally.

"It's in the tunnelling microscope," Mouze said.

"Looking at it this way is no good." Anthony crossed his legs stiffly and rested his heavy helm against the wall beside him. "We need to do some real tests on it, see what it does."

Corvax tried not to fidget. He hadn't told them about Tatresi but he was thinking that Tatresi probably had all the answers by now, damn him, and was still prepared to go right on pretending. That blue floor-cleaner boy should be here taking this on, not him. Even so, after his encounter with Tatresi's engine, and in spite of what it had done to save him, he was reluctant to touch Stuff again.

"I don't think that's a good idea," he said.

"You have knowledge to share?" Despite his casual pose the Strategos's eyes were keen as he stared at Corvax. "Or is this just your fear?"

Corvax thought about Xing and the knives. Maybe they'd got the pony to talk, to tell them everything he'd omitted to mention, or hadn't seen, and they were only toying with him before they decided he wasn't going to volunteer. There was no telling what Anthony knew. He recalled the fragment of time and sensation he'd had as the Stuff had left his hand.

"There have been two incidents," he began and slowly related to them everything he could remember, only omitting Tatresi's name from the account. They might as well find Xing and her crew, then ask the Dog what he thought had happened, for all the good that would do. They weren't going to exact any revenges now.

As he spoke he saw the Strategos move his head and the Shuriken Arrowhead's dagger profile turned and set off Belt-wards, no doubt to do exactly that.

Mouze tapped one of his forelegs on the rim of the radiator during the silence that followed Corvax's story and then said, "It seems to me there are two separate avenues here that may be investigated. First of all there is the question of how this substance does what it does, apparently defying our known physical laws. Secondly, there is the question of why it appears to interact with us and what the reasons for that may be. I believe these may be tackled alone. I'll explore the first, if I may bring in the Gaiasol science primary AI and a group of academics from the system. I suggest that TwoPi and Corvax are better suited to the second. Corvax's relationship with Uluru in particular . . ." He hesitated, not sure of what he could really say to the MekTek Strategos.

Anthony nodded. "Your recommendation?" He looked at Corvax and if he thought anything of the illegal developments in the Dreamtime, or knew of its new ability to react to unconscious impulses creatively, he said nothing.

"I think these two things are really the same thing, but I can see your point," Corvax said. "It's like TwoPi tried to say. What is and what seems to be are identical, but the surface and the underlying nature are not. At least, I think that's what she meant. But if our reality is the surface, then the real action has to be taking place somewhere else that we don't see. And I can think of only one place."

"Yes." Mouze drummed his feet in anticipation. "Seven-D."

"The hidden dimensions are only mathematical descriptions of theoretical spaces," Anthony said, voice gravelly with too much talking over too short a time. "Progressions towards M-Theory suggest that at least two of these membranes are real, but the others are negligible for any tests we have ever done. We have no way of looking for them except for the fact that equations suggest things are vanishing into areas we cannot perceive in any way."

"Ordinary humans using ordinary human technology cannot see them," Mouze agreed, "but we need to think in a different way. Let us pretend that it is the case that this substance is a four-dimensional manifestation of a greater artefact that also exists in the other seven membranes: an iceberg situation. Our only access to what it does there is for us to feed it a stimulus and witness the results here. But that explains nothing, except perhaps the basic motivating force that causes it to act. We know that it will form itself into structures that we also do not understand, yet which appear to function. Therefore the design of these structures is not coming from us, but from it. Only the *purpose* of the structure is drawn from us, by some means we also do not understand. And finally we also know that we can conjoin, in the manner of Forging, with this substance and be affected by its operations, like any other matter. So, for the sake of a quick study, and in spite of the obvious danger, I suggest that we divine ourselves a technology for positive interaction with Eleven-D."

Corvax watched the spidery form with a heavy heart. He'd only ever thought of simulating situations in the Dreamtime for himself, not even wanting to think about the chances of future real-world interactions. But the obvious solution was to ask the magic bunny to produce a nonexistent technology out of its invisible hat. Of course.

"We could just ask," he added after another thought. "We could imagine a person who talks, made of Stuff, who could answer."

"This too." The Strategos sighed and shuffled uncomfortably in his suit. He laughed quietly. "It's like playing a game, like being children—but we never expected the wizard to answer."

"It may not answer," Mouze observed. "Corvax carried it around quite a long time, and it remained inert."

"As far as I know," Corvax said, flexing his hands unwillingly as they tingled with the memory of the quartz pebble. "You know, this looks like a contact technology to me. Them leaving it where they did and its method of working. It's like an open invitation that waits for you to make the obvious jump. Just don't know to what."

"If the Voyager knows, then that may explain her choice of world and her urgency," the Strategos said. "She's been exposed to it the longest, and she's become intimately connected to it. So far it hasn't exceeded her expectations, as far as we know."

"Something happened," Corvax interrupted him, not able to keep it to himself any longer, "when it became the wasp-blades." He saw them both still and silent, fixated on his words, and felt suddenly like a cheap act. "I felt—I don't know, maybe that's why I can't express it—there was a kind of a crossing, a moment when I think that *I* was Shinjuku Library and *it* was the painting, yet also that we were one thing."

"We must assume, then, that it knows everything that you know, or that anybody knows who has had contact with it—as much as that may make sense or not," Anthony said, signalling in fast-data mode that he was prepared to accept any analysis as plausible in the circumstances for the time being. "It's therefore pointless to try and move it all out of system, but it still has to stay under regulated quarantine." He turned to look at Corvax. "I'll have the name of that other ship now, by the way."

"If they feel very threatened," Corvax said, "and they understand how to use Stuff, then it may not matter what you try to do to them."

"That can be my concern. I get the picture." Anthony grinned humourlessly.

Corvax sighed. He knew there was no other choice, but it was hard to reveal it and break faith with the rest of the Independence Forged and his own moral code, sketchy as that was. "Tatresi."

"And no others?"

"Not to my knowledge, though I guess there's nothing to stop them."

"Then get on with it." The Strategos stood up and nodded curtly towards Mouze. He turned on his heel and marched out as fast as the mag boots would let him move across the floor.

Within a minute he and Ironhorse Morningstar Dao had peeled away from the station and become only a dot of light.

The Shuriken Death-Angel did not move from its position twenty kilometres out. Corvax then realized who it was waiting for. Despite the heat, a penetrating chill ran through his fragile bones.

Mouze, also shivering atop the heater unit, wasn't in any great rush to start either. Their private thoughts were both interrupted then by the gentle voice of TwoPi, issuing politely from the lab speakers that she controlled with the assistance of the AI.

"Gentlemen," she said. "There is a further problem that you have noticed but not really embraced. It's central to the situation."

Guiltily Corvax realized that she had been present all the time, but that they had spoken of her as though she weren't there or was asleep, mostly because she had no distinctive form as a single entity. Even the Strategos had not acknowledged her, although she was the best mind of any of them. He shuffled around to face the wall where many of her bodies lay, and Mouze also made himself attentive.

"Despite our physical differences," she said, "we have human minds. Not necessarily all the same, nor even structured the same way mechanically, biologically, but in our identities and the very design of our consciousness we are all bound in the human mould. Even those of us with enhanced intellect, or greater memory, or superior sensitivity to all kinds of stimuli both within and without, are not significantly different from this fundamental paradigm. We have evolved ourselves in many physical ways, but we have not made much progress in this part of ourselves over the last ten thousand years.

"Our lives are short and we search for meaning. When we find none, we create it. If we agree with each other, our meanings become a dogma, and when we disagree then we become enemies and fight, or sit at a distance in an attempt at tolerance. It is the rare person who can stand aside and observe that our minds and identities are largely constructs of our social order, that we are abstract and arbitrary collections of ideas that resemble dusty archives in the galleries of a museum, visited by nobody, and maintained by a series of those insensible robots that are our habits. We live by our own agreement inside these miserable prisons that are our selves, and suffer the results as the Forged who believe in the doctrine of Form and Function now suffer, as the Unevolved who believe they are lesser beings now suffer. Our minds are full of confusion and conflicts from which we separate only with the greatest difficulty, and for short periods.

"Corvax, in your adaptation of Uluru, you have found a way to expose these inner conflicts to an outer reality, but you haven't resolved them. You don't want to be as you are, so you are blind to it.

"Mouze, in your experiments into the nature of matter, you've gone as far as you can go, without altering the edifice of modern physical theory. You don't want to be uncertain and take a risk, so you stick with the same old line and you are blind to it.

"To come to any conclusion with such limited efforts would be premature and false. We cannot do as the Strategos asks us to do, if we remain as we are now. I do not think that Stuff may be understood with minds such as ours, which will not step outside the bounds of all they have been told—and which cannot. We must have minds that are completely free for that, and even then the very alien nature of this substance may elude all explanation, although, as we have already witnessed, it will not elude observation.

"If we attempt to create anything out of Stuff, we will make only what we ourselves have already imagined. We'll see nothing of what may lie outside our imagination. We wouldn't be witnessing the alien, we'd be determining it. There's the problem."

Corvax didn't know what the emotional range of an Arachno was, but if Mouze was feeling the chagrin and disturbance that he was feeling then it was going to be damned hard to be able to do or say anything in the next five minutes. TwoPi was right, of course.

"Don't *you* have this kind of mind?" he asked her, unable to stop the resentment in his voice since he felt she had criticized them, but not herself.

"Rarely," she said. "And the next question will be, who does? The answer is that none of us do in any reliable way. But we can't do nothing, so what shall we do?"

"It seems as though you're saying we have to become something else," Mouze said. "We are Forged, so there is a potential, but you've already dismissed all current designs as erroneous."

"I don't think we can blame the blueprint," TwoPi said. "It could be that the very having of a mind at all necessitates that it form a *coherent* understanding of the world, however flawed that may be. There's no rule to say that an understanding cannot be entirely false from top to bottom. Many ideas seem to fit the facts before they are disproved. Our goal isn't to understand everything, but to understand Stuff. We guess that it is the product of people who can somehow perceive Eleven-D and we guess that it is able to understand us intuitively, perhaps telepathically, perhaps via a method we don't know. Therefore, to know it, we must become like it or we will have to just sit here on our fat asses and guess."

Corvax stared at the wall of cells. "Run that through me one more time? I thought you just said we should assimilate the sample and ask it to reformat us in the manner of a thing that resembles whoever the hell made it."

"Something of that order," she said.

"Is there some mistake in simply asking it for answers?" Mouze suggested, folding and refolding his legs uneasily.

"We're going to get the answers we expect." Corvax thought he'd finally got it and waited for TwoPi's confirmation.

"Which is no answers at all, except for those of us on a self-discovery mission," TwoPi assented. "And that is also necessary, even to begin this task. However, for the sake of efficiency and security I think it should be only one of us who undertakes this experiment."

"I'll do it," Corvax muttered. A curious change had come over him in the last few seconds. As he'd listened to her speaking and had run fractionally ahead to her conclusion, his heart had jumped with sudden energy and restlessness.

He saw in his mind's eye the desultory theatre of the marsh-land refugee camp. But this time it was the dilapidated shed containing the aeroplane that captured his attention. The old bird had never flown. Its pieces were scattered. He'd sabotaged the work a hundred times to stay with Dani and to torment Caspar, to loiter and discover the appalling and fascinating violence of the cranes. But it could fly, could have flown, if he'd ever had the courage to leave.

Mouze jumped around and stared at him. The Hive hummed audibly, each sister now focused upon him in her curiosity.

Corvax stood up wonkily, heavily, in the wretched 0.2G. "I was made for this." His beak cracked open in a difficult and unfamiliar gape, which it took him some time to recognize as an unprompted smile of delight.

Kincaid awoke. It was night. He was lying in the marshes. Beneath his skin the nursery ranks of seedlings rustled with movements of growth and respiration, comforting him briefly as he listened for the call to come again.

Above him he checked the stars and calculated how long he had slept. A while. And he did not need sleep. But there had been a lullaby, a kind of chant or murmur, not in his mind but in his bones, and it had slowed his thoughts, extended the wavelengths of his heart into the long, slow phases of sleep he'd last experienced in his Dormancy, after Mars was complete.

A systems check revealed that he was healthy. The usual minor problems of working were there. Two Hands had failed, clogged with the fine silts he'd disturbed from the river beds higher upstream, which were themselves choked with the earth run-off of a continent's abandoned soil. Countless other limbs had small faults, and repair lists awaiting. A portion of his green-housing had outdated UV protection—the sun here was very strong—and needed regrowth. He itched with the sloughing of dead cells because of the night's inactivity. Waking with him, his armies of Mites returned quickly to work, nibbling his hide and then excreting it as useful compost and fertilizer compounds, which they bonded with nitrogen from the atmosphere.

This news passed Kincaid in a moment and he ignored it. He stared accusingly at the two false Moons with their strange, regular shadows, two crescents scything the clear night sky. They said nothing to him.

Then he saw the fields around him in the fragile moonlight, the plains of water and mud. They were bare, as empty as a desert, without a root or a blade anywhere. A gentle sea wind blew in over him, quietly. The whole of his fen was gone.

A feeling like sickness and cold and the death of love crept outward from Kincaid's core to the tips of his fingers and toes. He put out his tongues and tasted that they had been there—in the soft dirt, the osmosis of fine roots had leached all available phosphates from localized areas with greedy abandon—and this confused him. He searched, stupidly, using senses that hadn't been stretched in years, to scan the distance and the cloud overhead, looking for what he knew didn't exist. The world's sudden emptiness was all the worse because whatever had reaped so thoroughly of his work had left him untouched. What for? Because he was himself alien? But the grass was such. Because it had another plan for him?

He racked his mind, but recalled nothing of the escaped hours he'd slept. No telltale noise or disturbance: no shifts of the mud, no ripples of anything in the water.

He cast about him everywhere, and there was no answer.

"Who's there?" he said and silenced himself, feeling a fool for even whispering it. *Nobody is there, you idiot. Nobody and nothing.* Had the voices taken the living things? Where? Why? Did the planet itself live, breathe and want? Was he—the largest being he'd ever known—a parasite on the face of a far larger entity that was showing its displeasure at his activity by brushing it away? Perhaps, mercifully, it let him live, to give him a chance to escape, or to see what he would do next? This world might have *eaten* its people.

He summoned Bara, and told him what had happened. Through the radio connection Bara's momentary silence made him feel the first real fear. Then Bara spoke, the ideas wrung out of him, if the hesitancy of the words was anything to judge.

"You'd better stop working. It's too soon anyway. And the investigator is here. She shouldn't see we're here. If she flew over, what would she think? You'd better hide out for now—rest."

Coming from another Gaiaform, as it did, Kincaid didn't take this as a slur. Rest was the last thing they were fit for. Inactivity created critical immune disturbances, led to breakdown and toxic build-up, anxiety, poisoning, death. "And you?"

"I have sent an Arm to the city on the west coast. She's making a base there for now. All the machines we thought we saw are ruins. The remains of other things—" he couldn't bring himself to say "people" "—have perished to such an extent there's no telling what they were."

At a level other than speech, in high-access mode, the two shared their feelings about the process and their betrayal of Earth, about Isol's cagey and glib assurances, about their doubts of her understanding of the modern age and their real position, about their own lack of knowledge of the place they had come to and what they had found. They suffered because they needed to work, but the work went nowhere no matter how hard they tried.

"Twenty kilotonnes an hour," Bara whispered at last. "I measured it out by the centilitre. Gases from ice, carbon dioxide I built, oxygen separated, hydrogen freed. I cut vast acres. I work without resting, but behind my back—I turn around and it's all there again, and in the atmosphere not one millilitre has changed in all this time. It's as though I don't exist, but here I am, all power out. I want to stop. I have stopped for a time. But how long can that last?"

"I'll bring on the nursery," Kincaid said. "I won't plant it out. It can wait a few weeks until we find out who does this."

"I've changed some Arms over to sampling ice cores," Bara acknowledged, with an unease that Kincaid felt in his own flesh. "I wondered if they might show us what happened here."

Both paused to consider the unknown world's past.

"Self-maintenance can be most absorbing," Kincaid offered.

"Especially in these winds up here," Bara agreed. "And you must have problems?"

"The silt."

"Yes."

"If we befriended this investigator, helped her out," Kincaid said, "she might speak up for us when Earth—"

"But Isol wouldn't trust us," Bara interrupted him quickly.

"She brought us here and said it would be a lifetime's work

in the service of freedom," Kincaid said, sharp and angry. "Yet all we do is sit and rot and listen to those damned voices from nowhere that she says are our imagination. She gets to flit back and forth like Queen Muck, and what does she know about it here? Nothing. She knew nothing when she brought us. She took one look and said, 'That'll do,' without understanding anything about the place. She doesn't even know if the previous inhabitants have gone, or if they're coming back. That's the trouble with the early ones, they've got no sense of proportion. It's all politics to them. They hate the Unevolved, and anything that's a poke in the eye for the Monkeys is a benefit to them. They have no minds worth connecting to."

"We're early," Bara said—meaning as colonizers—but without disagreement.

"So we are. And *old* now."

Kincaid transmitted his feelings about the life in the empty wind, the barren soil so thin, the minerals and the rocks. He told Bara about Isol shooting his Finger. "It's waiting," he said, "whatever she says. She lies all the time. I can feel her fear in every frequency she uses."

" 'It'? There is no 'it,' " Bara said with false confidence.

"Tell me you don't hear it and I'll believe you," Kincaid dared him.

Bara said, and sent, nothing.

Kincaid broke the line and lay in his silence, sinking deeper into the mud and not struggling to free himself at all. He stretched out several Fingers and checked their systems. He wasn't going to sit there and wait forever. Instead he'd stretch his hand and get back his old grip on things, a finger in every pie, just like the old days. Let this world try to stop him.

He laughed, making jets of water plume and spray suddenly out of the swampland, and shaking the clay far below him. And as for the gardens, this hell could stand more work. He could plant gardens and see what *it* would do with them. He had enough storage to plant a billion such: fountains, forests, parklands, savannahs . . . What was a marsh compared with that?

Yes, he felt better already at the thought, and he sensed his invisible tormentors agreed with him, their will a strengthening concurrence that ran alongside his own.

We'll make a contest of it, then, they said. *Show us what you can do.*

Kincaid lifted himself, and set to it.

From the Wind Tor, Zephyr looked down across Tanelorn, using her binoculars. They provided a map overlaid on the landscape for her as she scanned the city and focused her attention towards the harbour area. She thought there might be remnants of machinery there. Even if that was below the waterline, she could attempt an analysis. Anything would do—she needed a time-out from staring at the buildings without comprehension, and from trying to figure out whether the fossilized forms and microforms they contained held any more suggestion than the elusive touch of lives long gone.

She switched on the Abacand and fed it the binoculars' information. Both she and it awaited some kind of reply signal from the Gaiaforms before setting out. The journey might be far too long, and she had no idea where they were. Isol might have blocked it, for the Roach made frequent appearances. Her moment of grand action had passed and she was working hard so as not to feel deflated.

"Look there, along the beach," the Abacand said after a moment, its visual processing better than Zephyr's. It sent the location to the binoculars and she obediently adjusted her position until she was looking directly at the target.

"You're right, as usual," she said to it, humming a tune for a second of satisfaction. "What *is* that?"

Knowing she was being rhetorical, by analysing her vocal inference, the Abacand didn't answer.

Zephyr moved to maximum magnification and resolution. There was some cliff in the way of her line of vision, which made it difficult to be sure, but she thought that whatever it was had a skeletal look. Things that might have been bones showed ragged fragments hanging in the wind. They seemed to be set up high, above the tide mark. She checked her scale, not sure that it was reading right.

"How big is that thing in the front, the one that looks like a vertebra?"

"Half a metre across at the narrowest point," the Abacand said immediately.

"That's huge, even for this gravity." She dragged up her knowledge of palaeontology. "How does it factor up compared to Earth gigantiforms?"

"It would be in excess of their size. Also, as you say, excessive for this gravity."

"But if it's a fossil, what's it doing lying on the beach?"

"If I may?" the Abacand asked politely. "I have a conjecture."

"Fire away."

"There's no reason to suppose it's of this world. We're here—and we're not."

"If it really is a skeleton." But Zephyr was already stowing the binoculars in her pack and reaching out for the Abacand, which she dropped in her top pocket. Within a minute she had got the stiff sled harness over her shoulders and set off.

"Perhaps we should ask Isol if she has already scanned this—" the Abacand began.

"No," Zephyr said, getting into her stride, her breath deepening quickly. "We'll go see first, and talk about it later." She wanted to get there as fast as she could. At last there was something she could recognize and work with.

Zephyr began to breathe harder, a familiar giddiness building up as she towed the sled along one of the main drives, avoiding a crater where the surface had collapsed. She slowed to look into the holes, which gaped at her, utterly black.

"See anything down there?"

"More of the same."

"Check." She resumed her towing towards the shoreline, moving down through squares and rotundas, beneath high verandas and the tracery of bridges where a few spars were all that remained of their span, until she came to a long straight downhill stretch. Here, feeling hot and in need of light relief, she gave the sled a shove and jumped on top of her gear to ride it down.

The sled was equipped with its own steering gear that prevented it having a collision, and it ran smoothly on its six wheels. Plumes of grit whirled to either side as it banked and curved around the obstacles in its way. Zephyr had to hang on as hard as she could.

"A bit thoughtless," the Abacand observed, falling from her pocket as the sled, now a toboggan on an invisible run, swooped and juddered. Zephyr caught the cube and jammed one of its softer edges between her teeth, grabbing back on to the sled's side in time to save herself from being dumped on the stone paving.

"Do you think the stone here really is smart?" she shouted above the noise of the wind. "I was thinking it may be the lost technology we haven't been finding anywhere else."

The Abacand made an expletive sound. "You can still brake."

"Let's see what happens."

"Your anger with Isol, understandable though it is, is getting the better of you, if I might be so—"

The sled swept into line with the hill and plummeted down the steeply inclined road. Glancing at the control readout, Zephyr saw that they were approaching the existing rim rubble of the harbour wall in excess of forty kilometres per hour. There were no more stacks of rock to deflect their progress. With a curious sense of freedom, she slid her finger away from the brake button.

"It's time we tested something," she shouted to no one in particular, trying to convince herself. There was a strange glee in her. She was an Amazon hurling herself into battle in an honest fight against a visible enemy after so long spent waiting and wondering, being lied to and shuffled about by others. It was surely foolish, but she had to do it.

"You're going to die!" shrieked the Abacand. "And eventually, when my solar cells have eroded, then by extension—"

"Tell me something I don't know," she muttered through her teeth.

A horseless chariot, thundering with the sound of its hollow wheels on the minor roughs of the road, the sled skimmed eagerly towards the mountainous rocks. A spear of doubt fell and lodged in Zephyr's stomach, and then quickly another as they hurtled on unchecked. She hit the button before she thought it over. They slowed and began to slew left, in an attempt by the sled's basic programming to force a run along the quayside instead of into the obstacle. But it was far too late.

As the rubble rushed up to meet them, Zephyr flung herself sideways and fell into the road, rolling and sliding in an uncontrolled tangle of her own arms and legs. At every point she expected to strike hard edges and jagged points, to feel the ground scrape her skin off her bones and tear her suit to pieces, but she rolled on something like moss, and rebounded off rubbery masses here and there until she fetched up somehow under the sled, with its various boxes piling down around her. They had sharp corners and they *did* hurt. Off a way, she heard the Abacand railing crossly, and smelled the chemical odour of the red-hot brakes drift past her on the sea breeze.

A light sifting of breakfast cereal rained down over her head. She stuck her tongue out and retrieved a cornflake and then started laughing. Flapping her hands to the floor, she found it stony. She felt things digging into her ribs. Her leg was at a difficult angle and her muscles were complaining, but she thought her sides were going to split with the pain and exhaustion of her hilarity. Finally she managed to push the luggage off herself and sit up, checking for damage. There was none.

She got up and retrieved the Abacand. "That was one smart road."

"Variable resistance. Real-time situation assessment. Knows the breaking strain not only of your clothes, but also your skeleton, internal organs and muscle. And as I can see from here, a perfectly inert material," the Abacand said, switching through a series of modes with a flash of lights. "And even the sled is okay."

Zephyr ran through its data logs of the event with it a few

more times, standing in the hot sun, and then looked around, counting boxes. The surf was breaking on the beach below, with white horses dancing in joyful rows.

"I'm thinking that maybe this definition of 'inert' could use some work," she said. "Can you detect any structural changes in the stone?"

"As we were in full flight, there was shifting at the molecular levels, but now there is no evidence of a change having taken place. During my fall I noticed the ground reacting just prior to impact at the points of collision, as you saw. I assume the same thing has occurred to you."

Zephyr took a deep breath, and rubbed her arm where a solar charger had thumped it. "What would you need, to have that happen? Apart from the ability to do the changing?"

"You'd have to be watching," the Abacand said. "And have feedback from the reaction of me, you, and the ground."

"Doesn't sound like that *needs* a mind. Could our AIs do that?"

"Sure, if they had the methods. The calculations are straightforward, as long as they had the right memory and processing powers."

"So, no need to theorize intelligence?"

"No, not necessarily."

"Except for Kincaid's testimony, and he might be misunderstanding it," she concluded, putting the Abacand in her pocket and beginning to repack the sled.

"There is that disturbing factor," the AI allowed. "We should now test materials that do NOT appear to be part of the city."

"I'm with you, Sherlock," she said. Zephyr felt better with the Abacand secured to her person. Even though it was a machine that ran a composite personality program, she'd long since discarded all formality with it or any notion of it as simply a tool. Anthropomorphize at your peril, she knew, especially when you can buy another one of these and set it up exactly the same. Probably over a million people had one just like hers, all identical, so that if there was an Abacand convention they'd all speak in unison.

With the sled reloaded and parked properly by the wall, she climbed up to the summit of the rubble and looked down for a first close-up view of the natural bay, where Tanelorn's elegant foot set itself to the water's edge. The harbour wall was an extension of natural basalt formations that reared vertically from the long slope of a sandy shore where particles of gold, white and black mingled in a vast sweep of salt and pepper, occasionally punctuated by the sudden rise of monolithic black columns. These looked as though they had supported structures that reached out far into the deep blue water, where Zephyr's binoculars told her that the land shelf ran slowly down before dropping sharply to considerable depth, some two kilometres out.

"This beach is odd," she said, savouring the salty air, although she noticed it lacked the richness of Earth's onshore wind. Perhaps that was due to the lack of organic forms. "Why build this wall so big and high, if you then have a long gradient out to sea? Why has it been allowed to fall down, when everything else is in such good condition?"

"Let's sample some sand," the Abacand said. "That'll tell us something."

"Hmm." She turned and looked towards the object of their desire some half a kilometre away, near the gaping mouths of a series of sea caves that opened into the natural cliff. From this viewpoint she could see its vertebrate definition, and the dark colour of the bones. The tatters hanging from the vaults of the ribs looked more like skin than cloth; she had high hopes of a biological sample at last.

In spite of her excitement, she made herself pause on the beach itself and scoop sand grains into the Abacand's small analysis tray. The black motes were local basalt. The gold and white were a mixture of imported stones from elsewhere on this continent, assembled by deliberation rather than accident since no currents or local phenomena suggested the sea could have transported them.

Zephyr frowned, and looked along the vast sweep and out to sea. The waves sighed and bubbled, sounding alive. "Definitely nonlocal. Possibly not even sand at the time of occupation. These stones must have been pounded by natural erosion, do you think?"

"It's at least a good guess that they made up the structures no longer evident," the Abacand said. "Although we should expect to find less degraded elements than we have. Unless the erosion is particularly powerful here."

"I give you the evidence." Zephyr gestured at the peaceful tide, moving slowly out to low water. To the horizon, the blue ran unchecked and flat, the odd whitecap rising and falling like the wave of a hand.

"We might look for signs of recent climate changes," the Abacand began, but Zephyr silenced it with a tap of her finger.

"Not our job," she said. "We're strictly looking for civilization—intelligent life or the lack of. Everything else, though fascinating, must wait." And, without another second's hesitation, she began striding out towards the sand where it was still wet and easier to walk on, making her way along the strand to the dead thing, taking photographs of various kinds with the binoculars as she approached.

The skeleton was mostly buried in the sand, high and dry above recent tidelines. As she got within a few metres, Zephyr saw how old it was—the bone on the seaward side was worn and had lost its outer layers, exposing the bubblelike structures of its core. The ribs, one side of the body, arched up and over her in a twenty-metre-high cage, stiff and formal, vulnerable and fragile. She touched one hand-wide spar and felt its incredible lightness, like a kind of paper. Beneath the tip of her finger its ash-dry surface crumbled into dust and grit, which trickled down into the cuff of her sleeve before she had time to draw away in surprise.

Beneath the damage of her fingerprint she saw into the tiny caves and whirls of the bone's deep structure, where no other creature had ever seen. The mineralized remains were thin, larger voids criss-crossed with supports as fine as spider silk, which themselves fanned and vanished almost immediately in the vigour of the onshore breeze and were swept away. It looked avian, sort of.

She took out the Abacand again, to allow it to make its own examination. Meanwhile she looked up to the high curve of two ribs, where a flag of something flew. Fragments of the same semi-translucent material were attached to the bones of the vertebrae where they were sunk into the beach. Zephyr knelt down in the shadow of one massive block and took pictures, first to record the find, before reaching out towards the grey surface where the material lay like a fine snakeskin, diamond patterned. A scan revealed it was not skin. It was a constructed material that might once have been bonded to actual hide, and it was, as it appeared, made of diamond lattices. It was further impregnated with the microscopic fossils of living phages and biological technology that had once allowed this sheen to coat the surface of the creature and intelligently repel toxins, harmful molecules and microorganisms. Now it was merely information seized by time, being unpicked by entropy.

Zephyr broke a piece of bone off and deliberately crumbled it in her gloves. Nothing happened to prevent the decay. She touched a fresh piece of the lattice where it was stuck to the bone. It did not powder. It felt hard and smooth, perfect, until she reached its torn edge, which sliced open her thumb so easily she didn't feel a thing or even notice, until she saw the bright blood run down into the bone's empty channel and stain it red.

"Bugger." She yanked her glove off and stuck the thumb in her mouth quickly. "Anoth' contamination."

"As if that's important, considering," the Abacand said from its place on the sand. "You're breathing the air."

"Mmn." She found the bandages in her belt pack and quickly sealed up the cut, feeling the cool gel of the quick-healing patch firm up the edges to optimum pressure, slowly numbing the wounded area. "Wow, though—this is advanced technology." She looked down as the Abacand provided a high-resolution picture of the substance and traced out its design. Her heart skipped a beat. "More to the point, this is an environment suit.

And it hurt me, unlike the city rock. So whoever this was didn't live here, I'm guessing. It's alien."

The Abacand made a smug noise. "Most likely."

"Long dead."

"Carbon readings suggest at least three thousand years."

"So, long after our Tanelorn people have allegedly gone. Think it's been in the sea?"

"Almost certainly."

"Possibly buried on this beach and then, after some high tide, exposed and eroded. How does erosion get through something like this diamond coat, though?" Zephyr got up and walked along through the barred shadows of the cage to the smallest rib, where it was broken and lay on the sand. The breaks were worn smooth, she noticed. Following the line of vertebral bones, she knelt down and began to dig, recklessly at first, but then, feeling her thumb throb, more cautiously, using a trowel instead of her fingers.

Within a few inches she felt something resist, and then used brushes to uncover a piece of what she hoped would be a skull. But then she paused, sat back on her heels and looked over the coastline.

"This doesn't make sense," she said. "If the shore can be this violent, how has something so fragile survived?"

"Look at the rocks here," the Abacand suggested.

Zephyr scanned with the binoculars on high res. "I see." The stone scattered here beneath the cliff and leading up to the caves beyond was less worn, by a considerable margin, in what appeared to be a strictly localized area centred on the skeleton. "That makes even less sense. Unless it's deliberate? If someone put this here?"

"Like another kind of monument?"

"Yeah. Or a memorial. Or a . . ." She didn't know what, but suddenly she was thinking of her great-aunt Johanna and the dead crow she used to hang from the scarecrow's arms. "Or a warning, like a fetish. If you can protect this area from weather and storms, but let the rest of the place go to ruin, you must still have an interest here, right?"

And then she was thinking: dead crows don't make much difference to the others. It's a show, but it doesn't work—because the crows don't know what it means. Scares people off better than birds. The dead animal is totemic, but only to the person who put it there, and I don't know who put *this* here.

"I'm not detecting any power sources."

"What a surprise." Zephyr resumed digging, slowly now, but after fifteen minutes had passed she began to realize the size of the thing she was trying to uncover and also, for the first time, its significance. She sat back again, hands on hips.

"This is an *alien,*" she said. "Hot damn."

"Apparently," the Abacand agreed.

"Apparently," she snorted. "I touched an alien bone. This is *alien.*"

"The whole planet—"

"—Is dead as a door knocker. Not a thing here but buildings. And this is a body, a real alien. Alien even to here. Meaning: there is even more life in the galaxy than there was here. That's two aliens in one. Maybe they met. Someone died. They parted. A story. A story not involving us. People from yet other worlds who came here too. First. Before us. And this place was the same then: it was empty like this. And here he is, dead." She stared out at the ocean in awe. Then: "But it's *dead.* Yet I just interacted with that road that saved me from even a bruise."

She didn't understand at all. "Maybe he died for other reasons. But the edges of this lattice—according to your readings they've been disrupted by an energy weapon?"

"He may not have come alone. Perhaps there was a fight involving others of his kind and he was left here."

"Yeah." Zephyr glanced down at her theoretical skull bone: a surface of diamond skin stretched over some harder material. No features were yet visible.

"I haven't detected anything new," the Abacand reassured her. "Isol continues to act as satellite, and the Roach is over by the sled. She hasn't said anything about any weapons setup, or that sort of hostile response to our presence from anywhere in the system."

Zephyr snorted. "She wouldn't." But she didn't mean that. It was a snipe at Isol, because Zephyr herself was sitting here with this old skeleton, not understanding and possibly fantasizing a most ludicrous scenario out of pure desire.

"Hang fire," the Abacand interrupted her, thinking suddenly. "I'm getting a message from Bara at last. Hah, that Roach is in a tizzy! Probably Isol hasn't cracked this code yet."

"Professor Duquesne," the Abacand translated, "we have made some discoveries that warrant your attention. I have an Arm not far from your site, which has been my distant eyes and ears. If you meet it at these coordinates, we can talk there."

Zephyr reluctantly began to cover over her find again. "What about the Roach? It'll follow us." She knew that Bara didn't intend Isol to join the conversation.

"There's nothing to be done about it," the Abacand said. Then it showed her some files the VanaShiva had sent: pictures of other creatures, other machines—dead and broken.

"Let's go." She was up in a minute, and moving as fast as she could to the place where she'd first clambered onto the sands.

It was a hard journey to the rendezvous and she abandoned the sled halfway there. Puffing and sweating, she climbed back up towards the Tor and then followed the Abacand's instructions, through various areas, until she came to a place right on the edge where the last few constructions gave way to a bleak plateau of sand and rock. Where there was shade cast by the outer wall of some small building, a peculiar sphere was settled, metallic and unmoving. As she approached, longing for a rest, it unrolled itself and opened out into the Arm of VanaShiva Bara. Sections of its dorsal side fanned up into parasols or solar collectors, creating further shelter from the afternoon sun. It was bigger than the Finger had been, and sleeker. It had no head or tail to distinguish as features, but resembled a segmented caterpillar in its present shape, more machine than animal, its antennae taut in the light breezes.

"Professor," it said, "I regret the hasty actions of our friend, the Voyager Isol."

"You're not the only one," Zephyr said, coming into the

shadow of its long body and sitting down on a boulder to rest. She took out the Abacand. "How long have you been here?"

"Fourteen solar days."

"And you came to terraform?"

"It is our only function," the Arm said, ending with a remonstrative pause. "But in fact all our efforts have been wasted: this place has chosen not to change." It stiffened suddenly. "Isol is here."

The Roach scurried out of a hole in a nearby section of wall and sat in the sun. It didn't say anything, but crouched there, its long feelers moving very slightly back and forth.

"She may as well hear us." Zephyr sighed. "She knows I'm at her mercy anyway. Whatever we speak of here isn't going to find its way into my report—since I want to go back to Earth—but seeing as she's here and so are we then I think we may as well take advantage of our time and get to the bottom of what's going on. Whether or not anyone in-system ever figures it out." She had begun to discern various functional items within the Arm's structure—but its whole shape and design were a peculiar conglomeration.

It settled back into a posture of rest. "My Arm is a scout unit. It locates and tests various mineral and organic deposits for mapping purposes and historical climate data," Bara said. "I've used it here because of our curiosity: mine and Kincaid's. We wanted to see these cities for ourselves. He came too—you saw that."

Zephyr glanced at the Roach. It didn't look smart. She wasn't sure if it was only an instrument or not. She looked back at the Arm in its scratched metal casings.

"What did you find?"

Bara paused. "If I could make use of your Abacand, I can show you," he said.

As the Abacand relayed Zephyr the visual footage of the incidents, Bara narrated for her.

Nobility Bara's secondary free limb, Arm #36, tracked west along the heavy pavement of the primary city that Isol had named

Tanelorn. The Arm was in constant radio contact with Bara, but at this moment was at a great distance from his body and so had taken the tidying step of incorporating a temporary mind into its neural cores—a copy—that would later be reintegrated with his primary memory. As such, he presently experienced himself as the Arm alone, in the knowledge that he was also scattered in many other places, having experiences of which he knew nothing but would eventually come to remember. This division didn't bother him; in fact, as the situation with the voices went on, he was glad of it. The vulnerability of becoming separated from the main body was made up for by the knowledge that a fatal accident to any portion of him would not be the end of his life, but only of a small piece of it, which would represent hardly more than one of the Unevolved might expect to forget in an ordinary lifetime.

The Arm was a unit, which folded up neatly into a tough metal sphere for long-distance travelling, so that it could roll as a ball over any kind of terrain. At present he was exploring, and was half unrolled, his primary segments moving with fluid grace along the street, avoiding areas of crashed rubble and stone where towers and other structures had succumbed to the erosions of the weather. He was looking for evidence of a conflict here in the ruins of Tanelorn, and he was finding none.

Bara alternated between unknown side streets of minor interest and large regions of major development. His favourite point was a high redoubt that overlooked most of the city from a natural rocky promontory to the north. He burned with a soft, oily heat as he moved uphill towards it, relishing the simplicity and easy power of the Arm, folding up to roll where its snakelike undulations proved too inefficient.

From his vantage he surveyed the wind-softened rubble that stretched for mile after mile down the steep hillsides towards the sea. Nothing stirred among the rocks: they lay where they had fallen, peacefully, surrendered to the weather. Here and there metal machinery rotted, crumpled by massive blocks that had dropped from on high wherever they were outdoors, or hidden within the larger buildings, their frames and engineering crushed beyond analysis. His sortie would take him to them, yet he lingered awhile, watching the ocean and the beach. It wasn't physical fear that made him hesitate. It was an existential fear that went deeper than the possibility of losing his Arm. This fear niggled at him like a tiny itch in his nerves and circuits, the wobble of electrons in his mind. He couldn't define it, and equally he couldn't escape it. He didn't want to see the machines they'd left or butchered. He didn't want to face them. Thoughts of *the whispers* ran through his mind—he recalled the Secta reports from the twin Moons and the rambling, dissociated worries that Kincaid communicated: the mutterings of people lost far from home.

Bara hadn't heard a whisper yet and he didn't want to. But time ran on and he eventually curled up and again began a controlled roll downhill, towards the first of the dead things. It was little more than a skeleton: struts and ribs that had once supported a sort of flesh were bare and worn. By the imprints of tendon and relay he could recognize that this thing was more like him than not. It was *made* and it was machine and animal fused together. Its tracks were whole, their tread pattern subtle and intended for these stone roads, but the skin was long gone from them.

He surveyed its body scientifically, making conjectures as to its function—a long-distance transport vehicle?—whilst he looked at it as a fellow and as an alien at the same time. He reached out with his fingers and felt the ridges of one of its spinal structures, tasted the carbon nanotubules, and read their formation and its design in a moment, felt a sadness he didn't understand. From deep within its trailing segments he heard two pieces of metal swinging loosely together in the breeze from the shore, and before he could do any more he had to find and silence that noise, because it sounded of too many things: abandonment, wreckage, graveyards and warnings. It sounded as if someone might have put it there just for him.

The clanging spoke clearly. *Ba. Ra.*

As he tore apart the pieces of it and flung them aside Bara prayed for this machine. He mumbled the words out of the back of his head, pretending he wasn't really doing it. That made him feel better, as if he could talk to its soul and soothe its unquiet rest. Why *unquiet*? How could he think such a thing?

But he did. The tickle of it lay on his mind.

Isol called down to Bara the next day, informing him of the Unevolved investigator's plans to stay and explore the city. "If you found anything to suggest an error on our part," she said— meaning, he knew, anything that worked or hinted at a return of the planet's natives—"then remove it immediately. She has set up her camp on the hill above the sea, in one of those homes that has a tunnel way into the labyrinth beneath, although whether she has found this I don't know. Keep away from her."

"I know, I know," he grumbled, abandoning his examination of the dead behemoth and retreating carefully. His discomfort blossomed and he had to struggle with it momentarily. "I'm leaving now."

He withdrew his limbs and rolled up tightly, sealing his exterior against the tough grit of the road and country that lay between him and the rest of his body. "You haven't told the professor about the voices, I take it?"

"It remains to be seen whether or not she'll hear them for herself." The Voyager's tone was clipped and he didn't want to argue. If the Unevolved didn't hear them, then that must mean her kind were not susceptible, or whatever it was.

Bara spoke angrily. "We have to figure this out."

"Later," Isol snapped.

"I think Kincaid is going mad," he said. The whole planet's suitability was obviously in question. And he knew what that meant: back to the sleep death, probably forever. "Do *you* hear them?"

"Just stay away from the inspector until she's done, that's all you've got to do," she replied. "Kincaid will be fine. The voice doesn't worry me. It's probably some kind of neural illusion. Hallucinations."

"These machines. These *people*." He sent her images of the tracked creature and of the other thing he'd found, the one by the shore. "I'm thinking they're non-native. Everything else is gone, even the weeds. Why leave these? They must have come afterwards. I think they're aliens. We should try to find out."

"Don't worry about that now," Isol said. "They're all long dead, so what difference do they make? The important thing is that this world has a technology that we can use to free ourselves forever from the slavery of Form and Function."

"It's because they're dead that it bothers me," he said, now crumpled into a semisphere. Her ranting ideology tired him. It made him think she wasn't sane either. He felt he was alone and automatically began to initiate a Dreamtime cast to find a sympathetic soul in the vicinity, only stopping himself when he realized what he was doing. "Why would the others leave them here? What are they doing here? She's bound to find at least one. It wouldn't surprise me if Kincaid—"

"He's fine!"

Bara broke the link, a gesture of anger, then reconnected with, "Kincaid is planting the marshes. He thinks he is building a new world, but every night the planet consumes his work and mine. It really does it. And you say this place is ours to take over. How is that not mad?"

"Kincaid's conditioning is what he turns to in his weakness," Isol said. "What harm can it do anyway? Work is good for you." She broke transmission and he was left in silence, except for the sea's thunder as it rose to high tide far below.

The planet ate their work. That was not right. It wasn't even possible. But it ate their work. He was baffled by her lack of interest in that terrible fact.

What harm indeed? Bara didn't know. He didn't want to be responsible for Grip, but their old association as colleagues and friends made turning his back impossible. What story could he make up that would convince Kincaid not to try and found a world on this place, when he'd only woken because of Isol's promise of a forever home? What indeed?

Half the planet over, where Kincaid worked diligently by moonlight, Bara activated another Hand that Kincaid had borrowed from him, its job to test the gas fractions of the local atmosphere, to watch the weather, and advise. He ambled over to where Kincaid's Finger #2578 was grubbing in the squelchy loam, feeding chunks of dripping earth to its mandibles and busily processing them. Deep within its bowels, gases and microbes gurgled through the slurry, transforming it into a medium for plant growth. At the Finger's rear a sporipositor excreted large balls of compost, each containing a single seed, deep into the paddy field. Bara could tell that Kincaid was planting rice.

Bara beamed a greeting across and the Finger paused momentarily, backsignalling to the main body for an updated personality before it spoke.

"Bara, good news from the city?"

"Well. News." Bara's discomfort with the activity of the Fingers made him feel guilty. "The inspection is going ahead. Isol seems to think it will be all right. She expects to be validated, in spite of what's happening to us."

"And you're worried."

Bara watched the Finger delve with its claws and shuffle forward a few metres, resting its bulk in the shallow water with a large splash. To his left and right, other Fingers continued planting, their backs glowing silvery and greenish in the light of the two false Moons, whose orbits always brought them overhead in an unnatural parallel, one directly above the other. The light made the water seem icy, although the night was humid. Due to Bara's own work on the polar ice, the poisonous tang of ammonia on his tongue was dropping to negligible levels, as it always did in the early hours. The oxygen count was up now. By morning it would be down and the ammonia would return.

"Kincaid, have you paused to consider what we'll do if she's wrong?"

"There'll be other planets, now she's got the drive," Kincaid said easily. "An infinity of worlds."

The Finger grubbed up another chunk of black mineral clay in its pincers, and began masticating with the speed of a newly hatched caterpillar. Its skin rippled with pleasure. "Even if we have to leave this one, the maths says there are other worlds similar enough to old Earth, and systems similar enough to Sol that we can find work and a living there that would outlast many generations of us." He chuckled. "So I don't worry. I like to work. It doesn't matter if this crop fails as well. It doesn't matter how many fail here. If it's not to be, at least it's keeping us in shape."

Bara uncoiled one of his Hand's sensitive tactile feelers and rested it against the soft hide of the Finger where the heavy head was joined to the torso with folds of neck flesh. The Finger paused and trilled, gripping the feeler gently in one of its feeding pincers. "I hope you're right, old man."

"I am right," Kincaid assured him, pinching the Arm's central nerve with pressure calibrated to assure and console.

"To work, then," Bara said unhappily, and they broke their brief contact. "Form and Function be damned."

"Form and Function," said the Finger and made the salute of the Forged Independence party with a clod of earth held in its claw.

Bara let his Hand return to its business, and withdrew to his main geographical position on the continental highlands close to the northern polar cap. There, and within his Arm at Tanelorn, he thought that perhaps Grip was right after all. No big deal if they did have to leave. And they might survive that long. The only possible problem would occur from any surviving natives who might return, and the signs Isol reported from the Sectae up on the Moons all signalled that this was unlikely, if not impossible.

If he trusted her.

The sound of his drill boring into the deep ice, taking core samples, retuned to an unhappy note and, in the moment of his hesitation and concentration shift, the drill snapped in two. Bara spent the next twelve hours recovering it and making repairs.

It was almost dark as Zephyr looked up from this story. She rubbed her sore eyes. It seemed clear to her now that Isol and Kincaid, and maybe this person with her now, were all quite mad. Their dreams persisted dumbly, walked roughshod over all evidence. But her heart felt for them, because the undercurrent of their story was simple animal *need*, a thing she knew in herself was not easily answered, not easily admitted.

"The planet speaks and eats," she said, "and catches and protects. What else does it do? How could it do any of those things? How could a rock become an engine, and how could an engine talk?"

"Do you hear it?" Bara asked her quietly, his dorsal sails lowering as the last sunlight faded.

"No," she said.

"Oh." He paused. "Then it must be a result of something other than just contact."

Zephyr looked again at the Abacand, which held all the finds, all the data, all the answers, somewhere. An unpleasant idea had just occurred to her.

What if this entire planet were made of the same substance as Isol's engine? What if the whole system was too? Suppose it wasn't ordinary matter, but only looked like it at certain levels? Then a planet might talk, might think, might do as it wanted.

But what was the *it*?

There was a moment, before he started, when Corvax realized the difficulty of forming an untainted, single intent to act. His dream in Uluru had set out as an easy escape to a better life—he'd thought—in which he could be another person whose trials wouldn't cast any shadow on real others or on his real self. Now he wanted the same again, but from this alien thing. He wanted it to grant him the power, but nothing else. *Transform me,* he wanted to say, but then he had to think about the disease that was Caspar, and the old Tom who never fixed the plane, and then he had to wonder about his true motivation. If he hid such dangerous secrets as those, even from himself, couldn't they stand an equal chance of *becoming*?

He had to return to the dream to make it, he reckoned on instinct. He'd go there and resolve the thing, and build the plane.

With TwoPi's assistance he was allowed to upgrade and develop his MekTek adaptation for an even greater totality of interface between himself and the laboratory's AI, which would run the Uluru engine. They gave him the lump of Stuff to hold, seeing as they didn't know what else to do with it, and left him well alone in a cubic room sealed off from the rest of the universe—at least from most of it, from what they could perceive.

"Good luck, Corvax," TwoPi said as the door closed on him. "You're very brave."

He tried to speak, but couldn't get a word out before the door was shut. He'd have said, *I'm not brave, I'm only where I was going all along.* However, the unspoken promise of the Shuriken Death-Angel was in his throat, blocking it. A certain end, a quick end, if things didn't work out.

The AI waited until TwoPi and Mouze had temporarily

retreated from the station, and then requested access. In his brain the new growth of microtendrils seemed to tingle like Xing's hair.

"Let's go," he said . . .

He stood between the two massive boarding houses, where the tiny shack in which he'd lived crouched in submission. He faced its buckling porch and broken steps. A breeze full of stinging salt blew against the side of his human face, and bit the soft skin. Sand and wispy grass had buried him up to his ankles, as though he'd stood there weeks without moving.

From the house on his left he heard the heavy thud of boots on hollow stairs, and in the distance the shimmering heat-haze shape of a crane stepped mechanically across the shining wastes of water, where a grey sky met the grey sea and the land. Corvax looked down into his single small hand, where a pinkish kind of stone was clutched tightly, the roughness of its initial fractured faces worn away by time into an almost perfect egg.

Caspar appeared to his right, a bear of youth and arrogance, his blond hair wild and his sneer so pronounced that it might have been painted on. Taller, meaner in aspect than Corvax recognized, he swung himself around the high column standing by the door of the house built of burnt ship's timbers, and strode over the sand. His belt was stiff with ammunition and there was a gun on his hip, its holster unfastened.

"You've been gone awhile," Caspar said as he stopped a few metres away, pretending to start a pleasant conversation.

Corvax held out the egg. "I brought you this."

"A rock?" Caspar looked worried as well as contemptuous. He drew the gun and pointed it at Corvax. "How about I trade you that for the bullet in this?"

"You've tried to kill me before," Corvax said. "Don't you wonder why you've never succeeded?"

"I was hoping the cranes would do that for me," Caspar replied. But he glanced around him warily for any sign of the big birds. His own sudden fear made the gun shake.

"I die, you die," Corvax promised him. "They're my wingmen—" Although he wasn't sure.

"You're afraid of them," Caspar retorted, eyeing the stone. "Toss it here, then, whatever it is. And remember, I can shoot anytime."

Corvax threw the stone gently and it landed near Caspar's foot. Before either of them could react, a long sharp beak stabbed upwards from the ground and seized it. The crane's head bulged from the sand. It chugged the stone back into its throat, then swallowed and viciously thrust its beak towards Caspar, before sliding back and disappearing.

"You hoped I'd touch it and the thing would come for me!" shrieked Caspar.

Corvax just stared at the spot where the crane had vanished. He hadn't planned for that at all. *Now* what was he going to do? He looked up at Caspar's fury—and was punched hard in the chest by something. It flung him flat on his back. A numbness expanded into his lungs, so that he couldn't breathe. He lay and gaped as Caspar stood over him and pointed the gun towards his face. Only then did he realize that he'd been shot.

Caspar looked puzzled and stunned at what he'd done. "Why did you do that? You knew I'd shoot. She'll be mine now, and you'll be gone for good."

"But . . ." Corvax tried to speak but his mouth was filling up from the back, choking him on blood. "The plane. I'ff to . . . build it."

"That shit heap?" Caspar snorted. "If you'd any strength, it'd be long gone from here. I waited all this time for you to fix the fucking thing, hoping that when the day came I'd be flying out of this hole anywhere I wanted. But you didn't know how to fix it, did you? And they all know, Pete and the others. They all know you don't know, or you can't. And she knows. Dani. She knows you're full of lies. So we'll stay and rot here without you now, you miserable little fuck." He drew his foot back and kicked Corvax in the ribs.

His sight beginning to fade, breath finished, dying, Corvax

could only agree with him. He thought it might be better to die in this test than have to expose possession of a self like that to any kind of inspection, alien or human. He was a failure. He'd created this hell, and he'd made it without assistance. Now it would consume him, and there was no justice better. But with his last glance he looked up at the handsome, savage figure standing over him—so strong in its barbaric, Monkey way and so impotent, stuck in the cage of the marsh—and a sort of humour floated to the surface of his mind. Caspar had been a kind of idol, even if a hated one, despised for being effectively human. And Corvax thought he was funny now. He pointed a finger-and-thumb gun at Caspar and mouthed *Bang!* He died laughing and his body lay there on the sand, feet still rooted in the ground and, as night fell and Caspar and Dani lit the rooms of the empty house, the cranes came one by one and picked his bones.

Working with their terrible bills, they strung his skeleton together anew and made him a body from grass and feathers. All the while they spoke his name very quietly, intoning it in a kind of song.

> *"Tom. Tom. Back you come.*
> *No sleep 'til work is done.*
> *No rest 'til the hour is passed*
> *And you'll be home with us, at last."*

He stood up as dawn broke and went into the aeroplane shed, turning back in the doorway. The lead crane, a grey-headed creature hardly different in colour from the land, turned its beak of razor-sharp metal and regurgitated an egg-shaped stone, which hit the ground with a small thud. The crane nodded at Tom and then, with the others, spread its enormous white wings and flapped heavily into the sodden air.

Tom Corvax picked up the stone and watched them going, until they were lost in the clouds.

At the sound of his engine starting people came running from the flophouses; Pete and his mate, and Dani in her festoons of pink rags. Caspar came last, but he stepped aboard into the curious hold of the craft's long body. When they were all inside, Tom closed his mouth and spread the creaking vastness of his metal wings. He stooped and picked up the egg stone in his long, sharp beak—then, with a flick of his neck, swallowed it whole.

The wind came and lifted him into the air. He was as light as a piece of down.

The Uluru subroutine stopped of its own accord once the AI had determined it could no longer distinguish between Corvax and the stone. The AI then detached itself from the connections and firewalled itself in as best it could, leaving the physical body of the Roc on the isolation-chamber floor, no longer connected to anything by transmission or contact that it could detect. Feathers stirred slowly.

Tom was at one second afloat in the skies of a vast landscape, then he was sitting in the small cubic room of a laboratory, wingless and about as physically cranky as ever. His old feathers rustled and smelled of preening oil. His MekTek ran hot within his skin. He stood up and looked at himself in the reflective wall of his cube, and saw no change. But there was an acceptance of his shape and bearing that hadn't been there before, and there was the vastness of what lay behind his simple form now that he and the Stuff were one—suspended below him like a weightless balloon of possibilities, a brimming capsule of infinite time.

The AI opened the door for him and he walked wearily out into the lab proper. It was very empty without the wall that had been the Comb, and without Mouze's peppery and vital presence. TwoPi spoke from their distant transport via the AI's speakers.

"Is it as you imagined?"

"No," he said. "There are two things at once. I am Tom Corvax. And there is no 'I'—there is a greater mind, a superposition of all minds that have ever entered this state of being Stuff. These two states exist simultaneously because the mind that is Tom is here, made of this body, but the matter of this body is a part of a greater ocean of matter interpenetrated by the minds of the others who live within imaginary time, volumeless and occupying the whole universe."

There was a pause greeting this announcement, and he wasn't surprised. He waited for a reaction, giving them time to take it in.

"What is the intention of these minds?" TwoPi asked finally.

"They/it is . . ." And now words were starting to fail him, as he knew they would. "Looking," he said. "Discovering. Seeing what is there. The only way to understand is to become—you were right, TwoPi. And that is what Stuff is. It's them, becoming. And when *we* interact with Stuff, then we are begun becoming."

"Can it be removed?" Mouze said gently, as if afraid.

Corvax, for once in his life, had all the answers. "No," he said. "There is no possibility of return once living material accepts this translation. It—they—are in the process of evolving, and to assimilate Stuff—that is, to assimilate them—is to become them. They will not destroy parts of themselves. But until the fusion is complete, then there is a chance for me—or whoever—to destroy myself, if I don't want to carry on and be consumed."

"What is this critical period?" Mouze asked, as TwoPi hummed in thought.

"Hard to define," Corvax said. "But once it comes, there will not be any distinction left between me and it. I will be . . . All of my mind and memories and experiences will still exist, but the single linear consciousness that is my present mind will not exist in this coherency. It will be distributed, and the multiple will all be aware of it, be part of it, and I will be all of them, and none. Individuation and expression in Four-D will then be governed by interaction with individual minds—yours, perhaps."

"So, when you created the wasp-blades from Stuff, it responded to you, but does nothing unless someone is to ask?" TwoPi mused. "And why would it respond? Will it do *anything* a person requests?"

"Except destroy itself," Corvax said, hesitating. "Ourselves, that is. To learn the truth, intents are followed, and thus discovery is authentic. I'm not telling this all that well, I know. Sorry, it's very hard to explain. The Stuff really doesn't care in any moral sense about who or what is interacting with it. It's not interested in anything except the gathering of experience and knowledge and the qualities of other minds. It doesn't have a singular thing like a personality or intents of its own, but it's densely populated with fragments that do, although the purpose of the whole mostly dissuades the individuated parts from any overt actions of interference on their own behalf. Strangely . . ." He shook his heavy head. "I believe there is something like a war on within us. Between impulses that want to be re-created as individuals, who want to do all kinds of wilful things, and a greater force that is simply this watchfulness. Elsewhere in our galaxy and the wider universe there is much being acted out, and now that Earth has come into the realm, then there will be other places where people like us will be . . . played."

TwoPi made a gentle sound of sympathy that Corvax didn't expect. "How can we know that this has not already occurred?"

"You can only ask *me,* and I can tell you that Stuff had not come across us before Isol picked up the block."

"Of course, that's an academic and trivial question," Mouze added. "So what if we were all simulations? It doesn't make our predicament the less. Are we all to be assimilated to this state?"

"No, no," Tom said. "It's purely voluntary. That is, the initial use of Stuff is voluntary. After you accept it, then it becomes." He paused. "I can hear the others. Isol and Kincaid. Bara. Trini. They're like echoes." A sadness crept into his old hide and he sat down on the floor. "They don't understand what's happening, so they're fighting."

"Why don't they understand?" TwoPi said bluntly.

"They won't listen," he answered, and fell silent. The awareness of the Eleven-D and the alien was so encompassing that he couldn't express it. "We speak, they hear. They don't want to become us, they want to use us. They want to be us, but they don't understand what we are saying."

"But you must have drawn them to you quite deliberately. Why else was Isol so keen to go to that planet?" Mouze said.

"*They* wanted it," Tom said. "Like I wanted Dani. It was something they thought would complete them."

"Did you make that world for them?" TwoPi asked.

"No. The planet in question was the home of the First to Translate Into Other Space. It is both a navigational point and a library. There everything is interpenetrated by our awareness. We keep it so, to remind us of our origin. The matter is organized to retain memory in a physical form, so that our awareness of real time past is not tainted by times present. All the pasts of all who are Translated exist as data held by the material of the planet and its system. The Moons are the two scribes of that natural history, the generators of the Translation. Trini has understood some of this, because she is not as desperate as the others to retain her individuality."

Tom was a surface tension on the greater whole: he looked at his frailty and began to wonder at his own design. Had Tupac seen him as he could see it now: a fusion of genes giving instructions for his formation, a series of codes at all levels, a construction of materials, flawed and confused in their intent? And to change, all he had to do was ask.

Mouze and TwoPi conferred briefly about him—he heard them distantly, even though they didn't use the AI—and then Mouze said:

"How is the physical transformation in Four-D created? How was Isol's engine made? How does it work?"

"That cannot be explained to anyone who does not have a perception that can encompass the Eleven-D," Corvax said simply. It was the truth, but he knew it couldn't be satisfying—it sounded like a put-off. "Changes made effortlessly within the seven dimensions beyond your access cause the shifts of physical structure in the other remaining four. To answer your question about the engine, it uses the same ability, but transfers matter from one state to another, taking it to a form and a plane where there is no distance between the points in question. It is then re-Translated into its original state, give or take a few minor errors that are an inevitable consequence of all Translations of any complexity."

"And you have this ability now?"

"Not exactly. I could change myself, but for anything to be

altered it must be a manifestation of the greater entity—let's call it Stuff, for the sake of ease. All matter exists in Seven-D but not all of Seven-D is a part of Stuff."

"The nature of Stuff?" TwoPi enquired.

Corvax sighed. "Stuff is a technology and it is also people, indivisibly fused. You could not define it, one way or another, at any particular moment. It has no consciousness as you assume individuals must, nor does it have the insensible responses of a tool—but properties of both and also neither. It is intelligent, responsive, compassionate, but it does not have an identity of its own, although it contains the fragments of many identities and is capable of creating individuals who could act and exist as ordinary people. Part of that dualistic strife concerns this process of individuation and return, within Stuff itself. In the beginning, Stuff was a kind of Forging technology that was to use the Seven-D to facilitate movement and transformation, but it began a critical fusion with the organic life that invented it, as they used it to transport themselves, and now they are one."

"Why was it left at the axial crossroad where Isol found it?"

"It was there to be found. Stuff *watches*. It chooses points where life of a certain developmental stage is sure to come across it, seeding the universe with points of access."

"And why couldn't this have been done with intermediaries?" TwoPi insisted. "Emissaries?"

"Stuff has found that this method reveals the true nature of the finder far more . . . watchably. If it manifested and spoke from the outset, then the contacted race would behave untypically, and its intents and thoughts then couldn't be known."

"There's a sinister side to that kind of calculation," TwoPi said. "Don't you feel that now, Corvax? You killed with Stuff, before you understood it. Isol has created the circumstances for a civil war because she has apparently mistaken it."

"Stuff creates nothing that isn't already in the heart and mind of the observer," Tom said and shrugged. "And, personally speaking, I'd have been dead without it, so my reservations are limited. As for Isol, she isn't mistaken: she suspected all along what it could do. She wanted to bring the Forged out to Zia in order to equip them all with the means to shape their own destiny. She really *meant* that. She thought of them as becoming infinitely malleable."

"And when Stuff provides infinite power for those with no control of their desires—do others suffer and die then?"

Corvax stared down into the new levels within and of himself. "It has happened. I told you it was a morality-free kind of substance. To Stuff, good and evil has no distinction. There is regret for suffering and death, but it is not the agent of these things. It lives and it considers life a sufficient . . . condition."

"So the gun says it doesn't shoot," TwoPi replied. "Is that what you're saying? This thing has all the power, and does nothing with it but give guns to children?"

Corvax wished he had an answer that could refute her accusation, even though he sensed she was playing devil's advocate. "That's a way of seeing it, but the gun is a consequence of our minds. If we were in love with peace, and had no will to destroy each other, there would be no gun."

Mouze broke in. "Without using Stuff itself, can there be any way of destroying it?"

"Yes," Tom replied. "A quark-gluon plasma, or certain other forms of essential quantum instability, focused on a reasonably tight region can disperse us irretrievably if directed at us in our Four-D manifestation. And there are other ways within the Seven-D. I know Gaiasol haven't got any such weapon, so I don't mind telling you this. But you needn't worry about an invasion, Stuff only assimilates to those who *want* it."

"But before you tell them the drawback," TwoPi added. "Evolve or die?"

Tom said nothing. What could he say? He waited.

"Suppose a Translated Forge like Isol decides to destroy Earth," Mouze asked. "Will you do that?"

"It could be done," Tom admitted. "But we would not."

"So now you have a scruple? Why?" TwoPi demanded.

"Because I don't wish it," Tom said. "And I am who you're dealing with—sort of."

"*Your* intent is enough to sway this enormous collective?"

The Hive Queen was astounded. Clearly she'd been thinking of him as some kind of drone feature, or of minimal consequence.

"If Isol was Translated and wished to destroy Earth—she would have had to retain her current patterning in completeness, which is impossible. In any case, she's ambivalent. She might be made again, individuated, and then try to use her power for destructive purposes, but having been within Stuff, such a wish is almost definitely impossible."

"*Almost* definitely?"

"Free agents with infinite capability are a strong problem we are now dealing with. We do not create free agents of that nature and Translate them to Four-D, because of their potential for critical damage."

"Big of you."

"Although there *are* experiments of that nature made, very controlled ones, now and again. Destruction of this particular universe is possible, if the Eleven-D is abused significantly. We are investigating the possibility of shifting to other Universes, should such an event occur."

The conversation was stopped by a new voice. It was very chilly and matter-of-fact. None of them recognized it, and all fell silent in surprise.

It said, "How far away is the Ironhorse Timespan Tatresi from full realization of Stuff?"

Corvax felt his way to the answer. "Depending on his usage of the engine, about four solar days."

"Thanks."

"Who was that?" Mouze asked the AI.

It replied, "Who?"

"The person who asked about Tatresi."

"No such question has been asked."

But on the screens Tom Corvax could see the blurred image of the Shuriken Death-Angel peel away from its position, silently. Within a fraction of a second it was gone.

"Do you know what that was about?" TwoPi said.

Tom put his head in his hands. "I can't hear Tatresi very well.

But he understands the potential, like Isol did. I think . . . I think he intends to sell Stuff across the system and precipitate a far faster revolution. Machen will have to try and stop him."

"And you, Corvax," TwoPi asked, "will you warn Tatresi now?"

Tom looked up at the camera. "No, of course not. This is *his* struggle, not yet ours."

"So, whose side are you on?" Mouze said.

"Side?" Tom shook his head. "Nobody's. Never was. Not even when I was a boy." He stood up and flexed the stubs of his once-grand wings, withdrawing them into his body and thus assuming a more human form. It was easy. He lost his beak and made a nose and mouth. He copied a handsome form from an Unevolved clothing catalogue. Technically it couldn't breathe or survive the pressure in the lab's vacuum as Corvax once had, but he adapted it not to need to.

"You know," he said, "the whole issue of what shape you're in is really much more trivial than I thought." Then he looked up to see where TwoPi and Mouze were at. "So, shall I stay? Or is that enough? I'll have to go soon anyway. A day or so. Any more questions? You'll have to be quick." He turned around, floating in big steps as the minimal gravity plucked weakly at him, and felt his lips smile their way into a huge grin. He turned a pirouette above the floor, and set down lightly.

"Lest we forget," he said to himself, "the pleasure of simple things."

"Hello, sister," said the Moon.

It had been saying that for about half an hour. It said it to Trini—sometimes as a sound made by reverberating plates of its own structure, sometimes by reverberating parts of her body, sometimes by shivering light or electromagnetic waves or pulsing air.

It had started while she stood in the central chamber and looked at the space it contained. Although it seemed quite empty on some levels, when Trini made herself sensitive to dark matter she knew it was far from that.

She had understood at some point that the language system of the Moon's owners was written in a complex form of surface-texture changes—like a Braille, or a script visible to senses that were a combination of sight and touch. She collected sequences and made likely guesses at them, although, without the Hive, she was a poor calculator. She reckoned this room was where a process had begun. She thought it was directed and focused in the Fifth Chamber—a position out on the Moon's surface, facing the planet.

The Moon's repeated phrase washed through her, tidal and encompassing. She steeled her courage and set one hand into the raw bed of connections she'd freed up from a piece of the wall, with an antenna tuned to discharge any sudden jolts of electricity that might result, hoping this would be enough to save her.

Hello, sisters, Trini said to the circuits.

Trini was enveloped in a web of heat that seemed to close in on her, and then there was a quiet moment. She was aware of the systems far away from her, and those close to. She felt along the connections and experienced a strange but welcome sense of relief. Here was a Hive of a kind, a billion voices speaking as one voice, an ocean of possibilities cresting into a single point of consciousness to speak to her.

Abruptly there was a surge, a tsunami of energy and enthusiasm, boisterous as a puppy and powerful as the sun. It came towards her suddenly, but building from a great volume and distance. It crashed through her and she was swept up in it. What distance there had been between the machine Moon and herself was gone in that instant. She felt the sudden presence of seven hidden zones, each joined to each through her centre. Senses without names informed her of their depth and pressure, their essential relation to her own common space-time.

Then Trini knew the Zians had not gone. They were here, around the crinkly corners of the hidden seven, their presence removed from ordinary expansion, to this obstinate mixture of near-spaceless and -timeless regions where, unlimited by the laws of the Four, they waxed and waned as a seething tide. She knew what they knew, and they knew what she knew. There was now no difference between them.

Abruptly a signal from outside the Moon's surface startled her, and snapped her back to her physical position. She let go of the interface with the alien world and heard it repeated.

"Trini!" It was Isol. There was a clang as the Voyager's body docked clumsily against the Comb's frozen side. "You have to help me—help me get rid of it."

Trini opened a wider band so she could transmit some calming sonics alongside her voice. "Calm down. I'll come and—"

"I can't be calm! I can't do anything except . . . hang on to myself. They're trying to kill me! You have to help me. I know you can do it—you're a Ticktock. There must be all kinds of equipment in the Comb that you could use to get it disconnected. Hurry up! Come on come on come on!"

Trini paused and came to a halt in her walk back towards the Comb. "Isol, listen to me. What you're hearing is nothing to be afraid of. Try to stop panicking for a second." Back along the connection came the garbled response of Isol's terror, a furious noise.

"What do you know? Just get it out of me. Come on, please, Trini. Why are you taking so long? Open the door."

Trini stood still. "There's no way," she said quietly, emphasizing her sorrow for Isol's situation as she sent the words. "I can't do it. You've already gone too far. The bulk of you has already been translated into the Seven." She added a batch of explanatory maps, diagrams, schematics for Isol to read, to explain how it was.

There was a brief and complete silence as the Voyager digested the information they contained; then came the sound of her disengaging with the Comb. Trini listened with all her senses, and with the dull perceptions of the alien that were slowly becoming more true inside her. She realized Isol's intent, even as the small creature turned back to aim its weapon at the Moon.

"No! Isol, don't!" she screamed with every terawatt of power she could muster on every frequency she could use, hoping to at least blast Isol's sockets and throw her off her aim. "If you attack us—" the part of her that had become Isol's mind realized what to say, "—you end up as roadkill! You'll be dead before you can do it!"

No reply. Trini snatched a connection to the Moon's observational technology and searched the sky, finding Isol at close range, an energy weapon never imagined by human minds bulging out of her flank like a metallic cancerous growth.

"If I attack *us*?" The question came out of a fresh, sterile calm. "Are you with them now, Trini?"

Trini understood that Isol had been the toughest of them all, the last to respond, the most strongly in denial. They had left her alone as much as they could because, of all the things Isol had ever wanted, to be a part of someone or something else was not it. Isol was the individualist. She was alone. It was her nature and they could not change it, although they were about to be changed by it. Nor could they stop the inevitable connections that their technological aspect was forming with her. Isol was now a part of the whole, whether she or they liked it or not.

With all the processing speed of her Ticktock heritage Trini racked her knowledge for a clue and her experience for an insight. Quietly, from within the Moon's core, she sang:

A long, long time ago, I can still remember how that music used to make me smile. . . .

"Don't you dare," hissed the Voyager. "That's mine. My memories. My time. My life. Nothing to do with you!"

"You won't lose it," Trini pleaded with her.

"And if I blow myself to hell—or you do—will I still be there with you in some way? Will you have all of me except that song? Have you *already* stolen anything you wanted?"

"We don't want you to—"

"And I don't want you! Can't you understand that? I don't want you or anything to do with you! If I join you, I'm as good as dead anyway."

Trini said, "Gaiasol already knows about your plan, and about us. Corvax, the MekTek Roc, has translated into the Eleven. They're going to arrest Tatresi. Isol, if you try to use us to accelerate your own development, you will not be able to exert an individual control on that evolution. That's the nature of the Eleven, of Stuff."

Isol withdrew her gun. It slid back into a heavy abscess on her side. "Oh yeah? Well, you don't have me yet, you bug-faced bitch."

Trini watched her make the transit back to the Solar System, crossing the invisible, the timeless, which bound her closer, tighter. Isol's anguish coloured all her feelings. She experienced a stiffening of the breath and a plunging sensation of grey: the Secta equivalent of sadness. On the surface of Origin, Kincaid was going the same way—Bara, too. If only they'd possessed the bliss of Hive mentality to fall back on, she thought, then this wouldn't seem so threatening to them. On the contrary, to her it seemed like the arms of all the mothers there ever were. She wished they could see it that way, but for that to happen they would have to *listen,* and they didn't want to.

The only person she didn't yet hear was the lonely woman

whom Isol had shipped here to make a study of the Origin. Unlike the others, she had struggled not to ask anything of Stuff and had fought to impose no meaning. They had touched very briefly after the sled had run out of control, but to Trini this incident was no more than a blurred impression. It was strongly possible that the others would destroy themselves rather than Translate, as many had before them, and that the Unevolved investigator would be stranded on the planet's surface.

Trini found the correct frequency for transmission to the woman's Abacand, and began to speak.

Isol located Tatresi in Martian orbit, in the midst of delivering a speech to some of his favourite radicals from Independence. He was waxing lyrical about the future of them all on ZDN, explaining the use of Stuff, and their glorious destiny as shape-shifting free individuals with a universe to explore, or some such. She didn't really listen to the details. Instead she shot out the satellite relay station he was using for his broadcast, cutting off 99 percent of his audience in a split second.

"Shut the hell up!" she snarled at him, spinning into view from the planet's dark side as he turned in rage to find out who'd pulled his plug.

"Isol," he stuttered.

"The technology is poison," she interrupted whatever it was he was going to say. "You have to stop."

"But we agreed. Everything is in motion already. Thousands have signed up in the last twenty-four hours. Distribution centres—"

"Your idea!" she snorted. "And don't think I don't know what you're up to. You thought you'd wait for me to break the ice, and then you take over with your popularity vote and your chit-chat with the hobnobs, and you'd sell it all for a profitable little cheque and a place at the top of the tree, you limbless fuck! Well, too bad for you, you're in the early stages of a bad disease, Tatresi, old man. You're dying and you don't even know it!"

"If you're talking about the voices, then at first, yes, I was worried by them. But I've spoken with experts in MekTek and neuroscience from all over the system and it's all down to neural hallucinations. In time, these will be understood and developed out of the—"

"Really. Well, here's the science on that." And she downloaded all Trini's work to him. The pressure of the alien was a crushing weight on her, every moment. If she let her control slip for an instant, she knew she'd be lost. Tatresi was going through what she'd already been through, and now she despised him more than she could stand. How she'd chosen him as any kind of ally amazed her. He would have done this before—stabbed her in the back, and the whole movement, too—if only he'd had the guts for it.

His reaction was totally unexpected—although if she'd recalled her own militancy perhaps it shouldn't have been. He flipped the data back at her in a jumble.

"And you believe this traumatized insect and her claim? She could have made it up. There on her own, a drone, cut off from the rest of the world and from most of her mind. Typical Ticktock fabrication! Maybe she wants the whole of the new system for herself and her kind—did you think of that? Get you out of the way, as you accuse me of trying to do to you, and then there's no one left there to dispose of except two has-been Gaiaforms, both of whom are well on the way to senility."

"Tatresi," she bellowed at him. "Nobody feels more strongly about the Forged Independence than I do, but this isn't going to free anyone! This is just another kind of slavery and it lasts forever. You're in the honeymoon now, but you can *hear* them, I know you can. Well, that's going to get louder and louder over the next few days, until you can either kill yourself or let it in, but there's no other choice. If you sell this to people—"

"For Tek's sake, *you* were going to!" he snapped. "You know what this sounds like? Like you're trying to get it all back for yourself. You don't care about the Forged except as a caste you can rule over, now that you've made a gun too, so you can be the perfect dictator. Isn't that right?"

"This is insane!" she was shrieking. Insanity—it was that—

was too much for her. The alien was a scream on the end of every nerve, in her senses, in her guts, in her heart. She levelled the gun at him, but a streak of light caught the side of her eye and in that moment of hesitation another person appeared, someone neither of them recognized at all. Its form was difficult to make out, on any magnification.

Then, to either side of them, police came swooping in and surrounded their position. Isol translated to Zian space instantly. Tatresi jumped towards the sun.

Picking up his signal from the Mercurian outpost, the Shuriken Death-Angel followed him at maximum speed.

30. COMMUNICATION FAILURE

During the night Bara spoke about his dreams. Sleeping and waking at the same time, he muttered quietly, his broadcasts varying their frequencies as parts of his mind wandered. Zephyr lay in her makeshift shelter beneath the upturned sled, and listened to him as the wind hissed across the sandy ground.

"They are calling me. Such things to tell me. Such visions to see. So many to hear. Follow the story and all is awaiting. I'm afraid."

Bara rambled on, uttering voiced fragments that connected momentarily with the inexpressible visions he was having, produced tantalizing metaphors, then stuttered into silence only to begin again a second later. He was an aural archaeology, and Zephyr tried to piece together anything that seemed to come from the same origin, but it was a hard task. The only consistent repetition was his terror, at varying strengths: it ebbed and flowed as the visions came and went. He swayed where he stood, a chromed icon reflecting the mercurial light of the two full Moons, his weight making the ground crunch as it shifted.

Zephyr must have fallen asleep as she lay thinking of what Earthly precedents she might use as a model for this situation, not afraid for herself as it was now far too interesting for that, and probably far too late. She couldn't remember a time when she'd been afraid once she'd realized there was to be no escaping a situation. Its certainty drew out her stubbornness, and she rose to its challenge without complaints. So she might die here—well, she could have died anywhere, so who cared where? That didn't interest her. Life and mystery, *that* interested her. Perhaps she would have been keener on death and its processes if she'd had a religious side, but to her the religions of the ages were all mixed up in her head, a ceaselessly overworked agglutination of thousands of years of responding to the fears she didn't possess.

She woke with her face feeling cold on one side, gasping for breath, and heard the sound of an engine and rotor blades in the air above.

Bara was silent, but he was still there as she put her head out of the shelter. His antennae were stiff and skyward-pointing, body braced firmly on the ground. Abruptly the Abacand switched on from sleep, and began pouring out transmissions. Kincaid and Bara were arguing fiercely, and the sound of the blades was one of Kincaid's limbs approaching through the darkness, helicopter fashion.

". . . Plotting against me in codes you think I don't know," Kincaid gabbled, static saturating the sounds like an onrushing wave. "But I've guessed it all. You're going to leave me here, with them, to be eaten while you get away, but I've found out now . . ."

And against this tide of determined anger Bara insisted:

". . . No such thing. We were only trying to piece together the truth of what's happening. You didn't want to talk about it earlier. You wanted to work, and what's wrong with that? Isol will be in contact again soon, and then you'll see everything is all right . . ."

But he was losing ground, and losing conviction too by the sound of it.

"Get up," the Abacand cut into the dialogue, aiming its voice precisely at Zephyr. "Get up now and let's go back into the walls. Leave everything. Move!"

Its tone was so urgent that she paused only to pull her boots on and grab its small shape before she used the moonlight's glare to back quickly away, towards the first building of Tanelorn.

"You can't leave!" shrilled Kincaid, his voice suddenly booming from overhead. "You can never leave!"

Zephyr saw a flash of yellowish light, which briefly illuminated enough of a doorway for her to dart through. She heard a sudden angry motor-whine from Bara's Arm and then there was an explosion that knocked her off her feet and flung her to the ground. The material of it gave beneath her, so she wasn't

hurt but lay there stunned, deafened and blinded, dimly understanding that the two Gaiaforms were fighting now, and that
Kincaid at least meant to kill. Another flash, and then the whap-
whap whining sound of a rotor blade whipping off fast overhead and away.

The grinding noise of metal dying. A jet scream. The roar of
furious words and more furious assaults of power, and then suddenly a tremendous concussion that tore the breath out of
Zephyr's lungs and thumped them hard.

The next minutes passed in a senseless blur. She got up, and
the Abacand was urging her to run. She ran and hit things, and
fell. There was no oxygen at all in the air, and her lungs gulped
and gasped in a total panic, because she might not fear death but
she did fear pain. There were more bright flashes and more
whining of debris. Explosions battered her numb eardrums. And
suddenly it was over. Fire from the sky rained down, and then
there was silence—a deafening silence of complete totality that
eclipsed everything that had gone before.

The Abacand screen informed her that Isol had shot both
Limbs dead from her orbital vantage. Then Zephyr, lying in a pit
of blackness and in the shelter of some unknown thing, felt the
Roach patter quickly across her hand.

She snatched her hand back and looked up automatically. A
grey gleam shone a few inches from her head, and a red light
winked next to it.

"Professor Duquesne," the Roach whispered through the
Abacand's intervention, in the quietest and most humble voice
Zephyr had ever heard Isol try. "Please help me."

"How?" Zephyr said, aware of herself lying exhausted, flattened and alone, far from this person whom she didn't trust,
who was virtually a psychopath. The absurdity made her want
to laugh, and she had to try hard not to because instinct yelled
that now was not the moment.

"I can't resist them any longer," Isol said matter-of-factly. "I'm
so tired. I want to sleep, but if I do I won't wake up again. *They*'ll
be here instead of me. I beg you. Anything you can do, please."

"Listen," Zephyr said, without any idea what she could say. "Stay calm. Can you contact Gaiasol? It may be able to send—"

"It's all over with them," Isol interrupted quickly. "They've come for Tatresi. He was trying to sell it on to the others—make a profit and seize control of the Party. I wanted to stop him, but he wouldn't listen. If I make one more transit, I won't be able to hold them away from me. I know . . . I know you want to go home. I know that. But do you see? If I take you there, it's too late for me then. Here I have . . . some time. And you can help me. Tell them to let me go."

Zephyr pushed herself slowly up onto her elbows, and then sat back on her heels. She was shaking with the onset of shock and felt herself shiver. Keying her suit to heat her, she wrapped her arms around herself and looked at the small red and green and grey lights emanating from the two tiny machines in the darkness.

"I can't hear them," she admitted at last, aware that every word might prove her final sentence.

Isol laughed, a haunting sound. "I thought you wouldn't. I knew you'd be safe. They won't get *you* unless you want them to. Maybe they'd swap us—you for me? Your head must be so much fuller than mine. History? Human life? You're a far better subject than I am."

At the campsite some fuel cell blew, shattering the peace and making Zephyr jump. She heard the vigorous roar of flames and the snap and crack of burning.

"You for me?" Zephyr repeated, just to keep the conversation going. If that ceased, there would be no more hope.

"I can tell you about them, a bit," Isol rushed on. "I can see them from here. They want to know, to live, to experience all lives. They want mine, but any life would do. Any at all, they don't care whose. They don't care what it's like. If I offered them you they might let me go. Do you think you would like that? I thought you would. You study people throughout the ages. You wanted a thousand lives. Now you can have a billion lives, in there with them. You can be anything in a hundred worlds—

more, even. You could be me. You could be Kincaid. Know it all, see it all, feel it all better than any Uluru. You've not even got MekTek, Professor—but imagine a universe of history and life, living it all, from every angle. And I can offer all of this, forever. Every answer, too. They like searching for knowledge. They like wanting to know. They like being together. They want to suck everything up together, to experience the fullness of the real mystery. I can't live with that, do you understand? I can't be that, even though they want me to be. They want me to change into them, and them into me. But I want to be alone. It doesn't make sense, yet they won't see sense. But they might take an exchange, do you think?"

Zephyr, bewildered, racked her mind for anything to say. "I need time—" she began.

"But," Isol broke in, breathless, giddy, "I don't have much time."

The silence of the pause rushed in on them.

"You don't know if it will work. What if it doesn't?" Zephyr's stalling was futile, but Isol seemed to bite.

"Then I have to . . . go. I could crash into this planet's atmosphere hard and fast enough to be sure. They won't get me, in the end. Hah, Kincaid says so too. He has his pride. We didn't come here for this."

"Is that what these others have done?" Zephyr insisted, latching on to the clue on offer. "Are these dead aliens all suicides?"

"I don't know. I suppose so. Maybe they came here for their answers, or to offer someone else for their life or their world. Professor, I don't care about any of that now. I want to go from here, *alone*. I want to live and die as myself."

"You'd better ask them if they can let you go. Have you done that?" She felt like a mother talking to a stubborn child who doesn't want to make a request of a stranger.

The Roach fell quiet. The time of its pause stretched out and Zephyr's exhausted mind began to wander. She rested against a wall and closed her eyes on the darkness. As if through a heavy fog, she heard the splutter of the body outside as it burnt. Her musing was interrupted by a harsh flash of light, and a few seconds later a movement in the earth and air, like a gulp.

"What was that?"

There were no lights in the darkness. The Roach and the Abacand had vanished. Zephyr froze in position. Outside the blaze continued, casting leaping shadows through an opening above her. The wind changed as the minutes passed, and she thought she could hear a noise, but it was hard to be sure.

The Abacand's green light winked on. "EM pulse," it said tetchily. "Kincaid's wiped himself off the face—or spread himself all over it. That just leaves you, me, a depressed VanaShiva, an ecstatic Secta and a psychotic in-system. The Roach is fried, but I believe the Hand may still be okay. Of course it's part of Lady Loopy, so that hardly counts. If we can contact Trini directly, she might be able to do something about that . . ." It hesitated. "I'm rambling hysterically, aren't I?"

Zephyr didn't answer. "You and I are the only ones not affected by whatever," she said after a time. "Why is that?"

"From what Trini says, it's because we haven't engaged with it directly. We haven't had a conscious communication with it— as you wouldn't in a normal situation with what you consider to be inanimate furniture. Unless you're a neutron short of an atom."

"So how can Kincaid and Bara have become directly involved with it? I thought they only treated it as physical matter."

"Ah, no," the Abacand said. "To an Asevenday the soil and water are practically gods—they talk to them all the time. And for a VanaShiva all gases are sacred. Gaiaforms aren't just a fleet of forklifts and reactors. They have soul. They have a personal relationship with their inanimate materials that is built into their beings from day one. It's certain that both of them 'invited' this . . . material to respond to them, at least by *its* terms of invitation."

Zephyr thought of the old profs she'd studied under, babbling away to their skeletons and potsherds as they worked on

digs, or pottered in the lab. She thought of herself piecing together the splinters of a five-thousand-year-old bow, hour on
hour, giving it a history, a name, several owners, a billion adventures, talking to it as though it wanted to be reassembled . . .

"If I came here expecting Tanelorn," she said, "would it still
have been here just this way? Or is this Isol's fantasy of a lost
city?"

"Good question," the Abacand said. "Or Kincaid's, or
Bara's? I don't know."

"The road . . ." she began.

"Was unexpected to you. It reacted before you thought it
would."

"I was looking for language traces," she said.

"But we only *thought* we saw something in the patterns of
the stone."

"If I stay, will it appear?"

"Very possibly."

"And then I'll hear them?"

The Abacand seemed to take a breath. "You might. But I
won't."

"Why not?"

"Pure AI does not dream," it said. "I have no fantasies, no
desire. Even my will to live is a simulation. Quite a convincing
one, maybe."

Zephyr leaned forward slowly, body aching, and picked up
the small block, holding it fast in her hand. "Would they be interested in you? Isol said something about the mystery."

"I believe she meant the mystery of experiencing a life, as opposed to my existence."

"Which is?"

"Fabricated," it said after a thought. "Secondary. Regulated
entirely by my form and function."

"And I'm not like you, but built instead by insentient blocks
of chemicals instead of the hands of humans?"

"It is the arising of sentience from insentience that is the
heart of the mystery, I think," the Abacand hazarded. "That and

the assignment of meaningful importance to random matter. I do not do this last thing. I do not need a meaning to my existence, nor do I impose one on the universe. In that sense I have no creativity, and nothing to contribute to this collective consciousness. So, I am uninteresting to them and incapable of communicating with them."

Zephyr listened to the burning and the wind outside, together sounding like heavy sheets flapping and booming. *Everything is gone in a flash,* she thought—*transient. It leaves echoes for a time, then it's gone. This planet is the storehouse of everything. They keep it this way because to change it is to change the memories . . . and I have searched for the traces of memory all my life. Would I be terrorized like Isol, if that were my prospect of survival?*

She decided the opposite was true. For an hour or so she was upset, thinking of her family and friends, who even now couldn't have any idea what had happened to her, or where she was. Nor would they. Her place would be filled by another professor, her classes taught by senior lecturers, her office recycled, her effects picked over and thrown out. Perhaps Gaiasol military would send someone to speak to her sister, and leave some informative data in the record of all the people who lived and died on Earth: her name, the day she was born and the day she left. Conferences would go on, arguments would go on, people would still not know what Stonehenge was built for. Kalu would find someone else to talk to about Trilobites and send scarves to.

"Contact Isol," Zephyr said to the Abacand, as dawn finally began to colour the walls a faint shade of grey. "Tell her I'll go."

Gritter sat in the cell, alone except for the Strategos and the dog-faced agent who was now wearing his wretched Gaiasol insignia badge over his tatty velveteen coat, his long mouth slightly open as he panted in the room's heat—with what Gritter thought was an unseemly excitement at his big minute in the Strategos's eye. His perch was not in itself uncomfortable, but it was gripping his feet with its padded restraints rather harder than he'd have liked—hard enough that Gritter couldn't slip out a claw here or there.

"Brian Brown," the Strategos said, his ugly flat face shimmering with the copper MekTek that penetrated his flesh in fractals and paisleys of varying depth and complexity. It gave Gritter a headache just to look at him.

"I dunno who that is."

The dog-boy barked a slight laugh and produced something from his pocket that he held out in one paw-hand, fingers as knobby and furry as a monkey's. Gritter saw a bloodstained postal ID. "Got your DNA on it."

"I want legal representation," Gritter said, withdrawing his neck turkey-style.

"In return for the waiving of your somewhat excessive criminal record, Gritter," the Strategos said, moving closer to him, "you might help us out with a matter of urgent security. If not, then I'm afraid the best lawyer on the planet will not be saving your ass from the fire."

"Spatchcock," snickered the dog, licking its chops.

"Excessive!" Gritter protested. "I never done nuffink to anyone that hadn't got more than that coming to them, and post Phaeries aren't anything like human—everyone knows they're mostly AI stuck into some bug hybrid. You probably got his mind out of the chipsets fair and square, dintcha? Not like a real genuine bit of violence when you turn out of the egg already ruined . . ." He paused. The Strategos's meaty face was within an inch of his own. It was smiling, baring its big blunt white teeth, and the eyes—close enough to stab out with his beak—weren't happy.

"The Ironhorse Tatresi is offering to sell alien technology to Forged and Degraded applicants for the price of a reasonable house, a Party membership, and sworn loyalty to his campaign to elect himself Leader of the Independence Movement," Anthony said. "We want you to apply to act as his agent to the Degraded Earth community, to purchase a significant shipment of Stuff and arrange for its immediate collection at a location we will give you."

"Oh yeah, and?"

"That's it," the dog said. "We'll take care of everything else. You make the call, verify yourself."

"And then what?" Gritter demanded, neck still telescoped back to the max, even as the Strategos moved away to look at the cell's very interesting blank walls. "You got some trap lined up for him? Scupper the movement just as it was getting started? They must have something good on you . . ."

"All right," the Strategos sighed. "Get the officer outside to book him on the four counts of murder, and the illegal contact with extraplanetary offenders."

"Corvax?" Gritter screeched. "That was on orders, that was. A smart bit of a move that served *you* all right!"

The dog and the tall man were both at the door. They opened it. Then it began to close.

"All right!" Gritter knew what this was going to mean, though: no job, no money, back living on the streets, and knowing all the time that he'd betrayed the leaders of . . . well, okay, the self-interested slimy, lying bastards who wanted to run the world for the Forged yet still wouldn't be interested in him. Tatresi—no, he wouldn't mind seeing that blue freak taken out of the picture. So, what had happened to Isol? Ever since he'd been transferred to this individual cell, he'd been suddenly longing to hear the news again. "So, where's the bird flown, that he gets to call the shots?"

But they didn't answer him. The door closed completely and locked itself. After a few hours officers came and thrust him rudely into another sack. He was carried out on someone's back and put in a vehicle. At an anonymous public comms service he made his call, the dog-man sitting at his side, stinking, the two contacts of an electro-gun stabbing into Gritter's sides like skewers. Tupac's AI consort confirmed his eligibility to Tatresi's encrypted intermediary server. So, bloody hell, it was bad if Tupac was in on this and willing to shaft Tatresi straight up the line.

The transactions passed in a blur for Gritter. They seemed to take forever. The almighty blue himself never made an appearance, so he didn't even get the satisfaction of seeing that smug phizog and of knowing in his own head just how utterly screwed it was at long last. Getting his!

During one of the pauses while they waited for Tatresi's AI intermediary to verify the deal, the dog muttered, "Enjoying yourself now?"

"I like anything that does those who haven't bothered to notice me," Gritter replied with a clack of his beak. "Only justice, ennit? For me and the hundreds of others. Surprised you turned your back on us." He glanced out of the corner of his eye.

"What makes you think *I* feel downtrodden?" the dog said. "I've got a good job, education, pay and prospects, thanks to looking like this. You never know what life'll give you if you never ask."

"Easy for you to say."

"Sure, life's a peach for a fake pound puppy, runt of the litter. Just like for you, eh?"

Gritter flipped his wings. "I got by on my wits. I ent ashamed."

The dog sneezed, said nothing, but his lip curled slightly and showed a tooth. Gritter didn't know what that meant. He felt uneasy, but then the line activated again and he got his verification. The deal went down, machine to machine—the deed was done, just like that.

"Right." The dog got up slowly, wearily, and put the gun back in his jacket. "That's you done. Free to go."

"Free?" Gritter laughed, a wheezing in-and-out gape. "Free as I ever was, to suffer and die in this shit hole?"

The dog shrugged and turned away. As it reached the door of the shop, an Unevolved woman let the door shut in its face, and Gritter laughed again as the dog-man had to catch the heavy swing of it with his paw.

"Free," he said to himself. "Ah, shit."

Tom Corvax, who now bore a remarkable resemblance to Caspar, walked with Anthony along the banks of the Thames, watching the heavy swirl of the opaque water roll restlessly past as they made their way upriver. He thrust his small, weak hands into the pockets of his coat—how they felt the cold, even though he'd lived all his life in temperatures much lower—and rounded his shoulders, missing his wings. The gravity made him feel a thousand years old.

"This is the last thing," he said to the MekTek. "As Corvax, I'll help you keep the system free for a while. But then I'm gone. I think that's me paid out."

"Yes," Anthony said with a rising tone that meant perhaps not.

"You're wondering what stops us from just seizing everything because of our curiosity. We have the power to take you all, so why don't we?" Corvax said. He looked around him at the fine trees and the sunlight coming through their leaves. He remembered other scenes like this that he'd never seen.

"It's crossed my mind."

"Now that would be a terrible imposition," Corvax said. "Making people in your own image. Coming in and taking without asking." He laughed, feeling his new throat vibrate and shudder, his soft, flat face open, and his tongue cool in the breeze.

"Mmn." The Strategos grinned briefly into his own collar. "There may still be a civil war. Rumour already has you experimented on and murdered by the secret service, and the Jovians are about to hold an apartheid referendum. One can only hope that moderate Independence factions will get cold feet when we are able to issue a statement."

They passed the palm trees that made a lane up to Downing Street, and took a smaller pathway towards the hidden site where government shuttles routinely lifted and landed through their own secure air corridors.

"There is a final problem greatly on my mind," the Strategos said, once they passed under the arch of Gateway House and came into the shadow of its heavy iron-oak branches. "We have stranded an innocent woman on the world you call Origin. I have no doubt that Isol cannot return her, and I don't know the status of any others who may be alive in that system." He stopped and turned to face Corvax as they reached the opening to the landing court.

"Zephyr Duquesne?" Corvax said. "Yes, I know her."

Tatresi's mind was unquiet as he prepared to follow Corvax's old instructions for the use of Stuff. He imagined it parcelling itself up into neat lumps, dividing and subdividing as amoeba would, slowly filling up Hold Twelve with a stockpile of individual doses. Despite his fresh conviction that this must be the way forward, he hadn't forgotten Corvax's laboratory contents, nor the peculiar whispering that sometimes came to his mind of late, as he cycled towards sleep. He was still convinced that Isol's rambling was the product of an overstressed mind—so much potential power could do that to anyone. The fact that she'd even developed a weapon with Stuff only went to show how paranoid she must have become. He'd taken on the responsibility as a matter of course, especially after his red-carpet reception at the Debate.

On the other hand, Tatresi was also drifting here, between Mercury and the sun, hot as hell, skulking like a common criminal as he waited for the contact agent representing the Degraded

Earth Forged to make themselves known. He loathed this soiled feeling it gave him. If there'd been another way, he would have taken it.

All the same, he wasn't exactly surprised to see the ship that turned up. It was no lightweight cargo carrier or pirate clipper, no Dog Legba with stuck-on armaments and the mentality of a charging rhino. The thing on his scanners was indistinct—the same person or whatever that had appeared with the police when Isol had quit system and left him to face everything on his own. Either it must be one of Earth's unknowns or it was, he was very afraid to contemplate, from the same place as Stuff.

That wasn't impossible, he well knew. In fact it might be Isol herself, in some new form entirely, a phenomenon he'd not yet contemplated. He turned his narrowest aspect towards its approach vector and moved around the planet, keeping an arc of it between himself and being in full view.

"Tatresi," said a voice in his head, much more distinctly than *it* had ever whispered. "Return the engine and material to us, and we will not prosecute."

If the message and the deal had been a trap, then he needn't worry, he realized, since he could come up with a gun anytime that could fix Gaiasol's best operator in the blink of an eye. On the other hand . . . why was there always an "other hand"?

"Who are you?" he demanded. The machine or person gave him no access to any communications mode other than straight talk—no hologram, no nothing. "If you want this back, why don't you just take it?"

There was a flicker in space, in his space, internally. The Stuff ceased to replicate. It folded in on itself and the engine's delicate forms shifted.

"Wait, what are you doing!"

"Tatresi."

This was Corvax's voice, he was sure of it!

"Surrender the material and you can leave for Zian space now. Try to go anywhere else and you will be shot."

"Corvy, where are you?" He flung himself about the frequencies, searching for the source of the vocalization, the mode that strung all Corvax's individual identifiers out in his unique personal verification. With horror he recognized the origin of it—the engine itself. "Where are you? Answer me!"

"You can still go on," Corvax said with encouragement, with sympathy, with full Tek-Mode authority. "We will evolve, but others need time to choose their fate."

As Tatresi was distracted, the shapeless thing had come round Mercury's seething silvery eight-ball, faster than Tatresi could have believed on any Gaian engine. Solar glare blasted out from its shielding like a massive halo, almost blinding every sense he had as it deflected extra radiation and heat towards him.

He dodged back, trying to avoid it. "What the hell are you talking about?"

"Isol tried to warn you before. You're undergoing translation into the Eleven-D," Corvax said. "There is no escape now—not for you. You can give up the engine, and your plan to disseminate us to the unwitting, or you can die here."

"What's that thing?" Tatresi wanted time—time time time to think. This had to be a fix. His skin was starting to burn now as the other person closed in. He tried to back away, but the engine wasn't functioning. Why the hell did they want him to choose when he had no choice? They had him like a fish in a barrel.

"Decide," Corvax insisted.

Tatresi decided that he didn't buy it, and created a new engine and a new weapon in the split moment that it took for Stuff to move, ready to defend himself and break free. Such was his temper that Corvax's voice was silenced and the forms took effortless shape. He felt a huge surge of the most enormous, limitless power and, since he had no sensation of coming to an end, the end itself being so quick, that experience of exultation lasted forever for him, or at least far longer than the split second it took for his body to fly into pieces.

The Shuriken Death-Angel looked at the mess it had made, and shot up the larger fragments into tidy dust before directing the mass into the sun's corona, where it would be recycled into something more useful. As the sparkling shards of the cargo carrier tumbled, a large number of them winked out of existence within the Four-D, and the Shuriken watched their going with intent curiosity. It privately thanked Corvax, wherever he was, with a brief blurt on various prayer frequencies tuned to the distant stars, and then turned and spun away into the cooler darkness, envying Tatresi his engine and its power—but not too much, it thought, not too much.

32. HOMECOMING

"What is Tanelorn?" Zephyr asked the Abacand. She had recovered the sled and packed her few things into it, eating a dried-fruit bar as she did so. It tasted of figs, cranberries and apple juice. All fruit snacks seemed to taste of apple juice to her; boiled-down apple juice that had become dark and sticky as treacle, thick as tar. Even the fact that it might be the last one she'd ever eat didn't endear it to her much. Thirsty, she opened her water collector and sucked in a long mouthful. It was brisk outside this morning, and the ground gave up a stink of ash, fat and melted plastic where Bara's Arm had met its end.

"City where heroes go to rest the rest of the justified and intolerably noble," the Abacand muttered. "Anyplace could be it. This place, even. I've finally figured out that it's based around Cuzco theory: a branch of fractal mathematics that has made attempts in the past on five-, six- and seven-space. So maybe Isol dreamed it for us and it's no more of here than we are. Hard to say. Could also be a physical representation of the underlying Eleven in Four-D. Bloody clever. *Too* clever."

They had not heard from the Voyager, and weren't sure where she was. Zephyr had decided to haul back to the Hand, in the hope that it might still be functional. She slung her water can over her shoulder and put on the sled harness. Within a few minutes they were back on a broad plaza, climbing slowly uphill towards the high spike of the Wind Tor.

"I was really starting to think this might be dwellings," Zephyr said as she moved on. "Looks like they could be. Sort of houses for wormy things or advanced aesthetes."

The machine said nothing but added her remark to the record.

"Whereas it's the biggest historical artefact ever seen," she said after a minute or two of hard work. "But no way to decode it. At least, no way without joining in."

"It isn't a *thing*," the Abacand suggested. "It's *people*. And it's a thing. And a technology of somewhat aggressively biological preponderance. With a mission. Rather dangerous."

"Mnn." She stopped for a breather and wiped perspiration from her forehead. "Still, it feels a lot like a deserted world. I miss trees."

"You don't seem lonely here, though," the machine observed, perhaps switching into one of its psych modes.

"There's you," Zephyr said, starting uphill again and cueing the battery pack to help her out. "I guess, over the years, you know me better than anyone else. I like my work. You're never lonely with something to do."

"That wasn't your story six months ago, in the arms of Mister Married Lawyer."

"Ah, but you note he was never going to be a threat to the main purpose," Zephyr panted, feeling strangely exhilarated. "I mean, passion's a nice bit of diversion, a clue into the heart of Medea, et cetera. But it's not like a lost city of gold or the first line of Linear B."

"So, you'd rather read bad bread recipes in cuneiform than date or socialize?"

"I socialize," she objected. "I have . . . well, had . . . probably still have a lot of friends. We don't need to be together all the time. Real friendship just picks up where it left off."

"True enough," the Abacand assented. "But they'll miss you if you stay here."

"Are you trying to advise me to leave? If you have a plan, I'll hear it."

"I worry that you haven't really considered the consequences."

"And what will happen to you?"

"Me? I'll just run on until something goes. Probably won't make it to the next visit by anyone. Meanwhile I can watch the stars—lots of things. In fact, I was wondering, if you wouldn't mind, if you'd leave me in the dark somewhere, so I don't have to keep waking up when the solar cells get full. I think I'd rather be in off-mode."

They came to a narrowing, where the way sloped to a flat and curled around the side of the hill for a few metres, before heading up again. Zephyr paused there in a spot of shade as the sun, bright as a Spanish orange, climbed the sky, and her suit now laboured to cool her down. She touched the cube where it sat in her breast pocket.

"I will miss them," she said quietly. "I'll miss it all."

"If they'll have you, of course," it said. "Maybe if you're not Forged then you're not suitable."

"Thanks for that reassuring thought." She glanced around at the structures with renewed interest. Deep within them pale colours seemed to shift as the sun ascended.

"It may just be me," the Abacand broke in, "but can you hear something?"

"No."

"Here." And it amplified the sound.

I knew that if I had my chance, I could make those people dance, and maybe they'd be happy, for a while . . .

"It's coming from the Tor," the Abacand said, and as she took out her binoculars it relayed information so that she could zoom in on the tower's high platform, where the Hand still stood at rest.

Zephyr took the instrument away from her eyes and shook it, then looked again.

On the broad balcony of the Hand's landing pad a small field of poppies waved their fine green stems, their flower heads plump, just beginning to burst in the sun's hot persuasion. Flimsy tatters of red scattered open to reveal huge dark hearts, black and glossy as stag beetles, heavy with purple pollen. Amid the field the Hand sat motionless, its door open to the elements and its skin already beginning to grey and mottle in death.

The music continued, faint and haunting and the Abacand identified its strangeness to her.

Did you write the book of love?

"I believe that this is one of the mystery's several hearts," the cube said.

"The book of love?" Zephyr repeated, stupefied, remembering that Kincaid had died here because nothing could grow.

"Yes," it said. "Trini confirms that I am correct in deducing this from her data. She is most excited to think that you wish to join her, as nobody else has had any reaction other than to reject that notion utterly."

"Bara?" Zephyr said, unable to stop staring at the poppy field. "How is he?"

"The Gaiaform VanaShiva Nobility Bara is no longer individual."

"He . . . joined?"

"He has been Translated successfully."

"Does Trini hear him?"

"No, he is immersed fully in the superposition of states. His voice is now in all voices."

She put the binoculars back in their bag. "Holy shit."

That said, there was nothing else to do but go on up. She abandoned the sled, taking only water and a food bar and the Abacand with her and, much lightened in body although heavy of heart, made her slow progress up to the tower.

"Can you hear Isol?" she asked after a minute.

"No," the Abacand replied.

"Well, maybe you should ask Trini whether or not I can enter the club."

It paused as the communications were made. "It's not a club you ever leave," it warned. "She wants you to know that. But if you want to join, then you are welcome."

Zephyr managed another two hundred metres and then paused to rest. She held the Abacand and said, "Take a letter.

Blah blah all hope of rescue blah—fill in the appropriate reasons. Since my arrival on this unknown world, in the city of Tanelorn, although I had expected to find the incomprehensible, and succeeded, I have also found a sense of belonging and purpose and interest that had been fading from my life on Earth. With these things in mind, I choose to go forward and continue in a different form, whatever that may be. Dear friends, don't think of me as dead. I understand that will be far from the truth—as far as I could possibly be.

"Send it to Kalu and everyone who needs to know."

"Earth is an unknown distance away," the Abacand informed her. "This message may take thousands of years . . ."

"Just send it anyway," she said, and thumbed the "off" button.

She found herself thinking of the Strategos. On her way out here she'd thought that she'd return, and maybe they would go out together. It was an intriguing thought that had cheered her in many low moments. She was sorry she would never get to tell him how nice that would have been.

She took a drink from her bottle and yawned vigorously. The day was a hot one and the sky an almost unbroken blue. The growling hum of an engine broke the quiet. Zephyr clicked the Abacand on but kept her place. The hum became a throatier noise, and after a few minutes a white truck, battered and scratched and ancient, clambered over the plaza and drove towards her. In the cab sat a tall woman, her hairless skin the polished ebony of Ti-bone, her elbow jutting out of the open window, through which a cheap and tinny radio blasted out the same old song.

The truck carefully skirted the sled and drew up alongside Zephyr's resting place. Zephyr stood up and saw that the woman had a pink carnation stuck between her black teeth, its long stem almost chewed through.

She removed the flower with a casual gesture and waved it at the passenger seat, her expression one of cool insouciance. "Well, are you coming or not?"

Zephyr recognized Isol without knowing quite how. The

diesel engine chugged in the background. A red petal blew down and stuck for a moment on the truck's worn flank. She put her hands on the driver's door and looked up into the delicate, haughty face.

"I'm sorry I couldn't help you."

The girl shrugged, as if it meant nothing. "What could you've done?" She looked through the windscreen and into the distance, her eyes narrow against the brilliant noon light.

"Can you . . . wait just a moment?"

Again the shrug. Do what you like.

Singin' this'll be the day that I die . . .

Zephyr moved into the lee of a high arch, and into a small room, at last locating a place where no sunlight would ever fall, no matter the season or the time. She set the Abacand down there and looked at its green and friendly light.

"I'll miss you," she said.

"It's been a pleasure," the Abacand's neutral, sexless, cheerful voice replied. "Goodbye, Zephyr."

"Bye." For some reason she was choked up, tears welling so fast in her eyes and her throat so tight that it hurt. Its light went out. She touched the machine's case and felt only the soft plastic cover of a mass-made object, one of billions. And her life was inside it, set in circuit like in stone, waiting for someone to find it and try to figure it out again, when all its sense would be long gone.

The truck had waited for her. The door handle was hot and cranky as she tugged on it, and the paintwork almost burned her hand as she slammed it shut after her. A worn seat belt dug into her back but Isol wasn't wearing one, so Zephyr left it there. On the dash the pink carnation was drying out. Isol reached over and flicked it at her.

"It's yours." She put the truck in gear and thumbed the radio louder.

With a bad transmission jerk the vehicle lurched into forward motion.

Zephyr sniffed her odourless flower—the pink ones never had any smell—and twirled it in her fingers. She watched the city passing them by and then watched Isol drive, her fine hands delicate on the wheel's thick vinyl.

Isol turned to her, and a faint smile cracked the cool veneer of her face. "Ready?"

Zephyr looked down at her own hands in her lap, the flower between them, against the heavy blue suit. "Ready."

From all around her she heard a thousand voices begin to sing a happy tune.

Machen sat in his office, his hands folded under his chin, Bob the dog asleep across his shoes.

"I wonder what it must be like to have found all the equations of the physical world and yet count them an insignificant feature of the universe," he said to Anthony, who sat in the other chair, looking glum and older than his forty-five years. Machen himself felt he had aged sufficiently to warrant a pension.

"To command matter and energy as if they were . . . putty," he continued, "but not to care about that. As if it were pointless, uninteresting."

Anthony stared at the empty perches outside the window where a fine rain was blowing past. He read again the final report on Corvax and of Trini, taking a second to cover the pages.

"Would you join in?" Machen probed him, his blue eyes drilling Anthony for clues. "Would you have done that?"

"I don't know," his friend finally replied, feeling empty and uncertain, not even sure what to do with his hands, so he gripped the arms of the chair.

"By God, *I* would," Machen said, thumping the desk lightly and waking Bob, who sat up and scratched behind his ear. The sound of his leg batting against the floor was the only noise between the three of them.

Anthony heard the dog yawn, and saw its black-and-white tail wave gently back and forth in the footwell.

"What bothers me," he said finally, "is that there's no guarantee they've gone."

"They could have been here all the time," Machen agreed.

At some time in the morning a secretary brought tea. An undersecretary tried to draw their attention to some matters about the Jovian secession. Five people turned up for meetings, waited outside, were given refreshments, but left unseen. The list of Forged claimants demanding compensation for Stuff-induced sickness and debts had grown to just over three thousand. Bob got up and took a turn around the office, apparently considered cocking a leg against the fig tree, thought better of it, and began to dig at the carpet to indicate the fact that even if it was raining he thought they'd be better off outside.

Machen got his coat and Anthony followed him.

The three of them took a promenade outdoors, walking together until they reached New Park, and ascended in the lift to the broad grassy plains of the Rec where other dogs and their owners, children and people of all descriptions were enjoying themselves. The two men continued their sombre parade, hands in pockets, while Bob expressed himself freely among the small trees and bushes. He sat down on the path and watched them walking away, and for a second or two found great amusement in their intensity. But his own speculation lasted barely a minute, for the day was a glorious explosion of smells and sights, people and activities, busy, vacant and idling minds. Here and there he investigated the little woodlands, rousted a squirrel and interrupted two lovers arguing, found the end of a discarded chicken burrito, watched the birds high above him and far out of reach.

After two thrilling hours of pure enjoyment, he was glad to return to the stuffy office, reclaim his place at his master's feet, and slide into a restful sleep safe in the knowledge that, tomorrow and tomorrow and tomorrow, life would carry on its limitless paradise of curious instants—each an essential contribution to the inexplicable mystery.

About the Author

Justina Robson was born and brought up in Leeds. She studied philosophy and linguistics before settling down to write in 1992. Her earlier novels, *Silver Screen* (1999) and *Mappa Mundi* (2001), were both shortlisted for the Arthur C. Clarke Award.